Confidante

Books by

E. M. Prazeman

THE LORD JESTER'S LEGACY

Masks

Confidante

Innocence & Silence

Coming soon:

THE KILHELLION

Confidante

BOOK TWO OF THE LORD JESTER'S LEGACY

E. M. Prazeman

Copyright © 2012 Wyrd Goat Press, LLC

This book is a work of fiction.
Names, characters, places and incidents
are the product of the author's imagination.
Any resemblence to actual events, locales or persons,
living or dead, is entirely coincidental.

All rights reserved, including the right of reproduction
of any part or the whole work in any form without
permission from the copyright owner.
For permission to reproduce part or all of this work contact
Wyrd Goat Press through the website wyrdgoat.com

Cover and interior book design by Kamila Miller

ISBN-13: 978-1482556384
ISBN-10: 1482556383

CreateSpace First Print Edition September 2013

Also available as an ebook. This book and other fiction and non-fiction books can
be purchased from the Wyrd Goat Press website and major online retailers.

Please support producers of art and content by taking freely only that
which is offered for free, and fairly compensating for that work which the
artists of the world create and ask for pay in exchange for the hours and
years of love and training and toil they've put into it.

If you find the cover stripped off of this or any other book, it may have been
reported as destroyed and the publisher and author have not been paid for it.

Dedicated to that crazy little thing called love.

Chapter One

Mark balanced on his hands, teaching them the ship's pitch and roll before he trusted to remove his foot from where it braced on a bookshelf. He carefully transferred his weight to his right hand—

A woman gasped. He controlled his collapse but still hit his knee on the table leg. It had nowhere else to go in the cramped navigator's quarters. His puppy, now approaching ninety pounds with no sign of slowing in her growth, came over and snuffled him to make certain he was all right. The dog's ginger mask, initially faint, had already begun to fade by comparison as her brilliant white puppy coat gradually turned ruddy.

"I'm sorry." Winsome stood in the doorway, dressed in a sailor's naval trousers, a frilly shirt and a curiously shortened overdress of an effect somewhere between a proper dress and a waistcoat. The islander lady's naval uniform suited her very well, but then Winsome looked well in pretty much anything, with her sun-warmed skin, fine but athletic figure and amber hair. He would have preferred to look more like her than his own pale, bland coloration, muddy green eyes, and of course it would help if he wasn't showing all the symptoms of starvation.

It hadn't taken Winsome long to acclimate to the ship's movements. She didn't even need to put a hand on the door frame as the ship peaked and then angled down a wave. "For a moment I thought you were hanging from your legs ...." She sighed. "I don't know what I thought."

2   E. M. Prazeman

He found it hard to imagine that she'd been a sharpshooter that routinely climbed into rigging to do her work. One of the sailors told Mark about a time when she'd been aloft when the ship was dismasted. She rode the broken mainmast down into the enemy's rigging. She should have been killed, but instead she recovered, fought, and distinguished herself in that battle. Winsome proved her bravery again and again in the war between Cathret and the Meriduan Islands.

Mark wished she'd stayed home to help his lord and master instead of following him to Cathret. Rohn needed her help. Besides, Mark wasn't sure he'd survive to see the mainland. Then what would she do? "I'm all right," he assured her. And he did feel a little stronger. It took him a while to get used to goat's milk, but it hurt him less than cow's milk. The cook's rough bread also seemed to settle easier in his belly.

"What were you doing?"

"It's just an exercise."

"Will you teach me?"

That made him smile. She wanted to learn everything. "Of course. But usually it's taught on level ground, and your arms need to strengthen to the work. Don't get discouraged if you can't do it."

"I won't." She took off her overdress. Mark gave her a belt to tie over her shirt tails so they wouldn't flop over her face. Unlike a man's shirt that tucked into trousers or breeches, her uniform shirt went down to her knees and tapered in back to her ankles to match the overdress.

"You have to trust me," Mark told her.

"I will." The sudden shyness and the way she lowered her lashes made him sad.

He did his best to treat her with cool but amiable civility, hoping to discourage her feelings toward him a bit, but he found it difficult. He liked her too much. "Put your hands on the ground, apart about the width of your shoulders, and test your weight on them." As she did he positioned himself. "Whenever you're ready, kick off hard and I'll catch your feet. Make sure you keep them together as much as you can."

That sounded a bit off-color, but she didn't seem to notice.

She failed the first time to kick hard enough, but the second time she managed it. She whooped in excitement, squeaked, and collapsed. He helped her fall safely. "My arms aren't strong enough!" she laughed.

"Then you'll have to practice. Here. Lay across my bed." He shouldn't have suggested it, but she gave him a coy smile and settled on her belly, knees bent up to avoid the wall. "Hang over and put your hands on the ground. That's it. Now brace up onto your feet with your hind end in the air. Oh, hello captain."

"Lord Jester," Captain Shuller said politely as Winsome hurriedly stood and tried to compose herself. The dark, striking gentleman wearing a naval uniform-style coat in black and gold had exquisite, deep blue eyes ringed in brown. Those eyes tended to distract Mark from what the captain was saying unless he deliberately focused on the man's words. "I apologize for the interruption." He turned aside so that he wasn't looking directly at either of them.

"You're not interrupting anything, captain," Winsome told him hastily. "We were just, that is, Lark was teaching me how to stand on my hands." Though her shirt modestly covered her chest, she crossed her arms to shelter herself.

"Yes." The captain flashed a rare smile that quickly faded. "Looks a little chancy up ahead, clouds pushing over, wind's brisking. We'll make better time but you should secure any loose belongings just in case. I don't like the way the glass is falling."

"Thank you, sir," Mark said.

"Yes, sir." Winsome threw on her overdress and hurried out of Mark's room.

Captain Shuller ducked his head. "I truly apologize for—"

"Not at all," Mark assured him.

Captain Shuller started to leave, but he steeled himself and leveled a dark look into Mark's eyes. "I thought I'd heard that she and Colonel Evan were courting."

Colonel Rohn Evan, Lark's lord and master. Mark missed him terribly. Just hearing his name made his throat and chest ache. "I'm trying to match them," Mark told him. "They just—they would suit each other so well if they just ... I think they both fear the other will wound them."

"She's quite fond of you," Captain Shuller said softly.

"I wish she wasn't."

"You seem fond of her as well."

Mark nodded. "But not enough, for which I'm very sorry. She's been the best of friends to me. I adore her. I just ... don't love her. Not as she seems to wish I would."

"I see." The captain started to leave again.

"Thank you, captain. For asking. I'm grateful that you feel protective of her." He might have just found a badly needed ally. "Would you consider speaking to her?"

The captain's expression tightened and he swallowed nervously. "Regarding?"

"Not what we just discussed. I'm hoping you could convince her to sail back to Meridua with you. Not just for her safety. For her sanity. She's—" He had to keep checking to make sure she was in her room and the door was closed. *Dainty* at sea was quite noisy, with the wind whistling through the shrouds and the creak of wood against wood and the groan of great beams bearing the wind's force, driving the hull against the potent sea. Men's footsteps drummed on her decks and the pound and rush of water against the bow rumbled through the whole ship. Still, a conversation could be overheard even in these conditions. "I think she's after her father. I don't know what you've heard—"

"Enough to understand, I think." Captain Shuller looked grim.

"She's implied that she intends to protect him from me, but I wonder who will protect him from her once she confronts him, and who will protect her if he decides his life is more important than his daughter's." Mark hadn't seen much of her father before Kilderkin fled the islands, but what he saw didn't impress him in regard to the man's scruples. Mark had no idea why everyone thought well of him. "Worse, she doesn't understand what I'm tangled in. I'm afraid that if I explained, it would make her even more determined to stay with me." The look on the captain's face assured Mark that he understood that she could be killed. "I just want her to be safe. There's little left of my own life to protect. But Winsome—she has a great future ahead of her, if she only allows it." Mark had to hang on to the chart table as a particularly large wave lifted the ship's massive weight high into the air as if she were a matchstick. *Dainty* plummeted at an alarming angle down the other side.

The captain only had to lean in the doorway to keep his balance. "I will see what I can do. Thankfully we have a good stretch of water ahead of us. That gives me time to perhaps craft something with Mr. Johns. I wouldn't hold out much hope, though, lord jester." Winsome opened her door. "Based on reputation," he said without missing a beat, "and from observation, a fool's errand would be simpler to achieve."

Captain Shuller would have made a good jester. "I must try nonetheless."

"Try what?" asked Winsome.

"To find some trace of my father."

As he'd expected she retreated back to her original course, most likely the private head they were allowed to use. They weren't so near the water, so she was less likely to get an ass full of spray from a rogue wave.

"Good luck," Captain Shuller told him.

Mark told Gale to stay and went to use the sailor's facilities below. He didn't mind. He'd grown used to it.

Captain Shuller had hired a navigator somewhere on the Cathretan coast. They'd all come to a comfortable arrangement. Mark stored his valuables in the navigator's room, the navigator and Mark shared the space during the day, and at night Mark slept in a hammock below with the rest of the men and the bulk of the ship's cargo.

Mark actually preferred the hammock to the bed, though below decks stank a bit of rotten seawater, aged sweat, sour wine and animals. Mark wasn't sure if it was out of courtesy or not, but the navigator spent little time in his own quarters during the day, allowing Mark rare hours of privacy. Usually the navigator stayed on deck or went over his charts with the captain in the captain's slightly more roomy chamber. Winsome had the first mate's quarters, and Mr. Johns shared with the captain. After every dinner they all pitched in to settle Mr. Johns in for the night, moving the table to make way for a hanging bed.

Mark had been told that war ships had quite a bit more room for officers. Quite a bit more room probably wouldn't have equaled Mark's suite at Hevether Hall. He could have divided his suite among a dozen men or even a great many more and still improved upon each individual's allotted space on *Dainty*. Mark didn't mind. The cramped conditions actually helped, especially on days when he felt particularly weak. There was almost always something within reach he could grab or brace against if he lost his balance, and someone close to help if he fell.

Only a few sailors slept below at the moment, just the night watch and a handful that had no duties and wanted a nap. A war ship might have more than two hundred men on a ship *Dainty's* size. *Dainty* carried cargo, not weapons and warriors, so she housed only thirty to fifty men, depending how many were sick, on leave, or had died. Mark was told that thirty was considered a generous number for a cargo ship. He wondered if the captain wanted the extras for fighting force. Like many Meriduan ships, *Dainty* and her crew saw action during the war.

And now, if Mark didn't do something to stop it, they might all be dragged into yet another war.

They had bins and crates and bolts of cloth carefully covered and stacked where marines had once slept and fought and died, and where cannons and boxes of ammunition had stood. *Dainty* still had cannons, but she'd kept only four eighteen pound longs below and four twelve pound cannonades topside. With cargo stowed everywhere, they seemed more like an afterthought.

Mark felt along a thick beam as he walked. His hand tingled as it traced over a lodged cannonball that had been there since the war. It reminded him too much that he'd narrowly missed fighting in that war as a child, and that he might have to fight in a war very soon if things went badly.

Unlike most of the largely Cathretan crew he didn't have to crouch very far when he was below decks. *Dainty* had one more lower deck even shorter than this one, and below that, though they tried to keep it more or less dry, was the bilge. The sailors didn't check it often. Apparently they could tell how full of water it was based on how *Dainty* traveled through the water.

After he wedged himself cozily into the head and completed his business there, Mark went topside for some fresh air.

The ship in that time hadn't protested at all from what he could tell below, but the wind's force surprised him. Now the rush of water against the bow roared and licked the rail, and the sailors were busy with the sails. Gale rejoined him and anxiously paced around his legs.

"Glass is still dropping," the captain said. He crouched to put a hand on Gale as she passed and she wagged her tail briefly in response. "You finally get to see some weather, lord jester."

Mostly he'd sailed in soft weather. It had been windy and rough when he'd first left the mainland at the end of Frevai—

Had it been only two months since he'd left Cathret? It seemed a lifetime ago—

—but no one had seemed alarmed at the time and the chop and pound didn't bother Mark, not even enough to disturb his sleep.

This felt different. The crew didn't seem afraid, but they wasted no time. Their movements had a crisp, edgy haste that made him want to help. "Is there anything I can do?"

"I can't say yes, lord jester. Before, I might have. I know how much sailing means to you, but I can't accept the responsibility, not in your weakened state."

"Maybe there's something small—"

"There is no small task in a storm, lord jester. I'm sorry, but for your own safety and my sanity I hope you will confine yourself to the navigator's quarters or below decks until this blows over."

"I will. I wouldn't want to be in your way," Mark assured him.

"You are never in the way, lord jester," Captain Shuller said kindly. "We're glad to have you aboard."

Mark woke to the keening, cracking and roaring horror they'd weathered the past several hours, but the way the ship moved seemed easier somehow. Cold and damp, he eased out of the leaning hammock and carefully made his way along the slick, slanted floor. The ship pitched violently and then slammed almost to a stop before he made it to the nearest overhead beam, but he caught himself in time. Gale skated and staggered after him, unsteady even on four legs. Most of the sailors seemed to be below, and many of them slept. The rest played cards or worked on fixing gear. Even the chickens and goats had settled, either in relief or from total exhaustion.

It seemed that the cook had decided it was safe enough to prepare a hot meal. The warmth from the stove wasn't quite enough to make him comfortable, but it helped ease the chill. And it actually smelled pleasant below decks. No doubt the bilge water had been refreshed with all the action.

Not that long ago water had squirted in between the planks and he'd helped man the pumps to keep the water from filling up the lower deck. At least he'd been too busy to be really afraid, and the relative calm the other men either owned or pretended helped him to stay calm as well.

"Don't touch the hatch!" cried Mr. Briggs as Mark reached for the bar. "Water'll come in and some of the cargo'll be spoilt."

"I thought the worst of the storm might have passed." Mark had to raise his voice over the wind and ocean's wild symphony.

"It's rougher than ever up there. We're hove to." Mr. Briggs settled back to stitching a pair of trousers that had torn. They had old blood stains on them.

"Meaning ...?"

"Sitting whichever way the wind and waves want it. I reckon we're not too far off, but it'll cost us some time. We'll make her up soon enough."

"I don't think I understand. We don't have any sails up?" Mark clung to the ladder as the ship lurched up and pitched down again. Something rattled alarmingly above and he heard a faint shout. He nearly went up to help, but then he heard the captain call and he didn't sound alarmed.

"Bless you, lord jester, there's sail up, not that it'd matter much. The wind'd push us about a good bit even if we ran naked. We're laying pretty." Apparently Mark's blank expression convinced him he ought to be more clear. "The gale's blowin' the wrong way, so rather than fight it out anymore, we're sitting a bit and waiting."

8   E. M. Prazeman

"So we're stationary?"

"As any can be in the thick of it!"

Mark frowned. "I feel utterly useless." No one heard him. "I'm useless!" His own passion startled him.

"You look a bit better, if you don't mind me sayin' lord jester. I'll see if the cook has anything for you, and maybe Glint can milk a goat for ye."

"Please don't trouble anyone Mr. Briggs." But the sailor had already gotten up to go to the cook.

Something wasn't right, though he couldn't say what. He felt uneasy. Maybe he was finally seasick. Three of *Dainty's* own crew had been seasick for much of the storm so he didn't feel ashamed of it. And yet he didn't exactly feel ill, though his stomach burned as it always did when it was empty. If anything he felt afraid, and the chill from the damp gripped him harder than ever. Gale stared intently at him. The ship rose and for a moment it felt as if everything slowed, even his own breathing. *Dainty* rushed downward but he felt as if he were floating.

"You feeling ill again, lord jester?" Magpie called, looking up from his cards.

"I'm—" He started to say fine, but the scent of spice and wine filled his senses. He started to fall and rushing filled his ears—

A strong, black wind enveloped him, mingled with golden and orange flames. The spice scent permeated his flesh and he couldn't breathe. He writhed and fought for air, dying. His skin tattered and tore in that wind, flesh parted from bone on his face, and his chest seemed to crack open.

"I have you. I have you," Winsome said. The blackness and pain faded into the pressure of strong arms and Winsome's jasmine and orange blossom perfume. She was soaked and ice cold and dripping with seawater that chilled his already damp clothes. Mark tried to move but he couldn't. It was all he do to draw in one staggering breath after another.

Gale growled. It was the first time Mark had heard her make such a noise.

"It's all right, Gale," Winsome told her sharply.

"I'm sorry, Lady Kilderkin. She won't let me near him," Mr. Briggs said, "and I don't dare manhandle her. Puppies have soft bones."

Winsome stroked Mark's face. Her frigid touch didn't soothe him. He wished she would stop. "Throw me a rag," she told Mr. Briggs. "Let me clean his face. And bring him some clean clothes. I'll wash him."

"It ain't proper for a lady to have to—"

"Please, just do as I say." Her voice sounded different, commanding, as it had the day that Grant died.

He hated being so weak, helpless, useless. He should have been at the peak of his strength. He'd turn twenty years old soon, and he'd become more debilitated than Lord Argenwain.

His growing frustration helped him move. He managed to catch Winsome's wrist and pulled her hand from his face. Gale came over and licked his hand. She'd learned not to lick his face, finally.

"I've never seen anything like it." Magpie sounded afraid.

"My brother had the kellai dances," Mr. Gerran said. "Killed him one day. Kept shakin' and shakin' and then he turned blue and that was it."

"That's enough, Mr. Gerran," Winsome told him. "This is from poison. The lord jester will recover in time."

Love's faith is a fallen hope. He'd read it in a sacred poetry book and the words lingered, attaching themselves to unexpected circumstances. The meaning kept changing nuances and fragmenting. Words of a broken mind, or sacred insight into what Winsome had come to mean to him?

He felt as if he could take a full breath at last. Mark sighed and closed his eyes.

"That's it," Winsome breathed, or something close to the words. "The storm mostly drowned her voice. "You're safe now."

The bolt slid and the hatch door opened. Water spilled down and the screaming wind battered wood against wood. The heavy hinges groaned.

Captain Shuller and Mr. Johns descended. Mr. Johns slammed the hatch shut and bolted it while sailors scrambled to mop the loose water before it could reach the cargo. "How is he?" Captain Shuller had Mark's spare clothes bundled under his heavy oilskin greatcoat.

"He's calmed," Winsome told them.

"We'll take care of him from here on, Lady Kilderkin."

"But—"

"I'm sure you know what's best," Captain Shuller told her, "but kindly allow the lord jester to receive care from a quarter that will not bring him shame or regret when he is well again. If you wish to be of use, perhaps you can direct the cook. He will be most anxious to hear what might be best to aid in Lord Jester Lark's recovery."

Winsome stood, flushing pink with fury in her gaze, but her shoulders lowered and her chin lifted and she walked away with dignity, her hands following the beam.

"Thank you," Mark managed to whisper. He doubted that they heard him over the storm's racket.

"Don't worry, lord jester," Mr. Johns told him brightly. "We've cared for the sick before, haven't we, captain?"

"Indeed we have, Mr. Johns. And if we do well here we may yet achieve some fame in the practice of our art, should the lord jester care to sing of it. Holt, if you would procure some hot water without scalding half the crew, I would be much obliged."

"Yes, sir!"

Gale stayed close, weaving among the men's legs as they carried Mark near to his hammock. They staggered a bit with the ship's roll, but it was a controlled side-stepping from long practice and he never felt in any danger of them falling with him.

"The weather," Mark said. He smiled in spite of everything. "It's a little rough."

"That it is," Mr. Johns said with a laugh.

"I wouldn't mind. If. I could be dry."

Captain Shuller laughed this time. "That's the truth. Storms would be much more pleasant if we could have a dry spot somewhere on the ship."

"And. If I had. A hot bath," Mark said as they helped him strip. Some of the strength was returning to his arms, though nothing like the strength he'd fought so hard to regain. He wondered if he'd lost it all again, and if any amount of fighting would get him back to where he'd been such a short time ago, helping at the pumps.

"A hot bath would seem contrary to being dry," Captain Shuller remarked loudly.

Something like a dream, but waking, made him think of music and jeweled dancers weaving and unweaving. There across the room stood the handsome, dark-haired Colonel Rohn Evan, motioning for him to come over but Mark was having too much fun. "A dance. Would suffice."

"Did he say a dance?" Mr. Johns asked.

"I think our friend the lord jester is a little drunk from the tall waves." Captain Shuller peeled off Mark's shirt and rubbed his skin with it. The rough and painful contact helped revive him. The dancing dream vanished entirely as the cold overtook him, making him shiver so hard his body spasmed.

Drinking. Mark missed wine. His painful gut wouldn't allow him even a small taste without swift retribution.

The wind raged and the ship swayed and beams creaked but didn't crack. He probably should have been afraid, but after he suffered a few bites of bread and a glass of milk, Mark curled around the searing pain in his belly and felt safe. The men helped him into his hammock and stood by while he dozed but didn't quite find sleep.

The real danger waited for him on the mainland. Though he wished he could stay on *Dainty* forever, he wanted to face that danger as soon as possible and get it over with.

Better to die in learning the truth than to wait for the poison that had wounded him finally kill him. And maybe, at last, Winsome would go home. Meridua needed a woman like her. Colonel Evan needed her, and if, or rather when Mark died, Colonel Rohn Evan would finally be forced to admit how much he loved her.

"You'll have your family," Mark wrote to him later that night, his handwriting wandering around the page more than he liked as the ship bowed, curtseyed and removed again and again at the brutally playful sea's direction. "You'll love again like you never knew you could love. You'll know the love a father has for his child. You'll know happiness." Mark caressed the paper, and wished it was Rohn.

Chapter Two

The first time Mark heard Captain Shuller speak in a foreign tongue, it sounded like a curse. The wind had dropped, switched, and built waves that slammed the hull so hard they all feared even the incredibly thick oak would snap. The changeable weather harassed the poor sailors such that no one got more than two hours sleep at a stretch for a week. The captain would command sails to be raised and a change of course, only to have to pull them down again, or change the angle of the booms, or heave to. They grew so desperate for relief that they even placed Mark at the helm to help Magpie, a fair-skinned new recruit with a natural-born burgundy stain over much of his face.

Magpie had done what Mark hadn't managed to do in his own life. The Church had claimed Magpie as an infant, declaring his birthmark sacred. When he was twelve Magpie escaped to the sea, and he'd been sailing ever since. The Church, he told Mark, still tried to lure him, steal him, imprison him, and bribe him but in the end he always escaped or forced them to let him go. "Last time they locked me up I starved myself," he'd told Mark early on their watch.

Mark had allowed his fear of Lord Jester Gutter and of the Church to make him retreat to what he thought of as safety—a bond with Colonel Evan. And most of the time he didn't regret it. But every time he looked at Magpie, he was reminded that he could have found another way to run, and if he was caught to escape and run again. He just didn't have the courage or the will. He wanted to be safe.

Or maybe he just wanted to be loved more than he wanted to be free.

That hadn't worked out very well either.

Confidante 13

Mark helped Magpie change course, their hands moving in a now-practiced rhythm together against the smooth spokes. He didn't have much strength to lend to it, but he had an important duty. If Magpie slipped Mark had to catch the wheel and, if it was too strong for them, lock it. He also helped Magpie keep watch on the instruments. Again, Magpie could do it on his own, but Mark was there in case he dozed off or his attention lapsed. The work helped mitigate the cold from the rain and wind, though it exposed his already icy hands to the weather.

Holt climbed aloft. Mark thought it might be to adjust or repair something, but the sailor scanned the horizon. How anyone could see anything with the wind tearing off the tops of the waves and sending them like swarms of needles into everyone's eyes, Mark had no idea.

"Land ho!" Holt scrambled down and went to confer with Captain Shuller, who sheltered in the cabin. The captain came out and strode to the bow. He ordered change after change in course.

"Can't just trot in," Magpie explained while Mark helped with the wheel, responding to the navigator's somewhat nervous directions. "There's not much sea room at the mouth. Go in wrong and the wind drives you onto the rocks, or you get bound up in sands, or end up in chains and get pushed to where you can't even row out. Once we're in a fair way, though, the bay is the place to be in weather like this."

Mark finally saw it. At first he noticed a faint dark line, and then as they drew closer, another line that separated the rough waves from the friendly, rounded water in Hullundy Bay. The elements were so radically different from one another, and so clearly defined, they could have been in two entirely different spheres of existence, like life and the hells.

The captain strode back and took the wheel. "Magpie, I want you forward. Lord jester, you may as well begin to pack your things. You're home."

Home probably meant a different thing to a sailor, though Mark couldn't deny that part of him still considered Seven Churches by the Sea as home. He'd grown up in the old port, one of many that ringed the vast body of Hullundy Bay, and had only recently fled her.

It was spring, a typical rain-sodden, gray and stormy spring. He didn't remember it being this cold. Living in the tropics had likely weakened his hardiness as much as the poison.

The cloaks he'd put away he now took out for the first time since he'd left. Obsidian's and Lake's cloaks were mended and clean. They would suffice for all but the most formal events, and he wasn't planning to go to any of those.

No, this journey would have no beauty in it.

"Lark." Winsome looked in his open doorway. "Mr. Johns just told me we've all but arrived."

"We have." Something about her tone gave him hope. "Have you changed your mind?"

Beneath her fragile calm, she looked frightened. "Please tell me you won't leave me somewhere. Don't you dare abandon me."

Winsome didn't have to tell him. He could see it in her eyes. She'd never been on the mainland, and she had begun to realize how vast it was. Perida's size and the main island's span had surprised Mark at first, but it didn't take long to explore the city to its limits. Several Peridas would fit in Seven Churches, and Seven Churches was only one of several substantial port towns that lined Hullundy Bay. The only reason there weren't more large ports in the great bay were because of the famed hundred mile stretch of daunting cliffs. As for the island itself, a pair of them could have fit in the bay and still left leeway for ships.

Mark averted his gaze and continued to pack, though he wasn't thinking about what he was doing anymore. "You should go back to Perida."

"And what if you have a seizure somewhere. Who's going to help you? Gale?"

He couldn't find a swift rebuttal. "It isn't like you'll be forced to stand over my body holding off the assassins until I recover. Either I'll be in a situation where the people around me will help, I'll recover on my own, or it will be over for me."

"I'm of no help to you whatsoever." She sounded more angry than hurt, but her eyes brightened.

"I don't require your help. That's all I'm attempting to tell you."

"So if you fail, you fail, and too bad for Meridua and too bad for the colonel and that's it."

He'd been so stupid. She didn't just want to find her father and either save him or whatever else she planned to do with him. She wanted to know, just as passionately as Mark did, who threatened Meridua's freedom, and find a way to stop them.

She'd been fighting for Meridua's freedom a lot longer than he had. She had more right to it than him.

Mark hadn't folded his clothes very well. They didn't fit in the chest like they had when he'd left. He lamely drew a few pieces out and refolded them.

"Will you at least tell me if you have any reliable and honest allies on the mainland?" she demanded.

He didn't, not really, but he didn't want to admit that. Mark sat heavily on the bed. "We can't talk here."

Her frustration faded into something more pale and pensive.

"You may change your mind after you hear what I have to say," Mark told her.

"I doubt it."

"Not because of them, but because of me. Who I am. What I am."

She got back some of that wary look that she had when they'd first met on the beach near Perida. "Who are you?"

"You should pack," Mark told her. "Oh, and take this." He gave her Obsidian's cloak. "You'll need it."

Winsome clutched the cloak to her chest and watched him for a while before she retreated. The ship settled into quieter water and rolled with sounds almost like sighs heaving along the hull. Gulls, barely in evidence in the storm, now flew wildly in the fierce wind all around them. They didn't sound any different from gulls in Perida, and yet they seemed lonelier here.

He wondered if he'd ever again hear the strange cries of exotic birds, or feel warm, or bask in the sun, or see Rohn again.

I shouldn't dwell. I have a job to do.

And he would see Gutter again. Behind the fear and dread, his heart shivered with a strange and unaccountable joy.

"What are those?" Winsome gasped.

"Aqueducts. Please, try not to point." Mark didn't mean to be short with her, but he was as nervous as if his soul had been targeted by a Hunt. He attracted the attention of the nearest coach. They'd only been out in the rain for a few minutes, but he was already shivering from cold. "University," he told the driver, and urged Winsome to go in ahead of him. Gale had learned how to go up steep steps on the ship and neatly piled in after Winsome.

As far as he could tell, they hadn't drawn any unusual notice. That may have been in part because he'd insisted that Winsome needed to dress in a proper gown without a pistol or dagger on her belt. He'd dressed well, but down, and carefully avoided any sign that he might be serving as a jester, which included leaving his rapier behind. He allowed himself his town sword housed in a plain sheath he'd borrowed, and a small dagger.

The coach bumped and slid on the slick streets up toward the university as soon as Mark shut the door. Gale braced against his legs. He ran his fingers through her coarse, rain-dampened fur, allowing himself to be distracted by her. He couldn't say that he depended on her, or that he felt particularly close to her, but the thought of leaving her behind scared him.

Because she warned me. She always warns me, whether it's an assassin at my door or a seizure coming or a rider with a message.

He kept the strap to his satchel looped over his shoulder in case they had to bolt.

"Why are the roads all rounded rock?" Winsome sounded confused. "It makes the carriage rattle and look how people slip on them when they cross."

"It's so you can walk on them when there's a lot of rainwater without getting as wet," Mark explained.

"Shouldn't we try to find a room first?"

"*Dainty* won't leave until tomorrow, and I don't know if we're staying in Seven Churches yet or not." Mark wished she'd stop asking so many questions.

"Then why the hurry?"

He didn't want Gutter to hear of his arrival before Mark actually knocked on the door, but he couldn't tell her that. There was a small chance the coachman might overhear.

"It never stops raining, does it." Winsome looked pensively out the window.

Mark smiled at that. "It does. Eventually."

"What's that?"

Mark remembered the night *Mairi* had burned with painful clarity. "The Bracken Watertower." He'd passed it on the way to the docks forever ago when *Mairi* had burned. It stood, as it had always stood, as a bright whiteness amid the jumble of dingy, white-washed walls and slate or red tile roofs. Mostly tradesmen and sailors and their families lived here. It wasn't the poorest place in Seven Churches, but it was cluttered and busy and crowded, with living quarters stacked three or more stories high and narrow streets that seldom saw sunlight.

When it shone, the sun always won through to play upon the elaborate bronze grate twenty yards wide all around the tower. Water gurgled under that grate year-round, sometimes almost right under his feet, or in the last throes of summer, far below. Especially in summer Mark loved to go there to get fresh drinking water. It might take him an hour, not because there was a long wait at one of the spigots, but because he'd meet his friends there more often than not and they'd chat like the adults all around them until duty to their families forced them to return.

The docks had been repaired and painted since the fire. Only a few charred places remained, but their sharp scent cut into him and poured in memories of fire, flesh burned black with delicate pink cracks, and blood on snow.

Gale licked his hand. He scratched her head and she stuck out her pink tongue, just the cutest little bit.

"We have cisterns. They're lined in mosaic tile." Winsome sounded as if she were defending the magnificence of Perida, to no avail.

"I didn't have a chance to see them. I'm sure they're beautiful."

Winsome sat back and stared at his gloved hands. She'd seen the strange scar on his hand. He wondered if she'd asked Rohn about it. He always wore gloves now, even to bed, but she'd seen him stripped.

And now, so had the captain. Captain Shuller hadn't said anything about it. Mark wondered if either of them had seen something like it before. For all he knew, all jesters had some sort of scar somewhere.

Yet another question for Professor Vinkin.

"Why are we going to the university?" she asked.

"You're staying in the coach."

"I am not." No childish petulance or hysterics. Just a low-spoken, hard fact.

Mark sat harder against the seat back and stared out the window. The rain blurred everything outside. Tenements gave way to townhouses and homes with small gardens. Soon they'd see manors.

"I wish—" she began. Winsome scratched behind Gale's ear, her fair face drawn with unhappiness. "I wish I could carry a pistol."

It didn't sound as if she'd meant to complain about not carrying her pistol, but he doubted that she would confess to her original thought if he asked. "I'll see what I can do."

"You mean that?"

Mark nodded. "There are smaller arms you can carry, small enough to hide in your clothes. I just don't want you to stand out if we can help it. Ladies don't usually carry weapons in Seven Churches."

"Short barrels are inaccurate." She crossed her arms. "But if that's all you'll allow me, I'll make do."

"It's not me, Winsome. It's this place. It's very different from the islands."

The coach drew up in front of the university. Mark got out and had to catch Gale before she hopped out right after him. Rohn and everyone else who groomed the Meriduan obsession with dogs had nagged him about being careful not to let her jump down from anything taller than a breadbox.

Meanwhile, Winsome drew the cloak's hood over her head and helped herself down rather than waiting for a hand. Mark paid the coachman, who drew up behind a line of other coaches to wait for jesters and jesters-in-training who might need a ride. Mark drew up his hood a bit belatedly. Usually the rain didn't bother him, but even the few drips that slipped from his hair onto his neck made him shiver.

"These drivers just sit around all day?" Winsome asked.

"They usually don't have to wait long," Mark assured her. "It's not a good living, but they survive." He gazed for a long time at the university gates. They stood two stories tall, some jester's masterwork eternally on display. He recognized the flowers from his journeys into the afterlife. The artist had depicted them with petals of silver flame with gold needles in the center. The flowers at the gate's base were painted but those higher up were done with precious metals.

"Whenever you stare like that, I worry that—" She bit her lip and hugged her arms over her ribs. "Never mind."

"What?" he asked.

She winced. "It's the same look you have when, well, right after. You know."

"After I've been struck down."

She nodded.

At least the seizures didn't happen often.

Classes must have been in session. No student jesters lingered outside. They passed the gates into the courtyard where fruit trees, arrayed in pink and white, spread limbs over beds brightened by tulips and daffodils. Only a few small groups of young men loitering about noticed them crossing toward the main building. One of the jesters, a boy no older than fifteen, let out a low whistle at Winsome. The others laughed, and she blushed.

Mark wasn't sure if the boy wanted to start a duel or had merely been inspired to pay her a crass compliment. He wasn't interested in finding out.

Two older boys, their fine clothes protected by oilskin cloaks, opened the doors to the main building for them. Four enormous cherrywood and iron staircases rose from the vast room's four corners, and a central staircase plunged downward. It was all lit with stained glass and gas lamps and adorned with paintings, musical and scientific instruments cased in glass, and incredible tapestries.

Winsome gaped. Mark wished he'd attended the university if only for the privilege of exploring all the halls and up all those staircases where no doubt even more beautiful marvels awaited.

A jester hurried toward them and took a deep bow with a flourish. "May I be of assistance?"

"I need to speak with Professor Vinkin as soon as possible," Mark told him.

"He has class at this hour."

"We'll wait."

"May I ask who is calling?"

Mark wondered if Professor Vinkin would even want to see him. "I'd rather we wait by his office." The jester started to look wary and Gale began to growl, so Mark had to relent. "Tell him the boy who was beaten and disappeared has returned, and requests one last lesson."

Winsome, to her credit, said nothing and stood close.

"If you would kindly wait here." The jester led them to a panel that slid open. It revealed a small, comfortable room. The jester lit a candle for them, saw them seated, slid the panel closed and left.

"The boy who w—"

Mark shook his head and tapped his ear. Winsome stiffened in her seat and folded her hands together. Anyone watching or listening would soon be bored.

Mark set the satchel on his lap, the strap still slung over his shoulder. He spent his time admiring a small statue of a horse on a marble pedestal. It reminded him of Rohn. Hells, sometimes everything reminded him of Rohn. The horse reared wildly, mane flared, neck arched in fierce display of its power and pride.

They'd only waited a few minutes when the door slid open. "Professor Vinkin wishes to meet you at the Lantern Garden in an hour."

"Thank you. I will be there." Mark handed Winsome up and left in a hurry. He hired another coach. He could have walked it but he didn't have enough time and he feared he wouldn't have the strength.

"Now where are we going?" she asked.

"Pickwelling," he told her tightly.

"Where? I thought we were supposed to go to—"

"I know, but we were seen and I don't know how quickly the news will spread if someone recognizes me. I want to arrive ahead of any warning."

Winsome, with uncharacteristic patience, just stared at him.

"Pickwelling is Lord Argenwain's manor," Mark told her. She paled but didn't ask any more questions. "Please, stay in the coach with Gale."

Winsome nodded.

He took her hand and squeezed. It was the wrong thing to do, but he needed it. In moments he might lose her.

In moments he might be swept away and carried out into a vast sea whose only shore would be the one man in the world he trusted the least.

Gutter.

Chapter Three

Holly hedges hid away the gardens on both sides save for a few tall cherry, apple and peach trees, their blossoms gone and their limbs filled out with tender leaves. The tallest lilacs teased the sky with lavender, plum and periwinkle blossoms. Beneath the hollies, shy anemones hid their blue, white and delicate pink blossoms from the rain. Near the house, rhododendrons blared pink trumpets. Behind the house, he remembered the red ones and even more rare, the pale yellow ones with maroon-speckled throats. They would likely be in full show as well.

Gutter's roses would wait awhile yet.

Home. Surrounded by the grandest of manors, Pickwelling hid away within its many acres, where deer roamed as if this were a wild place rather than a building in a crowded city. As they approached the brick turnabout, the rain finally pattered to a stop.

Mark unslung the strap to the satchel. Best to leave it behind. "Winsome. Please guard this well."

"You can depend on me."

Mark did, more than he dared to admit. He lifted Gale's fuzzy head with both hands and stroked her face. He looked into her brown eyes, mostly hidden by her bangs. "Stay." He spoke it softly and with care. She understood even without the command tone and didn't try to follow him out of the coach.

It had been a long time since he'd walked up to this door, usually ahead of Lord Argenwain to open it for him. He could almost see his younger self, not yet touched by Lord Argenwain's trembling hands or kissed by that drooping mouth, opening the way and then taking the old man's arm to make certain he wouldn't trip at the low threshold. *I'll fetch you your slippers!*

And up the stairs he'd dash ahead, never looking back to see the expression on his lord's face. Now Mark wished he had. Would he see sorrow, joy, laughter, pain, lust ... maybe all.

Mark had been happy here at times. More, he'd been healthy. He'd never imagined that he'd be weakened by poison, his belly burning or twisting in agony, with spells of weakness that sometimes kept him from managing stairs.

But at the moment he could walk, maybe even fight.

He rang the bell. So familiar, that fine chord, like a velvet hammer striking piano wires. Most house bells just rang something between a dinner bell and a cow bell.

A boy answered and Mark stepped back in shock.

It could have been Mark himself standing there, though the young man was maybe sixteen, and prettier, and of course he would be taller later though now they were about a height. Blond, like Mark, but without the darker hair at his neck and behind his ears. He wore Mark's old clothes. Was it because they suited him, or because he didn't warrant a separate identity?

The boy drew himself up a little taller and his ice blue eyes stared boldly at Mark for a moment before he dropped his gaze, as he must to someone who was theoretically his better. "Welcome to Pickwelling. May I ask who is calling?" His voice had little refinement, and a bit of a dockside swagger to it.

"Lark." But it wasn't Lark who stepped inside the house as the boy reluctantly backed out of his way. He should have worn his mask, protected himself from this. There was the hated statue of the boy reclining alongside the fawn. And there, the stairs that would lead him to Lord Argenwain's bedchamber. That familiar route. To the left, the study where he'd spent hours with tutors.

"Master jester." He sounded as if he didn't believe Mark could really be a jester, despite the jester's name. "May I—are you here to see someone?" the boy asked, sounding ruffled.

"Is Gutter home?"

The boy tensed. "No." He said it as if he was glad, and offended, and afraid. "Master jester," he added belatedly. "Would you—"

Mark handed him the card he'd made. "Is he in town?"

"I'm not sure I should tell you that." The boy stomped over to the butler's bell and rang it. "Would you like to wait for the butler in our sitting room? It's right over—"

"No, thank you. And I know where it is."

The boy sucked in a sharp breath and his hands began to tremble. "You're him. You're Mark."

Mark wanted to grab him and take him away from the house, and he wanted to slap him, and he wanted Gutter to be here and he wanted to run.

Lord Argenwain. He couldn't face him.

Mark went out the door. "I'll return," Mark called over his shoulder. "Tonight. And if Gutter is not in town then I would like to know so that I don't waste any more of my time."

The boy ran after him. "Master jester!"

"Lord jester," Mark corrected him. He started to climb into the coach but the boy brushed his sleeve in a desperate attempt to stall him. Even that slight contact stopped him, not because of the impropriety, but because he couldn't stand to be cruel and cold to the poor boy anymore.

"Lord jester, I'm so terribly sorry." The boy had paled so much his mouth had gone white. "Please forgive me. Please come into the house. Gutter is in town, but he's away for the day. He'll be back for dinner. Please. I'm sure Lord Argenwain would want to see you. He's been ...." The boy's gaze lowered to the ground. "Please."

"He's been what." Mark dreaded that the boy would tell him that Lord Argenwain was ill, even dying. Winsome's strong hand settled on his shoulder and steadied him.

"I shouldn't say." The boy tightened up again.

"He's not ill?"

"No. No. Just old. He's just old." The boy's voice hardened. "Will you come to the house, please." He finally noticed Winsome's feet. Mark got in his way when he craned his neck to try to see her. Gale hopped down from the coach seat and sat in the coach's doorway, looking very serious but not particularly threatening with her puppy softness.

"I will arrive as near dinnertime as I can manage," Mark told him.

"Where are you staying, lord jester, so that we can send a message if—"

"I'll be here near seven," Mark told him. Gale made way for him as he climbed up into the coach. He shut the door, patted the wall, and the coach took them away.

Winsome sat quietly across from him. She didn't venture a word. When they passed the gate she took his hand. "You're trembling."

Mark leaned over and pressed her hand to his forehead. He was sweating too. He usually could ignore the constant pain in his belly, but now it seemed to slice him in half. Her cool hand calmed him. He braced on his knees and closed his eyes and let the carriage's rough sway lull him.

The carriage had turned toward the church, and halted outside. Mark had often walked this distance to pay on his indenture. He needed to talk to the priest and see if it had been paid off, or if Dellai Bertram had betrayed him or played some other game.

Not now. He didn't want to deal with that priest yet. Besides, they had more pressing things to attend to.

"Excuse me, lord jester," the driver called. "Where to now?"

Home.

He couldn't go to the islands, but he had somewhere almost as dear to him nearby. "Walker Main."

"Thank you, lord jester." The carriage started rolling again.

Winsome ran the fingers of her free hand through his hair. "I'm here," she said softly. "Please, tell me what you need me to do."

He knew he shouldn't accept her comfort, but he didn't want to hurt her anymore, and her kindness soothed him. "Just this," he whispered.

They passed under the narrow aqueduct, the smallest one in Seven Churches, the one that served the Bracken Watertower. The coach stopped at the fountain where Courser Street and Tailor Street veed at Walker Main. Mark opened the door and the driver got down this time to help them out. "Here you go, lord jester," the driver said. "Shall I wait?"

"Yes. Here." Mark gave him a cupru. He probably would have stayed for two bits, but Mark wanted to be sure. They had to meet Professor Vinkin before too long.

First he wanted to find a place to retreat to. He'd originally meant to find a quiet inn somewhere, but this would be better.

He walked toward his mother's wine shop, only vaguely aware of the satchel bumping against his back and Gale at his heels. He would have passed it, only he noticed the old bakery across the way and stopped. It had been converted into a cheese shop. Mark touched the door, caressed the handle.

He couldn't dwell too long here.

His eyes closed. He could still smell the old wine, even past the ripe, exotic cheeses. He wondered whatever happened to his family's furniture. He had a wild need to find out if it was still upstairs so that he could buy it and send it to the islands.

Not now. Perhaps never would be better.

Mark took a good look around and ventured down the main. He crossed the street a few doors down. He went into the fish shop—a bell tinkled anemically—and stopped at the counter. Old Gosh Warner wouldn't remember him. "Excuse me."

Warner made a good living selling the best fish in town to wealthy patrons. It showed in his glass cases and the quality of the meat, set in salt and this time of year, in snow shipped in from the hills that arrived too dirty for making sherbet and ices. Everything was perfect and clean, all the fish filleted on the spot and never a single bone in it. The old, broad-backed man with the long face, white hair and smoke-stained mustache and beard turned from his work scrubbing down his cutting board. His yellowed eyes widened. "Why—aren't you little Mark Seaton, all grown up?"

That made Mark laugh. "Yes. Yes it is."

"And by my shiny buckles aren't you dressed as fine as Lord Argenwain himself."

Mark refused to let his smile falter. "Thank you. Mr. Warner. This is my good friend Lady Winsome Kilderkin."

Gosh bowed his head for a long moment. "A pleasure, my lady. Now what brings you to my shop after all these years?"

"Do you still have a room to let over your place?" Mark asked.

"Aw, I'm so sorry, but no. It's been rented to the same family for the past three years or so. But I know a place just a few down. It's rough, though, if you're thinking—"

"I'm sure it'll be fine," Mark said hastily. "Where is it?"

"Gerty's Jam's and Jellies. You remember it, don't you?"

"I'm afraid I don't. My mother made her own."

Gosh nodded, and the pain in his eyes made Mark tear up. So people still remembered. "I'm so sorry about—did they ever find out what happened?" Gosh asked.

"No."

Gosh's mouth tightened. "Figures." He tossed his scrubber in a soap bin. "Priests." He practically spat the word, and Winsome's head jerked. Gosh winced. "Sorry, my lady."

"I'm not offended," she assured him.

"I'll be back soon if I can," Mark promised him. He had so much he wanted to ask, and not just about what had happened to everyone he'd known. He wanted to know if anyone knew, or cared about what he'd been to Lord Argenwain. Part of him thought that of course they'd have to know, but then, he never came here after his indenture had been sold, and they would never have an occasion to see him up above the university. Not many of them could read well enough to read the gazette, even if they'd had any interest, and they wouldn't connect Lark to Mark to wonder if he might not be a bound jester now.

Gosh had been watching him. He averted his gaze when Mark looked up at him. "Do come back if it pleases you, son. I'll have a nice cut of fish waiting by for you. You're terrible thin, boy. You need some good dockside food in you."

Mark almost protested, but then he changed his mind. "Thank you." He fled, and hurried down the street looking for the jam shop.

"Wait. Wait!" Winsome caught up with him when Mark slowed for her. "I don't understand half of what you're doing."

"While I'm at the Rythan Gardens, I want you to find a room at an inn. I'll be staying here. We'll engage a messenger to run between us when we need it."

"I'm staying with you."

"No, you're not."

She hooked his elbow with surprising strength. Gale huffed an uncertain snarl at her. "I didn't come to be dragged about like this and then left to sit in a room at an inn. Don't forget. If something should happen ... if you're alone, or worse, in public when you next ... if you should fall ...."

Mark stared away, vaguely aware of people going about their business, the horses and carts and butlers and children and geese being herded through. "I know. I'm sorry. But you can't stay with me. Your reputation—"

"You don't even know my reputation, or whether I care about it, which I don't."

"The colonel cares, and he will care if some gazette makes its way into his hands about how we shared a room overlooking a trader's street."

"I'm sure it won't be just one large room. Even if it is, if he doesn't trust me with you then he oughtn't trust what I might or might not have done during the war." Her eyes widened as if she hadn't meant to admit so much, but she jutted her chin in a show of determination.

Mark's jumbled feelings settled, finally overruled by the cares and hurts of someone other than himself. It didn't matter if he'd instinctively wanted to punish her for following him or if it had all been part of his desire to drive her away back home and into the colonel's arms. She needed him. The few slips where she showed her fear no doubt spoke of her overall terror. Her father had abandoned her, and she was left with a legacy of disgrace, suspicion, and an uncertain offer of courtship.

He had to admit he needed her too. He took her hand, kissed it, and led it around his arm so they could walk together properly. "I'm sorry."

She let out a sigh. "Never mind," she told him softly.

As a child he'd dreamed of walking with a fine lady someday. He had his wish at last, though like most things of late, it didn't feel like he'd expected it would.

The husband of the jam shop lady showed them the rooms. There was a small common area. It had a stove suitable for cooking and heating the rooms, a large table but only two chairs, a coat and hat rack, and a bin for shoes and boots with a few cleaning brushes and an old tin of shoe polish thrown in. The rental had three other rooms: a bedroom, a washroom which included a large laundry tub and wringer, and a cramped little office barely large enough to hold the desk inside it. Mark wondered how they'd gotten it in there. All the furnishings were modest, but in good repair, though they were a bit dusty.

"It's yours for two cupru a week," the husband began.

"Done," Mark told him.

"You have to provide your own linens and curtains. Mum'll wash 'em, but not your clothes," he continued, seemingly unaffected by the quick agreement.

"Excellent. Thank you."

"And we expect payment in advance." The husband held out his hand.

Mark dropped the coin into it.

"Beggin' your pardon, my lady," the husband muttered briefly to Winsome before addressing Mark sternly. "No whorin' and no visitors after dark. This is a nice neighborhood and if my neighbors complain I'll evict ye, no matter how fine your clothes are."

Mark smiled. "Thank you. I assure you you'll have no trouble from us."

"We're not afraid of your like, you know. We do good business with some of the finest families in town."

"I'm sure you do," Mark assured him. "Now if you don't mind, I'll send for our things. Where can I buy some additional furniture?"

"On Welling Street at the corner of Thirteens."

"Thank you." Mark encouraged him to leave with a gesture toward the door. "I'll have locks installed. I hope you don't mind."

"If you leave the keys I don't mind, but if you take them with you I'll insist you replace these doors."

"I will see that you get the keys. Thank you." Mark shut the door behind him. He shook some more coin out of his purse. "Winsome, if you could please, buy me a bed, and something to screen off part of the room, along with any linens and curtains you might want. I'll sleep in here, and you can have the bedroom. Now, I have to go speak with Professor Vinkin."

"Are we really going to be here a week?"

"You'll at least be here one night, and I'd rather you were in some comfort."

"I might be—" She seemed to change her mind, took a breath, and started again. "You aren't going to leave me here by myself, and I'm not going to let you run off while I play house servant." She looked like she wanted to slap him. Mark would have let her get away with it. "At the very least I'm going with you to that manor house tonight."

Dizziness rushed through his head. He needed to eat, but he didn't want to. To hide his weakness he carefully measured his steps to the table and braced on a chair. "Please have a seat."

Winsome stared at him a moment before she walked over and settled down. The chair creaked even under her slight weight. Mark sat down. He traced a letter G in the dust before he realized what he was doing. Grant's loss cramped in his chest. He took a deep breath and tried to let it go.

He couldn't tell Winsome all of it.

"I was a servant in Lord Argenwain's house," he told her quietly so that no one downstairs could overhear. "And I was Gutter's pupil." She didn't react so he went on. "The day I left, a young jester named Obsidian came to me, and gave me—" She knew he had them. She'd seen the codes. He still hesitated telling her so much, when only he and the colonel knew all of it. "He gave me the code book that helped me decipher those messages your father traded with the mainland. Before Obsidian died he told me Gutter would have to be the one to salvage the situation."

"Did you kill him?" she asked softly, her voice betraying only idle curiosity.

The suggestion shocked him, but it shouldn't have. Winsome knew him as an efficient killer with quite a few corpses under his feet. "No. I didn't kill him." She wouldn't believe it if he told her that part of the reason everything had worked out the way it did was because he didn't want Obsidian to ambush and murder Lake, a jester Mark hadn't even met. "The difficult part of all this is that I don't know what Obsidian was trying to do, and I don't know what Gutter's part in all this might be. Worst of all, I don't know what my part was meant to be. Intrigues are dangerous not just because of the money and political power behind them, but because so much of what they are is unknown. I'm in the worst possible position.

I don't know anything. I'm walking in blind. The only reason I dare do that is because I'm arrogant enough to think that Gutter might spare my life if I get in his way. I might still be useful to him. And it's hard for me to believe that all our years together were a lie. I think he truly cares about me. Part of him does, anyway." He wondered if that might not be a deadly assumption. "But the trouble with wearing masks as long as he has is that there's no way of telling whether it's the mask or the man that loves you." Somehow that last admission had changed color along the way. He hoped Winsome had heard the warning, and understood that Lark wasn't a man. Mark was, and she didn't know either of them well enough to know what was a mask and what was human.

Winsome sat quietly. She traced little circles in the dust.

"That house." No amount of explaining could prepare her. "You don't want to walk into that house, and sit at the dining table with those men. Please trust me on this."

"I trust you," she said softly.

That surprised him. He'd expected more argument. "If they wanted to hurt me, you couldn't protect me anyway."

"But I can." She looked up. "I'm a sharpshooter. They have a garden. They have windows. I will be there."

The idea of Winsome shooting into Pickwelling didn't shock him nearly as much as the terrible image of a bullet piercing Gutter's face. "No. No!"

"I won't do a thing unless you signal me." She kept her voice low, but urgency sharpened it and a cold professionalism made his skin crawl.

"No." He covered his face but he couldn't hide from his imagination, and it tortured him with Gutter's death over and over.

"Let me help you." She tried to take his hand but he pushed away from the table, from her. The dizziness swept through him again but he managed to blink back the fuzziness and stand up straight. "At least tell me where the danger lies." Her commanding tone forced him to think.

"The danger." He focused on that. He had to consider where it might come from anyway. He should have from the start.

"Would they arrest you? Imprison you? Would they capture you and hold you in that house, or take you away?" Despite the ire in her gaze and the frustration written on her face she did a fair job of keeping her voice low. "You can't go into a situation like that, where no one willing to raise a hand to help you will hear you call for help. I won't wait around until you're overdue and then try to help without any idea of how to find you or what trouble you're in. You're not that stupid, and I'm not that weak."

"They wouldn't involve the Church. They've always acted above it," Mark told her. "They might hold me against my will, and they might take me from Seven Churches." It was long ago, but he remembered well. "To Saphir City."

"The famed Hasle city," she whispered.

"It's a long way away from here," he said. "I can tell them that I want to go. We might well want to go with them."

"But why?"

He'd talked freely about things so far because he doubted anyone could overhear, but this he didn't dare speak aloud. He balanced himself and walked to the table, where he traced a word in the dust.

King.

She'd been there. She knew the Cathretan King was in danger from this plot. She'd told him herself. What he didn't know was whether she cared.

He cared. The royal family represented and maintained all that was good about Cathret. Who or whatever might take their place would quickly be overwhelmed by long established connections, intrigues and corruption. That corruption apparently extended to the Church. That didn't shock him, but most people would be horrified, and rightly terrified at the idea. "If that which defines sin, law and justice is destroyed or corrupted, society itself will crumble."

It's already crumbling. The king's death will only cause it to crumble faster and reveal what's beneath the façade ....

He hadn't heard the voices in his mind for some time. Ruby's whisper, if it really was Ruby, startled him. And the king .... He couldn't be sure, but it sounded as if Ruby yearned for the king's death. Why? It seemed incomprehensible that a spiritual being would allow harm to come to anyone in the royal family, least of all His Royal Majesty Michael.

He had to be even more careful of what he said aloud, and who, or rather what, he trusted.

Social goodness is more than a façade. I've met too many good people to believe otherwise. Captain Shuller. Old Gosh.

Grant.

"We can't be responsible for this." Winsome jabbed the table next to the word. "This is what we're here for." She wrote Meridua in the dust. "And the colonel. Let the mainland take care of their own."

"I don't even know who is on what side. And these two are connected. We ignore one at the peril of the other."

You are wise to see this. The faith placed upon you is well given.

The praise made him want to grit his teeth, now that he knew absolutely that the voices couldn't be trusted.

"And what if these people are on the wrong side?" she asked. "You don't even know. I haven't forgotten. You asked me if I knew what side they were on that night—*you don't even know.*" Her voice choked off. "What do you think they'll do to you if they're part of the plot? I'd better be armed and waiting if for no other reason than to put a bullet through your heart. Better that than—" She took a deep breath and sat back. "Better that than torture."

He had the eerie suspicion that she calmed herself this swiftly and efficiently just before she shot at men during the war.

She didn't just shoot at them. She killed them. She might have even done it out of mercy before.

Mark took her hand and held it gently. She'd seen so much more than he ever would. He hadn't even considered that Gutter or the Church might lock him in a cell and have him tortured, possibly for years, to wring every last bit of information they could from him whether he had any that they wanted or not.

It wasn't done, of course. Jesters used to torture commoners, and sometimes each other in the olden days when jesters wore bells and knights reigned like little tyrant kings by rule of sword and only the royal family was thought to have everlasting souls, pieces of which could be loaned to favored subjects.

Lately he'd seen too much of the old ways, bad and good, glittering darkly in the shadows and cracks of things, to dismiss the idea that torturers still existed. Someone, somewhere would be willing to pour strange potions down his throat and peel his skin strip by strip.

That someone might even be Gutter.

No, not Gutter.

But perhaps Gutter wearing a mask.

Gutter had to have at least one death mask. And he'd do what had to be done for Lord Argenwain. He always did. He always would. He likely would do it for others, too. A priest, another noble ... a member of the royal family. Never under their orders in that case. The royal family had no corruption within it and would not even hint at the idea. But Gutter would do it for their own good. Especially His Royal Majesty King Michael. Gutter loved him like a brother.

If Gutter wants my help to save the king, I'm more than willing. But if Gutter is insane, and plots to kill the king he loves, will I have the strength and wit to stop him?

Winsome touched his cheek with the backs of her fingers. They were cool, and gentle, and reminded him of the first traces of soft stubble on his face. It made him want to shave, and to wash away the filth he'd become steeped in again. He hadn't been in Seven Churches for a whole day and he already felt soiled. He captured her hand, held both her hands in his, and looked into her eyes. "All right. Only on my signal. I won't let them take me into a room without windows." His heart quickened, but it wasn't him. The colonel's heart, bonded to his own, made itself felt though they were many hundreds of miles apart.

He couldn't do anything if Rohn was in trouble. Even if he leapt onto a ship this moment, it would take weeks to get there. Weeks too late.

Maybe Rohn was just having a nightmare. Mark had woken because of them before. Or it could be a fit of temper. They both had tempers, almost perfectly matched like a pair of carriage horses. It made him smile to think of it, but worry dragged him back down.

"We'll have to come up with signals so that I know who to aim for."

Mark would rather set himself as a target in all cases, but he knew better. He might discover something that would require a different target.

Long ago he had a hard time believing Gutter might kill him. Now he himself had to choose a signal that could end the great man's life.

I should have never become a jester.

Too late.

Of course Gutter will try to kill me too, if he has to.

Strangely, that certainty brought him comfort.

I suppose that makes us friends and equals in a way.

The cold humor in that thought felt foreign, but it wasn't. It came from Lark, from the blue eye.

No, Lark and Gutter were not equals. Fellow jesters, yes, but Gutter had no equal.

"I'll need a rifle," Winsome said. "Captain Shuller has a good one. I hope he'll loan it to me."

"If not, buy the best one you can find, through a sacred messenger if you can. I don't want anyone to come looking for you if you have to pull the trigger." He kissed her hand and slipped away from her. "I have to go."

"But what if we end up going to Saphir? This will be a waste of time and money."

"This was my home street. These people are not a waste of my time and money. They're good people. They knew my parents. I'll leave it all for them." Mark went out and shut the door behind him.

Chapter Four

Mark had the coachman wait at the Fall Gate, and gave him two more cupru in the hopes that the sum might hold him better.

The last time he'd come to this gate, the driver had left him, and Obsidian had died writhing in the snow.

That had been at night, and the driver had heard the shot. Mark trusted that this time there would be no danger. Even if this driver left, other coachmen ventured here and parked during the day, hoping to pick up a fare from visitors who wanted to explore the vast beauty from one side to the other without having to double back.

By daylight the Rythan Gardens seemed peaceful and innocent. Wisteria blossoms hung from the vines, thick as tree trunks, that threatened to overpower the tall iron fence surrounding the gardens. Some of the magnolia trees, the ones with the spidery flowers, had begun to bloom. The broad brick paths were clear save for a few tattered leaves left over from the prior autumn. A small scattering of pink blossoms dropped from ancient rhododendrons. Patches of forget-me-nots turned old perennial beds and sunny hollows a perfect sky blue, and made the glowing, fiery orange of large poppies seem even hotter. He walked, satchel bumping at his back, Gale exploring back and forth eagerly both in front and behind him, toward the Lantern Garden.

To the right a path veered off toward Swan Island, where Obsidian had killed Lake, and died. All that seemed to have happened some other place. The path there looked nothing like the shadowed, icy way Mark had hurried and then crawled through, worming on his belly. He thought he could smell the smoke on his clothes, from the fire he'd come from, though his eyes only saw irises adorning the shallows in the stream and delicate trilliums hiding beneath the evergreens. A small cluster of ducks paddled by, quacking softly to each other but in his mind Obsidian's begging for him to stay all but drowned them out.

If he hadn't talked Obsidian out of his original plan, the jester might still be alive. That thought had wormed in his head for a long time, but now it emerged bright and fat and sick with guilt and regret.

He'd stopped without realizing it. Mark pressed onward, through an oak grove with benches, over a bridge that crossed the small stream, and to the Lantern Garden.

No one seemed to be about. The grim, cloudy weather, wind, and frequent rain squalls had kept the usual visitors away despite the cheer offered from swaths of brilliant spring flowers planted in riotous disarray.

Either he was a bit early, or Professor Vinkin was late.

The iron lanterns, some of them over thirty feet high, formed centerpieces for the various annual flower beds on the wild and hilly ground. Paths led to tunnels under many of the hills. When Lord Argenwain came here he'd often sit on a bench and watch Mark explore the small rooms and caves under the hills, many of which interconnected. The spaces beneath were lit solely by natural light coming through the lantern filigree by day. At night the keepers lit the lanterns, which burned oil. Lord Argenwain wanted them to be converted to gas, but Mark talked him out of it. The pipes would be visible, if not from the outside, then within, and either way it would spoil their artful lines.

Once Mark had stumbled on a young couple inside one of the smaller chambers. Her hands had gripped the lantern above her, and her lover had his face buried in her bosom, pounding away with unschooled vigor. Mark backed out without them noticing. He probably could have tripped over them and they still wouldn't have noticed. At the time the sight had offended him, but now its memory made him smile.

He started to feel dizzy again, so Mark sat. Gale sat on his feet. He drew his cloak close—it had been Lake's cloak once, picked off the ground just a few feet from Lake's body not far from here—and waited. The benches were all wet, but the cloak was good wool and the water didn't soak through.

It likely wasn't that cold, but the chill numbed him. Gale helped keep his legs and feet warm. Her bulk braced against his legs made it hard to turn and watch for anyone who might come up behind him. He trusted her to warn him if someone did.

At last Professor Vinkin came walking in his characteristic stiff, high-shouldered stride down the path from the Fall Gate. He wore coarse trousers rather than breeches and stockings, that overly large brown coat and the matching floppy brown hat. He had his valise with him, unwieldy and battered with the outer pockets sagging and stretched, held closed by thick, ancient clasps.

Mark stood and bowed. Gale shifted just enough to keep him from falling over her. Her thick, short, feathered tail swept the ground. "Professor."

"So it is you." He stopped well away and held the valise with both hands in front of his chest as if it could shield him, his usual somber expression a little worried.

"Thank you for meeting with me. I have some questions for you."

The professor looked him over. "You've been poisoned."

Mark's throat tightened. He could barely swallow. It wasn't nervousness, or pain. Something closer to shame. "Can you tell which one?"

"By looking at you, no. The slight yellow to your skin and eyes, emaciation. Your hair and nails are in fair shape, though I—" His voice broke. "—I expect that is a result of careful labor and makeup rather than a sign of health."

"That's not why I asked you to see me today."

"Are you dying?"

Mark gestured to the bench. "Won't you have a seat? I'll move just as soon—"

"Answer the question, please."

I don't want to talk about this. Despite his reluctance, he appreciated the professor's concern too much to put the man off. "That depends on who you ask. I was to die that night, and then within a week. A month. The doctor says any time, most likely from starvation, though a seizure might take me." He tried not to let the words touch him as he spoke them, but the dread still worsened his chill. Mark managed to get Gale off his feet and moved from the bench. She trotted over toward the professor. "Gale, heel." She dashed back to him. "Please, have a seat."

"You need it more than me. What is the agent?"

"Professor—"

"Please. I may be of use."

Mark doubted it. It was a rare poison, and had only recently come into use. "Deatlall. It's a swamp flower, carnivorous. It's rare."

"I'll ask my colleagues about it."

"Thank you." Mark took in a deep breath, let it out with as much of his hopelessness as he could, and settled back on the bench. "I have a mask, and drawings of two others. I'm hoping you might recognize them and tell me something about them. I suspect at least one of them is quite old."

Professor Vinkin backed away and his shoulders rose up even higher. "Please don't tell me you've found it."

He probably meant the Gelantyne mask. "No, it's not. I don't think any of these will be particularly famous. But I want to be sure. I need to know what I'm carrying with me." He got out the drawings first. "I apologize for the quality. I'm not an artist like—" Gutter.

The Professor still hung back. "Have you worn them?"

"The masks? Just one of them."

"A death mask?"

"No."

Professor Vinkin finally ventured close. He often did the same thing at his lessons, keeping his distance until whatever it was inside him that kept him apart from others relaxed enough. He took the sketches and looked at them carefully. "This mask with the stripes. It's remarkable. It's reminiscent of some very old masks used by traditions that date back to periods prior to the invention of steel. Was it new?"

"Fairly, yes. It certainly wasn't more than a hundred years old. It looked almost brand new. I suppose it could have been very well preserved."

The professor nodded and flipped to the other sketch. "This one I know. Too Mon." His head bowed, and the muscles on his pale face jumped. "I heard about Obsidian's death. It's very hard, you know. You never grow used to hearing about students you nurtured and grew fond of meeting horrific deaths at the hands of others you've taught. I knew them both quite well." The professor wasn't looking at the paper anymore, though he held it as if he was still examining it. "Do you have it?"

Mark didn't know if it would be wise to answer him.

"I hope you do. This is a wonderful, but dangerous mask. You would do well to keep him safe, but I would recommend that you never use him."

"Is he known to have any unusual traits?"

"Yes." The professor handed him the sketches. "Too Mon is very calm and quiet. He's also quick. You only have to put him to your face once to acclimate to him. From that point on he will completely dominate. Some even say that he doesn't have to be on the wearer's face. They only have to summon him to their minds. And therein lies the danger. It doesn't require too much imagination to think of what might happen to a jester who has no memory of what he's done for hours, even days at a time, and who might surrender to him without conscious effort."

Mark shivered from more than the spring chill. The blue eye from the mask sometimes came to him with thoughts that didn't feel like his own. Did the mask he'd painted on his face damage his mind somehow?

"Too Mon is over two hundred years old. He has his own friendships, and his own enemies among the masks." Professor Vinkin's shoulders slowly lowered. "An ugly mask, but precious. If you have him, keep him safe. Make certain he never falls into unworthy hands. If you don't have him, this is one circumstance where I might engage the assistance of some noble of power and importance to get him back. If you're not in a situation to protect him or gain him from unworthy hands, I encourage you to enlist help from the university, or royalty if you can."

Someone had considered Obsidian worthy of this mask. That implied a great deal, including the thought that Obsidian would, if he was aware of a plot against the King, do everything he could to protect the royal family.

Maybe Obsidian had been uncertain of Gutter's role in the intrigue. That would explain some things, but complicate others.

"Mark? Or do you have some other name now?"

"You can always call me Mark. My jester's name is Lark." He carefully drew his own mask from the satchel. "Gutter gave me this."

Professor Vinkin set down his valise to accept the mask with both hands. He opened the silk wrapping and gazed at it, first the back side, then the front. "Oh." A faint smile lifted around his eyes. "Oh my."

"Is it a named mask?"

"No. But I know this maker. This must be a later work. It might be completely unknown to scholars." His hands started to tremble. "You do know who made this mask, don't you?"

Mark shook his head.

"We went over this in your early lessons. Come now. Think. Look at the back. Look at the materials." He offered it back to Mark.

He hadn't looked at it with an analytical eye. The first time he'd seen it he didn't even want to touch it, though he found it beautiful in a strange way. He didn't want to become a jester, and masks were their most potent and familiar symbol. Later, it seemed too much a part of him to examine it objectively. Even now it was hard to look at it with an eye to identify its maker.

"What are the materials?"

He didn't want to say it, but it had finally occurred to him when Professor Vinkin's excitement began to show. "It ... it almost looks like human skin on the front. Deerskin backing, Saphiran lacquer." His memory, usually very good, started to crack but didn't open.

Masks made from human hands.

Mark's heart jumped. "This isn't Domonic Velt's work!"

"No," Professor Vinkin admonished. "His student, Josiphena Grimathis. You're correct about the materials. This is human skin, most likely taken from the hands, carefully applied to the deerskin with a mysterious process still unknown to us. These tears are distinctive to her work. The minerals she used are still unknown, though many have theorized that she used some combination of ground blue and lavender pearls, rare oils, silver, and abalone."

Now that the professor mentioned it, he thought he vaguely remembered something about a secret pearl and precious metal amalgamate, but he wasn't sure. Rohn should have been here to witness the failure of Mark's memory. He seemed so certain it was perfect.

"Where did Gutter get this?" Professor Vinkin asked.

"I don't know what I should keep secret and what I shouldn't anymore," Mark admitted. He wished he'd brought his cane. He hated depending on it, and he thought he could do without it. Now, as another wave of dizziness passed through him, he wasn't sure he'd make the walk back. "But I honestly don't know. You'd have to ask him."

"That is one of many inconveniences that intrigues heap upon you. It's not important, I suppose. I was only curious. I'm an admirer of hers."

Mark started to put the mask away, then thought better of it. It had helped him during a time of weakness before.

The professor made a small, unhappy noise in his throat. "There's so much I wish I could ask you, and now I can't. I'm so sorry. I hope—well, I hope for the best for you." His shoulders drew up. "How can I contact you if my colleagues have something helpful to offer in regard to your condition?"

"I have a room over a jam and jelly merchant's on Walker Main near Grishall."

"I think I know the place. Not far from where that famous wine shop used to be. Tragic, what happened to the young lady there. Did you hear of it?"

Mark didn't think it was possible for the professor not to know that she'd been his mother. The man made so many other connections so readily.

Too much pain and no point in enlightening him. Mark put the mask on his face. Lark took hold swiftly, though a little shudder went through his neck as something that felt like teeth bit down at the base of his skull. His weakness faded to a minor inconvenience. As always he felt lithe and light and limber. "I did hear of it." Lark stood and stretched. Gale danced at his feet, eager to play. Lark bent and let her lick his hand before he rubbed her all over. She wiggled with delight. "I should go." Lark didn't want to, but he had more business to attend to. "Will you walk with me to the Fall Gate?"

"Of course." The professor accepted Lark's careful pace, but only after a few impatient strides ahead. "May I ask why you retreated behind the mask just now?"

Lark smiled. "It's personal, but I will blame my health."

"It's not safe to overextend yourself using a mask. You can't cheat your physical limits."

"Not so long ago you told me I couldn't cheat time. That was the day I left Seven Churches. A difficult day. Arguing with you ... I didn't want to argue. I needed a friend. And—" he said quickly before the professor could interrupt, "you were a friend. I didn't realize at the time what a favor you'd done me by forcing me to look at my life at Pickwelling objectively. I should thank you."

"Your calm is most disconcerting." The professor held his valise a little tighter and ducked his head. It made Lark sad.

"I have one more question for you." Lark remembered it, though Mark hadn't. "It's about scars. Unusual scars. Are they common among jesters?"

"I'm not certain what you're asking. Jesters are often scarred in duels, or during dangerous missions."

He might be treading on sacred ground, but Lark's curiosity had him by the throat and he wanted to know far more than he feared any repercussions from *morbai*. "I meant something more exotic. If I show you, will you promise not to tell anyone, or ask where I got it?"

The professor nodded reluctantly.

Have a care, jester. You tread upon my patience.

That wasn't Ruby.

Lark hesitated, but he realized that the voice hadn't exactly forbidden him from showing the professor. "A handful of people know about it. Be careful and think before you tell me anything about it, just in case." He slipped off his glove and turned his hand so that the professor could see both sides. The professor stopped hard and would have grabbed Lark's hand if Lark had let him. Lark pulled the glove on again.

"What—please, show me again."

"I take it that you haven't heard of such a thing." Lark asked.

"Where did you get that?"

"You promised," Lark reminded him.

The professor huffed. "I should have known better than to promise that."

They walked together in silence for a long stretch. Gale had plenty of time to relieve herself in several places and to explore a wide swath around the path. Lark loved watching her roam. She related to the world far less with her eyes and more with her nose and ears. He could explore it with her by watching her, at least in part, though he only noticed a fraction of what she discovered, and he'd never know what she thought of any of it.

Though the professor was clearly out of sorts, Lark enjoyed walking with him. It was peaceful, and strangely it eased some of his loneliness.

They'd nearly reached the gate when the professor stopped. "I do seem to remember something, though I don't know if it's anything like what you showed me. In fact I'm certain it's very different, so different I hate to mention it. But you have a fine mind. I know you won't rely exclusively on my instincts if I suggest there might be a weak connection."

Lark took the opportunity to sit on a nearby bench. He could move well enough, but somewhere inside him Mark sagged with weariness and there was no need to press on past his physical limits.

"We had little opportunity to discuss distant nations, but they're a hobby interest of mine. The Bela in particular fascinate me. They have what they call *oushai*, which are a sort of knight. Before they are ordained they go through three days of what amounts to torture, and at the end of it they have unusual scars upon them. They call them *grezhizai*. There is no one word that can translate. It refers to a seed, a seed of sacrifice, courage and pain. They call that *grezhi*, and the *zai* are the newly-sprouted roots."

The professor had no idea how much sense that made, but Lark didn't let him see his astonishment. "It sounds intensely arcane."

"*Oushai* pre-date jesters by thousands of years. You'll find those who believe that they have a role similar to our jesters and nobles, but both aspects coexist in one person, while others will say they are unique and entirely dissimilar. Perhaps even opposite. They have no Church. They govern themselves. You would think that they would quickly corrupt, but they are famously severe upon their own kind. Cathretans who have traveled to Bel have said they are like *morbai*—inhumanly ruthless and merciless, but pure, driven, and fearlessly dedicated to their work."

"What is their work?"

The professor smiled. "Justice, of course."

That scared him. He wished he hadn't asked. "The suffixes. They seem similar to words associated with the sacred in Hasle."

"Yes." The professor's shoulders jogged in an odd shrug. "Discussions in that direction might be dangerous and are best left to priests better acquainted with religious stricture."

Lark stood and made his way a little more quickly than he had before. "May I offer you a ride? I have a coach waiting."

"It's just a short walk," the professor assured him.

"Are you certain? Please. I've very much enjoyed our conversation. I've missed you." It was true, but mostly he wanted the distraction. Not that it would help. His thoughts circled wildly around his need for justice and the scar on his hand and the voices and how he'd killed ... not even Rohn had questioned what had happened during the massacre at Hevether Hall.

"Very well." The professor's shoulders relaxed down, but not entirely. They never did.

Ironically, they didn't exchange further words for some time, which gave Lark far too much time to dwell.

No one had asked him how he'd killed so many experienced soldiers in his weakened condition.

Rohn wouldn't have believed that Mark had felt no fear. The protection from fear and grief had allowed him to calculate his chances and weigh the risks as if death were an unimportant consequence should he make a mistake. And Mark certainly wouldn't tell Rohn, even if Rohn would have believed, that Mark had hunted those men. They thought they were hunting him, but that had only brought them within easy reach without any effort on his part.

Though he knew it was wrong, Lark didn't feel guilty about destroying them. Mark tried not to dwell on it, though later he dreamt of cutting that man's throat and then being dragged into the man's body so that it was his own throat being cut. The worst thing, though, had been Rohn's expression when Mark had first come down the stairs.

Rohn's fist had been buried inside the soldier's gut, his gaze locked on the dying man's eyes, his expression easing into a luxurious satiety as if he'd just finished a good meal. *Thir kra muomaveh. It kills for pleasure,* the creature in the other world had said before it chose to condemn Rohn to death, or madness—whatever that blade portended. And Mark had gotten in its way. The scar on his hand was proof of that reality. Why the contact had healed the wounds he'd gotten during the ambush near the docks, he might never know.

It had been odd, having to tug the sutures free of his leg and arm without any scars between them.

"You're very quiet."

By this time they'd reached the gate, and the coachman roused his horse in order to meet them at it. "I'm thinking about sin. I seem to remember you telling me that you had little to do with religious matters. You concerned yourself with human beings rather than the supernatural."

"That's true."

Lark motioned for him to go first and the professor obliged. "I wish I had someone I trusted to ask about sin and sacred matters." Gale bounded up behind the professor. "Take us to the university," Lark told the coachman. The man nodded acknowledgement.

"You'd do better to think for yourself," the professor told him. He propped his valise on his knees and took shelter behind it. "Priests, sacred poetry ... they're too limited. Your intellect and imagination are far superior to their indoctrination."

"But I have no information to go on," Lark protested.

"You have your own humanity, when you choose to be human."

Lark fingered the edges of his mask. "What am I when I'm ... this?"

"No one really knows. They like to pretend that they know. Who or what do you think you are when you are that mask?"

The coach started rolling. "I feel different." He had difficulty defining it. "I still feel like Mark. Parts of him, anyway. It's as if Mark is always a little drunk, and Lark is sober. Awake. I see so much. And I feel. I do feel. I care. I love. But it's too clean. I feel as if I'm missing all the wonderful colors of the world and see only the primaries, plain and flat."

"Be careful with masks." The professor tensed up as Gale put her feet on the coach seat beside him and sniffed his hand.

"Off," Lark told her, and Gale settled down on his feet. He didn't mind, but Rohn insisted he train her to keep her feet off of furniture in anticipation of the days when she'd weigh around two hundred pounds.

"Don't wear them too often," the professor went on. "Trust in your training. It's not that the masks themselves damage anyone, at least not that I've heard. Most of them are at least mildly protective. But you can damage *yourself* while you're wearing them, mind and body. Especially with that mask. You won't fully appreciate what you've done until the mask comes off and all those colors come rushing back. Even the masks that completely obliterate all conscious memory leave traces behind that sometimes emerge in terrible dreams. Those dreams can be worse than the reality, and there may be no way to find out what dreams are true, and what dreams are rooted in fears of what you might have done, or what the mask is capable of."

That made him glad of his memories, even the ugly ones. "Is Too Mon dangerous that way?" Lark asked.

The professor nodded. "Be careful, Lark. I fear for all my students, but especially you."

"Why especially me?"

The professor took a long blink to answer. "Children of noble lines with ignoble souls, commoners with exceptional ability, third sons with the inclination ... they come to the university from all directions and many purposes. But they all know why they're there, at least on the surface. You don't. I don't know why you were trained, and I don't like the way you were trained. Your circumstances are highly dangerous, and I don't think it's fair. You didn't want to be a jester. You deserve better. This is no life for a good person, and you've always been a very good person. One of the best I've ever had the privilege to know."

Lark let himself slip away because he wanted Mark to hear that, and remember it, though neither of them could believe it. "I've met far better men," Mark told him as he drew off his mask. Grant. He had no way of describing that loss except as a wound to his soul.

Mark turned aside to pretend to look out the window, and the professor, kindly, left him alone. His body felt heavy, but he could rest now, and he let the coach carry him away.

Chapter Five

Mark had to change on *Dainty*, as he and Winsome hadn't had time to send for their luggage. Along with his finest clothes, Mark wore his rapier, the matching pistol, and the dagger Juggler had given him. He kept his mask tucked inside his waistcoat. All the clothes he'd had fashioned for him on the island were far too light even for spring weather. The cloak helped shelter him from the chill. Though the cold weather made him shiver, he actually felt warmer than he had in days. For the first time since they'd weathered the storm at sea, he wore dry clothes and boots.

After a few hours in Pickwelling, the last of the damp would finally steam away. Lord Argenwain insisted that the servants keep his favorite rooms in Pickwelling summer-warm.

He checked and rechecked the fall of his ruffles, his hair, his hat, his gloves. He'd groomed Gale to perfection. Her slightly ginger fur felt softer than the stirring of air in a sheltered garden.

His heart leapt about like a mouse trying to escape a tall bucket.

Maybe a short walk will calm me down.

He had the coachman drop him off at the gate. Drops from the recent rain spattered down from the trees every time the wind rattled them. Seven o'clock, and full dark not just because sunset had melted away an hour ago, but also because of the endless clouds that smothered the sky. Gale seemed nervous, heeling close though he hadn't asked her to.

Somewhere in the garden Winsome watched him approach the front door. He soon left the lights at the gate and walked in shadows toward the mirrored crystal oil lamps framing the grand entrance. He wondered if the boy would open the door, or eat with them, assuming they would dine rather than proceed straight to torture. Maybe they'd hide the boy away.

Mark hadn't even learned his name.

I'm so selfish.

Before he could ring the bell, the boy opened the door and stood to one side, silent, gaze averted down. He bowed. "Welcome to Pickwelling, Lord Jester Lark."

Mark had to force himself to step inside. He dreaded what welcome he'd really find. He took a few steps in a half-circle as if admiring the furnishings, but he saw no sign of Gutter or Lord Argenwain.

"May I take your cloak and hat?" the boy asked. He glanced at Gale, uncertain.

Mark shed his cloak. Pickwelling's foyer was warm enough for him, but only just, and the fresh chill on his back and shoulders made him shudder. "Thank you."

"Lord Argenwain wishes to see you in private before you go to dinner, if you don't mind." The boy's voice betrayed a harshness Mark couldn't define. It could have been jealousy, anger, pain, fear—Mark didn't know him well enough.

Lark could have made a better guess.

He didn't want to hide behind his mask. Not yet. "Thank you. Is Gutter here?"

"Yes."

That answer sent a shock of alarm and pleasure through his gut.

The boy led the way toward the study. For a moment Mark couldn't move his feet, but he managed to follow, his heart dashing in search of hiding places. It took all his will to keep his breath from staggering. Gale hung even closer by his side, almost touching his leg.

Why am I afraid of him? He's just an old man.

The boy opened the study door, and there he was in all his crumbling splendor, fish-faced, gray skin and clouded, yellowed, bloodshot eyes, white hair, bent, too fat around the middle and too thin at his shoulders. Lord Argenwain had a beautiful embroidered blanket across his knees, partly to keep him warm, partly to protect him from the hearty fire. A faint odor of urine and wine permeated beyond the lord's favorite perfume.

Hard to believe he'd once been handsome, and strong, and that he and Gutter had gone hunting and fishing and carousing with His Royal Majesty King Michael of Cathret.

Those old eyes that had seen much and lost more than Mark could imagine traced their gaze over him. The instinct to respect his former master made him want to kneel and beg forgiveness, despite everything. Lord Argenwain's lip trembled. It could have been from sorrow, or rage—most likely both. "So. You've come back."

Mark bowed. He noticed, without allowing himself to glance, that the curtains were open. "Gale, stay." He touched her head briefly before he advanced farther into the room.

"Leave us," Lord Argenwain told the boy. "And shut the door. No listening, either, or you'll be sorry when you're caught at it."

The boy bowed and retreated.

Lord Argenwain stared at Mark, his expression slack. Mark wasn't fooled. The old man wasn't dull in mind. Lord Argenwain had to have a hundred questions, but he wouldn't stoop to demanding answers from a person he viewed as a servant when he had a lordly right to have the explanations offered without the asking.

Mark, as a jester, had a right not to offer those answers, but he owed the old man something. He'd been well cared for in this house, and except toward the end, gently treated for the most part.

Why do I always make excuses for him?

"I hope you're in good health," Mark offered. A coward's opening, but he didn't want to begin. Not yet.

Lord Argenwain grunted his dissatisfaction.

Fine, then. "Has the Church settled with you in regard to my indenture?"

"Is that why you're here?" Lord Argenwain asked.

"No, not entirely. I'm here to see Gutter." Mark thought he'd feel a little victory when those fish lips quivered again, but it only made him feel like a bully. "But since I'm here anyway, I thought I'd visit." Mark walked to the chair across from Lord Argenwain and sat without invitation. He would have preferred to stand, but he was still tired from his long day about town. The heat from the fire soothed him. He held his hands closer to the warmth. The light glowed through his fragile flesh, revealing the shadows of bones. "At times I missed you, if that matters to you."

"I waited. I waited until you reached the age of majority. I gave you everything." Lord Argenwain turned his gaze to the fire. "And this is how you treat me."

Lord Argenwain's sharp defense when Mark had made no accusation surprised him. "I didn't come here to discuss that. That—it's over."

"You have a woman."

The boy—he must have mentioned that Mark had Winsome inside the coach earlier in the day. "You have a new boy," Mark countered. His temper had faded somewhat in Rohn's service but it roared back to life now.

"I'm old and I'm dying. How I find comfort is my affair."

"I'm dying as well but I don't go around buying vulnerable youths desperate for shelter to warm my bed."

Lord Argenwain's breath caught. "You're dying?"

Mark tried to wet his mouth but he was dry all the way down to his belly. "Your eyesight has gotten worse in the past months."

The old man shivered and hugged his arms, gripping so hard his fingers turned white. "Get me some brandy," he said roughly.

Mark fetched it for him, grateful for something easy and familiar to do. He warmed it in his hands near the fire before he handed it over. "Here." Now that he'd wounded the old lord even more deeply he felt sorry, and more inclined to be gentle.

"You're not having any?"

"I can't." Mark sat back down. "If you want to know, I left Pickwelling because I had no reason to stay anymore. I longed for freedom. For love. For family. Yes, you treated me well enough for a servant. I've heard of worse happening to boys in my circumstance. I doubt I would have survived without your interference—"

"You would have died in service to the navy—" Lord Argenwain interrupted.

"—But you taught me to please you as if it were no more important or significant than showing me how to fold your clothes. You might call it love, but feeding a pig before sending it to slaughter ... it isn't kindness. It isn't care."

"Then what is?" Lord Argenwain demanded.

Could he really be that heartless? "I was a child. I needed real affection and guidance. I needed parents. You could have been a father to me, but instead you made me into your toy."

"I loved you," Lord Argenwain snarled.

Mark barely reined in a stream of vile expletives so shocking he was surprised they came from within him, inspired by an anger he didn't know had grown so hot and terrible.

"I didn't ask why you left, because I knew." Lord Argenwain sank deeper into his chair. His eyes seemed to sink as well.

"I didn't leave because of that. But I didn't stay because of how you treated me. If you'd loved me, if you really cared about me, I might have stayed. But you didn't."

"I loved you. I love you."

Mark choked. He wished he had some water. He looked about for some but the boy or whoever had set the study had forgotten it. "That isn't love. Do you know what love is? It's what you have with Gutter. That's love. What you feel is lust and possessiveness."

"How dare you. You know nothing of what I feel." He shook all over now. "And don't pretend that you weren't willing."

"Oh, I was willing." Mark's temper lifted again, and his breath came hard though his words barely whispered. "I would have done anything to be loved. Instead I was used and put back in my place again and again. I didn't sit at your dinner table. I served dinner to you. That's love?"

"You can hardly expect, due to your birth and your situation—"

"I think the only reason I had an education was thanks to Gutter. After all, someone of my birth would have no need of such. Is that right?"

Lord Argenwain's eyes glared dangerously. "I wouldn't be too quick to credit your comforts to my jester."

Mark wished he had Lark's calm. He sensed an opportunity, but his heart pounded and his thoughts hunted for rebuttals, not questions. By the time the right words finally came to him, the moment had passed. "He shouldn't do things with your awareness, my lord."

"I guess more than he realizes. We've been together a long time." Lord Argenwain's trembling eased and strength glowed in his eyes. "And you reveal no little arrogance in presuming to speak for or against my relationship with my closest friend."

Mark closed his eyes against his pain. It wasn't just his belly that hurt, and it hurt worse now from hunger and anxiety. He realized he still longed for love, or if not love, then at least a show of regret. Something. "Why did you want to see me in private?"

"To have it out at last. I didn't realize." Lord Argenwain seemed to shrink behind his own belly. "Tell me you lied. You sound strong enough. Tell me you said it just to hurt me."

"What? That I'm dying?" There was no point to rubbing his face in the truth. "Perhaps I exaggerated."

"You shit," he whispered.

Confidante 49

That made Mark smile, though the warmth never blossomed into any real joy. "Let's go to dinner. I hope you have fresh milk. I've grown rather fond of it." He'd need its soothing qualities to force a few mouthfuls of something down. With or without it, though, he'd be in agony later. He wasn't sure how he'd bear up to it. He hoped that if he couldn't conceal his pain, Lark might.

"I want you to stay at Pickwelling."

The old man had to be half-mad to think Mark would even consider it. "I have my own rooms in town, but thank you."

"You know what I meant. I want you back."

"Then Gutter hasn't told you." That puzzled him.

"Told me what?"

It seemed impossible. Hadn't the boy introduced ... but of course he didn't. Mark didn't need an introduction here. "I'm bonded."

The brandy glass fell from Lord Argenwain's hand, spilled over his lap and cracked on the floor. Instinctively Mark got up and picked it up, then went for linens from the liquor cabinet to clean up the mess.

"You're what?" Lord Argenwain gasped.

Mark patted down the blanket and the drips on the floor. He set the cracked brandy glass aside.

"To whom?" Lord Argenwain demanded.

"I won't stay with you," Mark told him quietly. "Never again. You have a new boy. I hope you treat him better than you treated me, though I have a feeling that he has it worse. But never mind. Your soul has never been my affair." Mark dumped the soiled linens on the table beside the brandy glass and walked out. "Gale, heel." She came to him too eagerly and nearly tripped him on her way out the door.

He would have run right out of the manor to the road and walked all the way to Walker Main if he couldn't find a coach, but he wanted to see Gutter. He was glad he'd had it out with Lord Argenwain, though it left him feeling shaken and weak. It hadn't changed anything, but at least his heart and mind were limber now for painful confrontation. He donned his mask. It took him with a sharp shudder, and woke him to a sense of remorse.

He'd accomplished nothing by fighting with that old man. Lord Argenwain wouldn't change, and hurting him served no purpose.

Could I change who I am if I wanted to?

Is what I am sinful? Can I really count myself a better person than Lord Argenwain in my tastes?

Professor Vinkin told him to think for himself. Lark's instincts assured him that love, real love, wasn't a sin. It couldn't be.

But how do I know if what I feel is real love?

Maybe real love was selfless. What Rohn and what Grant had been, had done for him, and what they'd done to him made no difference. What he did and what he wanted to be and do for them mattered, and he would have done anything for them. Even die, unfulfilled, alone, and unremembered.

Mark should have come to that conclusion a long time ago. He'd allowed his pain and his past to confuse him. Even calmer now, Lark straightened his posture and walked to the boy waiting in the foyer for him.

"You best see to Lord Argenwain," Lark told him. "Where is Gutter?"

"He's waiting upstairs in his room. I can—"

"I know the way." Lark trotted up the stairs, Gale fast on his heels. He should have been afraid, but he couldn't wait to greet the greatest of jesters once more and for the first time.

Lark stopped at the top of the stairs, keenly aware that Winsome was somewhere outside. She'd be worried and uncertain about where she'd find him next. He'd told her the rooms he'd likely visit.

Fortunately, Gutter's was one of them.

Lord Argenwain's suite wrapped one end of the main building upstairs, and Gutter's wrapped the opposite. Their doors faced each other across a long, grand hall. Mark used to sleep in a small room between them, nearer to Lord Argenwain's suite and with a connecting door into the lord's private rooms. Across from the top of the stairs a large bank of leaded glass doors with beveled edges opened onto a balcony that had an excellent view of the rose garden. The curtains were drawn. Lark waited long enough for Winsome to circle in the garden, then drew his hand along the curtains to move them as he walked toward Gutter's suite.

He knocked on the sitting room door.

I hope Winsome isn't cold and afraid.

He also hoped that she hadn't played him and planned to shoot Gutter from the start. He doubted that she'd lied to them all, but she'd damaged the trust he'd felt toward her when she'd confessed that she had been part of the conspiracy that threatened Meridua. It didn't help that he didn't know her very well, and that she seemed overly-protective of him.

Lark knocked again. "Gutter? It's me."

"Come in." That rich, deep voice still curled Mark's toes. It warmed well past his mask and rekindled all those feelings of love and betrayal and respect. Lark opened the door slowly and went in.

The walls were painted with roses, all perfect and in various stages of bloom. They billowed one on top of another, vast creations of delicate color, some as large and round as card tables.

And on a stand, to Lark's surprise, sat the portrait Gutter had done of Mark three years ago, or had it been four?

Gutter stood beside the portrait. The curtains were drawn, as usual. Lark knew he ought to contrive to open at least one, but he didn't want to. He strode to the large man in dark clothes that subtly glittered with wealth like a starry sky and hugged him close.

Gutter hugged him back, a large hand combing into Mark's hair with an intimacy as powerful as that moment Mark had shared with Rohn. But this wasn't sexual, much as he'd welcome that.

Mark had come home, a disobedient son returning to his father. He could try to deny it, but he'd be lying to himself.

They drew apart, both reluctant to let go, Lark dreading what would no doubt be a verbal sparring contest. Gutter leaned back against a buffet table. He was so tall he could have almost sat on it comfortably. Gale went to sniff at him, but didn't get close enough to touch before she retreated back to Lark. Lark stroked her head and sung her a low note of reassurance deep in his throat.

"Lord Argenwain didn't want it in his bedroom anymore?" Lark gestured to the portrait. He'd been so young. It was laughable to think of himself as that much older, or at least it had been before he'd been poisoned. He would never be that innocent or alive or healthy again.

I'm not young anymore. I'll never be young, and I'll never be old either.

Gutter's gaze, dark within the mask, darted all over him. "You've been poisoned." His breath hitched. "What was the agent?"

"Deatlal. But I—I didn't come here to talk about that."

"When? When did it happen?" Gutter's voice verged on a soft and terrible anger.

"Weeks ago. Please. I have a lot of questions, and I'm sure you have just as many if not more. But I've missed you, and ...." He gestured helplessly, then laughed and touched his mask. "Thank you again, for this. You were right. It's perfect."

Gutter closed his eyes. "It's alright, Thomas." It was the barest of whispers, but Lark heard the name clearly. It shocked his thoughts back to the estate sale the day after his mother died. Thomas, a regular patron at his mother's shop—at the time Mark had no idea he was Gutter—had come to warn him that the priests were coming to manage the indenture he'd inherited. Was Thomas the person Gutter had been before he became a jester?

That had to have been a long time ago, before Mark was born.

Mark and Gutter had wounded each other so many times since Mark had come to Pickwelling. It seemed so clear now, how much they cared for each other and how neither of them could afford to. Love, however, spared no expense and accepted all risks. Mark had nothing to fear from showing that he cared for this man when it was so obvious that Gutter suffered from shock at hearing the news. Lark stepped closer and took Gutter's hand in his. Squeezed. "I've already defied the doctor's predictions. There's no telling how long I'll last, but I'm sure I'll still be here tomorrow."

"Don't make me cry, Lark. It's dangerous." Gutter drew in a long, unsteady breath.

At first Lark thought he'd meant it as a joke, but Gutter was completely sober. "Dangerous?"

Gutter shook his head. "That's for another time. Are you hungry?"

"It can wait," Lark assured him.

"Good." Gutter slipped free of his grasp. "You left. And then, you paid your indenture. Very inconvenient, because now I need your signature to release your part of the hull fund."

"My part?" Lark had a number of uncomfortable questions he had to ask about *Mairi*, but this business was the least important to him. "I'm a little confused. I thought the hull fund was entirely mine."

"I've paid into it."

Lark wanted to ask why, but he doubted Gutter would answer, and besides, a more important question might give him the answer, if indirectly. "Why do you need it?"

"A ship. A new sort of ship. Here, I'll show you." He went to his drafting table and opened the broad drawer underneath.

The painting stole Lark's breath. A huge ship among wild waves, sails bulging with violent winds. Four masts gently sloped, an impressive arsenal of guns, and a graceful array of square and angular sails. "That's a war ship."

"No. No. A new sort of trade ship that can defend herself. Look, the bases of the masts are armored. She'll hold two hundred crew and safely carry the most precious cargo over vast distances. This ship will discover new islands, perhaps even new countries we've only heard of in legend. Your ship. Our ship. An explorer, an adventuress, a diplomat and a keen business woman. You will name her. She is ... she is my ... my plea. For forgiveness. I started construction on her almost as soon as you left."

Lark's heart tripped wildly inside him and his gut burned with searing pain. "Did you do it? Did you murder those men and destroy my future with them?"

Gutter retreated to the window and sheltered beside the curtain. Lark had never seen him so out of sorts. It only made him more afraid of the answer.

"Thomas." Gutter whispered it. "Thomas," he said more firmly. "Is going mad."

Lark fought to bury all that those words implied but the implications welled up out of the depths with an agonized fury. "Who do I love, then? A mask? That mask?" He gestured to Gutter's face. "Thomas. Thomas burned *Mairi*, and trapped her crew inside because he's insane, and the mask couldn't stop him?" He tried to stay calm but his blood raced ahead of his mind.

"It's not that simple, nor easy for me to explain," Gutter whispered.

Lark could almost hear the men scream. The phantom sounds mingled with Mark's unheard cries of horror. "And he, not you but he burned her and her crew because I was going to leave in three years, maybe—"

"You don't understand."

"Explain it to me." For a moment he felt a fleeting temptation to walk to that window and give the signal to end Gutter's life. It passed in a heartbeat. He couldn't unmake his love for the man, even if that wasn't really a man standing there. "Are you even human anymore?"

Yes, a voice whispered in his mind in a foreign tongue. ***He is a man. Like you are.***

This time, he knew for certain. Lark knew that voice. It was Ruby. He'd known it since childhood.

"You don't remember." Gutter leaned into the corner, slowly mastering his emotions. It deadened his voice. "When you were very small, your mother was robbed, and stabbed. Thomas found her, bleeding. She had you cradled in her arms. Thomas knew her. He'd often purchased wine from her. He helped her home, and sent for a doctor she couldn't afford. You were only two years old. We, he, spent much of every day helping see to you while she convalesced. He could have sent a servant, but he didn't want to give away who he was. He loved walking as an everyday, common

man among regular people too much. And that's when it happened."
Gutter made it sound like a guilty confession. "He fell in love with you."
For the briefest of moments Lark's emotions plunged with terror that
Gutter and his mother had had an affair, until the end of the sentence
relieved him ... but Gutter's tone still frightened him. "He adored you. You
were so precocious. Unbelievably bright. And gentle. If your mother had
let you, you would have adopted every kitten in the neighborhood. You
used to admonish people to be nice to each other. Men arguing, on the
verge of violence, would stop and apologize when you gazed up at them
with those large green eyes and told them that they had to stop fighting."

Lark had to sit. He'd never heard any of this, not from his mother, not
from anyone. She'd always treated Thomas like any other customer, with
kindness.

"You called me Mister Tom." Gutter drew another unsteady breath.
His hand toyed with the edge of the curtain. "Then your father came
home, and that was that. I visited as often as I could, but I wasn't family,
and your father was nervous about my presence. I know they argued often
about me. I'm sure he accused your mother of infidelity."

Mark had no memory of any argument except mundane ones about
how Mark ought to be raised and what they could and couldn't afford.

"You were better than the circumstances to which you were born,"
Gutter said. "Anyone could see it. You weren't a sailor. You deserved a
proper education, and opportunity to mingle with the highest-born society.
I thought initially that you would make a fine butler or perhaps a business
liaison or a seneschal, but then ... things changed. Everything changed."

Even past his makeup, Lark could see him pale.

"Did Thomas ...." He couldn't ask it aloud.

Did he kill my parents?

"No! Don't think that. He adored your mother. I adored your mother,
and I respected your father. Erril had a good life arranged for you, the best
he could manage. Please, believe me, I would never harm either of your
parents."

Lark almost sobbed with relief, though he feared it was all lies. "Do you
know what happened to them?"

"No."

That soft answer was a lie. Lark trembled. Somewhere behind the mask,
Mark railed and fought to keep himself hidden and sheltered, but even the
calm, gentle mask couldn't protect him from this. "You said everything
changed. What changed?"

"Before I can answer that, we have to go to Saphir."

Confidante 55

"I have other duties." After having his heart broken, it seemed a small thing to risk what little remained of his life to ask. "I need to ask you about Obsidian."

"No. No more answers unless you come with me." Gutter shuddered as if he'd put on a mask, but of course he only wore the one over the painted mask on his face, the famous Gutter Rose. Maybe the masks had switched places.

The skill in mental arts that possibility suggested made Lark feel small and stupid.

He didn't know the Gutter Rose very well, and he didn't like it or trust it. "Unless my business takes me there, I won't go."

"If your business is what I believe it may be, then Saphir is where you must go." Gutter strode to the door. "Dinner?"

Lark was tempted to leave, but he hoped that he could lure more from the lord jester after a few glasses of wine.

How could Thomas do it? All that murder and destruction, all that suffering ....

Just as I nearly asked for Gutter's death, knowing it would not bring them back, and though it would have ended all chance of saving other lives, royal lives, at risk. I'm not any better than him.

That knowledge didn't change the fact that love and hate tore him between them harder than ever before.

Gutter smiled and opened the door. "Don't fight me. You're smarter than that. Whether you like it or not, you're a jester, and it's usually best for a jester to be everyone's beloved friend until the day you decide it's time to slip in the knife. I just hope today is not the day you end me, my boy. It would be such a waste, when we're so close."

A shiver went through him. Gutter showed no sign of knowing or sensing that brief moment when he'd been in mortal danger, but still, the timing of that comment .... *We're so close,* he'd said. Close like friends, or close to a goal yet unnamed? Lark steadied under the warmth of that smile, his curiosity caught, unwilling, by the hook. He went out the door and led the way to the dining room, grateful that the mask smothered Mark's agonized confusion.

Chapter Six

"Lord Jesters." The yet-unnamed boy met them at the base of the stairs. He gave Lark a sharp but otherwise undefined look before he threw his gaze down. "Dellai Bertram has arrived."

Lark flinched, but no one seemed to notice.

"He's in the music room," the boy added.

"Thank you, Jeffrey." Gutter took over the lead toward the music room.

Considering that nearly all his fears had just been confirmed and that he had only begun to wrestle with what he was supposed to do now, Dellai Bertram's presence should have been of little consequence.

Then why does it feel like another betrayal?

The dellai, with his red tattoos and perpetually sour expression, stood up in shock when Lark came in. He looked to Gutter first. "*Morsha kevlay,*" he said formally in Hasle, an ancient greeting that roughly meant 'well met'. "Lark. I confess that I'm surprised to see you here."

Lark bowed. "Dellai. I thought you might have been on your way home by now." Gale made a soft noise in her throat that verged on a growl. He told her to hush softly under his breath and she retreated behind his legs.

"I had a great deal of business to attend to. But I am leaving for Meridua, tomorrow early, in fact."

"Jeffrey, let Lord Argenwain know that we've gathered," Gutter said. The boy hastened away. "Shall we sit?" When no one objected, Gutter once again led the way.

The staff had arranged the dining room for an intimate dinner for four, turning the remainder of the vast room into a comfortable sitting area. Fires burned at both ends. Two servers stood by. Lark approached Carrol and quietly asked for milk to be served with his dinner. It felt strange addressing the man from the lofty heights of a guest rather than as a fellow servant. Carrol bowed formally without comment and went to the kitchen.

Lord Argenwain kept his family portraits here, as well as one of himself as a young man. Rounded cheeks, a friendly chin and bright eyes were framed with expanses of luxurious dark brown hair falling loose around his shoulders. He'd been handsome in a jolly, approachable way, his expression overflowing with mirth.

Did Gutter know when they bonded what Lord Argenwain secretly lusted for?

Lord Argenwain had bastard children scattered throughout Cathret. As far as Lark knew, he never had any contact with any of them, but his sacred requirement to continue his noble line was officially fulfilled. Everyone who dared to comment on the lack of wife and children in the house referenced his dislike for children and his noble decision to provide richly for them from afar rather than expose them to his disdain.

Ha. If only they knew what he truly protected them from.

Here they were, depicted in masterful oils, usually dark-haired though he had a few fair ones, three girls and four boys. There was plenty of property to go around after he died. Michael, named after the King, would inherit Pickwelling, as well as Crysvale, the country estate about twenty miles outside of Seven Churches.

While Lark perused the familiar familial collection, the dellai and Gutter made small talk about travel by ship and how it would likely be some years before they saw each other again.

"I may visit sooner than you might expect, now that I have a bond connection to Meridua," Gutter remarked. "I would very much like to meet the young man who lured my beloved Lark away from me." The first hint of annoyance had finally worked its way into Gutter's voice.

What plans of yours have I foiled? Lark didn't feel guilty about that at all, especially now.

He burned my father's men alive. He couldn't let himself think about it too much, or he'd do something irrevocable. He walked to one of the dining room windows and looked out. A little of the crystalline candle chandelier's lights glowed on a few evergreen hedges. Beyond that, in the darkness, Winsome waited.

"Lark," the dellai called. "What news of the nominations?"

"The colonel is campaigning for the presidency," Lark told them.

"Then he may become president." Gutter sounded intrigued.

"It is likely. He is a favorite." Lark felt more daunted than proud.

"And all this time I believed it must have been love at first sight," Gutter remarked.

Bold, unflinching in his public remarks, bordering on cruel—this was the Gutter that others feared, should their less-than-perfect actions attract his comment. Lark had never been exposed to his sarcasm or the sharper edge of his wit. The dellai probably knew Lark was a staghorn, but still, it made too light of all the complicated, painful and beautiful things he felt toward Rohn and then twisted it into political ambition.

"They make an interesting pair," the dellai said.

"Is his master handsome?" Gutter asked.

"Perfectly," the dellai said. "One tall and dark, one fair and graceful—it is a good thing that only women of note will be permitted to vote."

Lark blushed, and not at the compliment. As if women could be moved by appearances to any more degree than men. If anything the vote would be more fair if common women were also allowed to vote. Unlike noble women, they had to be practical not just in the management of their households but in work that was often as difficult as any man's work. His mother and the maids in Pickwelling had proved that to him over and again.

Gutter's gaze sparkled darkly from behind his mask. He seemed to notice Lark's discomfort, and apparently took pleasure in it. "So this new common nobility will decide?"

"Barons," the dellai corrected him. "And commoners will vote as well. But with or without baronial status, they must be residents of at least five years. Sailors must prove at least seventy percent support to families who have been residents of at least five years to qualify," the dellai told him. "The offices of registration and census are still being formed. They will likely only just complete their work in time for the vote itself."

"Which will be held when?"

"The thirteenth of Fuller."

"Not this—"

"No, in over a year's time."

Gutter walked toward the table, forcing them to gather there, as Lord Argenwain arrived. "A fair month."

"It is the least likely for our infamous tropical storms," the dellai told him. He nodded to Lord Argenwain. "A pleasure to see you again so soon, Lord Argenwain."

The old man, supported by Jeffrey just as Mark had once supported him, made his slow, dignified way to the table and sat at its head nearest the fire. "Dellai Bertram," he acknowledged softly. He didn't give Lark a single glance.

Jeffrey left to help serve dinner. Lark gestured and Gale retreated under the table. When he sat, she moved so that she pinned his legs against the chair.

Servants poured water and a pale wine that Mark wished he could try. His first mouthful of the creamy soup, a delicate fish chowder with leek, was pure bliss. But then a burning began in his throat, followed by an acidic churning and pressure in his gut. He managed another spoonful and then cooled it with milk. The relief was only temporary. He started to sweat.

All familiar pain, pain he'd schooled himself to reveal as little as possible, threatened to crush his composure. The servants brought bread, still steaming from the oven. He remembered this bread well. He allotted himself a portion as large as the end of his thumb and savored it. It tasted so good, buttery and sweet with that exquisite crust that had a delicate, tender crispness to it. In his mouth it brought him joy, but once he swallowed he felt overfull. He stared at the glory of a meal, starving to death but too full and in too much pain to eat another bite.

Gutter had paused in the enjoyment of his own meal to watch him. Those dark, glittering eyes within the mask seemed to brighten when Lark looked back at him.

"You seem ill," Dellai Bertram remarked coldly. "Is something the matter."

Gutter, who'd only moments before enjoyed a little light torture at Lark's expense, turned red about his neck. "You haven't heard?" His rich voice had deepened.

"Heard what?"

"Someone poisoned him."

Dellai Bertram nearly upset his soup as his spoon came down hard against the edge of his bowl. He looked hard at Lark, perhaps only now seeing him.

"Do you know of a cure for deatlal?" Gutter asked.

"Deatlal? And you survived?" The dellai seemed more puzzled than upset.

Lark chuckled low in his throat. "Obviously." He watched the dellai carefully. The dellai's thoughts clearly focused hard down several avenues, his gaze shifting back and forth and away, darting. Lark wished he could read through those eyes into the man's mind. The dellai knew something.

Perhaps someone at the church had ordered it, or perhaps the dellai only suspected some of the many barons and jesters that he knew so well.

"There is no cure," the dellai told them. "We have searched. The poison has its origins on the main island in particular, and if we haven't found a cure, no one will. It is invariably fatal, though there are a handful of cases that linger on." His gaze focused back on Mark. Was that regret in his expression, or guilt, or just pity?

"I know a doctor in Saphir." Gutter gave Lark a significant glance. "He may be able to help."

"Mainland doctors have little experience with it, but I wish you luck."

Lord Argenwain pushed his soup away. "Take it," he told Jeffrey sharply. "Take it all away. I'm not well. I'm sorry, gentlemen, I have a sudden need to retire. Please continue without me." He shook as he stood on his own. Jeffrey turned back with the soup and helped him out. Carrol fetched the soup away in his stead.

Lark hesitated, then remembered it was his right. He nudged Gale so that she gave him some room and stood as well. "Thank you for the fine dinner, but I should leave as well. I apologize for upsetting everyone."

"Please stay. Stay the night," Gutter told him. "We'll leave for Saphir first thing in the morning."

"No thank you."

Gutter stood. "You must come to Saphir." His voice hardened. "Please."

"Give me a better reason than a faint hope of a cure."

"There are things you need to see."

"Gutter!" The dellai shot to his feet, knocking over his chair in the process.

"Shut up, Terrance." Gutter didn't even spare him a glance. His gaze kept Lark rooted in place. "Everything changed." He spoke the words softly, reminding Lark of their conversation upstairs. "All your questions, answered, but not here. In Saphir, City of Bridges. Eshku Fasemasq. The Shadow Circus. Come with me, if not for your own sake, then for political advantage. I don't imagine you've come all this way just to visit."

"I'll consider it." Lark bowed and walked out, trembling. Strangely, Gale hesitated before she followed him out of Pickwelling into the cold spring evening.

He wanted to drop the mask, but something afraid inside him kept him from removing it.

Not here. Not now.

He made it to the street and turned right toward the nearest avenue. There he had to go left, downhill, toward the university where he'd be more likely to find a waiting coach. He schooled himself not to look behind him to see if he could spot Winsome, and kept his pace slow to give her more time. A slow pace also lessened the possibility that his weakened body would collapse.

His grinding, burning belly rebelled and he slowed even more to keep the food down. Every little bit he managed to retain would give him that much longer to live.

I'm dying.

He stopped by the iron fence that edged the university grounds and held on until the weight of his mortality eased a little. The worst part was that he'd be separated from everything he knew and cared about. Those glimpses into the other world and its creatures didn't just terrify him. Though that foreign landscape was beautiful, he preferred the nuances of human faces, and blue skies, clear streams, songbirds .... He loved this world. All of it. Even with the blood and the cruelty and all its other flaws, he loved being alive in this place. He never wanted to leave.

Lark crouched and Gale came into his arms. He held her close, her soft, clean fur warming his face. She squirmed a little, still very much a dog rather than a human being, not knowing how to comfort someone who wanted so much to be held.

You can't bribe time, and forever is a cheat the world never allows.

He wished he could be braver.

Much to Gale's relief Lark let her go and started walking again. He noticed a coach just around the corner down the avenue, one of three. He made it there and hesitated.

There she was, walking around the other side of the university three long blocks away. He walked slowly up to the driver. "Walker Main," he said, and waited for the driver to come down and open the door. Lark gestured. "Go on," he said, and Gale hopped up into the coach. He took a moment as if steadying himself, and then allowed the driver to hand him up into the coach. He looked out. "Is that woman there looking for a coach, you think?"

The driver looked. "I believe so, milord."

"I think I recognize her. Let's see if she's going my way."

The driver climbed up and drove the carriage toward her, slowing as they neared. Mark pushed open the window. "Excuse me, miss. Are you on your way to Walker Main?"

Winsome hesitated. She looked pale, but otherwise all right, well-wrapped in a large cloak that covered the long rifle. "Excuse me?"

"I'm sorry," Lark said. "I don't mean to be forward but I thought I saw you near Walker Main and I'm on my way there. I thought I'd offer you a lift. I didn't mean to frighten you. Driver—"

"No, I mean, yes. Thank you. I appreciate the offer, and I accept."

The driver stepped down again and helped her in.

They didn't speak. Fortunately it didn't take long to get there. Lark dropped her off in front of their rooms, and had the driver let him off near Bartlee's Fish and Chips, better known for its brandy and desserts than its dinners. Lark went inside, ordered stew, waited a few minutes by the fire much to the curious stares of Bartlee's regular patrons, and then left well-wrapped in his cloak to hide his fine clothes with the stew in a box wrapped in several layers of oiled paper.

Winsome practically pounced him at the door. "Are you all right?"

"Yes. Thank you."

"You left early. What happened?"

"I need to feed Gale." He unwrapped the stew on the floor, checked it to make certain it wasn't too hot for her, and then straightened. "Good girl, Gale."

She set into it with a fury. He envied her abandon.

"Lark," Winsome pleaded.

He settled into a chair. She'd furnished the rooms well, if sparsely, and someone had dusted and swept—probably the wife from downstairs. The fierce cold hadn't yet yielded to a fresh fire in the stove. "I'm tired and I'm going to bed."

"Lark."

He sighed. "They didn't threaten me. We argued a bit, but mostly I upset them, and it was better to leave. You saw Dellai Bertram?"

"Yes."

The fire crackled. Gale started chewing on the paper, so he took it away from her and pitched it into the stove.

"Did they say anything about my father, or about the former mayor ... anyone?" she asked.

"I didn't ask about them. I never got that far." He released his cloak tie and pulled off his boots. "We'll talk in the morning."

"I would like to discuss it now." She crossed her arms.

He'd meant that he would speak with Gutter again tomorrow, but her interpretation was also true. "You have nothing to say about Dellai Bertram and his connection to Gutter. I have nothing to say about what we discussed at dinner until I've had a chance to sleep and think things over."

"I have nothing to say because I know nothing."

"I believe you," he said, though he didn't entirely trust her. "And I need time to appreciate what I've learned." He forced himself up and went to his bed behind the short screen she'd bought. He heard her walk away to her room. The door shut. After a moment he stripped down to his shirt. Gale hopped up on the sturdy bed Winsome had bought for him and panted, no doubt expecting him to tell her off. Instead he settled beside her and stroked her head.

He had to try and get some rest, and the room was cold. Lark wormed into bed, shifting Gale gently with his feet, and drew the feather blankets up. The mattress had a feather bed over it, and the cool comfort of it billowed up around his body.

He was afraid to take off his mask.

Is Gutter truly mad beneath his masks?

He didn't want to imagine it, but the night he'd told Gutter he didn't want to be a jester returned to him. He remembered the flinch, the smeared portion of the Gutter Rose showing beneath the mask, Gutter's hurry and agitation. He could imagine too easily how Thomas could have compelled Gutter toward the docks with no plan, driven by a remorseless sense of loss much like he'd felt when Grant had died. Thomas' beloved boy would leave him forever. Maybe Gutter had boarded the ship with some modicum of control. "I wonder if they knew they were in danger when Gutter came for them," Lark whispered to Gale. "I wonder if Thomas tore the mask free right in front of them—"

Not quite what happened, the foreign voice whispered. **He got the ones on watch drunk. The rest were asleep or weren't on board at all.**

What are you doing? a softer voice whispered.

Lark could have asked himself the same question. He didn't want to hear. He didn't want to know anymore. "Shut up," Lark whispered, and closed his eyes.

He didn't remember dozing off, but he woke to Winsome in a nightdress kneeling by his bed. "You were just dreaming. It's all right. I'm here," she whispered.

"Hmm?"

She touched his face near his ear. It was wet. He'd been crying in his sleep.

Winsome kissed the wetness, and again. She pressed him back and settled on the edge of the bed. Her body stretched alongside his and she kissed his neck. Her hand caressed his face again and she touched the mask.

"No."

"You shouldn't sleep with it," she whispered.

"No, Winsome." He wanted to say yes. He wanted to find out if he could be like other men and maybe someday have a wife and children and go for walks in the park in public without people making comments and looking askance, disapproving.

"Is it because of Rohn?"

"Yes." He wanted Rohn for himself, but he also wanted Rohn to have a family someday, and Winsome seemed ideal. The lie was also the truth was also a lie.

"If you wanted a virgin bride for him then you should have picked someone else to force upon him." She didn't sound bitter. If anything she sounded amused. "I'm cold, and you're cold. We could be warm together." She kissed him again. He let her press him back, yielding to her touch. She smoothed his shirt over his chest. He helped her pull it over his head. Her lush mouth traced down his body. It should have pleased him. When Rohn had done much the same every grazing touch lit his passions and made him cry out with need.

Her mouth was little different from Rohn's, but it took those memories of his lord and master to stir even the faintest warmth within him. She drew her body up against him and kissed him with abandon. Her lips may as well have been warm liver squirming around on his face.

"Winsome, stop. Please stop." He caught her hands.

Her breath shuddered and she shivered. Lark drew the blanket over them both and held her close. She hid her face against his neck.

"I can't," he told her. He wished he could. He didn't want to hurt her, and he didn't want to be alone, and he liked her so much ....

"You don't want me." He almost didn't hear the barely whispered words but he could hear her shame and pain.

"No." She squirmed but he held on. "Winsome. Listen to me. You're beautiful. Intelligent—"

"Just let me go."

He released her and she sat up beside him. "You're everything admirable and wonderful and I do love you." The last words fell flat. They held too much friendship and not enough passion. "But I can't, and it isn't just because of Rohn. It's just that ... you have breasts."

"Excuse me?" Her voice lifted to a growl. Gale shifted uneasily at the foot of the bed.

He waited, hoping she would come to the realization herself, but she just loomed beside him. In the darkness he could see little of her beyond shadows but he felt her hard regard. "I wish," he began lamely. "I had hoped. If anyone could, you could."

"Could what? Make you feel?"

"I haven't been with a woman before."

Her regard gentled. She touched his mouth with her fingers. "You haven't?"

"But I've been with men."

She tried to stand bolt upright, lost her balance and sat hard. She missed the edge of the bed and slid awkwardly askew beside it.

Lark sat up. "I'm sorry."

"You're lying."

"I'm sorry. I'm not lying."

"And Rohn knows?" Her voice raised higher.

"Yes."

She started to cry, then laughed, and pushed herself up, still sobbing. "I hate you."

"I don't blame you," Lark told her.

"I'm such an idiot."

Lark smiled. "We're two of a kind."

"Stop being so charming!" She laughed through another sob. "And take that damned mask off. Please."

"You can't see me anyway. It's dark."

"I can hear it in your voice."

Lark started to, but he couldn't. He couldn't any more than he could take the skin off his own face.

"Please," she whispered.

"I can't."

"Why not?" She ventured close again.

"I'm afraid."

She snuffled back tears. Her hands found his face. "I'll help you."

His hands settled over hers, following along as she traced the ribbon back and pulled the bow knot loose. His breath caught and he held the ribbon tight so the mask wouldn't slip off.

Slowly, gently, she drew his hands forward. The mask's pressure against his skin eased, and panic washed in with the cold air on his cheeks. His fingers clasped the mask's edge.

"I'm right here," Winsome soothed.

Lark let go with a shudder and Mark took off the mask. His heart thundered and he gasped for air. The pain in his belly had eased since it peaked shortly after the soup, but fresh awareness of it sliced through him.

He could hear sailors screaming. He saw the flames in the bay, and *Mairi's* figurehead drowning in fire and water, her ashes searing and blackening the snow that fell all around him.

Winsome kissed his face, his mouth. The memories and nightmare fantasies faded, but he felt nothing for her except a quiet gratitude for her care. "Don't," he said softly, ducking her kiss. "I'm sorry, but it's not fair to either of us if I try and pretend."

She drew away.

Mark held the mask in his lap. "I'm going to Saphir. I think it's best if you go back to the islands. Tell Rohn—tell him what you've seen."

"I haven't seen anything." She sniffed again, and wiped her face on her sleeve.

"You've seen me." He wished she knew how rare that was, how few he would have trusted to touch his mask, kiss his face, and see his fear. "I'll send a letter with you." When she didn't answer he tried again. "You might take the same ship Dellai Bertram is taking back to the islands. You could learn something from him. You're clever enough, and brave enough."

"You need me." Her voice sounded flat. "I won't leave you here alone."

"I'm not alone here." A lie, but he needed her to believe it.

"Because Gutter is your friend?" She made it sound like an accusation more than a question.

"I don't know, but—"

"Then I'm staying."

Mark set the mask aside. "You can't help me, Winsome. And I can't protect you from them. I do believe that Gutter will protect me, perhaps even at the expense of his own life. That's worth a great deal here. A lot more than that firearm of yours. But he won't protect you. He might even seek to harm you, or snare you into his intrigues."

Her breath hitched into sobs again. She stood up and retreated to her room.

Mark sat alone in the darkness. The stove, apparently out of fuel, made settling noises. He stood and added two large logs to the small bed of coals, along with a few bits of kindling to get it going.

Winsome startled him by bursting out of her room. She was dressed for travel.

"Where—" he began, but she went out the door and slammed it shut behind her. Gale jumped to her feet.

Mark paused long enough to pull on his breeches before he dashed after her. "Winsome, wait." She didn't stop so he followed her down the back stairs, the cold night air slithering over his skin. "Winsome." He couldn't catch up with her. The cold brick stabbed his bare tender feet. "Where are you going?"

Gale dashed ahead of him and caught up with Winsome, but then the dog stopped and waited for Mark. Winsome was almost a block ahead of him now, the rifle making a sharp tent of her cloak at her shoulder. His breath came up short. He walked to catch his breath and then tried trot after her, but a rush of weakness made him stumble and he had to catch himself on a wall.

He could go on without her, but that didn't matter. He needed to know that she'd be safe, even if she hated him for it, even if it meant begging her to come with him after all because at least he would know she wasn't alone and afraid and hurting somewhere in an uncaring city. Out of desperation he pointed at her. "Gale, fetch."

The dog chased after her, surprisingly quick for such a heavy and awkward puppy. She seized Winsome's cloak and pulled.

Winsome halted. Her shoulders sagged.

Mark caught up to her eventually, his feet numb, legs trembling with weakness.

"Let me go." Winsome stood there, face shadowed. Gale kept hold of her cloak, her short, feathered tail wagging wildly.

"Good girl," Mark told Gale under his breath. He tugged the cloak free from her mouth. "Winsome, I don't know what to do. Gutter is my best chance at discovering whatever it is that threatens Meridua. I could hunt for your father, or search for Feather, but I'm so far behind them that by the time I catch any hint of them they might be on the other side of the world. I could introduce you to Gutter. I could make certain they'd invite you—"

"I know. I'd be useless."

Mark stood there, helpless and far more useless than she could ever imagine herself. "You're brave, and you're strong. I'm weak and cowardly and blind and I'm so sorry, Winsome. I had no idea." That wasn't exactly true, but he hoped it would make her feel better. "I don't know what I've done to deserve you. I've been horrible to you. I wish I could be a friend, a lover, even a husband but I can't even be a man. I'm a boy, a toy, a broken thing wrecked on stormy, rocky shores that pretends it can sail."

"Stop it," she breathed. He tried to move to take her hand and look at her but she kept her back to him, one hand at her face, the other carrying a heavy satchel as if it weighed only as much as a purse.

He didn't want her to leave him, but he had to make her go back to Perida, either that or give up and go back home with her.

I'll never make it back home anyway.

His breath shortened. He forced it to stretch, and steadied his voice. "As much as I like you, and as little faith as I have in myself, I have to agree that you'd be less than useless in Saphir. I'll be dancing at royal courts. There's no amount of dressing up that will hide your lack of connection in those places. There are killers among them that priests turn a blind eye to because they're considered sacred, and men who duel for entertainment, and assassins that hunt for purposes that seem insane to us. And you'd be prey to any creature that might hope to influence Gutter, or hurt him. I won't be able to protect you."

"I don't intend to go to Saphir."

Then did she intend to go after her father herself? "If you try to go your own way through Cathret ... please don't, Winsome. Please." He no longer felt the cold. He ached with emptiness instead.

She stood there, trembling. Mark yearned to comfort her, but he had to find the right words to send her home instead.

Sink the knife in and be done.

"If you insist, I'll go with you." He measured his words carefully so the pain wouldn't voice itself. "It's probably too late to save anyone anyway. The colonel will let himself die the next time an assassin comes, so he can be with his men who died in the war. He had one chance for happiness, and I took you from him. It's all a waste. My life, your love, and his future, gone. So why not force a pointless confrontation with a minor element in a small part of the larger intrigue?"

"You little burr," she hissed. He forced himself to hold his head up though he wanted to flinch. "Go back to your mainland fops and your parties and pretend that you're a hero if it makes your dying breaths easier. None of us were anything more than a game to you anyway, and you lost. You've lost all of us."

"Goodbye, Winsome," he whispered. It took all his strength to turn from her and walk away. Gale trotted up and matched his stride.

Either she'd go home, or she'd hunt for her father on her own. If the former, he wouldn't want to stop her. If the latter, he'd never talk her out of it now.

It took Mark some time to work his way back to their rooms, dress properly, and pack a few things. He shouldered his satchel and went back out, making sure to leave the door unlocked and the keys on the table. Because of the late hour and his slow pace, it took him the better part of an hour to find a coachman dozing on the side of the road. The coach was parked by a tavern which most likely had been boisterous earlier but now the laughter and conversations burned low like the fires banked in the hearths. Mark paid him in advance and climbed in. Gale climbed inside after him, weary and shivering with uncertainty. He rubbed her neck and chest to try to comfort her.

The gas lamps at Pickwelling's gates and entryway still burned, but the lamps and candles in the house were out. At the front door, Mark carefully pulled on the chord so that it would play softly.

The wait seemed to stretch on and on. Finally the door opened. Gray-haired Janis, the downstairs maid, stared out blearily with a beautiful candle lamp in hand. It took her a moment to recognize him. "Mark?" she asked plaintively, then stepped back and opened the door wider. "Excuse me, lord jester. Please, come in."

Mark came inside. Gale circled his legs, so anxious now that she panted hard as if she'd been running. "Lord Argenwain invited me to stay the night," he told her. "I—I've changed my mind and gladly accept his generosity."

"Oh. Yes. Very good, my lord jester." The weariness fell away, replaced by nervous calculation. "If you'll give us but a moment—"

"Please don't rouse the house on my account. Any room will do. I'll even take a chair for the night. I'll probably not sleep anyway."

"We wouldn't treat you thus." She looked hurt by the suggestion. "Please. This way. Take my arm if you like, lord jester."

"There's no need, but thank you."

"May I take your bag?"

He clutched the satchel closer. "I have it, thank you."

It seemed like an entirely different house from the one he'd grown up in as she led him to the guest wing in the dark and sleepy manor. A few servants crept about their earliest duties—the baker warming up the ovens for the breakfast bread, chamber servants delicately adding fuel to stoves and hearths in the occupied rooms, wash attendants drowsily attending to the day's first wash water as it heated over the vast bath stove, the cook's assistants carrying the day's food up from the underground stores. Those familiar sounds made him feel like an intruder. He'd interrupted their extremely busy schedules. He'd very seldom been up during this hour when he'd lived here, less often as he grew older and the nightmares grew farther apart. Once he'd been ill and had wandered about. He didn't know why he hadn't rung a bell for help in any of the rooms he'd passed. By the time a wash servant had noticed him he was so cold and miserable that the hearth-warmed blankets they'd heaped on him had felt scalding-hot.

Janis had been there as she had always been in this house, not quite as gray-haired back then, with fewer of the fine lines that gave such lovely character to her eyes. In many ways she could still be considered a young, attractive woman but she was long past marrying age and would grow old and die in service at this house. It wasn't a bad fate, but he wondered if she wished for a husband and children instead.

She nurtured him as if he were a child now as she had back then, opening a guest room for him, lighting the lamps, hustling him to the bed, helping him stow the satchel into the low shelf of a nightstand, helping him with his cloak, his coat, his shoes. "Do you have nightclothes with you?" she asked. "If not I can fetch some."

"In the satchel, but I'll manage, thank you, Janis."

"I'll send for Morris."

Mark started to protest but then thought better of it. Janis bustled out.

"Gale," he whispered, doing his best to smother his loneliness. She perked her ears at her name. He settled on the floor beside the bed and sat with her.

What am I doing?

She knew better than to lick his face so she licked the air near his cheek. He put an arm around her and rubbed her side. Out in the hall, a servant walked quickly by, then another rushed the other way.

Dellai Bertram, he guessed, needed help to prepare for his journey. He wondered if Winsome would try to take the same ship back to Perida, or if she'd go another direction entirely. If it were him he'd try to stay on with *Dainty* until she finished her route around the bay and returned to the islands that way, but Winsome would likely be in a hurry to get home if his awful work had succeeded. Maybe she'd try to follow him at a distance. He hoped not. The dangers he'd described to her were all too true and real. At the same time, he missed her already and wanted to run after her and beg her to come with him.

Someone knocked and the door opened.

Jeffrey.

Gale trotted over to Jeffrey and circled him. He stood still while she sniffed his shoes and at his crotch.

Gale returned to Mark, apparently satisfied.

"Morris is busy and I heard the bell," Jeffrey explained. "I'm learning to be a valet. If you don't mind, it would be my honor to serve you." He was sleepy, which brought out more of the dockside swagger in his accent.

He looked a little unkempt too. Mark hated how that made him more attractive, especially after he'd rejected Winsome.

"You want to be a valet?" Mark asked.

"Very much, lord jester." Jeffrey's gaze sharpened, as if Mark had mocked him for it. "It may not seem like much to you—"

"I think you'll like being a valet. Come here. I'll show you."

Jeffrey walked over.

"My things are in my satchel." The benign role of teacher was a welcome distraction from thinking about Winsome, though he didn't actually stop worrying about her. "Have you done this before?"

Jeffrey hesitated. "No," he admitted.

"The important thing is to look like it's all business, and act as if you don't see anything personal. If you have to touch something that you shouldn't but you have to anyway, do it quickly and carefully. My mask is tucked on the side of my satchel. When you get out my nightclothes try not to disturb it."

Jeffrey carefully drew the satchel out from the nightstand.

"Be perfunctory, like you've done this a hundred times, but not in a way that looks like you're not being careful with my things." Mark's gut clenched as a particularly disturbing image of Winsome hunting for a coach in a dark neighborhood came to him.

"Have you done this before?" Jeffrey asked.

"I've helped the valet with Lord Argenwain before, but mostly I was what I think you may be. A companion. I read to him, and kept him company, and helped him with letters and such."

Jeffrey drew out Mark's nightclothes. He looked like he had a hundred more questions but was either afraid to ask or resented the desire to do it.

"Lay them out in order," Mark told him. "Did you ... meet Bainswell?"

"Bainswell? No. Who is he?"

"Lord Argenwain's previous valet. I was just curious." They probably threw him out on the street as soon as Mark was gone. Served him right, and yet, it didn't seem right to use a human being like that. Gutter had given Bainswell everything a poor man could dream of but as a pretense, and then took it away. If Mark had come back to them and asked for his old situation, they would do the same to Jeffrey.

Mark gazed at him.

Or perhaps not. What little beauty I have left will soon be gone, and I imagine this handsome creature is willing to do a great deal more than I ever did.

Jeffrey blushed, and though it was an irritated pink on a shy and sullen expression, it enhanced his beauty a thousandfold. "Am I doing this wrong?"

"You're doing fine. Now help me with my clothes."

Jeffrey helped him out of his waistcoat, then pulled Mark's shirt off over his head. His hands, long-fingered, would have been well-suited for the keyed instruments or cello.

"Fold the shirt and set it aside," Mark coached, trying not to let the breathless feeling he had carry into his voice. His worries over Winsome crested and fell away into even deeper loneliness. He yearned to fill that loneliness.

But not like this. Not now.

Jeffrey caressed the shirt as he folded it, and then ran his hands over the nightshirt. It was all deliberate temptation, done with the skill of a master craftsman but with far more cunning than love or desire. "This next?" His voice sounded husky.

Mark shivered with yearning. "With a nightshirt, you can bunch each side in your hands so that you can put the neck hole over my head, and then you hold out the sleeves one at a time so I can put my arms through. On a more fitted shirt the hands go through first, and then you guide the neck hole over my head. You can practice either way with the nightshirt."

Jeffrey took up the fabric. "Which way would you prefer?" He moved to stand close in front of Mark. Before Mark could answer he settled the nightshirt over his head. Mark slipped his hands into the sleeves without help. Jeffrey smoothed the delicate fabric, better-suited for the tropics than the chilly room, over his chest. "I took too long," he said softly. "You're cold. May I warm you, lord jester?"

It didn't matter that Jeffrey lacked subtlety. Those words were spoken with enough skill that they penetrated Mark's pitiful attempts to armor himself. "You don't want me." Mark certainly wanted him, more than he wanted a decent meal, more than he wanted sleep, or wine, or even his next breath. He very much wanted to be with a young man skilled in play who would help him forget briefly that he'd deliberately hurt and lost a loyal friend.

"It would be my honor and pleasure." Jeffrey knelt and Mark's heart started to pound. He felt faint. Long fingers skillfully unbuckled his belt. A hard, rich contraction pulsed through Mark and he gasped despite his best efforts to control himself. "Do I ask you to stand now?" Large blue eyes stared luxuriously, knowing eyes that had hungered and wept and smiled through pain and now saw only wealth and luxury and freedom from deprivation and desperation. "Or would you rather lay back?"

"Were you a dockside fawn?" It was Mark's one hope to prevent—

To prevent what? What might be my last moment of real pleasure?

Jeffrey darkened with irritation, but without a trace of shame. "You think Lord Argenwain would stoop so low? I am far more precious a jewel than that, lord jester."

"And well paid, I'm sure." He felt mean for saying it, but he hoped it would drive Jeffrey away.

Jeffrey smiled. "I wonder. You're not afraid of me, are you? I can't imagine why but I don't know how else to explain why someone so near to bursting would stab at one so willing. Unless ... no. You aren't the sort that feeds on humiliation, mine or your own. You have a gentle heart. You yearn for love." He lowered his lashes. "But I'm not worthy, am I."

All manipulation, all false but Jeffrey made it feel real. Mark longed to touch that face, to speak comforting words, and to kiss that mouth. "And what would Lord Argenwain say?" Mark reminded him.

"He worships you." For all his skill Jeffrey didn't manage to hide a note of bitterness there. Mark doubted that it was jealousy. More like foiled competition to be the one and only object that Lord Argenwain could not live without.

Because if you are loved and worshipped, you'll live in luxury for the rest of your life. Is that it, Jeffrey?

"And I can see why," Jeffrey continued, raking his gaze over Mark's half-dressed body. That gaze felt like fingers grazing his skin. "How could he deny you anything? You have always been the one with which he most longs to share his sins. And am I not sin embodied?" A slight change in his posture invited Mark to look and explore the depths of all things forbidden and all things feared by those who believed that men should never touch each other with sensual love. "And therefore, his to give to you to sate that which his aged body can no longer please?"

"So now you're a gift?"

A flash of irritation lit those blue eyes again. Mark hoped that Jeffrey didn't guess that it only made Mark more ardent. Those glimpses of real feeling revealed the real person, and the real person held Mark prisoner. He should have ordered Jeffrey out a long time ago. Jeffrey's expression warmed again and he lowered his lashes. His hand came to rest on Mark's knee and started to slide up his thigh.

Mark caught his hand. There was no resistance in those fingers, just supple grace and skill. They toyed with each other's hands. Jeffrey started to pull Mark's glove off, but Mark didn't let him. "I don't believe," Mark told him, "that you came here to seduce an emaciated, dying shadow of a man for no pay, and I know Lord Argenwain didn't send you. So what do you want?"

"We're to barter?" Jeffrey let a little more of himself show. Hope glowed behind those eyes, and more cunning.

"What are they paying you?" Mark carefully played his voice so he might set the trap without Jeffrey noticing.

"Two ar a week. It's a fortune to someone like me, but I wonder if you could make me a better offer." His other hand settled on Mark's thigh and pressed. He dragged his fingers toward Mark's knee.

He could have this boy for three ar a week. It galled him, and at the same time ... why not? Rohn would be appalled, of course. It was quite a different thing than bringing a puppy into the house.

But of course he wouldn't. It wasn't just that slavery was supposed to be a sin. The idea of lavishing his desire on someone who pretended to respond, someone who seemed to loathe him ... it repulsed him so much that nearly all his ardor drained away. He sprang the trap. "You should leave." The flat, cold tone would hopefully scare Jeffrey into believing that Mark would inform Lord Argenwain of Jeffrey's lack of loyalty at breakfast, with his pay rate as proof. Mark decided to spell it out, just in case he didn't catch it. "I'm not the sort of fool who believes he can buy a thing as precious as love. But even if I did, I would not rob someone like Lord Argenwain of his toy, only to misuse him in the same fashion. Do you often try to sell yourself on the side? I don't think he'd like that."

Alarm raced through Jeffrey's eyes. Too hastily, awkwardly, he leaned close. "But I do want you. It's not just the money. That's just to see how much you want me. Please. I don't want to leave you. You're the most magnificent—"

"Just go."

"We could have an understanding," Jeffrey said. "I—want us to be friends. I didn't mean to come on so fast and hard. I thought you wanted me as much as I wanted you."

"You'd be better off learning to be a valet," Mark told him. "You won't always be beautiful. Now, go on. I'll finish dressing myself for bed."

Jeffrey eased away to his feet. "Please. I didn't mean—"

Mark couldn't keep torturing him. "I'm not going to tell anyone. I know what's it's like to be trapped in luxury, and what it would mean if they threw you out."

"But I'm not trapped. I like it here. I love it. You don't understand. I'll do anything to stay. In ten years I can earn enough to live on for the rest of my life. Besides, I don't want to be old. I see what old age is." He let out a soft, ugly laugh. "Who wants it? I'll spend every bit, get blind drunk, swim in all the young flesh I want, and then end it quick. Right off a cliff." He laughed again, under his breath, caught in that nightmare of a wishful dream.

A shudder of revulsion raced through Mark. "I won't interfere with your scheme. I'm leaving soon anyway. In a few hours I'll be gone and it's likely I'll never return." Impending death seemed to push him toward the edge of his own cliff, but he was far from willing. He couldn't laugh like Jeffrey had.

Jeffrey backed away. "Are you sure you don't want me to stay?" He gestured. "You ... I know you're lonely. I wouldn't mind. He wouldn't mind either. He cried himself to sleep over you. He—he loves you." A hard note of contempt edged the words.

Mark shook his head. The entire situation reeked of death and lies and madness and he wished he were in the cold rooms above the jam shop. He wished he were anywhere but here.

Jeffrey's expression changed to something puzzled and a little affronted. "Sleep well, lord jester." Jeffrey backed out of the room, and shut the door behind him.

Mark wrestled out of the rest of his clothes and left them on the floor. He kept his gloves on to prevent anyone from seeing his scar. He wouldn't need socks or a nightcap tonight—he had two feet of down on all sides. It still took him some time to warm up. He traced a hand over the pillow and imagined it was Rohn.

He didn't want to die so far from home.

He didn't want to die at all.

Most of all he didn't want to die alone. At least now he'd have Gutter. That shouldn't have been a comfort, but it was.

Gale tried to scramble onto the bed, letting out little whines in the process. He knew he ought to tell her no, but she gazed at him with her soft puppy eyes, and there was plenty of room. He got back out of bed so that he could lift her properly. He was barely strong enough to do it.

She flopped onto her side, let out a swift, heavy sigh and groaned with exhausted satisfaction. Only the very end of her short, feathered tail lifted and dropped in a weary wag.

Her peacefulness and joy reminded him that at least for now he was still alive. He would finally see Saphir, the grand city. His memory painted him images gathered from artwork and books. The reality wouldn't be so splendid, but it would be something. It would be special.

He would spend what remained of his strength in the last place Rohn had been truly happy. Mark wove his fingers into Gale's fur, and closed his eyes. His gut burned with anxiety, he shivered from cold and his mind concocted evil ways in which Winsome might be suffering in loneliness, fear and heartache.

None of those thoughts would do anything for him, or for her. He had to rest and then focus all his will on the conspiracy, Meridua's safety, and anything else he could do. He made lists in his mind and memorized them, all the little steps he'd have to climb to find his way to success. The items seemed to go on forever. All the secrets he needed to pry from Gutter's mind. Letters he had to write. Escape routes he had to plan in case he needed to flee Gutter again.

The feather bed finally warmed him, and exhaustion bled him until he drowned in darkness.

Chapter Seven

Mark cut up his breakfast sausage, even though he couldn't eat it. He surreptitiously dropped a bit to Gale. She snuck it into her mouth without making a sound, as if she knew that any disgusting noise or excessive shifting would result in her eviction from under the table.

"Morris is already packing my things," Lord Argenwain told them, wiping his mouth.

"My lord," Gutter protested. "It will be dangerous." He was on his feet, gripping the back of his chair to restrain himself.

"Not to me."

"There will still be considerable snow in the mountains, and the risk of a dangerous storm is too great." Mark had never seen Gutter so anxious. Everything ceased to exist except Gutter's lord and master. Mark's presence at breakfast and agreement to go to Saphir had become so insignificant that he may as well have vanished.

And he preferred it that way.

Lord Argenwain gave Gutter a fond look. For once his expression won through his otherwise sour and fish-like face. "You will not deprive me of what may well be my last look at that great city where you and I had so much fun. And it's not my health you should most worry about. You and the boy will need protection. I can at least provide a safe haven to which you both can retreat."

"I've delayed too long as it is, and you can't be a party to this," Gutter told him. "I don't need a shelter. I need success."

"You can't keep me in a padded house forever." Lord Argenwain took a small bite of what passed for oranges here. The fruit didn't smell quite ripe.

The islands had spoiled Mark's appreciation of good food in more ways than one. "By next year I may not be able to travel at all."

"You're weary after a day at the park. I won't have it." Gutter started to walk out of the breakfast room.

"Stop right there." Lord Argenwain's voice halted the most powerful jester in the world without lifting beyond a calm drone. "I'm going to Saphir, my friend. And I'm inviting Mark to travel with me. Don't make me disinvite you from my carriage."

A shiver traveled up Mark's spine.

"He's not your companion anymore," Gutter told him.

"He's not either of ours. He's a bonded jester, a lord in his own right." Lord Argenwain looked Mark's way. Their gazes connected. Mark's heart skipped a beat, then thundered back to life. Old he might be, but Lord Argenwain still commanded tremendous power and wealth. And he was not stupid. He had craft, and will, and despite his terrible flaw, nobility. "He's not your child, nor your creature. If he arrives in Saphir at your elbow he will be a target for every intrigue ever developed against us. He will be, must be, and is what he truly is. An ambassador of Meridua and jester to a person who might soon be president of that new nation. As such, he should travel in exalted company. And as famed a jester as you are, my own fame and connection to His Royal Majesty is quite a different thing. As you well know. You need my reputation. Both of you."

Gutter made an outraged noise. "You think presenting him as an ambassador is any less dangerous? At least they fear, respect and love us in Saphir. Do you know what courtiers think of the United Islands of Meridua?" He focused his dark, glittering gaze on Mark. "Rabble. A mob with a collection of swords and toy ships worth little more than a handful of signatures. The gazettes spend only a line or two to mention the impending nominations. Meanwhile, His Royal Majesty farts and—"

"Stop." Mark had never heard Lord Argenwain speak so sharply to anyone who wasn't a servant. Gutter paled at his tone. "I warned you. And this is what it has come to. We have no choice now, and I can accept that. But you will not be so damned foolish as to speak irreverently and carelessly of His Most Noble and Sacred Majesty, even to illustrate a valid point."

"Yes, my lord." Gutter seemed to shrink in size. For a flicker of a moment Mark saw something in those eyes behind the mask, something afraid and lost and confused.

Thomas.

Mark didn't know if the thought was his own, or something else's.

"Will you do me the honor?" Lord Argenwain asked Mark.

Mark didn't dare hesitate. "Of course."

Jeffrey edged into the doorway. "The carriage is ready."

Lord Argenwain looked to Gutter. "Will we require two carriages?"

"No, my lord," Gutter said softly.

Mark had always seen Gutter coming and going as he pleased, informing Lord Argenwain only of whatever he wished his lord and master to learn, and then flitting off to some other task, or a party, or to paint, or vanishing altogether. He'd never seen the two men square off, and he would have never believed before now that Lord Argenwain would win an argument against Gutter, much less cow him.

"Tell them to prepare a wagon for all our effects," Lord Argenwain told Jeffrey. "I believe we're just about packed."

Jeffrey hesitated. "My lord, would you like me to accompany you?"

Lord Argenwain gave his full attention to Jeffrey, but only for a moment. "No. I will not require you."

Jeffrey should have been pleased. Full pay and no duties.

But Jeffrey wasn't pleased at all. He looked hurt. Maybe it was an act, necessary to ensure Lord Argenwain believed in their mutual theater. But Lord Argenwain wasn't watching him. No one was except Mark.

Jeffrey gave Mark an angry look, eyes too bright, and then left to his duty. Maybe he wanted to go to Saphir because it was part of his dream. Maybe he thought Mark had betrayed him, and feared that he'd be thrown out as soon as they left the city gates, or that Mark might try to take his place.

Mark didn't think it was any of those things. It seemed even someone that jaded and cold could be hurt by rejection, even a welcome rejection. Jeffrey, it appeared, would find no joy in being alone and unmolested. It baffled Mark, and yet, hadn't he himself been so lonely that he'd yearned for Lord Argenwain's bed?

Was it loneliness, or was it something more complicated that made a hateful thing into a thing of desire when it was taken away?

Maybe the both of them just didn't have anything better. Or maybe they couldn't feel, understand, or know real love, making its artifice the best thing they could hope for. He thought he loved Gutter, and Rohn, but they didn't seem to love him back, not the way he thought people loved each other. The closest thing he'd had to a lover, oddly, had been Grant, and they had never even kissed, never ever would have kissed, because

Grant wasn't a staghorn. So why did that friendship, that love, feel so true and real while everything else was convoluted and painful?

The front bell rang. Mark nearly jumped to answer it before he remembered he was a guest here. A few moments later Ames arrived.

Even in the short time Mark had spent here, he'd gathered that Ames, the new man, and Morris, Lord Argenwain's most favored footman, vied for the newly-opened position of valet. For the moment the two men traded back and forth between that duty and their everyday ones, depending on who could free himself to help Lord Argenwain first. Ames bowed with dignity. "Lord Jester Lark's baggage has arrived," he said.

"Very good," Lord Argenwain told him. "See to it that it's properly loaded onto the wagon. I don't want the carriage overloaded. And then pack your things. You will accompany us. Be quick, as I expect we'll leave within the hour."

"Very good, my lord." Ames bowed again with no change of expression, but he had a little extra lift to his step as he left.

"He's working out quite well," Lord Argenwain noted. "An excellent find." He looked to Mark. "He's related to an old staff member at Lady Brickholl's."

Mark nodded in acknowledgement.

"Do you have good staff at your manor, or whatever it is?"

He hadn't heard. It seemed impossible that he hadn't heard, but then again, as Gutter had pointed out, news from the islands wouldn't warrant much in Cathretan gazettes, and Lord Argenwain didn't care to read them. "I'm still developing the staff at Hevether."

"It was insufficient?"

"They were killed, my lord," Mark told him.

Gutter didn't say anything. He didn't have to. The massacre at Hevether Hall wasn't just a terrible tragedy and outrage. It clearly revealed Mark's failure as a jester.

"I'd heard the islands were terribly dangerous, and Perida in particular." Lord Argenwain sat back and waved away the remains of his breakfast. He hadn't eaten much, though far more than Mark had managed. "You could have chosen a better master, my boy." His voice held a note of sadness in it. "You could have had a fine one."

"I never wanted to be a jester," Mark reminded him.

"And yet you are."

"Yes. I suppose I am." The conversation had faded into something inconsequential and unworthy of his memories of finding Grant, Norbert and Philip murdered, and Trudy so grievously wounded he'd thought she had been killed as well. "But any shortcomings resulting from my bond are my own."

"Marta, send for Jeffrey. I have a few more preparations to make before we leave," Lord Argenwain commanded.

"Yes, my lord." The maid bowed and hurried off.

"I have some letters to send to Hevether," Mark told Lord Argenwain. Gutter watched them both with silent and grim interest.

"By post or messenger?" Lord Argenwain asked.

"Messenger."

With a gesture, another servant dashed off.

"If you'll excuse me, I'd like to try to write a few more words before we leave," Mark told him. Lord Argenwain nodded, and Mark left as quickly as his unsteady legs allowed.

The guest room had plenty of writing materials. Mark selected a plain white paper and black ink.

My dearest master,

I have lost her. I hope she goes home, but she may go deep into Cathret or follow me to Saphir. I'll do my best to find her and protect her if she yet remains on the mainland.

They offer hope for a cure. A vain one, I think, but I will investigate because I don't want to be parted from you. I wish you were with me. I wish you could show me Saphir. Selfish, I know. It would be too painful for you, I think. I'll write of it as if we were here together, with no troubles to worry us in the quiet hours.

I am well, so far. Gale is a comfort and a loyal friend. She's grown, not just in height, girth and weight but in solemnity. She makes me proud everywhere I take her, and I take her everywhere with me.

I fear for you sometimes. Your heart speaks to me. Write if you can, but know that it may be some time before any letter catches me. Let me know, if you can, if you're well. It would bring me some comfort.

I must go. I miss you.

He almost wrote I love you. Instead, he signed Lark with the flourish he'd been practicing, and sealed the letter with a blank in which he scribed his initial just before the wax fully hardened. He held it to his lips and closed his eyes. If he could have, he would have delivered himself into Rohn's hands, but he hadn't even begun to trace the path and purpose of the conspiracy.

He'd have plenty of time to ask questions on the way to Saphir. He'd have to be careful, or he might find Gutter's protection taxed beyond its limit.

If he misjudged Gutter, Mark's corpse would not be the first or the last to be buried in the mountains where so many jesters over the centuries had vanished forever into hidden graves.

By the time they left Seven Churches they had a mix of twenty sacred and private guards for an escort, three wagons, and a merchant noble who hastily gathered his wagons and employees in order to take advantage of the protection that would accompany a great lord. People stopped and gathered on the streets to watch. Some called out well-wishes. Lord Argenwain gave cupru and sometimes ar to beggars who pleaded at his window. Several times Lord Argenwain sent Ames with packages of food and a few coins to impoverished old men and women too weak to walk. A few young jesters that happened on the scene performed a drover's song with such finesse that Gutter motioned them to approach. They drank his praise greedily while they tried not to appear too curious about Mark.

The spectacle as they departed soon gave way to roads climbing into the hills beyond the city. The hills fell away into broad valleys, and more hills, each set of hills higher than the next. A great many farms and a few villages made an excellent living in the region generally known as Hindland County. The vineyards seemed especially prosperous, with elaborate gates, soaring fences to discourage deer, and large manor houses overlooking them. The villages themselves seemed peculiar in that they had few private homes but a great many common houses and taverns, as well as waystations where messengers from various services changed horses or slept for a few hours before moving on. The people acted as if everyone were a stranger, and they treated those strangers with unnatural if shallow warmth and welcome.

Few people that they met on the road or saw through the windows while passing through one of those villages gave Lord Argenwain's rich and well-guarded caravan a second glance. Mark supposed they were accustomed to such things.

The views from the road would inspire anyone to paint. The perpetual spring clouds at the coast broke into airy white brush strokes, drifting against an intense blue sky so bright it hurt to gaze at it too long. Though both wild hills and grain fields still stood as bare as winter, the north side slopes glazed with snow, waterfalls broke through their icy casts and ran into riotous, muddy rivers. In the valleys, the first leaves began opening on the trees in shades of bronze, yellow and brightest green. The earliest wildflowers—columbine, iris, daffodils, tulips, white starwort and amethyst faellia—bejeweled the last dry wisps of grass and first short, bright growth of it in the meadows. Despite the sun it was colder here than by the sea, and they all had to wrap up in cloaks to fend the chill.

Gutter sketched with watercolors in his travel book, his brush impatient to set down the most important elements that would nourish future paintings. No doubt he'd sketched these same valleys many times before, but Mark had seen only a few of the finished works. Gutter sold most of them before the paint dried, and he jealously reserved his painting time at home for his beloved roses. Those flowers faithfully bloomed for him every year during the social season, when he usually stayed at Pickwelling to help Lord Argenwain entertain.

But the spectacular beauty soon grew monotonous, especially since it often took two or three days to cross a single valley and as many to climb and descend the hills. Civilization failed altogether save for a lone military outpost at one of the passes and an occasional messenger's waystation. Most nights they were forced to camp by the road.

Camping proved unromantic. Even with Lord Argenwain's relatively posh travel tents and folding cots, it was cold, damp, windy and lonely. A full night's sleep proved impossible, with guards talking through their watches, sudden storms lashing at the fabric and blowing through floppy doors, and the cries of wild animals and strange birds. The strangest part, though, were not the bird calls but the lack of seagulls. He'd never been anywhere that didn't have gulls flying overhead, or the ocean's salty breath. His skin dried out and cracked around his fingers. His lips crusted and the lower one cracked in the center and bled. Thirst clawed his throat, and constant sipping at his water flask seemed to only make it worse. Every morning when he woke he was so dry he couldn't even swallow.

Even on those occasions where Gutter talked and bought their way into a messenger's wayroom for the night, Mark still didn't sleep well. Dark dreams and a perpetual light-headedness, broken at times by deep, pounding headaches, wore him thin.

Though everyone seemed pleased with the good time they made on their way, Mark couldn't help but notice that messengers and other travelers on the road readily passed them, most at a healthy trot but some at a swift gallop on sturdy, shaggy horses or driving two-wheeled carts that often carried sled runners along their sides for the snowy conditions that might lay ahead. He wished they could reach Saphir as quickly as that.

Mark didn't want to admit it, but he grew weaker by the day. When wolves howled and dogged their caravan for several days, it seemed to him that the animals sensed his fragile hold on life and hoped that he'd be left behind for them to finish off. He wasn't sure he'd reach Saphir at all.

His seizures came more often as well. He sang or cried out in the midst of them so he could see his surroundings, but sometimes he wished that he'd kept silent. Blue fire and depthless canyons of stars filled with soaring, lion-faced monsters haunted his dreams for days after his failing body released him into the other world. But something constant threaded through these seizures. He'd never seen them before, but they never failed to appear now. One, a vivid crimson being draped in white, sparkled with violet and sapphire. Those sparkling, commingled colors seemed to ooze from it like sweat and trickle down in rivulets. The other, a delicate emerald and straw gold being with large, sorrowful eyes of amber and umber, glimmered with diamond fire that curled off like steam from a cup of tea. The emerald creature decayed every feathery bloom and crystalline structure that its form happened to brush. The streams of light from Mark's voice shattered on it and fell away in a constant mist. The crimson being stood by and held at bay any other creature that dared approach with a single look, its sword-arms dripping that sparkling, amethyst-and-blue liquid. Where the liquid fell it bloomed into strange, spiraling crystals that swiftly crumbled away into darkness.

Mark couldn't say why, but it seemed that these beings had been wounded. Each time he saw them they seemed to bleed less, if in fact they were bleeding. Though he called out to them, they never answered.

The twenty first day Mark dozed uneasily as they traveled, resting under Gutter's arm, only faintly aware that they traveled slowly up a steep incline, and that it was cold, and that the carriage jarred over rocks. Ice formed inside the windows, and their breath blew misty. Lord Argenwain, who'd traveled fairly well up until this point, looked pale and hollow-cheeked. On that twenty first day, the wind took offense at their good progress and attacked, driving snow from the sky and chasing it back up again from the ground until they were blind.

Their caravan drew off the road at the nearest flat place. Their driver set the brake among shards of rock amid which a mostly-frozen flow of water skipped and fell down the steep mountainside. The guards lashed the wagons, carriages and carts together. They converted the tents to tarps and set them over the wheels on the windward side. It was all the protection they could provide for the horses, which they unhitched, fed grain, and kept together in the lee of their impromptu windbreak. The carriage swayed like a hanging lantern in the wind. The carriage and wagon drivers blanketed the horses, wrapped their legs and covered their heads with quilted gear. After tethering the carriage to the rocky ground with tent lines, the guards took shelter with the horses and huddled in groups of five under linked cloaks.

Mark had never felt such an evil cold, not in the depths of the worst winter in Seven Churches when hundreds froze in their beds and the city lay so thick in snow and ice that everyone was trapped inside their homes with whatever provisions they had on hand. During that storm, Mark hadn't been able to open the windows at the top of Pickwelling's small tower because they were frozen shut, and snow completely buried the lower windows. He'd been a little afraid, then, but he never felt so fragile as he did now.

This cold in a few short hours made his bones ache and feel brittle. Their lips all turned blue, and tiny crystals of ice formed in their hair, eyebrows and lashes. He had no idea that air could be so cold it hurt his lungs. It tasted stuffy at the same time. At least Gale kept their feet warm. She didn't seem terribly uncomfortable.

"I'm going to get some spare clothes," Mark told them.

"You're staying right there," Gutter said, his teeth chattering. "I'll go."

"We'll both go."

"Don't be foolish." Gutter opened the door on the lee side. Worse cold poured in and snow swept all around them. Gutter went out, shut the door, and vanished.

Mark forced himself to open his cloak so he could wrap an arm around Lord Argenwain. "Can you sit on the floor?"

"Hmm?" Lord Argenwain stared at him dully. He'd stopped shivering. For some reason, that frightened Mark more than the jerky shudders that racked them all.

"Sit on the floor."

"Whatever for?"

"I'll sit with you. Please. Sit by me." Mark helped him down. "There," he said, tucking the old man in close beside Gale. He pulled off his cloak and wrapped it around the old man's front so part of it draped over Gale. He rubbed his arms trying to stay warm. "Come on Gutter. Come on," he whispered. His anxiety made his heart stagger.

The door slammed open and Gutter barreled in with an armful of clothes and cloaks. Mark nearly pitched out of the carriage in his haste but he managed to catch the door and shut it before the storm tore it off.

They dressed in as many layers as they could and then crouched down on the carriage floor, everything left over piled on top of them. The floor felt like ice. "Let's get some of this under us," Mark suggested. He started to sweat, wrestling with loose clothes, his arms and legs stiff from too much cloth covering them. Gutter helped lift Lord Argenwain enough to shove wool clothes underneath him. Everyone put woolen nightcaps under their hats.

At last he could settle again. His remaining strength drained from him and he went limp against Gutter's shoulder, his legs tucked painfully between Gale and the bench. It was better, warmer anyway, than it had been before.

"How did you survive the crossing into Seven Churches?" Mark asked Gutter. "When you came, just before I left," he amended. His shivers had turned into a series of quaking shudders with long stretches of numb misery in between.

Gutter shuddered, then half-laughed, half-coughed. "I took the roundabout way through Vyenne. I used a horse service so that I could change mounts quite often. It was a long way, but it really wasn't very hard."

He'd forgotten. Gutter had told him that. "What was the hurry?"

Gutter's mouth went slack, and his eyes ceased to sparkle. "It's not important any more."

"Than it won't bother anything to tell me."

Gutter wormed his gloved hand into Mark's. "I had to move someone."

That made no sense. "What do you mean?"

He squeezed Mark's hand. "A good friend, and her daughter, died of sickness. The boy lived. He's almost five years old now. I had to fetch him from the neighbors and take him to a house where he'd be cared for."

"Your son?" Mark wondered aloud.

Gutter nodded. "I named him Mark."

He had a hundred questions, all of them painfully personal. Why such affection for a stranger's child if he had his own? Why didn't that family live in comfort in Pickwelling—

Oh. No. They couldn't live at Pickwelling, could they.

You shelter your children from Lord Argenwain, but you didn't shelter me, who you pretend to love best.

"I hope he's well." Mark gritted his teeth.

"Better than you are at the moment."

That made Mark chuckle despite everything. "Naturally. How are you bearing up, my Lord Argenwain?"

"Hmm?" Lord Argenwain lifted his head. "Better." His head lowered again.

"I was going to take Mark to Saphir with me this time," Gutter told Mark. "At a more rational time of the year. But you changed so many of my plans."

"And what is our hurry?"

Gutter smiled. "Why, you are, of course. Don't bother to ask any more questions about it. I won't answer them."

"It seems," Lord Argenwain grumbled, "our hurry will do us in."

"The storm might kill us, or leave us stranded if it kills the horses," Gutter agreed cheerfully. "The strongest of us might walk down, but that would not include either of you, so we must all hope this passes without too much snowfall to budge, because I'm not leaving either of you." Suddenly, Gale tensed beside Mark and her fur puffed up like a frightened cat's. Gutter smiled, oblivious to her, but then his eyes suddenly rolled back and his smile became a rictus.

Mark cradled his head. "Gutter!" Now he understood the horror of watching someone in a fit or seizure and being helpless to do anything for them. "Gutter." Gutter's body shuddered with tiny twitches. "My lord, what's happening?" Gale growled and whined and then barked several times.

"It's him," Lord Argenwain said unhelpfully, seemingly unconcerned.

"Gale!" Mark didn't mean to be short with her, but he needed her to settle.

"Mark," Gutter wheezed, and then he laughed an eerie laugh. "I will. I will. I know." His mouth relaxed and he laughed more naturally. "The hair does fly."

Madness.

Gutter's expression relaxed nearly to normal and he let out a sigh.

Mark shivered, still worried but less so. "Was that Thomas?"

"No, dear boy. No." Gutter took in too-even breaths and gradually relaxed. "I'll explain some other time."

"Was it poison?" How could Mark not have seen this before? Was it recent?

"Me? No, no." He let out another laugh, this one pained. "No, that was not a seizure."

Gale continued to whine, but she quieted and tried to worm her head under Mark's arm. "Then what was it?"

"A conversation."

Mark's skin prickled with alarm. "With who?"

"A mask." Gutter smiled a cheerful, toothy smile and then closed his eyes. "We should get some rest. Especially you. And then we'll eat."

Alarm and dread sparked pin prickles down his arms and back. He knew Gutter owned some dangerous masks. Mark had one as well, and he'd only been a jester a short time. Still, this seemed different. He didn't want to speak the name, so he ducked his head and tried to rest. It haunted his thoughts anyway. He didn't think it was the Gutter Rose.

Gelantyne? Did Gutter actually have it?

Another meal without milk. Sopping his bread in broth seemed to help, but he was able to eat even less than the minute amounts he'd kept down before. Gutter insisted that he eat beyond his fill and within a half hour he lost it all. A precious meal, wasted, and heat too as he opened the door to be sick outside the carriage.

Mark huddled against Gutter, shuddering not just from the cold but from everything, especially masks and the short future he faced among them. His thoughts shifted to Winsome—not exactly safe harbor, but not as grim and seemingly hopeless. He hoped with all his heart that she hadn't followed on foot, ignorant of how deadly the cold could be.

Ignorant of how dangerous Gutter and whatever secrets he carried with him might be.

Gutter put his heavy, warm arm over Mark's shoulders. "I'm afraid too," Gutter admitted softly in his ear. "Would you mind distracting me with an account of what happened in Perida?"

"If you tell me why you didn't take your son with us to Saphir, luckily as it happens to be."

"That's not fair." Gutter chuckled. "My reasons are quite private, while your tale will be related to me in some fashion or another, by gazette or connection. Eventually, anyway."

"Do you want to hear about it from me now, or later from someone else?" It felt very lonely saying those words, knowing it wasn't an idle threat.

Gutter tucked his head closer to Mark. "It's because of you."

"Me?" He might have understood not wanting his child anywhere near Lord Argenwain, but ... "why?"

Gutter hesitated. "Your relatively swift return to the mainland has re-created an opportunity I thought had passed us by. I dare say no more.

Besides, I want very much to show you my beloved Saphir, and I wouldn't have the time if I stayed with my son, or the nerve if I took him with us. There will be a great deal to see and none of it is suitable for a child's eyes. Are you satisfied with my answer?"

Mark wasn't, but he nodded and told him a little about the party and the poison and Juggler's attack on Hevether Hall. He left out his theories regarding Juggler's reasons for the attack, but he suspected Gutter could fill in the details, assuming he was as deeply involved as Mark guessed.

Recounting the tale made him look at it and the letters Winsome had stolen from a new direction. He had no trouble imagining that the Church was corrupt and that it wanted him either dead or in their power. He realized that there might be a real possibility that the king was in danger from the Church as well, though for obviously greater reasons than whatever inspired the Church to attack Mark. If so, Gutter might need Mark to draw the Church's corrupted actors into the open and deal with them before they killed the king.

It made sense, but Gutter's decaying mind and his involvement with the dellai and those coded letters also made it too possible that Gutter himself wanted the king dead for reasons Mark would never understand.

The talk wore him out. He hid against Gutter's deep chest and slept.

By nightfall the wind slowed and the snow stopped. The guards dug out starter paths for the carriages and wagons, hitched the horses and wrapped their legs and hooves in tough leather and steel snow gear. The caravan plowed as best they could through the snow. Fortunately, not much snow had drifted on the road. Most of it had blown up against the mountainside or spilled off the cliffs. Mark watched the drivers fuss over the horses, walking alongside them, clearing snow when the wheels on the carriages and wagons jammed, sometimes pushing the carriages and wagons to help the horses with the weight. He wondered how long the men and horses would last. He would have offered to walk as well, but he knew he'd only manage a short distance.

Over the long, cold night and into morning they crept up, over and down the harsh landscape. By afternoon they'd gotten past the worse of the snow and settled on a broad, grassy slope in the lee of a massive rocky ridge. Others had camped there many times before, leaving hundreds of fire rings, discarded rags, and tree stumps. Not many trees were left to grow, turning the area into a decent meadow in which animals could browse. The drivers turned the horses loose and everyone rested for three days.

Two days after they resumed their travel, still in the midst of mountains, climbing another ridge of great rocks and sharp peaks, they stopped at a crest at Gutter's command. "Mark," he urged. "You have to see this." He drew Mark from the carriage.

Mark's legs had grown so weak he could barely hobble along. Once he emerged from the carriage he took Gale into his arms and set her down, his back protesting, arms trembling all the while. Gale trotted stiffly around the carriage. Her legs trembled for a bit as well before she loosened up and began to sniff about. Lord Argenwain didn't venture to move at all.

Mark climbed one slow step at a time from the road to the top of a flat rock as large as all of Pickwelling Manor. Rings of stones from many campfires and an old, abandoned shack stood there, but they were of little notice.

Far below lay a long, narrow valley like a river of green, overflown by huge flocks of white swans and threatened on all sides by snow and ice. That ice groaned and cracked and shattered, as potent as lightning and cold and sharp as steel. Dozens of little rivers interwove into a knotwork of crystalline blue ribbons so pure they shamed the sky. Rocks in soaring spires, natural bridges and cliffs formed islands and walls, many with delicate, half-frozen waterfalls that faded into mist and rainbows. Pools, ringed in gold and fading from palest green to deep navy, glittered like precious gems set into the rocks. Amid all that natural magnificence, its towers like jeweled spindles, lay Saphir, City of Bridges, City of Jewels.

Mark stared in awe. He couldn't write about this and hope to convey that splendor. The greatest artists and writers had failed in their rapturous attempts to depict its beauty. "How," he whispered. He didn't even know what he was really asking.

"They say that something like this awaits us in the afterlife," Gutter murmured.

Mark shook his head. He knew better.

"I've seen it," Gutter added.

Mark looked at him sharply. Gutter's gaze shone so bright his eyes seemed to have an inner glow. He slipped off his mask, baring the Gutter Rose to the winds. The sharp, swift air drew tears from his eyes, but the paint, formulated for near-permanence against all but the most vigorous alchemical assaults, remained perfect. "Here's another look, Thomas," the Gutter Rose said. His voice revealed no sentimentality, just a possessive appreciation and a willingness to share it with the broken soul behind the paint.

Confidante 91

"Perhaps I can help Lord Argenwain—"

"No," Gutter told him. "Hunger has weakened you, but you're still a young man. He's more frail than you by far. A single slip could mean a broken ankle, or a painful end to his life far away from even the meanest comfort. Besides, he's seen it before."

They stood there for a long time. Several guards, the lord merchant and all his men joined them. Few words rose above the wind. When Gutter grew restless and replaced his mask, everyone climbed back down.

"Is it as wonderful as I remember?" Lord Argenwain asked as Mark settled heavily into the now-hated carriage seat.

"Alas, time has stained that fair city. Oh, for the brighter days of our youth," Gutter said, smiling. The carriage started rolling again, now traveling so steeply downhill that Mark felt a little alarmed. It wouldn't take much for the horses to slip and for the whole of it to tumble out of control off the nearest cliff.

Between fits of terror every time the carriage slid or tilted sideways toward a precipice, Mark's thoughts returned to the tears in the eyes of the Gutter Rose as they'd taken in the view.

"Will you let me speak to Thomas?" Mark wanted desperately to have answers to his questions before he died, and death felt terribly close.

"No."

"I don't mean take off the mask. I mean, can you ... can we communicate at all?"

Gutter gave him a sidelong look. "Why would you want to do that?"

Mark had no clear answer for him. "You said everything changed. Was it because my mother died? Did he love her? Did she love him? Or did she die because everything changed?"

"You can ask me that, but it's not time to answer. As for Thomas, he appreciates your interest in him, but he can't come out to play anymore. He's too dangerous."

Lord Argenwain sniffed. "That's a laugh."

Gutter looked uncertain. "My lord?"

"You're killing our boy with this abrupt change of plan, and you're worried about Thomas?" Lord Argenwain's gaze slid to Mark. "I don't know what's worse—if you should live and we succeed, or you die before my eyes before we even reach Saphir."

"Please, my lord," Gutter protested.

Lord Argenwain tipped his head back and closed his eyes, as if he might try to nap again despite the carriage's alarming angle and sway. "I won't give away what you intend, but you best inform the boy soon."

Gutter spoke to Lord Argenwain, but his gaze rooted into Mark's eyes. "If the other elements are not in place in time, there will be nothing to inform him of, my lord." He settled back to gaze out the window. "We will be forced to enjoy ourselves and form innocent political connections for our boy's beloved Meridua instead."

Mark leaned back and tried not to think about going off a cliff. If the carriage started to tumble it was likely that none of them would get out in time. Not that he wouldn't try. But it seemed stupid to fret about something he had no control over.

As he had no control over Gutter's plans. Actually, he felt a little better about the situation, now that he'd heard Lord Argenwain and Gutter argue about it. He didn't know anything specific, but he'd heard enough hints that when real information came his way he might be prepared to understand it.

Mark sweated anyway, sweated and shivered until he felt numb. He worried about Gutter's plans, and shuddered at the idea that none of them would live to see Saphir should the carriage go off the cliff. He stared out at the rugged scenery, impassable save this passage cut from solid stone broad enough for three carriages abreast, and wished he'd seen what Gutter had seen in his visions instead of the hellish beauty he knew as the afterlife.

Chapter Eight

They arrived in the city late at night. Thousands of gas lamps and the light passing through countless glass windows lit the crowded streets. Delicate stone bridges supported layers of ironwork arches that linked the upper floors of towers. Those towers framed every river crossing and adorned every major building in the city. Few coaches were in evidence. Young men pulled carts holding up to four people along the streets. Most of the populace, though, walked.

Despite the cold and gusty wind most of the people strolled about without cloaks, in keeping with the fact that it was early summer, resplendent in countless fashions. He even saw some woven straw hats from the islands. Many wore clothes of nationalities he couldn't place, and he could only make poor guesses about a person's origins based on skin, hair, height and language. He recognized only a few of the many tongues spoken all around the carriage when Gutter opened the window so he could get a better look. Somewhere, someone played a violin very well, reminding him of Pickwelling from what seemed a lifetime ago.

An unusual couple caught his attention and Mark stared in shock. The two men, walking alongside a third, held hands. At the corner they stopped and one leaned over and kissed his friend's cheek.

A few moments later he noticed two other men speaking very intimately, their faces almost touching. Not twenty paces away two beautiful women, one dressed in a man's coat and waistcoat and trousers but tailored well to her sleek figure, walked side by side at a slow, courting pace.

A hand on his shoulder startled him. "Be careful. Your tongue might dry out if you leave your mouth open like that."

Mark closed his mouth. "But ... Saphir is the center of the Church."

"You'll find the Church is more varied than you might think, and that Cathret is a bit strange in its in uniformity. Besides, Saphir is special. There are things permitted to certain people under certain circumstances."

"What about me and my circumstances?"

"Mark," he said with a small laugh. "We're jesters. The only sins we need fear are those that our masters won't forgive."

It didn't fit with what Gutter had implied when he gave Mark his first mask. "I want to be a good person. I don't want to do evil and then depend on someone else to protect me."

"My sweet boy. You are a good person." Gutter took off his hat and ruffled his hair. "One of the best I've ever known. Any sin you might actually perpetrate would be naughty, not evil."

People used to say things like that about Grant. It sullied Mark's mood even more. "The whole journey you haven't mentioned anything about this. I can understand leaving out something like who can fondle who, but—I can't go to court in total ignorance of sacred matters in Saphir. It could be dangerous." He thought specifically of the *Mrallai Uss*, though his tutors had held that the sect had become so rare as to be insignificant. Still, hardly a year went by without some murder in Saphir being blamed on them.

"Don't worry about such things," Gutter told him.

"Because you'll protect me?"

"And if I can't, it won't help to worry anyway."

That small but important confession of fallibility shook Mark's sense of delight at finally entering the great jeweled city, and reminded him that civilization didn't secure a person's safety. It only guarded against some dangers and opened him to others.

Quite a few people had dueling scars. Almost all of them were men, most often jesters but he saw at least one noble with an eye patch. Cheek scars, missing ears, nose scars ... A young man had a gloved hand with two stiff, unmoving fingers stuffed to fill in for the flesh ones no longer a part of his hand. "It's strange," Mark realized aloud.

"What? That I have less power in Saphir than in Cathret?" Gutter gave Mark a look that unsettled him even more. "Why would that be strange?"

"No." Mark had touched on something more important than his original observation, but he didn't know enough to ask the proper questions to discover more. Best to follow his first point of curiosity. "In Seven Churches we had our share of war veterans, but it's nothing compared to Perida. I'd say one in ten men in Perida is visibly disfigured from the war."

"That's a shame," Lord Argenwain noted without emotion.

"I haven't seen a single missing limb on anyone here, which makes sense. Publicly anyway, Hasla didn't involve itself in the war. Dueling scars, on the other hand, are in great profusion, maybe even more common than war wounds in Perida."

"I don't see why you would find that surprising," Gutter said.

"I thought dueling was illegal."

"Dueling to the death is illegal," Gutter clarified.

It seemed that when men had no war to occupy them, they turned to other means to hurt each other. Perhaps there was no such thing as peace, the thing most sane people claimed to want.

He hoped it was his mood that made the world seem like that. He wanted to live so badly. Life was priceless. Why did people do these things to each other? When denied war, did they somehow long for the pain of mortality, or did they just not care or consider the real consequences of battle until the fear of death gripped them by throat?

"They are adept at drawing first blood without killing." Gutter continued idly, as if he might be discussing the merits of a breed of horse or a hunting hound instead of human beings. "Very adept, in fact, at disfiguring and shaming their opponent without killing. But deaths do still occur, as do duels to the death. When two people are determined to kill each other, even threat of castration or the lopping off of breasts won't deter them."

It was an unthinkable punishment from a Cathretan point of view, a view that only one who had been born and raised in Cathret could feel, he supposed. Unusually uniform, Gutter had called Cathret's religion. Mark hadn't realized how that constancy had given him comfort, even as he'd struggled under its yoke. An ugly trade—freedom for people who loved their own gender coexisting with a law that permitted removal not only of a man's ability and sacred requirement to sire children, but the center of his being, his pleasure, and his ability to receive and accept physical love. Even with death breathing so close and passionately beside him, Mark didn't think he would want to cling to life after losing his manhood.

"You must be very careful here. Saphir is deceptively civilized and welcoming, but she has a hot temper and is quick to take insult." Gutter sat back, his eyes lit with fond memories and a smile on his lips. "The duels ... mine were often written into the gazette, and hundreds would come to watch." He sobered and sat up again. "You mustn't allow anyone to lure you into a duel. You aren't trained for it. But don't be offended by your lack of education in this arena. It wouldn't have served you as well as you might think to learn how to outsmart a man trained to this." He gestured out the window to a man with a false nose and a scar that split his lips at a near-perfect vertical line.

"Instead of teaching me how to duel, you trained me to kill." The battles he'd fought rushed back to him. He tried to smother them by focusing on Gutter's expression but the scent of blood and the agonal cries remained.

"I trained you to survive. You can survive a pissing match over who has the longer rod. An ambush, on the other hand, or multiple opponents, or a fight with pistols and rapiers and broad weapons against armored or partly armored foes, is something I worry about far more. Those happen here as well. They happen all over the world in alleys and on battlefields, often without warning, and are all too often perpetrated by someone we think of as a friend."

I learned that lesson too well.

The merchant lord split away from them and they stopped in front of a large town house tucked between two others large townhouses. The three of them together covered the length of a long block. The middle story had a broad balcony divided by beautiful iron gates, while the uppermost had a shared balcony with an arched bridge in the center that connected it to a busy building across the street. The roof appeared to be a shared space of some sort. He thought he saw large trees growing there, but it was hard to tell. The roof wasn't lit as brightly as everything else.

"That is the famous Erothis Banre," Gutter told him as they climbed out of the carriage. Gutter gestured broadly to the building across the street. "And this," he said, turning to face to the center townhouse, "is Avwan Trofal." He strode to the door and rang the bell, then returned to gaze on it at Mark's side. "This is my home when I am in Saphir, and you, from now on, are my guest." He held out his arm for Lord Argenwain. The two men took the stairs at Argenwain's pace, side by side, like the old friends they were. The door opened and a tall, pale man slightly older than Gutter bowed before he stepped aside for them. "Welcome home, lord jester. And welcome, Lord Argenwain. The messenger arrived in plenty of time and all is in readiness." Mark barely managed to follow along with the Hasle. The expected and familiar niceties helped him understand.

"Bert, this is Lord Jester Lark of Perida, Meridua's most important ambassador. Please extend our best hospitality to him." Gutter's Hasle was flawless.

"Absolutely, my lord jester." Bert bowed to Lark.

"Be sure to procure for him a full pass to the banre," Gutter said. "And send a message to Doctor Ulaleh. I would like him to visit at his earliest convenience."

"It will be done, lord jester."

As Mark stepped inside the bright crystal and silver interior, a woman of exceptional auburn-haired beauty, despite owning at least four decades, threw herself into Gutter's arms and hugged him hard. "Where is Mark?" she asked breathlessly.

"He's still home. But I've brought the original." Gutter gestured to Mark, who bowed, uncertain.

She looked suddenly uncertain as well, and shy. "The confidante?"

"Don't call him that." Gutter told her under his breath.

She gave Gutter an admonishing look that would send fear into the hearts of most men. Even Gutter avoided her direct gaze, and set a soothing hand on her arm.

"Mark, may I present my friend Sroh's wife, Gzem."

A servant led Mark through lightly-peopled marble halls and comfortable sitting rooms scented of rose, bergamot and heavy with steam. The upper floor of the Erothis Banre was only open to the elite, wealthy, and most noble, and as Gutter's guest the bathhouse's doorkeeper accepted him without question. For some reason, Mark felt that his father would be ashamed of him for being here under that pretense.

The doctor was waiting just outside a pair of flat, gilded doors that dripped with condensation. He had a friendly but serious smile. "You must be Lark."

"Doctor." Mark bowed his head in respectful greeting. Servants began to strip them, and ensconced them each in a towel wrapped around the waist. Mark didn't consider himself shy, but his prominent ribs and yellowed skin offended his own eyes and he dreaded what other people would think of him. He ducked his head and kept his gaze low to avoid any chance of noticing how anyone else might react to him.

The doctor was only about forty, fit, and judging by his scars, experienced and well-traveled. He wore his straight, long hair tied back in a ribbon. Judging by the ragged ends, it had never been cut. It trailed down to his waist in heavy, sinuous lengths. He had coarse, brown skin with a little pale mottling on the backs of his hands, and his nails were black. If someone had forced Mark to guess the doctor's nationality, he might have offered the far southern tip of Osia as a possibility. He'd learned about so many cultures and peoples of Osia in so short a time during his lessons, he couldn't count on his memory to help him much.

Mark followed the servants, removed his towel and slid into the hot, salted bath beside Doctor Ulaleh onto a submerged stone bench. For a moment neither of them did anything but luxuriate in the perfect heat that flushed their skin with bright rose tones and made sweat flow in rivers as it mingled with water and steam. The slightest movement increased the sense of heat snaking over his skin. Wood slats protected their feet and backs from the hot copper tub. The wood at his feet was still too hot to bear at first. He floated his feet a few inches up until his toes warmed enough to endure the water's temperature. Gradually, seductively, the moisture in the air and the salted water softened his parched skin. He closed his eyes and drank in the bliss.

An hour before Mark had stared at a collection of portraits in the Family Room. Gzem's children grew up in frozen bounds from gray-eyed, round-cheeked beauties with terrifying mischief in their gazes to handsome adults. The boys were about Mark's age in the latest portraits, which had been painted about five years ago.

He wanted to assume that the boys were Sroh's, but they had a striking resemblance to Gutter. Their tall, heavy statures, handsome, strong-jawed faces, and dark, rippled hair echoed Gutter's more aged but graceful form too closely to be ignored.

Gzem had told Mark with pride that the twin boys both had families. Gzem's youngest, an auburn-haired girl, had apparently become feral and was last heard of leaving from Southern Osia on a ship bound for Bel where the warriors Professor Vinkin has talked about lived.

Warriors that might bear scars like Mark's. He'd wrapped his hand and wrist in gauze at the house before he walked over the bridge to the Erothis Banre to keep his scar hidden. The sodden bandage had loosened in the tub's relentless heat. He carefully unbound it only just enough to tighten the top layers.

A young woman settled on the edge of the tub behind him, her legs touching his sides. She encouraged him to rest his arms on her knees and began to rub his shoulders and neck. The broad, immaculate room began to fill with the scent of mint and something powerful but pleasantly nasal-clearing. It had several baths like the one he shared with the doctor, all large enough to fit a baker's dozen of clients. Even the air in the room was warm and humid enough to ease some of the perpetual chill Mark had tried to ignore ever since he'd left the islands. Combined with the bath, he finally felt truly warm.

Doctor Ulaleh slipped off his bench to crouch in front of Mark, head and neck above the water, and began to examine him. "Unfortunately I don't have a cure for your condition," he said in passable Cathretan. He checked Mark's feet.

Mark didn't expect the disappointment to wound him as deeply as it did. It was, after all, the expected response. Nonetheless he very much wanted to be alone for a moment to recover his composure.

"Still, there are things I can do while we wait."

"Wait for me to die?" Mark asked, more than a little shocked.

The doctor looked offended. "Of course not. What's this?" He touched the bandage.

"It's not an injury. It's—something I prefer to leave covered. It has nothing to do with the poisoning."

The doctor grunted, dissatisfied.

"What are we waiting for?" Mark asked him.

"We'll be waiting for a response." His hands played over Mark's legs with too much efficiency to inspire anything but renewed shame of his shabby, emaciated condition.

"Response? I don't understand."

"I have a colleague in Barrutan." When Mark continued to look at him blankly, the doctor added, "a small town in southern Vyenne. It's nearly at the same latitude as Cutring, the northernmost island in Meridua." He felt over Mark's shoulders and arms, briefly interrupting the ever-deepening, glorious massage.

Mark considered himself a fair student of geography but he hadn't heard of Cutring or Barrutan. He should have known the island, especially since he presumably needed to serve as an ambassador of sorts at least part of the time. He'd have to study Meridua, if a book could be found about it in Saphir somewhere, or shame might be the least of his troubles should someone question his competence or credentials as ambassador.

"There's a swamp flower that grows near Barrutan, possibly related to deatlal," the doctor told him. "It's a problem for the locals during the dry season because the blood-like smell of the decaying flower attracts bears and pigs, which eat it and die. For some reason true carnivores are immune to its lure, but certain omnivores find it irresistible. Anyway, these animals die deep in the swamp and then other things feed on the corpses and die—between the loss of livestock and the flies and vermin and difficulty of cleanup thanks to the dangerous muck formed by a half-dried swamp ....." The doctor seemed to realize he was rambling and stopped. Mark didn't mind. The story held his full attention, and echoed what Juggler had told him, almost to the word. "This colleague of mine studies the local remedies for rtutru poisoning. I've already written him. We'll see if he can offer any help."

"Thank you." It still seemed like a faint hope. "I doubt he can help me, though. If there was a cure, I'm sure the islanders would have heard of it."

"You'd be surprised. There isn't much call for it. Most deatlal poisoning cases are invariably fatal within minutes. Those that survive beyond a day are rare. I've heard of only a handful of cases lasting as long as you, and all of them predate my friend's work." He pinched the skin on the back of Mark's hand. "Your blood is too thick. Have you been gradually becoming more yellow?"

"Actually it's the one thing that's getting better. I've been adding oils and lemon to my baths and soaps." The oils helped with the peeling, cracked skin on the sides of his fingers. Sometimes the dry skin extended to his palms, the backs of his hands, and the soles of his feet. The lemon seemed to help bleach some of the yellow from his skin. Unfortunately it had all gotten much worse during their crossing over the mountains.

"It's not the lemon that's improving your color. Your organs were damaged, but they appear to be healing, or at least adapting. That's very unusual. The trouble is that you're healing too slowly. Your ribs are stark, there's some show of vertebrae, hollowness around your collarbones ... I've seen worse, but this will not end well. We have to get more food into you."

"I can't force it. I just lose it if I try to eat more."

"Interesting," he said softly in Hasle. "Is there blood in the vomit or in your stools?" he asked aloud in Cathretan.

"Sometimes."

"What do you tolerate the best?"

"Milk."

"The island remedy, I believe."

"They gave it to me right after I collapsed," Mark told him.

"What else?"

He hated talking about it, especially since he craved so much more, especially meat. Any kind of meat. "Bread. Rice. Oatmeal mash."

The doctor prodded along his ribs. "Most people don't like to think about it, but human beings are animals. We breed like animals, eat like animals, and we fatten up just like our four-footed friends when we have too much of ... what?"

Mark wasn't sure why the doctor was asking him. "Gravies. Sweets—"

"Gravies. Fat, and grain. You're alive because of the fat in the milk, and the bread. Sweets will help you, especially pastries because they have loads of butter."

"I can't keep anything sweet or acid down. No wine, no oranges, no pastries. And if I have too much butter or fat it sits in my belly forever and I don't feel like eating at all."

"That's a problem." The doctor sighed. "How often do you eat?"

"Usually twice or three times a day."

"Let's aim for ten."

"Ten?" He didn't want to think about how much that would cost him in pain.

"Ten. I want you nibbling as much as possible. And liquids, lord jester. Your case is not hopeless. We have something to strive for now. The answer to a letter. I sent it by express as soon as I received Gutter's message about your situation." The doctor smiled at him. "We'll invent the most unhealthy, rich, gout-inducing recipes the world has ever seen. Gutter has a good cook. We'll all three of us sit together and concoct a variety of comestibles sufficient that you won't quickly tire of ten meals a day." He touched the arm of the woman rubbing Mark's shoulders. "Bring a pitcher of water and a large glass." The doctor sank into the bath until he'd completely dunked his head, and then rose up, his expression soft with relaxation. "I want to see how much water you can drink in an hour. Impress me, lord jester. Prove to me your island courage."

Mark woke braced on a kitchen table. It was warm and smelled of flour and butter and exotic, earthy spices. The cook had put away anything scented even remotely of cinnamon, clove or allspice. They all reminded Mark too much of the poison's fragrance.

The cook.

The cook slowly kneaded bread on a marble counter trimmed in ebony. The kitchen's width accommodated two ample aisles. It was at least forty feet long, not quite as large as Pickwelling's, or Hevether's, which in addition to the short order kitchen had its own building, but it was arranged so beautifully it could produce equally large feasts. Its two ovens

102   E. M. Prazeman

had sculptured faces built so that the openings looked like mouths, and the doors had teeth formed into the metal. The stoves, counters, cupboards, flour bins and pantries were built as artfully as the finest furniture.

Petren was its lord and master. He had strong shoulders, strong hands, and a bit of a gut that hung over his belt. He wore his muddy brown hair short, and kept a very brief beard and mustache.

The way he moved, and spoke so softly, and the way he smiled more on one side than the other fascinated Mark. And his eyes ... muddy brown like his hair, but they were large and wide and slanted up a little at the outside corners. His lashes were short, but thick, like his brows. Thick but tidy.

Petren looked over his shoulder and smiled that crooked smile. "You're awake."

Mark realized Gale was gone. "Where's my dog?"

"I let her out into the courtyard. Here she is." He answered a scratch at the door and let her in. "Don't you shake!" he admonished her, dashing for his bread counter. He covered a mound of dough with a clean cloth.

She walked under the kitchen table and flopped down.

"Good girl," Petren told her. He pushed his thumb into the dough and transferred it into a glass bowl. Mark had never seen such a thing as that artful glass, blown such that it had enough strength to endure the power in Petren's arms. It was beautiful. Petren set it on a counter between the two ovens and covered it with a fresh cloth, though the one he'd just used looked perfectly clean. "I didn't want to disturb you," he told Mark. "You looked like you needed the sleep."

"Thank you." Mark stood. He didn't want to leave. "And thank you for all the work you did. I already feel better."

Those large, brown eyes gazed at Mark with unabashed admiration. "You look very well, lord jester."

Mark's cheeks warmed. It was a friendly and kindly-spoken lie.

"He blushes." Again, the uneven smile, and this time Petren blushed as well. "I hope your room is comfortable. Do they have you in the Dahlia Suite?"

"I think so, yes."

"What a climb. Sometimes I'm grateful I'm just a servant. My room is just adjacent, here, and I hardly have any need to climb those awful stairs." He gestured to the far door. "The ovens keep my room warm. Would—"

"Would you—" Mark began at the same time and stopped, gratefully, before he made a fool of himself. "You first."

"I must yield to rank."

"And I must yield to the first, and to hospitality. Please." Mark bowed.

"He bows to me!" Petren blushed hotter. "I only meant to ask if you would like a little more to eat. The oven is warm enough still to bake a little something. Perhaps a biscuit, not too sweet." Before Mark could protest he scooped up a small amount of flour, cleaned his hands in yet another clean towel, and dipped into a butter crock with his fingers. Sugar went in, and spices, and salt, and a dash of cream, and baking powder. Before a minute had passed he'd shaped it and put it in the oven on one of several baking stones he kept stored in the oven's mouth.

Mark usually had no trouble making small talk, but everything he came up with seemed stupid and dull. "This is a beautiful kitchen."

"Thank you. I remade it. Everything except the ovens." He cleaned the counters yet again. "They're a bit old-fashioned, but they work well and I wouldn't part with them even if the modern ovens look so much nicer."

"Can I help?"

"I'm shocked." He didn't sound shocked. "You can help dust the counters." He fetched a towel and walked over, stood close, offered it. Their hands touched.

Mark wished he didn't have gloves. Petren smelled so good ....

"Tell me," Petren said huskily. "Are you close to Lord Argenwain?"

Mark didn't want to answer. He didn't have to. It was a very forward question for a servant, even as highly-placed a servant as Petren, to ask. But Mark didn't want to rebuke him either. "In some ways, yes. In most ways, no. No." *Not in the way I hope you mean.*

"He is jealous?" Petren asked softly.

Mark caressed the skin on those strong hands. They flexed under his touch, reached but didn't dare to touch him back. Mark's heart skipped and thundered in wild alternation. "He denies me nothing." Mark leaned up and miraculously the exquisite, talented cook bent his head and they kissed, sweetly at first, then hungrily. Mark's desire roared and rushed inside him. He pressed close, his hands dragging as if he could claw away Petren's clothes. "I think," Mark gasped, "we're going to burn that biscuit."

Petren laughed, a stream of foreign words that sounded like cussing spewing out. He drew Mark with him, reached into the oven with a towel and pulled the biscuit out. "It's safe," he breathed, and crushed Mark to him.

They stumbled into Petren's bedroom and fell into his bed, tangling in their own clothes in their desperation to get out of them.

Fuck the gloves. Mark yanked them off and touched him everywhere, trembling but not afraid. Alive, he was alive. His belly hurt and his body was weak but he could caress and kiss and hold and grip and stroke and stroke—

Suddenly there was oil smeared on his chest, on his belly. They bathed in the luxury of hot skin sliding against hot skin. Petren gripped and stroked him and then opened to him. Mark hesitated. He'd never ... and never wanted to yield to that himself. But Petren's eyes were lush with need as if he yearned for it more than anything else Mark could give him. And it was tight and hot and Mark was careful but a violent urge rippled through him. He surged in and in, Petren's muffled moans and Mark's desperate cries mingling until Mark crested and shuddered with a strength he didn't know he owned anymore.

Petren spilled over in Mark's hands as Mark receded in waves of warmth.

For long moments the only things that existed were Petren's body and Mark's own heartbeat bathed in golden languor. Then, in the distance, another heartbeat matched not-quite-in-time with his, as elusive but as real as dreams felt when he was in them.

Mark thought of Rohn, his heart beating in silken harmony with Rohn's. He thought of Hevether too, and felt a moment of wishful homesickness. If only it could be like this with Rohn. Always.

But it would be a guilty joy after long deprivation, if it ever happened again.

I won't live long enough to be with Rohn again.

Unless the doctor's friend has a cure.

A cure seemed unlikely, but against his better judgment he had hope again.

His weary, sweaty, oiled body sagged against Petren's comfortable belly. Petren's large hands stroked his back, sliding up, down, slowly up, slowly down. Mark nestled against his side and pillowed his head on Petren's heavily-shouldered arm. The pain, forgotten for a moment, returned to his belly. Before it could overwhelm his tranquility, he drifted off to sleep, only vaguely aware of Gale as she climbed awkwardly onto the bed and pushed her nose under his hand.

They woke and played twice more in the night. The last time, after, Mark reclined in a dazed stupor for at least an hour. His limbs glowed with pleasant memories of ecstasy while his belly protested his hunger with fire and slashing cramps. When the pain grew too fierce to bear, Mark washed and dressed. Petren tried to tease from him one more moment of passion. But his strength had fled, and ... at least Petren seemed unaware that it was pain that hampered him. Mark simply begged that it was weariness, and that he'd be expected in his own bed by morning.

With Petren's instructions, Mark and Gale were able to take a set of servants' stairs and a pair of little-used halls to get to his room. He slid out of his clothes once more and climbed into the heavy down bed, naked, perfumed by fine oil and Petren's scent. Gale scrambled onto the bed and fell into a weary heap that kept his side warm. It felt like he hadn't slept for more than an hour when someone knocked on the door. "Lord Jester Lark, Lord Jester Gutter is here to see you."

Nauseated by lack of sleep and that terrible acid hunger that hurt almost as badly as trying to sate it, Mark slipped out of bed into the cold air and draped on a robe. Gale lifted her head briefly, then slumped back down. "Thank you. Please let him in."

Gutter smiled as he came in, his dark eyes bright behind his perpetually masked face. "He's accepted my invitation." Whatever other news he'd planned to tell Mark faded. "You look much worse this morning."

"I—" It hadn't exactly been a bad night. Mark's smile warmed his face. "I need breakfast. Unfortunately." The smile and blush faded together. The thought of food made his belly twist tighter even as his body ached for sustenance.

"We should talk a great deal more about what happened to you in Perida. I need to know."

Mark wanted to talk as well, but he was afraid now. He needed Lark's steadiness and calm and his perceptive empathy. "Let me bathe and dress."

"You don't trust me."

He couldn't let Gutter lead them down that path. "We both have questions and we both don't want to give answers until we're satisfied as to where the other stands. I don't think we'll make any progress until you can answer my questions, and I doubt you're willing to do that. Not yet."

"You want your questions answered?" Gutter's exquisite, deep voice carried a warning note in it. "I don't think you do."

It felt like years had passed since Mark's temper had last quickened his heart and mind and tinged the world a little red. He felt stronger, lighter, and too willing to say anything he wished. "Why am I here? You said you'd show me something. So far all I've seen is a beautiful house, an even more beautiful mistress, and a bath."

Gutter's mouth tightened into a line when Mark said mistress. It relaxed into a well-sculpted but unconvincing smile. "You'll have part of your answer tonight."

Mark's temper flared hotter. He fought it as best he could, but he wanted to lose control and that made it harder than it should have been. "Then leave so I can prepare."

"You're dismissing me?" Anger and shock rang in that awe-inspiring voice. "You are still very much a child, Mark. You don't want to play this game with me."

"Mark? You made me into Lark. Against my will—"

"You made yourself. You ran off and ruined your future, your health, your life and I'm dividing all my resources to repair the damage you've caused—"

"Your madness destroyed *Mairi*. You killed—"

"You slept through your life hoping for a dream that would never come again and was never yours to begin with." Gutter's eyes showed too much white and he showed too many teeth. "Your father should have had you on that ship years before but you were too small and too weak. Sailors your age have already spent half their lives at sea, while you've spent your days in a wine shop and in a manor house, both of which far exceed a sailor's lot but you yearn for sailing like an ancient decrepit yearns to stuff a woman with mad and impotent desire—"

"You blame Thomas but you took him to the docks. I saw you leave. Don't tell me you lost all control because you had ample faculty to talk with me on your way out. I wonder what other blood is on your hands. Who else do you blame? This mask? Another? The Gutter Rose? You have a great variety of excuses available, enough that I might not see the lie when you tell me that Thomas, you, whoever you are, would have never hurt my mother."

Gutter's eyes went cold. "I didn't kill her." His voice had gone cold as well.

"What happened to my father?" If he could have crushed the truth from him Mark would have seized him by the throat.

"Your mother, your father, your ship! They're gone forever. What matters now is what's here, in front of you. I look at what you've done and I can't understand how the intelligent young man I raised could be so stupid. And you can't even stand by a single decision. You're newly bonded to an islander and where are you? Here, with me." Gutter halted his tirade and lowered his gaze along with his voice. "What happened in Perida? Explain it to me so that I can help you. You do want me to help you, don't you? Isn't that why you came here?"

The sting of that truth sobered him. "Yes," Mark admitted.

Gutter's voice shook with passion. "Then tell me enough that I can do what you want."

The seductive offer perfumed his mind like the rich scents of a feast. He hungered for it so much he couldn't think rationally. "You'll help me? I wish I could believe that. I think you want me to help you. You've wanted it from the beginning, before I ever set foot in Pickwelling."

Gutter took a step closer, looming, his dark eyes bright with power but he seemed caged, a lion surrounded by spears and guns. "Just one thing." Gutter had softened his voice but the impending admission of his ulterior motive shocked through Mark's body like lightning. "I want you to sing for someone, when the time comes."

"You need my voice." Nausea thickened in Mark's throat. "You heard me singing in my mother's shop and you decided, I need that voice. Is that it? What did you do? Did you offer voice lessons, and she refused, sensing a trap and so you had to take it—"

"That's not what happened."

"Then *what*? Gzem called me a confidante. She meant a Confidante, like a Seer, or a Hand, or a Speaker." He'd wondered if Feather might not be a Seer, or if madness made her seem that way. She'd called Mark a Confidante, and she knew Gutter. "Are you collecting Stricken for some arcane purpose?" The idea that he actually might be a Confidante shook him, but it also gave him hope that the voices he heard weren't an indication that he was insane.

Not that Gutter's belief gave the idea that much more credence, and didn't Confidantes slowly go insane anyway?

"You're not ready for any of this." Gutter backed away. "I will see you at dinner."

Mark strode after him, alive with the power of all his fears and all his anger. "Whether I'm ready or not I'm in the thick of things. I thought they tried to poison me because I uncovered a plot to take the islands but they wanted to foil you, didn't they? Did Baron Newell and Feather flee the islands because they had been implicated in an intrigue? Or was it because the same murderer, not Juggler but someone in the Church, might try to destroy your Seer as well as your Confidante?"

The flesh around Gutter's mouth paled to the delicate shade of mist in autumn. "I should be proud. You're a little askew, but you know all the players, don't you."

He wanted to ask about the letters. He needed to know the identities of the cup, the moon, the star and the blade. Unfortunately it would give too much of what he knew away.

"So you suspect the Church poisoned you? I wasn't sure ...." Gutter reached for the door. "I wish I did know."

Claiming that much insight might be dangerous for both of them, and Rohn as well. He couldn't lead Gutter down that path without knowing for certain. "I have no evidence, just a feeling, and it's not one I intend to act upon until I know more," Mark admitted. "Juggler may have had his own reasons. His master may have been corrupted. But I don't think that's why Juggler tried to kill me. I had been in Perida just long enough."

"Long enough for a message to reach Cathret, and an order crafted by the Cathretan Church to be sent back to the islands." Gutter's hand slipped from the door handle. "Dellai Bertram should have never left you alone there, but he didn't dare send a message to me and there wasn't time for exchanges over such a great distance anyway. He had to come himself."

"Gutter, what have you done?"

"I can't tell you. You have to trust me, and be patient. It's almost over." Gutter's hand trembled. It was only a moment, but it frightened Mark even more than the fit he'd seen in the carriage. "I can't tell you, but I can show you. Beginning tonight. We start in the safest place tonight. I just wish I could send you to Tundrelle—you might have to shelter there before you return to your master."

"Who, or where is that?"

"Both a who, and a where, in northern Vyenne."

Probably some old man. Long ago, before he'd left Pickwelling, they'd promised him a comfortable life. Gutter wouldn't have chosen a place outside Cathret unless he wanted wealth, safety and obscurity for his protégé, and the best way to achieve that would be to bond him to some lonely, unwanted old lord near enough to death that Lark would shortly inherit everything from him. "That's a long way from the sea, isn't it."

"Don't think I haven't noticed that you had the access to wealth, the cleverness and the desire to steal yourself away, escape and sail from Pickwelling for some time, but you didn't take it until after *Mairi* burned. It's rather petty to accuse me of denying you your natural right when you don't even seize it for yourself," Gutter pointed out.

And what plans did Gutter have for the other jesters he'd nurtured? "What happened to Obsidian?" Mark asked.

Gutter shook his head. "That shouldn't have happened. That is what comes of not obeying those who have seen the spine beneath the flesh and skin. I asked him to do a simple thing, and I still don't know how it could have come to that. I think we may never know. But since you mentioned it, I hope you will trust me enough to answer a simple question. Do you have a certain book and ring?"

Mark hesitated.

"Do you have either of them with you?"

He hadn't even answered, but Gutter was sure. Mark could see the certainty in his eyes. "No."

"You have it memorized?"

Mark nodded.

"Good." Gutter opened the door. He started to say something else, then stopped himself. "Good." With that he went out the door and shut it behind him.

What little anger he had left in him fled, leaving only a terrible suspicion that he was making one mistake after another. He wanted to run home to Perida. But there were mountains in his way if he traveled the most direct route, a dangerous journey through Vyenne if he went the south way around the worst of the mountains, or he'd have to cross a very large stretch of wild and dangerous territory followed by a long sea voyage if he went the other. He paced his room, legs watery, gut burning with pain. If he could have clawed his way home he would have torn his hands down to the bone against solid stone to get there.

Steady. A king's life hangs by a thread.

Gale circled anxiously around his legs. He nearly tripped over her. She forced him to stop pacing. He crouched beside her and she leaned into him, eager for comfort. His hands, now familiar to the task, rubbed around her ears and massaged the loose skin around her neck and head. He steadied more than she did. He pressed his face into her fur, rubbing her sides, taking in her mildly unpleasant but comforting dog scent.

His voice had likely gotten his mother killed.

He wasn't ready to believe he that he was a Confidante, but he did hear voices sometimes. He didn't remember hearing them before his mother's death, but then again his mother used to complain about him talking to himself. She said it wasn't healthy to have imaginary friends. He remembered only one, and only the name, not the games they used to play. Mark called him Ruby.

But he'd stopped talking to Ruby long before ....

Thomas knew Mark from age two. That predated everything Mark could remember. And though they no longer spoke to each other, Mark still recognized Ruby's voice. He didn't know what that meant, if anything.

He'd come here to learn more about the plot that threatened the king. He thought he'd discover more of the players, and perhaps a hint of when, where and how they intended to harm the king, or at least why. Instead, everything so far had circled back to Mark himself.

He had to learn more, as much as he could tonight.

And he had to eat.

Mark washed, shaved and dressed with the help of two servants, not because he needed their aid but because he wanted to look as well as he could as quickly as he could manage. He might change once more before dinner, but between now and then anyone might arrive to visit Gutter, even His Royal Majesty King Michael, who often traveled to Saphir in early summer for the Masked Theater. Mark couldn't allow himself to make a poor first impression.

Gale had breakfast in the room, and a servant let her out in the back garden, which he hadn't even seen yet. He met Gale on the back stairs. She heeled prettily and stopped dead when he froze at the laughter and words coming from the kitchen.

"—and he popped like warm sparkling wine," Petren said in Hasle.

"Hsst! We'll lose both our jobs," a young man whispered.

"I think he'll be back for more, once he sleeps it off," Petren said gaily. "The poor, sickly thing isn't just starved for food. No doubt no one's been inclined to touch him. But what a victory. I'll be the talk of *shrefmetyne*."

"You better keep your mouth shut about it. I mean it." The young man clattered lids and carried something that sloshed.

"They wouldn't dare touch me. I give them fame. My creations are without equal."

"You can still cook if you have no tongue."

"You don't know how these people work. You don't keep an unhappy cook, not if you want to live." Others in the kitchen laughed in agreement.

Mark motioned for Gale to stay and quietly backed up the stairs.

"I feel sorry for him. What a beautiful face, and those eyes. Wasted," Petren said. "It's just as well. I wouldn't have had a chance at him otherwise. The *trerashefral* would have swarmed him at the banre. No doubt instead of wondering how tight he is they're all discussing whether or not he's contagious."

"There's not a few that might risk it in hopes of making a connection or three."

Mark had to cool his shame before he went back down. He thought about Grant, and *Dainty*, and the portrait he'd commissioned for Rohn. That made him think of his own portrait, that innocent boy that no longer existed, staring with lonely eyes out on a summer's day. Though it made him sad, he no longer burned with embarrassment. He motioned to Gale. "Go fetch," he whispered.

She seemed to decide that she didn't have to know what to fetch to go get something and trundled down the stairs.

"Perhaps make a connection to Gerson Lowell," Petren said. "I hear he—" A string of curses erupted as Gale pushed her way in. The curses changed timbre and Petren opened the kitchen door. He looked a little too pink around the cheeks and pale everywhere else. He stared only for an instant and then he bowed. "Lord jester. My kitchen is at your command."

Mark made a show of a shy smile and made his way slowly down the stairs, allowing Petren plenty of time to assume that he hadn't heard anything. "Thank you. Your hospitality is most welcome." A few snickers came from the kitchen but Mark didn't let himself blush. It wasn't hard. Shame had given way to hurt.

He shouldn't have been surprised to be a source of gossip. It hadn't even been particularly cruel.

Petren's nervousness eased. "I have something special for you this morning," he said. "It's not quite ready, though. I hadn't expected you to be awake at this hour."

"I have trouble sleeping sometimes." Especially when awakened by half-insane jesters. "I can wait, if you don't mind. I'm a little chilled."

"The kitchen is very busy," Petren told him. He seemed to debate between one thing and another before he went on. "But you're welcome to sit wherever you like, if you don't find it too uncomfortable." He opened the kitchen door wide. Gale stood under the table Mark had slept at the night before, tail tucked, head low. They'd probably frightened her with their reaction to her coming into the kitchen.

"I'll breakfast in my room. Thank you anyway. Come, Gale."

Gale sped out of the kitchen and hurried up the stairs ahead of him.

"Lord jester," Petren said before Mark could turn away. He held the door close to his face, those large, strong hands perfectly clean save for a light coating of oil that emphasized the warm, healthy color of his skin. "I wanted to thank you. For trusting me. I'll do everything I can to restore your health. It is my honor, and a true privilege."

Mark nodded and went up the stairs. He'd only gone partway when someone let out a laugh. "Shut up!" Petren snarled. "We have work to do. This is serious business. I'll fire the lot of you if tonight is not a perfect success. If you think I don't mean it, ask Haldro the next time you pass him in the street."

Mark sat in his room and wrote until his hands ached. He wrote to Winsome, hoping she'd gone home while fearing she hadn't, and to Bell and Fine and every other jester he could think of in Perida that he trusted even a little. And he wrote to Rohn. He said little but wrote pages and pages about trivial things and beautiful things and things that made him marvel and feel small, but nothing that mattered. Six pages in his smallest print, both sides, of idle talk. When he finished he rested his head in his arms and forced himself to think of nothing at all. He just watched the shifting darkness and unformed shapes behind his eyelids and listened to the house. Every so often he heard a whisper in his mind, but nothing he could understand.

Breakfast arrived, some sort of meat pie, and thickened milk with a rich vanilla scent. The meat pie was half the size of his fist but it looked monstrously large. He craved it so much that hot saliva poured unrelenting down his throat.

I can't eat this.

He cut away some of the crust. The meat inside looked strange. Bright red in color, and it had the consistency of fine squash pie.

Maybe.

He tasted it. Glorious meat seasoned with mild, sweet pepper and something indescribably mellow and savory suffused his senses, like sage and paprika that had no heat to it. Before he could stop himself he'd taken several forkfuls into his mouth and chewed reverently. He washed it down with the milk—barely sweet, scented with vanilla. Egg and something far more fragrant than flour gave it the texture of a thin custard.

Too much. He knew it in a few seconds. He tightened his throat trying to keep the food down while his belly threatened to tear itself apart. He curled against his knees but not too tightly because any pressure was even more excruciating.

Gale whined and circled him anxiously. "Go on," he rasped at her. "Go lay down."

She obeyed by settling less than a foot away and stared at him intently, her head between her front feet.

Mark managed to lower himself to the ground beside her. Noises emerged from his throat. It didn't sound like his voice. The pain didn't ease but he got used to it.

A servant found him. He told her to leave him alone and to say nothing to anyone about it. She must have obeyed because no one disturbed him.

Every minute passed so slowly it felt like the hours he'd need to recover would never end.

Eventually he got up, still hunched with pain, and went back to his letters to keep himself distracted. "I ate half a pie today," he wrote to Rohn. "It was delicious." He penned the words with anger and sorrow, but a moment later it made him chuckle. It made him feel better, not in his belly, but in his heart.

He turned lunch away. As he'd feared, the meat lingered in his belly for a long time. By mid-afternoon he managed to eat and keep down four spoons of oatmeal mash, heavy with cream.

"Looks like I'll have three meals today," he told Gale. "As always." He concluded his letter to Rohn with one arm tucked around his belly.

I'll be at an important dinner tonight. I promise I won't do or say anything to make you ashamed of me. I know I'm young, and more and more I'm realizing I'm not as intelligent as I'd allowed myself to believe, but I'm learning. I'll learn quickly and put my lessons to use.

I'm close to the center of things here. My business may conclude sooner than I expected. If so, I hope to see Perida once more.

Your faithful friend and servant,

He folded it and sealed it, then asked a servant for a letter case. He placed all his letters inside and locked it. After perusing the room he decided to place it in a drawer that had a small splinter showing in the very back. He slid one of his hairs under the splinter, then wound the ends around the underside of the clasp. Anyone who picked up the case would either break the splinter or the hair. Either one would let him know, and the letters weren't of any importance even if someone did read them.

It was almost time for dinner. He took off his waistcoat and shirt to shave once more, lined his eyes in a rosy black, and smoothed a little cover-up on his face and neck to disguise the yellowing of his skin. He brushed his hair with a tiny bit of oil on the bristles to keep it smooth, and tied it back.

He almost looked healthy. Fear of death rushed him with unexpected vigor, slicing down his throat and making his heart beat too fast and too light against his ribs. He hated Saphir, and loved it with an agonized passion. He would have left if he could have, but part of him rejoiced that he had no choice but to stay even if it meant having nowhere safe to retreat to and no one he could trust.

A servant knocked. "Lord jester? The guests have arrived."

"I'll be there in a moment. I'm going to take my dog out first."

He took the back way, but he heard nothing from the kitchen except the chaos of a feast in the last throes of preparation. He found a back door and opened it for Gale.

She trotted out into a lush, fragrant darkness lit only by an eerie blue-green sky glinting with the first few stars of evening. The scent of snow mingled with a hint of wood smoke from Petren's ovens and food and some exotic night-blooming flower hidden from his eyes. The courtyard was less than half an acre, but it had a large tree in each corner and gates and a fountain and trellises in an artful arrangement.

Petren came up behind him. He pulled his apron off over his head and tossed it aside in the hall's corner. "How are you feeling?" he asked.

Mark shrugged.

Petren stopped less than a foot away. "I—I made Liz tell me. I'm sorry about the pie. I thought if I ground the meat to a paste—"

"It's all right. It's not your fault."

Petren edged closer. His hand touched Mark's gloved one, the one with the scar. "You should come to the kitchen tonight, after. I'll make you another biscuit."

Mark smiled past the hurt. "I don't think so."

Petren moved away and returned to his kitchen. Gale came back inside, and Mark led the way toward the dining hall, his yearning more powerful than his hunger had ever been.

Chapter Nine

"I've always wanted to see the islands."

The graceful, exquisite man sitting close beside his equally exquisite wife spoke those words with genuine longing, and strangely as if, in spite of all their wealth and influence, it was out of their reach. They were both Cathretan nobles, but to Mark they seemed like something more eternal, like art or music. They both had light brown hair and delicate but not pale skin. His Grace the Duke Farevren, Lord of Kenwallick and Duthring, had an understated way about him that had charmed away all of Mark's fears. He asked Mark to call him Geoff. Her Grace the Duchess of Jessrill, Lady Dyanne of Prussmyle, Angcheswere and Nort, had a boisterous, infectious laugh and a fearless amicability. "I'm just Anne," she had told Mark when Grand Jester Legend proudly introduced her.

He'd never met them before, of course, but he knew of them. The Duke and Duchess married in Saphir, and famously never left. And Legend, though the story went that he earned the name through study and had been mocked for his vast memory of inconsequential things, lived up to his name in time as the jester who kept the peace among nations, and helped settle the war between Meridua and Cathret. The tall, slender, bookish jester with thin black hair and shy blue eyes held himself with quiet dignity when he was introduced, but once he relaxed he spoke seldom and devoted almost all his attention to his lord and lady. He wore gray with soft orange and cream. His silk mask was the same soft orange, longer on one side to partially cover a scar on his jaw. The mask was written over with gray calligraphy in a style that made it even harder to read the Hasle, aside from the challenge of the low contrast between paint and silk.

"But travel is so difficult," Anne told them. "As soon as our youngest child becomes old enough to risk the travel ...." She laughed and smoothed her hands over her broad belly. She seemed more than alive, better than happy, but something wasn't right. Like Mark sometimes felt as he gazed upon a meal he couldn't eat, she seemed vulnerable, like frost to sunlight. She yearned for the sun, needed it, but couldn't have it. "We could stop, but I'm still young enough, and four seems too few." She spoke Hasle slowly so Mark could understand better. They'd agreed he needed the practice, and so he struggled along and they kindly indulged him without teasing him.

Gzem glanced at her husband as if she expected to see something in his dour, impassive expression. A huge brute of a man with scarred arms, Sroh seemed at first to be of a sour disposition, but the more Mark watched him the more convinced he became that Sroh suffered from painful shyness far more profound than Legend's companionable reticence.

Bert opened the dining room doors, letting in a draft that bothered no one but Mark. "Excuse me, Your Graces and Lords Jester, but Gerson Lowell has arrived." Mark felt another twinge of irritation. Gutter hadn't mentioned that Gzem was a duchess as well, and Sroh her duke-by-marriage, when he'd introduced her on their arrival the day before.

"Very good, Bert," Gutter said. "Shall we retire to the salon?"

"Yes, please," Anne said. Mark realized belatedly that she was likely uncomfortable in a dining room chair in her condition. They'd lingered too long at the table even for him. The time had just passed so swiftly he'd hardly noticed.

Bert led them to the salon, where one of the famous and beautiful Saphir gas stoves warmed the room. The lacquered iron had been decorated well enough to be considered a work of art as fine as any master potter's vase.

Mark still hadn't gotten used to the things. All he'd ever read about them mentioned how often they blew up. They did heat well, though, and without smoke, which supposedly gave Saphir its pure air. The only wood and coal smoke came from ovens and cook stoves. He'd been told earlier in the evening that the poor, who lived better in Saphir than anyone else of modest means in the world, couldn't afford firewood. When they didn't have access to gas heat or coal they burned other things, including dry horse waste, and usually only during the hardest part of winter. Sometimes the tenements had a steam heating system they all shared, a contraption Mark had also heard about and also had read about how they dangerously blew up from time to time. But no one seemed ill at ease to be in the room with a gas stove. In fact Lord Argenwain sat near it to warm his hands.

Maybe he did so out of necessity. It seemed he was all for everyone else having gas, but he still refused to have it piped to the interior of Pickwelling.

Gale started sniffing around the room, as she sniffed around most rooms, and then settled beside the stove as well and laid her heavy head on her front feet. Mark hoped she was all right. She seemed to spend most of her time sleeping.

Gutter's salon featured light cherry furnishings, blue cloth, amber embellishments and robin's egg walls painted with cloud-like forms that suggested roses touched with gold. Mark recognized the handiwork—Gutter had painted it himself.

Gutter had the requisite number of musical instruments displayed conveniently about the room, but the salon's real charm lay in the paintings, including one of Lord Argenwain in his youth, one of Mark as a boy of perhaps twelve that he didn't remember posing for, and a self-portrait of Gutter himself.

Gutter's self-portrait drew him unwillingly to gaze on the handsome, strong-jawed face completely barren of face paint. The brush strokes were cruelly done, marring the mouth into an ungraceful line, smudging the eyes such that no white showed at all, Gutter's favorite hat scrawled into a series of dark lines and bent feathers, ruffled shirt just a scrumble, shoulders rougher still as dark blocks studded with impure white dots to indicate the sparkle of blue diamonds. It was as much self-mockery as a self-portrait, maybe even self-hatred, but honest in admitting his undeniable charms. The style was so different from everything else Gutter had painted that Mark checked the signature twice to make sure it was his work.

He heard Gerson Lowell come in and the others greeted him with joy, but he wasn't quite ready to turn away from Gutter's naked face.

Gutter had been innocent then too, though he hadn't been a young man. Perhaps it was rough because it was only a memory. It hadn't been rendered with a mirror, unless Gutter had managed not to reverse his own image somehow. Perhaps another artist had roughed it for him. Mark checked the date in the lower left. The painting was five years old. It had been after the change, whatever the change had been.

Maybe this wasn't self-hatred, then, but desperation. Maybe he'd been trying to cling to his sanity.

"Lark."

Gutter had called to him. Mark pulled himself away from the painting with effort. "I'm sorry—" He couldn't finish the apology.

If Rohn's dead lover had had a more handsome older brother, Gerson Lowell would be that. Dark curls touched with gray spiraled neatly back into a bun. He kept his beard and mustache in tidy trim and confined to an artistic and beautiful shape around his mouth and chin. He wore red and white, as all priests did, but his robes weren't divided. They were mostly white with red revealed through slashes in his sleeves and in gores. He wore a heavy gold belt as well as an ornate chain of office around his neck, marking him as head of a constabulary order, perhaps the prime master, though Mark couldn't tell at the moment. He couldn't look away from those dark eyes that gazed back at him with intelligence and curiosity. When the gerson moved the slight sound of countless keys jingled softly from beneath his robes at his waist.

"Gerson Lowell, may I present the Meriduan ambassador, Lord Jester Lark of Perida," Gutter said warmly. Something about Gutter's regard stung Mark's heart. *He believes in me.* "Once known as Mark Seaton, of whom I've spoken of at long length." The addition of his birth name was so irregular as to make Mark wonder what Gutter meant by it.

"Well met. I'm sorry I'm late," Gerson Lowell said.

"No one mentioned it," Mark told him, and then blushed. "I mean, you were missed but no one—" He was babbling like an idiot and had badly botched his pronunciation of most of the Hasle words. He suddenly felt horribly ashamed of his appearance. "May I offer you something—to drink?"

What's the matter with me?

"Yes, thank you. Some wine."

"Do you have a preference?" Mark's heart thundered in his ears.

"The gerson prefers grismotael abarti," Gutter told him.

"But if you don't have one open, please, pour something you like," the gerson told Mark earnestly.

Gutter strode to the cabinet and reached it about the time that Mark realized he didn't know which of the several cabinet doors held the evening's stock of wine.

Gutter shot him a look as if to ask if he'd lost his mind, and then his eyes widened. "Oh no," he said very quietly his breath. "You will not."

Will not what? Embarrass you? Too late. Mark collected a crystal glass from a beautiful set hanging upside down from a rack in the topmost compartment in the cabinet while Gutter opened a fresh bottle of wine. "Anyone else for some abarti?" Mark called.

"One for my husband, please," Anne said, laughing at something the duke had told the gerson.

"Did you hear me?" Gutter asked under his breath.

"As if I—" But Gutter's expression seemed more forbidding than a mere reprimand for botching his introduction. "You think I might try to win—you don't mean to say he leans that way?" Mark's heart beat even faster.

"Not as far as you're concerned." Gutter poured the wine. "Besides, he has a lover."

"What a remarkable dog," the gerson said. "Is she yours, lord jester?"

"Yes, thank you. She's a rare breed employed by sailors in Meridua." Mark hushed his voice down to speak to Gutter. "Why did you put the two of us in the same room if you didn't want me to—"

"I want you to meet him, not to fawn in front of him."

Mark's face flamed. "You had to know I'd be impressed."

"What are you two whispering about?" Anne called.

Gutter cast her a swift smile and went back to ignoring her. "I'm sorry," he relented softly. "I didn't think about it."

Mark had a childish urge to kick him in the shin, but he had to laugh. "I don't know why it makes me happy to know that you make mistakes sometimes, but it does. I suppose it means there's still a human being in there. But of all the mistakes—just look at him."

Gutter glanced surreptitiously at the gerson. "His nose isn't straight and his brows are too thick, and he's a priest. I thought you hated priests. Besides, I thought you favored large blonds."

"What are you talking about?" Mark whispered that more harshly and loudly than he'd intended.

"Oh please. I know what turns your head. And that one soldier—I thought you'd broken your own neck, your head snapped back around for a second glance so hard."

He knew about that? He blushed so hot he thought he'd permanently scalded his cheeks. He had to wait a moment and take a few deep breaths before he dared turn around. He wished he'd worn his mask.

Mark carried the wine to where the guests had begun to settle near Lord Argenwain. He gave the duke his wine first, and tried to hand the glass casually to the gerson. He barely managed without dropping it and retreated to Lord Argenwain's side. He never thought the old lord would serve as a refuge but the slight acid scent of his skin and his familiar bored slouch helped calm Mark down to something less than a fluttery panic.

"If you'll excuse me." Sroh bowed and left, shutting the doors behind him.

The conversation failed, and Anne looked expectantly at Gutter. The room held a deathly silence broken only by the faint sounds of servants moving about the manor and the tick of a clock. The last time he'd seen such haunted expressions and so many solemn faces were at his mother's estate sale. These beautiful people, like his memory of that day, seemed brushed over with ashes and tears invisible to the eye but easily seen by a heart that knew grief.

Gutter strode over to stand between Mark and the duchess.

The gerson braced his elbows on his knees and wove his hand together. He had very graceful hands with slender, flexible fingers. "You can sing." The gerson focused his grim, introspective gaze on Mark.

Mark's knees threatened to buckle under the strength of that gaze. "I've heard better," Mark said.

"I will allow that," the gerson said, though it sounded odd—it may have been a turn of phrase in Hasle that meant something slightly different. "Though I suspect modesty. You hear other things as well. Things we cannot."

Mark's heart pounded hard again, though this time it wasn't from awe. They let him stand there, exposed, expecting an answer for something he didn't understand well enough to lie about. Only Gzem seemed more uncomfortable than he felt.

"Have you heard anything while you've been here?" the gerson asked.

"No." That at least he could answer without fear. They wouldn't know any better.

"Do you have a guardian?"

Mark wasn't sure what he meant. "Gutter, I sup—"

"I mean, is there a voice that protects you? Do you have a name for it?"

He thought of the beings he'd seen during his seizures, but even if he wanted to mention them, which he didn't, the gerson had asked about a voice that protected him. The voices he heard seemed to have no protectiveness to them at all. "No."

He wanted to leave. Gutter hadn't brought him here to show him anything. He'd brought Mark here for an interrogation by a priest who knew something of Confidantes.

No doubt the charming duke and duchess were involved in something to do with the king as well, and they needed Mark. He had a sick feeling that they didn't intend to protect His Royal Majesty, though he desperately wanted these good, charming people to protect King Michael with their lives, hearts and souls. "No," Mark said again. "I don't even know what it is that I hear." Maybe they would tell him. He wasn't sure he'd believe them even if they did.

"Does it sound like this?" The gerson altered his Hasle, and his voice so that they almost, not quite, sounded like the sort of words he'd heard whispered in his mind and in his vision when he was bonded. The intonation and accent gave him chills, though the language wasn't identical, at least not compared to what he'd heard so far. *We are unheard, unseen, and unreal,* the gerson said in that language. Mark wouldn't have been able to understand, except for the similarity to Hasle and that it came from sacred poetry. As far as he could tell, the verse didn't refer to the *allolai* and *morbai*, but to human beings.

"Isn't it dangerous to ask that, and dangerous for me to answer?" Mark demanded.

"Not here."

"Because Saphir is special?" He was on the verge of shouting at them all, not out of anger but terror.

"Yes." The gerson stared at him as if he were fascinated by this strange creature rather than reacting to Mark's anger.

Mark had to look away from those dark, beautiful eyes. "What's going to happen when I sing?"

The duke and duchess clasped hands. She looked afraid, and the duke closed his eyes and bowed his head. "His Royal Majesty will come to Saphir, and we wish for him to hear you."

His Royal Majesty Michael often came to Saphir to enjoy its arts, but this year would be different. Mark tried to stay calm. He would have an answer to his most important of questions if he just stayed calm. "But first, you have to know if I'm really a Confidante."

"Yes," the gerson said.

"That's all I have to do. Sing." Mark gazed at each of them. Their grim expressions convinced him that he would not be singing for the king's health. The wonderful duke and his charming wife, Gutter, Lord Argenwain, the fiery Gzem and the heart-breaking gerson intended somehow to end the king's life.

Why?!

"Yes," Gzem said. She gave Gutter a hard look that could chip ice.

It was a good thing that Gutter didn't know that Mark had learned about the plot, or Mark's life would be worth less than a nit's.

It was madness, literal madness, as anyone within striking distance who had even a trace of ill intent toward the king would go insane. Assassins of old against the kings and queens of the world sometimes tried to elude the inevitable through wearing masks and setting buildings on fire from a distance or using longbows or conscripting servants to unwittingly serve poison. It didn't save a single one, and only one regicide long ago succeeded, at the cost of the assassin's sanity, and his life.

That had been on a battlefield, and not one soldier left that place unscathed.

Now he knew, and he would live out the rest of his short life as a madman if he tried to help these people.

Why are they doing this? Gutter I can understand because he's losing his mind, but why the duke and duchess, and why the gerson?

"You won't be alone," the gerson told him. "We have collected a small choir. It will be the most important performance of our Age."

"Has Gutter told you I'm dying?" He'd mispronounced at least two words but judging by their expressions they'd understood him.

The gerson looked to Gutter, his expression carefully guarded.

"We're trying to save him." Gutter smoothed a hand over his hair. "Not just for this. He's a good man. There is no one more worthy. And I love him like a son." Gutter's voice caught, but then he smiled and looked over at Mark. "A very disobedient son, and far more impetuous than I'd suspected. But I couldn't be prouder of him."

"What's being done?" Anne asked.

"As much as is possible," Gutter assured her.

Lord Argenwain took a breath and rubbed his hands together. "In the meantime, we must allow him to rest and gather his strength. And he needs time to practice."

"This is too soon and too sudden," the duke said. "Lark, I fear you may not be strong enough to endure what lies ahead, even if we can make all the arrangements in time. A performance for royalty is arduous to begin with, and this will be an especially long and difficult performance. Gutter, take him away from here. I don't like how this feels in my fingers."

"One more year." Anne's voice sounded shaky. "I don't know if I can endure another summer of this, especially not like the one we had last time."

"We'll go to Osia. Or Bel."

"I can't travel," she reminded him. "And it will seem strange. It will attract his attention."

"She's right." Gzem's low voice sounded sure from hard experience. "You don't want him to suspect that either of you knows something is amiss. It will only encourage him to move more quickly."

Confidante

Gutter went to the duchess and knelt down. He took her hands into his and pressed them palms together. "Anne. They won't hurt you. They've never ventured to hurt you."

"I don't care about that. I trust that I'm protected. I fear for my children and most of all I fear for him. I'm afraid that this time he will be the one that disappears. I have this feeling. I dream about it."

"We won't let that happen," the duke told her roughly.

She sniffed back tears and let out an uneasy laugh. "You can't promise that."

"She's right," Lord Argenwain said. "We already know he is vulnerable to our dear friend's unfortunate interests."

They couldn't be talking about the duke being in danger from the king, but Mark didn't know who else it could be. And what did she mean about disappearing? He wished he could make himself believe that this was all theater staged for his benefit. Unfortunately they all had a look of exhaustion about them, a weariness of a depth that he hadn't experienced himself despite all he'd been through. While he'd struggled for only a few months, for them it had been a long war. How many years?

It explained why the duchess seemed so fragile, and why her smile at dinner seemed both exuberant and thin.

"I confess I'm confused," Mark admitted. "And I'm more than a little nervous about all this."

"As well you should be," Lord Argenwain told him gravely. "But it's best if you know as little as possible. Your confusion will be your best ally."

"I'm sorry, boy," Gutter said. "But for now you must trust me. Please trust me. Or if not me, then Anne and Geoff. They are more than trustworthy. They define all that is good. You don't have to rely on their reputations. You can see for yourself."

Anne opened her mouth to protest, but then sagged. "May I have a little water, please?"

"Of course." Gutter hurried to get it.

For his part, the duke sat by calm as a summer afternoon, his gaze faraway while he gently rested his hand on his wife's small white hand as if his life didn't matter.

"I should go," the gerson told them, standing. "If we are to move forward, I must continue with the necessary preparations. Lark, I would like to speak with you alone tomorrow, if I may. It's nothing so dire as all this. It's just music. Also I need to show you the venue. You should hear your voice in it so that you can tune your practice."

Gutter returned with the water and gave Mark a warning look. He didn't need to. Lust was the furthest thing from Mark's mind. "Gerson, you may consider me in your service," Mark said.

Against his better judgment, Mark visited the kitchen after dinner. Sitting in a room among what he feared were the sweetest assassins a man could hope to meet had more than unnerved him. It put everything he thought he knew into doubt.

He wasn't sure if he'd ventured toward the kitchen for a meal, or comfort, or just to talk. He only knew that he didn't want to sit in his room alone with death.

He slowly pushed the door open. Petren and two other cooks were packing leftovers into bags and piling them into the arms of waiting servants while the scullery crew scrubbed the floor. Mark watched them awhile, stepping aside and holding the door for exiting servants, largely unnoticed except with brief genuflections as they passed. Petren spoke at least three languages with ease and humor. Mark could read as many and more, and had been proud of that, but here in Saphir he felt only that he had a great deal more to learn, and not just linguistically.

He wished he could hate Petren, but he felt as drawn as ever to the handsome cook.

"Lord Jester." Petren's shoulders jumped and he took a step back from his work. He tidied his hands in a fresh towel. "Mirk, Obelai—be sure this kitchen is clean before you leave tonight." He went out into the hall with Mark. After a moment of staring into each other's eyes that made Mark's chest ache, Petren lowered his gaze. "I hope you enjoyed dinner."

"Yes." He'd only managed a few bites of bread and a glass of thick milk, but he'd never admit it to Petren.

Petren started back toward the kitchen. "I can bake you some—"

"No, thank you."

Petren stopped in the midst of an inviting gesture toward the door. He leaned back against the wall in defeat. "Lord jester, perhaps you were too exhausted to remember the doctor's orders, but I remember, and I've been keeping count of your meals."

Mark had no response to that.

"Whatever pain you experience, surely starving is worse."

"Starving isn't worse than the pain. It just accompanies it, like a bad harmony." Mark stopped resisting—he didn't even know why he tried—and went into the kitchen. "I can try." He doubted he could keep anything down. He always felt weak and shaky after he lost a meal, but maybe it was worth an attempt if for no other reason than to stay alive long enough for the doctor's friend to answer.

"Where's Gale?" Petren asked.

"Sleeping in our room. I think everyone must have been feeding her under the table. She's exhausted." He chuckled. "It's a little strange walking around without her, but I have to admit I miss being by myself, without having to consider her. Not that I don't consider her when she's not with me. As I came down the stairs I started to worry about whether she'd panic with me out of her sight."

Petren gave him a long, sober look before he offered a smile. "Then whatever I do, I shouldn't keep you too long, hmm?" All the food had been packed out and the cooks were in the midst of dusting the room from top to bottom. Flour hung in the air and built up a sneeze. Mark suppressed it by pressing his sleeve to his face. "That's enough for now," Petren told them. "I have work to do. Go on, I'll finish on my own. Good night, Obelai. Vre temb, Mirk." He herded them out and shut the door behind them. He stood a moment with his back turned, then bustled to his bins to gather eggs, flour, salt and butter. "One thing I like about men is that I never have to ask if they enjoyed my company. You are the first to make me doubt."

"You don't have to doubt," Mark assured him. He felt cold and uncomfortable talking about it. "I'd welcome another night like the last." Except that he didn't, but only because it wouldn't be like last night. He'd have those words he'd overheard playing in his mind. For the sake of comfort and pleasure he might bear the humiliation, but it wouldn't be a beautiful experience. Just a carnal one.

Petren made a simple batter using cream, flour and water. "I find it frustrating that everything that would make this better than bread will make you even more ill than you are." He beat the egg whites until they frothed and folded them into the batter, then started on a crust. He chopped and pressed it into a mold in moments. "We will try this, and see. If it works better than the meat pie I will consider it my greatest victory."

"What can you tell me about Gerson Lowell?"

Petren smiled at his batter. "Ah, the beautiful constable. I've heard much gossip about him. I'm sure they're all lies. But he is handsome, isn't he."

Mark felt a double wave of jealousy, that he would never garner a compliment that was given without pity again, and that some unnamed lover had the privilege of the gerson's companionship. Probably another pretty Hasle-born gentleman with large but fierce eyes. They'd be like incestuous twins admiring each other's good looks. "Is he a good man?"

"They say he can draw honey from old, dry wax."

"I mean, is he honorable. Does he have a reputation for being cruel, or manipulative?"

"Gerson Lowell?" Petren placed the pie in the oven. "Don't tell me he's already broken your heart."

"I'm not talking about him in that way." Mark couldn't disguise his impatience. "I'm talking about his character."

Petren gave him a curious look, one hand braced on his hip, the other on the broad marble counter. "He's known for his great mercy." Petren worked his jaw. "What is this about?"

Mercy. Was the gerson's compassion a mask, or had Mark leapt to one too many conclusions? "Nothing."

Petren approached like he expected to be slapped back at any moment. "It's very difficult watching you suffer. Extremely difficult. I have this constant desire to help you. It's like watching a bird with a broken wing."

Mark blushed with shame but found a trace of strength in anger. "The only thing worse than pity is mockery."

Petren blanched. "I didn't mean—that is, I—lord jester, I have the greatest respect—"

Mark couldn't suppress the bitter laugh that welled up from his throat. "Thank you. I'm finished here. Please send that egg thing up to my room when it's ready."

Petren blocked his way. "Please don't be angry with me."

Mark ducked his head so that he wouldn't have to look directly at Petren. "You don't have to be afraid of me. I won't hurt you. Now let me by."

"I should be afraid, but I'm not." He smiled his crooked smile. "Well, I am, but I don't care. Here." He took Mark's hand and placed it on his chest. "Feel that?" A steady, strong heart drummed under Mark's palm. Maybe Petren had meant to be seductive, or he'd wanted to show his desire, but to Mark it seemed little more than a ploy.

Mark pulled his hand away. "I've been a toy all my life, and it seems here I'm no different. I'm as sick of it as I'm sick from poison, but I let it happen anyway." *For love, or love's poor second cousin in this case.*

Confidante

127

"You're just lonely. That's all," Petren soothed. "That doesn't make you a toy. I'm lonely too sometimes. We all get lonely. Even your friend Lord Jester Gutter. Maybe especially him."

If anything, Petren's observation made his longing worse and his sense of loneliness plunged into terrible depths. Mark looked up. Staring into each other's eyes again didn't feel like lust or play or even agreement. Petren became a thing of mystery and emptiness, a void into which Mark was willing to fall just to get away from himself. He took his gloves off and slid his hands over the thin fabric hanging against Petren's strong back. Large hands settled around Mark's hips, and they kissed. It was awkward, strange, learning the contours of mouth and tongue as if they were novices too shy to plunge and explore. They may as well have never had any familiarity with each other at all, despite their unfettered intimacy the night before.

Fresh worry that Gale might be pacing and scratching at the door interrupted the slow, weak build toward lust. "If you want me, make it quick. I can't stay long."

Petren drew back, drawing in cold air between them. "I like games. I thought you like to play as well, but you turn everything into a duel to the death, don't you. You make men feel like they matter to you and play the part of the hurt lover and then you turn it around. Why? Do you think you will matter more to me if you hurt me?"

"I don't want to hurt you. I—"

"But you come at me like you want something more than a night or two. I can't be that to you. It's impossible. I'm a cook. Even if I believed for a moment you wanted something lasting I'd be a fool to love you."

"But—"

"If you didn't destroy me yourself, then one of your friends would. No thank you. We are finished here." Petren took both of Mark's hands as if he wanted to use them to push Mark away, but then their fingers twined together.

I only didn't want you to hurt me again. "You're right." Mark wished it wasn't true. "I hadn't thought it through." Grant's death should have impressed a greater need for caution. He'd let lust dull his reason. He'd been expecting far too much from Petren. "I should go." But he nuzzled Petren's neck. He smelled so sweet and clean. "In a little while, if you want me to stay. I'll stay for just a moment longer and then I'll go."

Petren's gently lopsided smile glowed until it reached his eyes. Their bodies conformed to each other, full of unbearable promise and need. "I'm going to burn your food."

"I don't think so." Mark gripped the back of his neck and kissed him hard. He pushed him against a cupboard and they undressed only as far as they needed to. Hands kneaded skin and drew it over hardness. They pulled and pushed and kissed and bit until their breathing broke apart into gasps and every touch made their bodies arch with a pleasure deeper than a morning's first stretch. They pressed into each other, mirrored in perfect harmony. It was so natural, and so easy to feel what they knew the other also felt and to reach, to battle their way closer and closer to bliss. Mark tried to muffle his cries as he fought his way to the other side of that pillowed, intimate barrier within himself. It suddenly gave way and he overflowed with hot pulses. They surged together—

—ebbed together ...

... and stood together in weak-kneed and disheveled calm.

Mark stood against him, heart still pounding, breath hitching, for just a moment before he thought about putting his clothes back together.

Petren kissed the side of Mark's forehead. "You were right. That was quick."

Mark chuckled, suddenly shy. He didn't know the first thing about what he was doing with Petren, or with any man. But he'd begun to learn.

The hot water Petren had sitting by had long cooled, but it wasn't ice cold. They cleaned off and mostly ordered their clothing in case anyone came in. Mark put on his gloves.

"So, what is that on your hand?" Petren asked, checking on the pie.

Such a casual question about a scar whose making still haunted him. "Can you keep a secret?" Not that he intended to tell Petren anything about it. That he knew of its existence was enough.

Petren gave him a sidelong look. "Now I'm sorry I asked. Secrets are dangerous."

"I don't think it matters too much. Just don't brag about it. Or me. It might not be safe." *And I don't want to feel any more stupid than I already do.*

Petren blushed. "I can be discreet."

Mark had more than a few doubts about that. "I would be grateful if you didn't mention it to anyone."

Petren went to the oven and opened one of the doors. He stared at the pie through the great open maw. The coals still gave off waves of heat, but little light—the interior was almost pitch black. Only the gas lights in the kitchen revealed any sign of what lay inside. "If you want a lover, I will always be here, but never look for love from me."

Mark hadn't intended to, but Petren's statement still bothered him.

"I doubt you want my advice, but I would suggest that you don't look for love from anyone. Love ... it's something invented by women to try to keep men, who innately seek variety, to stay in their beds through guilt, or fear of growing old alone. Better to be friends with many than to love only one. I'm sure you've noticed that friendship is far better than the romantic theater some couples try to play."

Mark wanted to argue, but he let it go. It wasn't as if he knew anything about love himself. The nearest things he knew to love existed only as half-remembered dreams, and they would never be brought to life. Rohn wouldn't allow it, and Grant was dead.

What Petren had said of friends made him think more of Grant. If Grant had lived .... Not that they would have ever been lovers. Grant had attacked Mark when he'd found out Mark's bend, and it had ended their friendship. But if he'd lived, maybe they could have repaired that break and become friends again.

Given time.

The newly-bonded jester Mark had been had no idea how little time they'd have.

"I hope I haven't offended you," Petren said.

"No. I'm just remembering a friend." Time hadn't faded the memory of Grant's smile, but it would, just as time had obliterated all but a few traces of Mark's parents. "I need to make sure Gale isn't tearing up the room. Please send the pie up when it's ready."

Mark went up the back way to his room. Gale raised her head from where she sprawled in the center of his bed, then went limp again with a contented sigh. Mark wished he could sleep as well, but he needed to try to eat at least a little first, so he settled to write.

Rohn would probably think him insane to put so much work into a fisherman's grave. The idea brought him pain as he put it into words, but long after Mark was gone, others could visit Grant's memorial and touch a face of stone that might acquaint them with that rare smile and the kindness in Grant's haunted green eyes.

Chapter Ten

Something like thunder rumbled in the distance as Mark and Gerson Lowell stepped out of the carriage in front of an enormous gatehouse under clear and cold blue skies. The sun's intense glare reflected off of glass and tile and gold on the grand buildings nearest the thick wall. Though it was bright as any late spring day, the air smelled of snow. The light breezes bit hard enough that he was grateful for the many layers of clothes he wore.

Beyond the broad iron gates a slight arch in the road indicated a bridge under which one of Saphir's many crystalline rivers flowed. "Stay," Mark told Gale. Her tail thumped and she set her head down between her feet as he closed the carriage door. His hand, unused to checking the swing of his rapier with the automatic grace of someone who always wore one wherever he traveled, rested on the pommel as a make do.

"This is the Guilbarabb," the gerson told him. "No carriages are permitted except under royal command." A fast, white and ice green river formed a kind of moat, but with thick, fortified walls on both sides complete with towers. The towers directly across the river from each other often had a high and narrow bridge that traveled between them, while the infrequent low bridges like the one Mark now faced had heavy doubled gatehouses connected to each other with elaborate and daunting ironworks that barred the way from the river. Anyone who fell in from the tops of the walls wouldn't last for more than a breath against the brutal current, but even if they did, they'd find no way out.

They crossed the bridge and passed through into an immense commons. The flat, multicolored stones formed a vast mosaic of brights and darks and reds and golds and earth colors. Thousands of people milled about in casual conversations or quickly strode in straight lines toward some business, but they seemed like a handful of gravel flung over a vast field.

"What is the figure?" Mark asked awkwardly in Hasle, gesturing to the mosaic, and then he remembered he'd read of it. "Is that the Falleon Orb?"

The handsome gerson grinned as if Mark had paid him a personal compliment. "Yes. Here. Here it is, small enough to see." The gerson led him to a section of wall. It was only an orb in that the delicate tendrils curved as if they had been applied to a perfect but invisible globe. Rays burst from the globe's center. The fresco had aged well, but it still lacked the brilliance of the perfect, clean stone.

Strange that only something that could fly would ever appreciate the Falleon Orb in its entire. Did *morbai* and *allolai* see some version of it in the other world? Or had a madman conceived and built it out of some sense of spite?

Gerson Lowell only gave him a few seconds to admire the Guilbarabb from their vantage before he hurried them across the commons toward one of many large buildings. All the buildings seemed to attempt to be the one with the most towers or the one with the largest dome. Faced with so many architectural challenges in their efforts to be the most magnificent, they couldn't be compared directly with one another or simply measured from end to end. Would the greater height of one count against the width of another, and did columns on that one cheat the prize from this vast arched and open expanse for the greatest span at the entryway? Could a massive lantern count for the height of one tower when another, lacking the same adornment, soared over the first tower's last habitable space?

Birds fluttered in broad arcs and circles or pecked at the flagstones, soft coos mingling with harsh caws and sweet peeps. Other than the people, they were the only signs of life in a place of marvelous and deathly-still stone.

"That is the Deshommbra Fael, and that is Wheillass," the gerson said as they crossed the commons. He pointed out more and more as they made their way, so many famed buildings Mark had to rely on memorization tricks to hold them all in his mind even though their names were all familiar to him. "Don't worry. No one will mock you if you can't remember them all," the gerson assured him. "A man rarely knows himself well enough to trust whether he will be brave or a coward in battle. How could a man then know the heart of Saphir?" His glorious eyes glowed with joy. "I had the honor of helping in the repair of the Veiavra Fael. She took one hundred years to build, and stood for nearly a thousand before she began to falter. No one noticed until she broke one of her own windows. They wanted me to reinforce her architecture. Instead, I chose to invent a machine. The workings took the course of a summer to lift the place that had settled. It revealed a water issue that we corrected. It was a lucky thing to discover it, though I doubt she would have settled much farther in a dozen lifetimes. By then, I have little doubt someone wiser than me would make a better correction, but perhaps I saved the loss of another window in a hundred year's time." He chuckled under his breath. "My small contribution to Saphir, briefly noted, and soon forgotten."

"The greatest deeds are often unknown and unremembered by men," Mark reminded him.

"Don't mistake my meaning. I don't crave recognition. All fame belongs to them and the genius of their architectural and *zhellavai* creators. I only patched a tiny spot."

"*Zhellavai*. I have not heard their word."

"Oh. Hmm. It refers to someone who builds. Like a stone mason, or a carpenter. That sort of artist, as opposed to a composer or architect, whose accomplishments are experienced by secondary means." He laughed low in his throat. The sound made Mark tingle all over. "When I was a young man we used to have debates about whether poets were *zhellavai* or *ambrai*."

Their course took them toward a building in a fine, pale gray stone adorned with what looked like shockingly large sections of lapis and a gold-spattered red stone. Its delicate spires and fluted walls surrounded a long peaked roof that had to shelter at least two acres. Among the other buildings, this one didn't seem outstanding, but looking up under its eaves humbled Mark utterly.

"In Cathret, this is known as Summer Sky Hall."

A jolt shocked through Mark. The idea of performing for the king hadn't affected him beyond the political and physical danger. The idea of singing in Summer Sky Hall, however, made his insides and knees feel like water-filled sausage skins.

He'd always taken his own voice for granted. He might not feel particularly proud of a performance, but he'd never doubted it or felt like he'd failed a piece of music even on a bad day. But this ... this was Summer Sky Hall.

"Is something wrong? Are you ill? Do you need to sit down?" The gerson had gone pale with worry.

Mark did need to sit, but not because he felt ill. "Summer Sky Hall."

"Yes. It is the very best music hall in the world, though lately both Osia and Bel have made some proud claims of their own. But of course you've heard of it. Oh." The gerson seemed to finally realize. "Oh. But I thought you had performed many times and in front of a great many very important people."

Not this many, and certainly not in there.

"You must feel ten times worse than I did when they asked me to help repair the Veiavra Fael."

Mark felt faint. "How did you come up with that number?"

"What number?" The gerson looked confused.

"Ten times." Mark giggled to help some of the panic escape.

"Oh. It's a turn of phrase. I didn't even think about it."

Mark tried to bite his lip but it trembled too much for him to manage it. It made him giggle again.

"Come inside." The gerson lightly touched Mark's elbow. The contact only unnerved him more. "A look may not settle your jitters, but at least you can enjoy the view."

The reception room had a vaulted ceiling that soared at least three stories. A series of three balconies on each of the higher levels looked down upon a golden and jeweled chandelier of lions that had been converted from candles to gas light. There were so many frescoes and painted curtains he could only allow himself a brief glance at each and he still stood there for a long time, turning in place, trying to grasp it as a whole.

"There are various places to dine and have a little something before and between performances in the front two towers," the gerson told him. "The rear towers are for storage and administration, of which there is a great deal required. Like a beloved *ennai*, she is under the duress of constant adoration." The context more than memory reminded Mark of the meaning of *ennai*, a sort of noble whore that had no equivalent in Cathret.

The gerson led Mark to a side door. "This is one of two hallways that lead to the stage." He applied one key of the many on his heavy chatelaine's ring to the lock, and greeted a sacred guardsman who sat and read in a comfortable office space tucked beside the door. The poorly-lit hallway revealed some of the stonework that connected the building above to the foundation. "She is quite peaceful and content," the gerson told him. "As is proper for a fine lady of her generous age. But we watch. We always watch." His hand traced along the wall as they walked onward for a long stretch. The floor curved down, and then back up where it terminated at a set of broad stairs.

"It sounds as if you're involved with quite a few of the undersides ..." Mark began, and then realized he hadn't used the correct Hasle word for foundation. "... of these buildings." He didn't try to explain himself for fear of making more of a fool of himself, though he blushed.

"Architecture is my passion, but my duty is to their security. By rank I have charge of the entire city, but almost all my time is spent here at the Guilbarabb." The gerson led the way up the stairs. They passed a large room lined with doors and stairways down and up in every direction, and then abruptly they arrived behind the rearmost curtain. The gerson slipped between curtains out onto the stage. Mark hesitated, then followed.

"Dwith Vareetta will be here to practice in an hour. This hour is yours alone."

The summer blue ceiling was streaked with lavender and blue-green and sparkled with quartz-studded silver medallions. Balconies layered like open leaves in a puzzle scroll gleamed with gilding. Glass lamps glowed blue and gold in long lines in the aisles. Overheard rows of gas lights bound in silver filigree and crystal made graceful arches and glowed against their mirror backings. At the moment, most of the lines were dark.

It would be magnificent when it was all lit.

His steps sounded strange. They didn't echo at all. Nothing echoed at all in a room so large it should have been filled with echoes from every slight sound.

He couldn't imagine filling this place with his voice.

The gerson took a flight of stairs down from the stage, skirted the orchestra pit and walked up an aisle where he sat on the edge of what would be the Royal Court. His hands folded over his belly and he leaned back in the plush chair. And waited. A few caretakers sweeping and dusting paused to have a look at Mark. Unimpressed, they returned to their work.

> *I wish for you*
> > *That we had never met*
> *That you were happy*
> > *But I will never forget*
> *Wine and sunlight*

Mark's voice rang the hall like a fine bell. The last note of each line hung suspended for a moment longer than expected but didn't echo back at him.

A whisper could fill this hall.

He hadn't sung even a bit of the song he'd written for Grant's funeral since the first and last time he'd performed it. Part of him wanted to start at its beginning, but it didn't belong here. It was an island song with an island rhythm he'd only just begun to feel but didn't yet understand.

He reverted to something familiar, though it pained him to sing it again.

Cold the sea of northern gray
Cold the ice and sky
Cold the rain and cold the hands
Trim the sails to fly

Fly we fly beyond the waves
Where stars and waters meet
And float for many a thousand days
The free and gallant fleet

Hot the sea of tropicans
Hot the sun and sky
Hot the rain and hot the hands
Trim the sails to fly

Fly we fly beyond the waves
Where stars and waters kiss
And long a many thousand times
For lovers we all miss

Blood the color of our pain
Bloody storm and sky
Blood rains down, blood on our hands
Trim the sails to fly

Fly we fly beyond the waves
Where stars and waters die
And mourn a many thousands times
When we must say goodbye

Bless the sea of sailor men
Bless the earth and sky
Bless the rain and bless the hands
Trim the sails to fly

Fly we fly beyond the waves
Where stars and waters greet
The weary, happy sailor men
The free and gallant fleet

The melody haunted him long after the last notes faded into the velvet and gilding. The last time he'd sung it he hadn't been alone. The sailors on *Dainty* had sung it with him, and taught him a dozen other verses, most of which didn't rhyme very well but he was fond of some of them anyway. There was a bawdy one with fuck, mate and gate that Mr. Briggs always sang right after the blood verse.

You're here to practice.

"How does my voice carry?" Mark asked.

The gerson stirred as if Mark had woken him. "You don't need to force it, Lark. Your voice could carry very well even in a stable. You may ... I shouldn't advise you."

That annoyed him. "Is there anyone here that can give me advice?"

"You can be a little more subtle," offered one of the caretakers. "New performers worry too much about being heard. Show your trust in the grand lady and caress her with nuance."

The caretaker's boldness surprised Mark, but he was grateful. They'd likely heard thousands of performances and would give good counsel. "Thank you."

"And don't sing Gra Farata Obelai," another caretaker said. They all groaned. "Everyone always wants to sing Gra Farata to prove that they have seven octaves and can interval better than the reeds."

He hated Gra Farata. "You have nothing to fear. No Gra Farata, and no Ode to a Dying Lover, either." With death close by at all times, that one had lost what little romance remained in it after years of using it as an exercise.

The caretakers applauded.

"I see no reason to practice here," Mark admitted. "It's a great privilege, but I'm wasting time better spent on someone—"

"Who needs the practice!" a caretaker called, and they laughed.

"—who has more complicated things to do than just stand here," Mark amended.

"You could do more than just stand there," the gerson suggested.

"I'm not going to dance." Mark felt a little faint at the suggestion. And faint he certainly would when the room was full of people and all the lights burned while the poison's weight stole his strength.

"Use the Vicalli Stair," a caretaker suggested, and the others clapped.

"Request it and it will be arranged," the gerson told him.

"What's the Vicalli Stair?"

"A glass stair," the gerson said. "A beautiful glass stair on which one can walk up, down, or sit as one chooses. It's a good idea. It hasn't been used in a long time. And it would suit your voice well."

"If it's not too much trouble." He'd forgotten for a moment that he might be party to an assassination attempt. It came back to him after he spoke, not before, so the gerson was spared the sarcasm that could have laced his words.

"I'll have it assembled a few days before your performance, and arrange practice time for you. In the meantime, I have some music you should look over."

When they emerged, Saphir's unnaturally clear air smelled even less of a city, with little smoke and even less of midden air and almost nothing of horse to pollute it. Its cold purity at this moment rivaled the wilderness they'd crossed. "Will I be alone on stage?" Mark asked as they walked back to the gatehouse and their waiting carriage.

"No."

He should have been relieved, but he didn't care about the performance so much as he wanted to be able to act in the king's defense if he had to. "I admit I was intimidated at first—"

"You turned whiter than ash." The gerson had an elegant, self-effacing smile that made Mark's unwilling heart flutter.

"But I think I can manage without support, if need be. When will I get a chance to rehearse with the others?"

"Soon. I mustn't be more specific than that. And you—" The gerson briefly set a hand on his shoulder. "You have to be careful about what you say."

"I have no one to gossip with," Mark reminded him.

"I mean ...." The gerson might have been struggling with his Cathretan vocabulary, but Mark had a feeling that he was trying to say something without giving too much away. "Your voice is very clear, and may be overheard."

As a priest he may have meant *morbai* and *allolai*. As a conspirator, he might have simply suggested that there could be spies closer than Mark might otherwise guess. As both ....

There was so much he didn't understand.

"It will be a magnificent performance," the gerson told him, apparently trying to inspire a little idle conversation.

As if that mattered to them. "It's not as if I'm being honored by being asked to perform."

The gerson's brows rumpled. "He wouldn't have asked you if your voice would not please all who heard it. It is very much a tremendous honor."

"It's political. My voice serves a purpose here, and it isn't artistic."

"You're jaded for one so young." The gerson walked close, his elbow occasionally rubbing Mark's. "And you're also wrong. If you weren't bound I would have tried to bring you into the Church."

That made Mark smile. "Gutter must not have mentioned how I feel about the Church." He'd said it gently, but he regretted it instantly, worried that he'd offended the gerson. "Anyway," he went on, trying to smooth any feathers he might have ruffled, "I'm just ... out of my depth here. This intrigue ...."

The gerson stepped in front of him, forcing him to stop. "How much do you know?"

More than I should.

"Lark." The gerson put his hands on Mark's shoulders.

Mark pressed him away and started walking too fast. It made him light-headed.

The gerson caught up with him. "Lord jester, please. Let me speak with you. Please. Over here. It will be safe over here." Mark reluctantly followed him into an alcove set into the wall beneath a painted rendition of the Falleon Orb.

Young men fall in love a hundred times crossing a commons, the old saying said. Mark couldn't afford this attraction, even if it might be welcomed. He didn't welcome it himself. The only person he'd felt more tangled about than the gerson was Gutter, and he hated everything about that love.

He heard Gutter's astonishment in his own thoughts.

But he's a priest. You hate priests.

It would have been easier to resist the gerson's invitation if Mark had hated priests more, or if he could at least blame them for the loss of his parents. At least what little they did back then to solve his mother's murder was done for the sake of justice. He couldn't extend the same considerations to Gutter.

He didn't want to, but he trusted the gerson more than the lord jester.

Let him try to convert me to the cause. It won't matter anyway.

And maybe Mark would learn something.

The gerson had him cornered in the alcove. Mark's fingers brushed over his rapier. His own touch on the frigid steel startled him.

What's the matter with me? He didn't feel in danger, not on the surface, but his hand wanted to stay near the pommel, and he was afraid to move it away.

The gerson didn't notice. "Don't answer with anything more but yes or no. Have the *morbai* and *allolai* whispered to you about Gutter?"

That wasn't the question he expected. He couldn't answer either way. "No. I don't know. I don't even know if what happens is real, or just ...." Madness.

"It's not madness."

Mark hoped that the gerson was merely insightful and didn't have some otherworldly thing whispering Mark's thoughts into his ear. "Not yet?"

The gerson avoided looking at him. "Yes or no, have they mentioned Gelantyne?"

"The mask?" The thought made him sicker in his belly than the damage the poison had done. "Please don't tell me he has it." Of course everyone suspected Gutter would, and Mark's unconscious belief that Gutter actually had it had grown with every passing day. It shouldn't have bothered him to hear yet another hint that Gutter possessed the most dangerous mask in the world, but it horrified him.

Maybe Gutter didn't have it. Maybe he was looking for it. Or maybe the King ... but the King would lock the evil thing up. Wouldn't he?

Maybe Gelantyne and king were connected somehow. It would be such a relief if he learned that this entire plot revolved around the mask and the king had gotten caught up in it somehow. If that were true he could help them in good conscience.

"Please answer the question."

"No. I've heard nothing. I haven't heard anything since I've come here, at least nothing I can understand, so there's no point in asking me more questions like that. I can't help you. I'm not some sort of prophet." Mark started to leave but the gerson got in his way. "If you want answers, ask Gutter. I don't know anything."

"I don't believe you."

Those words made Mark's teeth press tight against each other. When he forced them to relax his jaw slid forward. His familiar friend—his temper—had come to visit. "Then why bother talking to me? What could you possibly learn from me that Gutter doesn't know better?"

"I want—" The gerson winced. "I'm trying to protect you."

So that was it. The gerson suspected he knew that King Michael was in danger. And the only reason Mark's mind might be at risk so far in advance of the performance had to be because they intended to harm His Royal Majesty.

His hopes that this might not have so much to do with the king sank away into darkness. "Why would you bother? I'm dying anyway. What does it matter if I go mad before then?" It mattered to Mark, of course, but the gerson had him flustered again.

"Gutter." The gerson spat the name like a curse and strode off toward the gates.

Mark hurried to keep pace with him, though he couldn't quite catch up. "You want to protect me? That's not possible, even if I wanted it, which I don't."

The gerson halted. Mark was too aware of how exposed they were, with passersby watching curiously. No doubt all the jesters in earshot or who could read lips were trying to piece together the conversation so that they could learn something useful for themselves.

"You won't even look at me," Mark pointed out. "How in the hells do you expect me to trust you?"

"I'm a priest."

"Do you know what priests have been to me? Bankers. Slavers. Ignorant judges. Guards so tied by mundane duty that they can't or won't pursue the injustice and heal the pain all around them. I have a difficult time considering them instruments of good."

A flash of temper lit the gerson's eyes. "Is that what I am to you?"

"I don't know you well enough to say whether there's a person behind your eyes or if you're just another stone in a court wall." His anger melted into heartache.

"All priests are people." The gerson's warm voice hardened. "It's easy to judge when it isn't your duty to right wrongs and stand fast when any sane person would flee."

Mark started to argue, but then he remembered with ugly detail the fire that had destroyed *Mairi*, and how all those guards had gone to help. Certainly some had stood by to keep order, but some had helped and bled and burned alongside the sailors. And perhaps if the guards that stood by hadn't placed themselves there, a sudden turn of events for the worse might have killed every guard in the city, leaving her without protection of any kind. There would be no one to keep watch over the wounded, and the valuables in the dock buildings, and to keep paths of escape clear if the entire city caught fire.

"Or maybe you don't even give me that much credit. After all, all I do is lock and unlock buildings." Most of the heat had cooled from the gerson's voice, but he still cut his syllables with sharp edges.

"I don't know you," Mark reminded him.

Their intimate stillness amid the grand, jeweled buildings of the Guilbarabb enhanced Gerson Lowell's extraordinary beauty to the point where he seemed too perfect to be anything but a work of art. "I suppose it doesn't matter what you think of me," the gerson told him. "We'll just have to ... try not to interfere with each other."

Interfere. In Hasle the word probably didn't have the same sexual suggestion as it did in Cathretan, though they were almost alike in pronunciation. Still, it made Mark smile.

"Now he smiles," the gerson remarked.

"I'm cold." Mark started toward the gates again, his thoughts playing hide and seek and finding neither answers nor hiding places. All he knew was that he wanted to be a friend, a lover, something, maybe even everything to the gerson. For both their sakes he couldn't be, even if the gerson had wanted it.

Once they'd settled back in the carriage, Gale's happy panting steaming Mark's knees, he relaxed and the unnatural weariness that came from his long illness overwhelmed him. He propped himself in the seat's corner and closed his eyes.

"Why did you run away to the islands?" the gerson asked.

Mark didn't open his eyes to answer. "Is that what Gutter told you I did?"

"He wrote to me of it."

"I wanted justice." It sounded stupid now. "I have to say, I had no success. In light of that, I know I shouldn't be so quick to judge priests."

"Everyone does."

"He who judges most is judged the most." He spoke it in Cathretan because it had better rhythm than it did in Hasle. "I used to think that was a comment on judges, but after our conversation today I realize it applies better to me." He knew of a great crime, *Mairi's* burning, and he'd done nothing about it. He didn't even know why he hesitated to demand a trial.

"Is that an apology?"

Mark smiled. "Stop being so companionable. "

"I didn't think it was a particularly friendly question." His voice had warmed again, but this time Mark could hear his self-effacing smile in it.

"You're forcing me to make amends so that we can enjoy each other's company, and I don't want to enjoy your company. I want to hate you."

"You don't sound very serious about your pursuit."

"Let me be more—" His Hasle failed him again. "Obvious. I know you have a lover, and I have a friend, and I have a lord and master far from here. But I want to invite you to the *banre*, and make you show me Saphir, and play cards with you and go with you to the Masked Theater, and most of all I want to live." That last admission made his breath catch. Long ago it might have been a word of drama, or a comment about existence versus exuberance, but now it was too literal and sharp and cold. "You make the feeling of a close death go away. But I can't afford to wish for you. I have to concentrate on what I have to do before I die. You're just so ... distracting." The understatement in that made him chuckle.

Gerson Lowell moved to Mark's side of the carriage, and his hand cupped over Mark's on the seat. "I want you to live. I want to show you Saphir, and play cards, and listen to your voice. Not only your music, but your voice." He squeezed Mark's hand, and then let go. "Eventually, someone will probably tell you that my lover rejected me when his wife became pregnant. That's true. But I don't want another lover. I don't even want to be your friend. You confound me too much." That made Mark laugh again, but he still kept his eyes closed. "Yet, I want—" Gerson Lowell touched Mark's face, startling him into opening his eyes. "—I want to be someone you can depend upon. If you're willing to trust me, I promise you, I'll never do anything to hurt you." He winced. "Not deliberately."

Mark took the gerson's hand in his own and held it. "I believe you." For the first time in forever, he didn't feel alone. He wasn't sure he could trust the gerson. It didn't matter. He had no choice anymore. Whether he wanted to or not, he believed that if he had asked, Gerson Lowell would abandon whatever alliance he had with Gutter and help Mark instead.

He held Gerson Lowell's hand all the way back to Gutter's home. After he stepped out, he stood in front of the steps and watched the carriage go. Gale sat beside him, watching his face.

It didn't take long for his hunger and dread of starvation and all his other worries to clench up inside him again. Mark let himself into the house.

"—choice!" Gzem's voice rang from the next level upstairs.

Gutter murmured something Mark couldn't catch before he strode into view at the top of the stairs. "Welcome home. Did you have a pleasant tour of the venue?"

"Yes, thank you." Gutter seemed little more than a thin veneer of humanity compared to Gerson Lowell's depth. Whatever Gutter and Gzem had argued about had made Gutter's façade of sanity more fragile. "Is everything all right?" Mark asked.

Gzem strode out, all fire and femininity, with a determination Mark had never seen in any other woman. He believed she could hold her own against any man, not just intellectually but physically through finesse and skillfully applied strength. "If he doesn't understand," she told Gutter, "he won't be able to protect anyone." She gave Mark a strange look that wasn't quite pity, and walked off toward the stairway leading up to the third story.

Gutter made his way down the stairs. "She thinks that because she can withstand damned near anything, so can you." Gale bounded up the stairs to meet Gutter, then hurried back down ahead of him as if Gutter needed her to show him the way.

"I won't know until you try me," Mark said. "And neither will you."

"I don't want you to have to endure this. You were chosen for a task. Not by me. I have no choice but to give that task to you. But I do have a choice about whether or not to expose you to more danger than you'll already face, and I choose to protect you. Gzem thinks—well, I think you have a fair idea what Gzem thinks. She hopes you will choose to fight with us on your own, but wants you to have the chance to resist if you decide you want no part of this."

"I remember you saying that you had delayed too long in whatever this is." That sense of standing near the edge of a cliff overtook him, but Mark pressed on. "I believe that you're reluctant, and that worries me. Not because of any danger, but because maybe something within you doubts that what you're doing is right. That is my real objection to all this. Because I doubt it too, charming and honorable dukes and duchesses apparently in danger or no, the same nobles willingly involved or not."

"Trust me. You don't want to be convinced." Gutter rubbed behind Gale's ears.

Something twitched through the lord jester. Gutter shocked up straight and his eyes rolled back. A spasm rocked him. Mark grabbed Gutter's sleeve to keep him from falling.

Whatever held Gutter released him an instant later. He gazed at Mark, something darker than defeat shining in his eyes.

It was an old, resigned anger, but it wasn't directed at Mark. Gutter's gaze slid up the stairs. "It seems," he said, "that I'm overridden in more ways than I care to count."

Chapter Eleven

Small shocks and chills darted through Mark's body as they walked to Gutter's suite. "What are you?" Mark asked.

"I could answer that in a lot of ways, but I suspect you have a more specific question in mind." Gutter slid a sly look in his direction just long enough for Mark to catch him at it.

"Are you a Confidante?" *Is this what I will become the longer I listen to the voices?*

"That's an interesting notion." Gutter allowed Mark to catch up with him and put his arm around Mark's shoulders. Instead of feeling comfort or camaraderie, Mark felt like he was being compelled to move forward against his will. "I'm not, but you're the first person to ask me almost the right question." He chuckled. "No one has thought about me in any way except as a jester. They think so many terrible things about me, but never consider the sacred. Not that I am, or have any right to pretend that I do the things I do for Good." He leaned close. "But I am a Hand, my boy," he whispered. "Not even Gzem knows that."

"They can touch you?" Mark gasped the words, trying to keep them low so that even a nearby servant couldn't overhear.

"They can thresh me like wheat." Gutter straightened and let out an unpleasant laugh.

The main doors to Gutter's suite led into a large reception room done in reds and browns. Bright summer light came through windows set in alcoves in the ceiling, illuminating rich, burgundy rugs with subtle floral designs and leaving the rest of the room in shadow. The dark colors should have made it seem cozy, but instead it seemed small and dangerously crowded, with too many hiding places behind rare tapestries and heavy curtains.

Gale let out a whine, tucked her tail, and sat out in the hall. "Come on," Mark urged. She inched forward, dragging her belly, ears held low. Her whole body shook. "It's all right," Mark soothed, stroking her face. He didn't want to force her. "Stay." Gale retreated into the corner between the door and wall, still trembling. Mark took a few steadying breaths. They didn't help. He forced himself to go inside.

Gutter took a side door into a large closet, generously lit by the white-gold glow of alcove windows that reflected off of white marble well enough to see by. Mark lingered in the doorway a moment before he managed to force himself to follow Gutter inside.

"Close the door." Gutter walked to a tremendous locked wardrobe. Mark had never seen its like before. It had iron doors and oak thick enough to daunt any axe, but it wasn't a crude thing. Delicate flowers and vines adorned the wood, and the iron had been cast into an ornate mold with strange trees whose roots also had leaves on them.

Something behind those doors made Mark feel even more uneasy. His stomach made a soft fist and squeezed. His hair prickled up on his neck.

Gutter pulled out a key that hung from a hidden ribbon around his neck. Mark stepped back as the lord jester fitted the key to the lock and turned it left, then right, then center, and right again as if he were opening a puzzle box. With each turn the lock made a heavy liquid steel-on-steel sound. Gutter left the key in the lock and opened the doors.

At first Mark didn't see anything past him, but then something deep red, almost wine, like part of a thick silk shirt, caught the light. A faint ruby design glimmered in the heavy fabric. Gutter bent and slipped something like a hood over his head and Mark took another step back. His belly plunged.

A gold mask draped with cloth whirled with animal grace and fixed its inhuman gaze on Mark's face. An ancient instinct within closed off Mark's thoughts and held him perfectly still like a rabbit hiding from death in the grass.

The gold wasn't entirely naked, but lacquered. The colors and metal formed into large amber eyes with no whites. Sharp cheeks crested over long, hungry hollows. It had no mouth, but a golden chin that dovetailed in a cleft. Cream, black and gold curved beneath the eyes and formed a design like a crown over the bare brows. The ancient design made him think of old kings and ruthless warriors. Gutter would not be able to see, and his voice would be muffled, if he could speak at all. He'd been obliterated, and in his place this silent creature stood—

The room plunged into sudden darkness with the mask at center providing the only thing of form, not so much a source of light but as if only the mask existed and everything else had become a forgotten dream. Mark's pain faded, and then his hunger. The being's terrible, beautiful gaze rested on him gently, judging him without mercy but understanding him with a kindness that transcended all his hopes of what true love might be.

e'illoathai

He knew it meant 'you will sing' though he couldn't say how he knew. It didn't speak. No sound had touched his ears but this wasn't a vision or in some space he fell into during a seizure where Mark's consciousness could see in all directions at once. This thing existed in Gutter's room with Mark's all-too-physical and vulnerable body. Mark's fragile heart tried to simultaneously pound its way through his ribs and out of his throat. He tried to back away and ended up with his back pressed into velvet and silk waistcoats. Left with nowhere to hide, he knelt and looked up into its eyes.

The mask's cloth billowed and formed spikes of sharp, golden steel like a horrible mane.

Morbai. Allolai. It didn't matter if it was a destroyer or a creator, it terrified and fascinated him, as if the sun and moon had bred a being of lightning and molten gold.

e'illoathai

"Why?" The word came out more clearly than he expected.

The answer cracked through his mind like hammer blows breaking his skull.

To shatter humanity's ignorance and bring down the Trokellestrai. Cathret has suffered long enough beneath the weight of their folly and arrogance.

In that agonizing answer the mask sliced deep into his mind. The scar from that wound left something that felt like a memory, but Mark knew he'd never learned it, not from book or word.

Trokellestrai were *allolai* who upheld the Law of Knowledge.

He didn't want to challenge it but he had no choice if he wanted to save the king. "Cathret isn't suffering. It's prospering."

Only as you prosper now, your body shriveled from poison, your mind crippled by what you do not know. You must learn before you can heal, become whole, and thrive.

Your king is a monster, a creature bred for beauty and intelligence at the expense of its soul.

Mark didn't know whether his heart or his head would explode first. "I don't believe it." The Gelantyne mask was evil, dangerous ... he probably shouldn't have told it that he didn't believe it.

Would you risk your life to have it proved?

He'd rather defy it and die here, now, than have anything to do with a creature that would condemn both a beloved King and Mark's own cherished lord and master. *I'm dying anyway.* That didn't make the prospect of being destroyed by this thing any less terrifying. If anything it made death seem more horrible and close, but the mathematics won over his terror. "My master was attacked during our bonding. If he is what you would call a monster, then the king—"

The Trokellestrai might want your bond master dead. I don't.

That shocked him. He wanted to ask more about Rohn—how the mask knew about him, why they wanted him dead, but he couldn't afford to pursue personal matters. At least, not now. "You would not condemn Rohn, but you would condemn the king?"

Your master offends their sensibilities with his predatory grace. They have no regard to his place in humanity. Mark's mind tried to pick up on the nuances of the creature's thoughts but apparently he'd reached the limits of human understanding. *He hunts and destroys that which they prize,* it added, apparently in an effort to help him. *The Trokellestrai count his kind as less than human, as if being a lion were an offense, and a sheep's existence superior. They do not see the hypocrisy in their own champion line because they feed their beast the sheep he craves in his cage rather than let him run loose to seize his own prey.*

They do not recognize what you know in your heart, even if you don't know why. Their so-called natural world is a lie. They don't care that fear and helplessness uphold their mockery of peace. They pretend that ignorance is the same as innocence.

"I know something is wrong, and I believe you're trying to help somehow, but I don't know how regicide—"

A war claims many lives. Will this king's death count as a greater tragedy than Grant Roadman's? Mark flinched. *And what of the jester you slew? Would it make it easier if this monstrous king came to murder you with Gzem's blood on his hands?*

Mark couldn't tell if it was trying to help him discover hidden truths or just manipulating him. "That would depend on if he knew we were all plotting against him," he pointed out. "We are, technically speaking, foul assassins."

A slight shift in the angle on the mask made it seem to smile. ***You are worthy.***

He didn't want to be flattered, but his heart glowed with pleasure anyway. He didn't want to believe a word Gelantyne said, but it made terrible sense. Was it a good liar, lacing its falsehoods with truth, was it both sincere and insane ... or did Mark believe in a king that didn't deserve his faith and trust?

You will sing, because you love your master, and truth, and most of all you seek justice. Perhaps one day, should your voice succeed, you might even learn what justice is.

The mane of swords drew in, splitting into golden rays of light that obliterated the darkness around him. Mark's dazzled eyes adjusted back to the closet, where Gutter bent forward to slip off the hood-mask. Sweat streaked his face and he sat heavily on a bench. "You're bleeding," he said. His voice sounded muffled and faraway.

Mark felt wetness at his ears. He touched his fingers. Blood. He stood up and his balance wandered sideways. He had to catch himself on a waistcoat.

"It will heal." Gutter reached into a drawer and handed Mark a pair of handkerchiefs. "What did Gelantyne tell you?"

Mark settled onto a short stool meant for servants who polished shoes or adjusted hems. He dabbed at his ears with the handkerchief. He remembered every word, every nuance he'd managed to comprehend, but it still seemed indescribable. He'd been groping in the dark for so long, and now he'd seen too much to really understand.

I've faced Gelantyne. I spoke to Gelantyne. It was both more and less terrifying than he'd expected it to be, and far more personal.

"He did ... speak ...?" Gutter ventured.

Mark nodded. "We talked."

"You spoke to him?" Gutter's eyes went wide.

"I forgot to ask him an important question," Mark realized. He felt light-headed.

"You asked questions?" Gutter stood, his face going from pale to pink. "Gzem is the only other person I know who's dared. Did he answer your questions?"

"Why my voice? Dwith Vareetta is in Saphir practicing at this very moment in Summer Sky Hall. Her voice is far better than mine."

"Even if that was true, she is—" Gutter turned away with the mask cradled against his chest.

Mark couldn't make out what he'd said. "I couldn't hear that. She's what?"

Gutter faced him. "She's not a Confidante." Gutter put the Gelantyne mask into the wardrobe and began to lock it very carefully. "The *allolai* and *morbai* can hear human voices to a certain extent on the other side, but your voice ... clear to them, and ... Gelantyne refers to as engraced vibrations. I don't understand—"

"Gutter, I can't hear half of what you're saying."

Gutter put the key away and finally focused all his attention on Mark. "When you scream—when you and the others scream, it will be like a symphonic wildfire. It will help us."

Mark dabbed at his ears again. He wanted to hate Gutter for all of this and rail and defy and refuse, but he was starting to understand too much while still not knowing enough. "How many others will be at the performance?"

Gutter went to Mark and gently took a handkerchief from him. "I think you've met Feather." He dipped the handkerchief in a light cream sitting on a dresser and started cleaning Mark's ear.

"Yes, I've met Feather."

"She is one. There are others."

She must be here already. She left ahead of me, and probably traveled with something faster than our caravan.

Did I destroy one of Gutter's ... whatever we are ... when I killed Juggler?

Mark remembered with regret that Juggler had a fine voice. Mark liked him very much, despite everything, and Perida felt emptier without him.

The King is a monster because Gelantyne says he is, or is this the result of political games among the morbai *and* allolai? *Did Juggler and I end up on opposite sides because of what we believed in, or because neither of us understood what was really going on?*

Politics. Wasn't the other world supposed to be a place of grace and clarity that existed beyond petty mortal society?

The answer may be no. If so, can I do this in good conscience without understanding the context? Gelantyne had said Mark would do it because he loved Rohn, but Mark didn't know if he could fight this *Trokellestrai* just because they attacked Rohn, assuming Gelantyne didn't lie about that. Gelantyne claimed it was because they didn't like who Rohn killed, and Mark suspected that how Rohn went about it bothered them. *It more than bothered me when I saw him killing ... I don't know how I'm supposed to work out what's right and wrong in this.*

At the party, Feather had said, *I should hate you, but I can't. I will miss you.*

He couldn't tell what she'd meant by any of that—not why she wanted to hate him, nor whether she knew he'd be poisoned or if she'd referred to her leaving for Saphir, or something entirely different.

I can't forget that she might not be entirely sane, either.

Gutter said something too softly to hear.

"I can't hear very well," Mark reminded him.

"I said I wish you would share your thoughts with me," Gutter said.

"If *morbai* and *allolai* can hear my voice so clearly, aren't you worried that one of the enemy side might overhear us?"

"Not here, not now."

"Because of Gelantyne?"

Gutter took Mark's chin in his hot hand and made Mark look into his eyes. "Gelantyne is trapped on our world. He can't protect us. Never, ever trust that he can protect you." Gutter released him. "But he has allies, and they control much of Saphir. With the king, however, will come an army loyal to the *Trokellestrai*. They've come before, and in eras past they've always left in peace. We may ignite the first true battle after a hundred years of skirmishes and who knows how many more centuries of uneasy and often-broken truces. The outcome will be of no concern to us. All that matters is that we do our part for Gelantyne. You will sing, and when the time is right you will scream. Beyond that—the less you know the more likely it is we will succeed."

I will not do this blind. "I know about what you intend to do to the King. I want to know why. Why would you do this to your friend?"

"He told you?" Gutter recoiled and he gasped a few times before he composed himself. "It's all right, Thomas," he whispered.

Mark wished he didn't have to press him. "I need an answer, Gutter. You can't expect me to lose my sanity and get cut to pieces by guards unless I know this is the best way, the only way to spend the last days of my life. It's not like I'm going to last anyway. You might as well tell me everything."

"You still look at me like the boy I've always loved, but by damnation and destruction I can't tell if you're just cruel or foolish," Gutter growled. "I told you Thomas is dangerous, but you keep slapping his face."

Mark's temper sparked to life. He took a breath to counter with a long litany of doubts and fears and hurts when a stray thought stopped him. *Will I get my answer this way?* It seemed so ugly and cold and manipulative to think in terms of getting his way instead of opening his heart and speaking his mind, but wasn't that what he'd been trained to do? *Like it or not, I'm a jester now. I have to start acting like one. When it serves a purpose, anyway.*

"I'm sorry," Mark told him. "You're right. I didn't think before I spoke. Nonetheless, I must know why you're doing this to a man you've known and cared for much of your life. You know it's not only to satisfy my curiosity. In fact, I'd rather not know. But this is too great a commitment. My soul ...." He didn't know how to describe what had become a vague but too-real sensation. He'd become aware of his soul's value and fragility the same way a man whose arm hung by a few ligaments understood how precious it was, how very much his it was, and how much it was a part of who he believed himself to be. Only in the case of his soul, if he lost it, there would be nothing else of him that would survive, never mind heal.

One of Gutter's shoulders twitched up and he shook his head. But then, unexpectedly, he spoke. "He was my friend. Is. But for a long time I suspected that his favorite pastimes weren't restricted to riding, hunting and betting on horse races." Gutter turned his attention to a long line of silk shirts. His hands smoothed over them and his gaze fell to shadowed places. "He doesn't just torture and rape. His mother didn't die peacefully in her bed. His children ... they're under guard, to protect them from each other, and to protect him from them and them from him."

Torture. Rape. Mark tried to say something but he couldn't form a complete thought, never mind a word.

"He's a harsh disciplinarian. If I didn't see the need, I would pity them. He wants to shape them into something that passes for what the duke and duchess really are, just as he was shaped to deceive the world and hide his true nature. And so, another generation of twisted souls inflict themselves upon our world not as mere predators, but as our regents. They make us love them even as they take us from our homes one by one and destroy us in secret for their pleasure. Sometimes I fear it is his only true pleasure, and everything else is a mask in every sense of the word."

It didn't seem possible. Everyone loved His Royal Majesty Michael. With so many priests and courtiers and not a few nobles who wouldn't hesitate to bring him and his entire family down if such a thing were known, how could he have hidden this? "What about Duchess Anne? How is she involved?"

"Any woman that catches his eye is in real danger, and she is even more vulnerable because of her relationship to the duke. His Royal Majesty has self-control, and patience. But I won't wait for him to create an opportunity. I adore her. I adore her husband. They are what I thought the king was, and what he should have been. And I will see them on the Cathretan throne, even if it means madness and death. I am a jester. It's my duty to do these things."

"The duke and duchess ... he wants to kill him to get to her?" So many different parts of things that seemed to fit together—he felt like the world had broken apart and he'd only begun to start piecing it back together again with half of what he needed still missing.

"It's not that simple, and no, I will not go into it with you. It's a very private matter."

"And Lord Argenwain?" The only way he could keep himself from trembling apart was to hug his own arms.

"My lord and master." The edge of a fond smile tugged at his mouth. "Always sensed something was wrong with Michael. Some might say that Merrin recognized his own kind. But despite your opinion of my lord, Lark, I've never known Merrin to harm, force, abuse or coerce a child. It would make him ill to even consider it. He despises his own desires, but he can't master them entirely, so he ... he has young men past their age of majority dress up and play the part. I hate him for it too, sometimes. I think it's vile, especially the way he lured you despite my begging against it. But he isn't evil. Not like Michael."

Mark wanted to agree, though he had his doubts about how benign Lord Argenwain was or wasn't. "Will the *morbai* destroy Lord Argenwain's soul for what he is?" Gutter had to know, or at least have a guess.

"I believe so, yes." He said it so mildly, as if he'd remarked on the likelihood of some distant relation marrying well.

"Could you save his soul?" *If Lord Argenwain can be saved, then maybe I could save Rohn from the Trokellestrai ....*

Gutter looked startled at the suggestion. "My dear boy, I have done far worse than him, and I will do far worse before the month has ended. But it will not be so bad an end for Thomas. The shreds of my soul will become part of all that is beyond this world. Nothing is ever utterly destroyed. And I ... I think Thomas will not mind so much. As for Merrin, I think he is more afraid than I, but he has no illusions that he will be spared, just because he tried to be good and feels remorseful. You must be good to be worthy. All he and I are worthy of is to feed the flowers of the Sykathan Hell."

Right after Thomas destroyed *Mairi* and burned alive much of her crew, Mark might have agreed with him. Now he desperately wanted to believe in redemption.

Gutter tipped his head and offered a pale smile. "My best comfort is that I have had a multitude of privileges in my time. I have seen what might have been my destiny if I had made better choices. I have loved and lived in luxury, and half the reason I have been so remarkably successful and widely feared is due in part because I stopped trying to be good and instead did my best to be effective in the name of a greater good. And I have known you, my dear, dear boy. That has made a great many things worthwhile."

All his efforts to keep from shaking overcame him at last. Mark shuddered violently, overwhelmed by his mortality and the painful realization that not only was Gutter damned, but he wouldn't even fight it.

Gutter had begun to shake as well. "I rather enjoy this part," he remarked wryly, digging inside his waistcoat.

"What part?"

"The trembling after I've had my wits terrified away from me. It lets me know I haven't lost all of my humanity, and it's a rather interesting ride, don't you think?" He drew out a tiny flask and after some careful maneuvering to get the opening to his mouth without sprinkling the contents liberally all over himself, he took a sip. He offered it to Mark.

"What is it?"

"Muoduo." Mark had never heard of it. "Vanilla cognac," Gutter added helpfully. "Very stiff. It's distilled by Belan mountain men and then flavored in Osia with the world's best vanilla. A truly worldly drink. Many have tried to imitate it and failed."

"No thank you. My stomach."

Gutter's expression sank. "Oh. Yes. I'm sorry." He took another sip and his expression lifted again. The light in his eyes and the suggestion of laughter around his mouth—he seemed to be enjoying himself immensely. It took him a bit of work to fasten the cork and steel cap back on the flask and to snap the guard shut.

"I'll sing," Mark told him. He didn't want to, but perhaps it was the right thing to do. More importantly, his voice now gave him much-needed leverage.

"By all the hells you'd better. Gelantyne will not accept anything less." Gutter replaced the flask in his waistcoat's inner pocket.

"If."

That got Gutter's attention. "If what?"

He'd find no better time to press his advantage. "You understand that I'm not here to help you. I'm here for Meridua."

"Yes, of course," Gutter said dismissively.

"I mean it. I want to know what all of this has to do with Meridua. The code. The signet ring." Without Mark's voice, Gutter and his cohorts would have a harder time seeing all their finely-laid plans through to harvest. Gutter had to answer, though of course he might lie if he thought he had to.

"Your sense of timing makes me proud, but you and I will not play this game. I won't do it." Gutter got up and left the closet.

Mark chased after him, his knees unsteady. "Gutter."

"This you should be able to determine on your own, with a little thought." Gutter stabbed a finger against his own head.

"How is the Church connected? Why would they try to kill me there, and help me here? What is Dellai Bertram's part in this?"

Gutter whirled to face him. "You won't need any of those answers if you make certain your little soldier isn't elected to the presidency. You may think you will die here but I won't let you. You must live, and you will harness all your strength to this cause or Meridua's freedom will be a sham, and a short-lived one besides. No one in the world will be free, if they can even call themselves that now."

Little soldier. Heat rushed to his face. "I want those answers. I will not sing without them."

"All of Saphir could have been yours." The fire in Gutter's voice set him back on his heels. "But now you have your little island and your little colonel and I suggest you go home as soon as the last scream dies in your throat and fuck in the bed you've bonded to your ass."

"I won't live just because you refuse to admit I might die."

"Do you even want to live? Sometimes it seems like you want to die."

Mark had already allowed himself to be sidetracked too far. He had to come back to the point. "Why hold back information on what must be an insignificant intrigue in the face of everything else you've planned unless *my little soldier* is an actual threat?"

"I'm in a very good mood. Let's not fight over this," Gutter muttered.

"I'm sorry if the lives of thousands of people aren't as important to you than your good humor, but I won't leave this alone. Before I do anything for you, I want to know what will happen to Meridua."

"Then talk to the duke and duchess. Leave me out of it."

That suited Mark better than well. "With pleasure." He rushed to leave.

"I hope you've considered what your arrival at their home might suggest to anyone who might be watching them closely," Gutter called after him.

Mark paused at the double doors that opened the way to the hall, his hand on the door handle. He wondered when Gutter had taken charge of the argument and whether he'd intended to manipulate Mark to this very point.

I'm not going to beat him at this.

"You're young." Gutter gentled his voice as he settled into a large chair in his reception room. "Everything seems so easy when you're young, and so hard at the same time. You want to do something. Everyone seems to be standing around wasting time, keeping secrets that should be shouted across every town square in the world. But the problems you face are so monumental that you feel like you're scaling a cliff and at any moment you'll tumble down, carrying everything below with you to shatter on the ground."

"Poetic metaphor is not your strongest skill," Mark told him.

"No. I'm very much a painter. And it is paint that purchased this house, paint that maintains it. Paint that maintains what is left of my sanity." He made a loose gesture with his hand toward Mark. "You don't wear your mask very much. I approve. It should be something applied at the proper time. It shouldn't be a crutch, and never a shelter."

Gutter's praise always warmed Mark through and through, even when he didn't want it to. "What is happening with the Church? Will you tell me at least that much?"

Gutter slouched back deeper into his chair and stretched his legs out. "There have always been facets to spirituality, or factions if you prefer. They call each other cults during their uglier arguments. Sometimes the word heresy is bandied about. But they all know, and you and I know, that every sect is imperfect. We all face the same problem. As Lord Argenwain and I have sacrificed ourselves for the sake of humankind—and we are certainly the best to be sacrificed, being the worst example of humanity second only to a few rare others—prophets have sacrificed their sanity to try to transmit the truth. We all want to know what really matters. Can men change their natures? Do our actions truly outweigh who and what we are inside?" His gaze sank until no light reflected from his eyes and the holes in his mask seemed like pits in his face. "We want to know, can our actions be forgiven, and if they can, *should they be*." His hand rubbed the chair's padded arm, smoothing and roughing the crimson velvet in alternate strokes. "Since the time of Raphira it seemed that we shouldn't know. Being disobedient, we searched for the answers anyway, resulting in her madness, and the madness of countless other Seers, Confidantes, Hands and Speakers. But then a few hundred years ago someone made a mask."

The Gelantyne Mask.

"History remembers the mask as the most perfect and powerful death mask ever created. It seemed to make the wearer impervious to harm. It destroyed documents, started wars, created an army of worshippers, and nearly conquered the known world until the wearer, little more than a gibbering skeleton by then, died. The mask's power died with him, history tells us. To be sure that no one could ever revive it, the mask was locked away. Then about a hundred years ago, during the reign of Ian the Faithful, Michael's great grandfather, it vanished."

Mark wondered what any of this had to do with the islands, but he was willing to be patient, especially since he sensed the story would soon change from what he'd been taught.

"What actually happened is that Gelantyne, an ancient *allolai*, and his lover Furyl, a young *morbai*, started a war. They believed that humanity could be uplifted and enlightened through education. The *Trokellestrai* want us to remain ignorant so that we develop into our true selves. They want us to glorify ourselves or damn ourselves by our own effort and merits, so that we don't twist our actions and muddy our intentions by adhering to a set of rules that we would bend and manipulate regardless of how well written they might be. Gelantyne maintained, and maintains to this day that we have not been innocent of trying to escape the hells by false action and insincere goodness for some time, and that we should at least understand the truth of Good and Evil rather than flail about in the dark. He could not touch us, or speak to us without harming us, so he ... he came here. A human body would be too short-lived—"

"So he became a mask?" How was that even possible? At least intellectually he could at least allow for the possibility that a spiritual being could enter a human body somehow ....

That implied weird, confusing things about *morbai* and *allolai*.

"He gave up his immortal existence to inhabit it. And yes, I see by your expression that you understand that he has all the limitations of a mask. He can be destroyed, though I wouldn't want to be the one to try it even if I wished to." Gutter raised his gaze. The light coming from the ceiling brightened his eyes.

Mark had no such understanding. His thoughts flew elsewhere.

Mark had fought to end his own ignorance all his life. He should have felt grateful to Gelantyne, but he remembered how the Gelantyne Mask had marched so ruthlessly and relentlessly, its heretical Church spreading like a plague.

Of course, history would be remembered in the manner in which the victors would choose.

"Then of course there are the breeders among the *allolai* and *morbai*, turning our royalty into pets that show well, but are hardly human anymore." Gutter sank down again. "The Church of Meridua has a number of important persons who are part of a secret sect relating the teachings of Gelantyne, including Dellai Bertram. The problem is that the islands and their *allolai* guardians are not strong enough to resist should the *Trokellestrai* come for them. To make matters worse, the priests are certainly not all of one mind as to when and how various teachings should be disseminated. Perhaps some of them find the whole matter heretical. If your poisoning was in fact instructed by someone within the Church of Meridua, then we know what we've always suspected. There are those within it loyal to Cathret and Her Church. Unless ... unless you know something different about what might have happened that night."

"Wait a minute. Gelantyne implied that the *Trokellestrai* were the ones who—" He wondered if he wanted to admit it. "Gave me the scar on my hand. They're on the island?"

"Servants to the *Trokellestrai* are everywhere. On the islands, that presence is more like that of sacred guards in the living world than the Trokellestrai itself. In other places, the full span of that monstrosity exists in ways I don't understand, but I know enough that it frightens me." He took another sip from his flask. "Will you tell me what happened the night you were poisoned?"

Mark had to sit as the implications of what he'd learned knitted and unwound various imperfect theories. "My guess is that the Church offered salvation to a jester who had no other recourse. It would make more sense, based on what you've told me about Gelantyne, if that offer came from a priest loyal to the Cathretan Church. Either that, or some sect that is fighting Gelantyne's cause within the Meriduan Church considered me a threat. Maybe someone knew, or someone told them, that I was a Confidante, and that made them afraid of me." *If so, they knew before I did.* While his thoughts jumped from guess to guess, Gutter sat and listened patiently in perfect silence. "Or .... I prevented a plot that threatened Meridua's independence from the mainland. Perhaps the answer depends on whether the conspirators wanted the King, and therefore Cathret's Church, to reclaim Meridua, or whether they wanted me out of the way because I prevented the followers of Gelantyne in Saphir from solidifying their presence in Meridua. What I don't understand is whether they were the ones who sent send military men and weapons to the islands."

"Oh." The sound groaned from deep in Gutter's chest. "So you discovered that."

"Yes. And I made it hard, if not impossible for them to maintain their presence and supply lines. "

"In that case, assuming the poisoning and your unfortunate success are connected, your answer would come from our side. I helped arrange those things, but they were not placed there to help us take control of Meridua, although we would, of course, secure as much political power as we could to get what we needed. And we wouldn't have minded if our control became complete—not to rule her, Mark. Not to bring her back under mainland control. I actually prefer a free Meridua, especially a Meridua that acts in accordance to our purpose."

Mark wondered if it bothered Gutter in the slightest that his allies may have been responsible for Mark's poisoning.

He wondered which was more valuable, his voice or Meridua's resources. Sugar wouldn't have been enough to tempt Gutter to take part in such a thing. Ships, on the other hand .... "You need Meridua's ships for the coming war."

Gutter nodded. "We need ships and money and control of the trade routes. You have neutralized our best candidate for president, a person who would have helped save Cathret, preserved Meridua's freedom, and hopefully helped us bring the war to a swift end."

Kilderkin? Seriously? If so, then Juggler felt he was truly in the right. He was trying to keep Meridua free.

No. Maybe it was the mayor that they intended to shoehorn into the presidency.

Both households were involved in the plot. Kilderkin had the papers. The mayor, no doubt, had more.

And it was very likely that none of them, aside from Feather, had any idea of who Mark really was, or his importance to Gutter and the rest of the intrigue. Gutter couldn't have predicted that Mark would flee for the islands and unravel things, and Gutter would want the secret of his Confidante preserved.

Gutter broke the long silence. "Meridua's loss will cost many thousands of lives, and might cost us the war. But if your master becomes president, we have another chance. Through you."

The thought of Meridua aiding in a mainland war repulsed him. "Gutter, Meridua isn't stable enough to provide military support to unseat the royal family. The only way it would be capable of helping in a war of that magnitude would be to revert the government to a tested and true system." He spoke as if he intended to help them with the regicide, but Mark still wasn't convinced, never mind manipulating Rohn into backing a war with the mainland.

"You have little faith in your chosen nation."

Mark surged up to his feet. "I believe in her, but we aren't ready. As you've pointed out, we don't even have a president yet." A realization made him smile. "Though Meridua didn't need a president to hold the mainland back."

"She is strong, but you're right. She needs either a king or a president, and the elections may not come soon enough. Even if they do, will the president be able and willing to make the rapid decisions required? We need a president who is willing to put every life in Meridua at risk regardless of which way the decision is made."

"The colonel could, and wisely." That much Mark was sure of, though he knew Rohn would disagree with him. "He's experienced in war. He would know who to consult, and the people would believe in him."

He would do well in war. It's peace he has trouble with.

Gutter got a calculating look in his eyes. "You think I should support him?"

"I won't sell him to you in exchange for making him president," Mark warned him. He regretted his words as soon as he spoke them. He shouldn't have given away his feelings like that. It would have been better if he'd let Gutter believe Mark would help them convince Rohn to do whatever they wanted.

"If you don't win on your own, then somehow it's not valid? Doesn't the best man for political work employ all his resources to do the best for his people?" Gutter asked.

"The vote belongs to the people, not to jesters or even the nobles."

Gutter laughed. "You sound so much like one of them. I wonder what they did to you that made your fine mind so soft, dripping with weak doctrine meant to herd the ignorant and lazy into an army of zealots."

He'd already made his objection. He didn't mind telling Gutter the reason. "You taught me my principles, not them. A nobleman, and especially a president, must serve his people, not the men who have the power to make him a nation's leader. I could, as his jester, negotiate and arrange and scuttle about like a political leech but I won't because my lord and I work together for good without sacrificing another good to ensure success. I will not sell him to you or anyone else."

Gutter shrugged, as if he didn't care one way or another. "Then you have removed the man you believe is best for Meridua from any chance at the presidency, and whoever takes his place will be another's creature."

"Who's? Gelantyne's?" The idea of the mask coming to Meridua repulsed him even more than the thought that no matter what he chose, the mainland jesters would not only influence but outright choose Meridua's leader, not the people of Meridua itself. "Is Gelantyne that deeply involved in politics? Or is it you?"

"You should speak to the duke and duchess about Gelantyne's influence."

Had Mark just witnessed the slightest of missteps? It seemed to him that Gutter didn't think his own political powers were sufficient to bully Mark, as if the greatest jester of their age needed a duke and duchess to back his threats. He'd invoked them once before. That could have just been a ploy, and it seemed so at the time. A second mention seemed to suggest weakness. "That won't be necessary." Mark tightly held on to hope. If Juggler's death and the mayor's flight from Perida had truly gutted the mainland plot, and Gutter was Gelantyne's best instrument, Meridua might in fact be capable of deciding her own fate. The colonel would help the duke and duchess only if it was the right thing, not just for the mainland and Meridua, but the common men and women who comprised every nation's heart. Mark just had to keep Gutter's focus on Lark so that he'd hopefully neglect any other strings he might have tied to other Meriduan men of influence.

But if I die—

When I die ...

—I have to help Rohn. I have to write of this, and I need to choose someone there that he can go to for help. But who? Bell? Jog? Any or all of them could be tied to Gutter or to the Cathretan Church. At this point I don't know which is worse.

He knew the intricacies of this plot went deeper than he could comprehend at the moment. As it stood, even what little he knew made his head spin.

Mark wished he knew what Rohn would think of Gelantyne. He didn't trust his own feelings about it. He couldn't even define that terrible awe that had suffused him when Gelantyne inhabited Gutter.

Monstrous good. It is a monstrous, horrific Good, much as Gutter is himself.

"*If* I live ... I want to discuss this with Rohn before anything is decided," Mark told Gutter.

"I can tell that you love and trust your lord and master," Gutter ventured. "Young men—"

"Fall in love a hundred times crossing a commons." Mark returned to the door. His hearing had already improved, but his gut burned and pain sliced through it. "Stay away from Meridua. Keep them all away, and I'll sing."

"I can't promise to keep them all away. I can't even be sure I know who they all are."

"You are the greatest jester in the world. You can do anything." Mark went out and shut the door hard behind him. He stood in the hall a moment, trying to absorb all he'd seen, and said, and heard. Only one thing made him feel a small bit of hope.

He'd stood firm.

He may have very well helped Meridua after all.

Gale waited, a shivering mess of frightened dog. Mark bent down and stroked her. "Good girl. You're a very good girl. It's all right. Come along." She hurried after him as Mark walked slowly toward his room.

He had to get a message to Winsome, especially if she hadn't left the mainland, and Rohn. Most of all, his stubborn, introverted, murderous and beloved Rohn.

Chapter Twelve

Mark wrote the letters quickly, and sealed them with blank seals into which he sketched his monogram.

He needed to speak to Gzem. She and Sroh seemed the most sane of anyone in the household, and he didn't feel comfortable approaching the shy and grim Sroh.

Mark found Gzem in a simple but elegant office on the third floor, writing at a small cherrywood desk. She noticed him immediately and fanned the journal pages to help the ink dry. "Yes?"

"I need a messenger, one that knows Cathret extremely well. I need him to find a young woman, a friend of mine. I don't know where she is. I only know where she might have gone."

"Your best chance is with a sacred messenger. If it were me, I would ask Gerson Lowell. He likely knows who has the best reputation for finding someone under the sort of circumstances you describe." Her gaze settled on the letter in his hand. "If I could I would take it ... but I'm needed here."

"You were a sacred messenger?"

She laughed. "Oh there's nothing sacred about me." Her bright expression yielded to something softly sorrowful, though she kept her smile. "I have to stay here, in case Gutter needs my help so he can then not ask me for it."

Mark ventured in, Gale heeling neatly beside him. Gzem didn't seem to mind. He shut the door softly behind him. "It's none of my business—"

"Yes, it is." She got up, shut the journal, and sat against the desk's glossy surface.

"You don't even know what I'm going to ask," he pointed out.

"Why I'm here as his guest instead of at my own house in town, why those portraits of my children resemble him ...."

"I wouldn't expect you to answer such personal questions." Mainly he'd wanted to know how she and Gutter had met, and how long she'd known about Gelantyne. He knew very little of Gutter, though he'd lived under the jester's influence for nearly half his life, and he knew even less of what Gelantyne had done to Gutter over the years. Without that knowledge, how could Mark trust him?

Gzem smiled and made a soft noise in her throat. "You only consider it a presumption because Gutter never mentioned me to you, while he constantly spoke of you to me. I have no right to claim that I know you, but in many ways you're part of our strange family. In some ways I think of you as his son more than his actual children."

"Did you carry messages for him?" Mark asked. It would seem the most likely way for them to have met.

"Actually, Sroh and he were very good friends. Sroh—" A soft laugh escaped her. "He's very honorable and dutiful. Gutter loved that. In his own way Gutter is the same, though no one would believe it of him."

Mark wondered if the two men had both courted her, even fought over her. Something had come between them, because Sroh didn't seem to treat Gutter like a friend at all. "How did you meet Gutter?"

She folded her hands together and set them on her knees. "I don't seem like much, I know. But my grandmother married a very highly-placed, highly-regarded nobleman and I carry a valuable bloodline. I had many offers, but I chose Sroh—more noble of heart and mind and body than of blood. But we had no children." Her voice murmured in her throat when she paused, as if she restrained moans of pain. If she felt sorrow, though, it didn't touch her mouth or eyes.

"I'm sorry."

She smiled at his words. "At first everyone blamed it on my occupation, so I left the service." She ducked her head, still serene, but that slight noise sounded in her throat again. "But it was Sroh," she continued. "Sroh knew Gutter very well. He asked if Gutter might not know someone who could help us. Sroh feared his family might do something rash to rid themselves of me. They knew if I divorced him and had children, it would prove he wasn't fertile and destroy his chances to marry well again. I of course feared my family's jester would take Sroh away, or force me to leave him. They didn't care so much if I might be the infertile one. They just wanted to keep the family fortune and good name from being tangled with Sroh's. Gutter offered a solution neither of us expected. And here we are. And here I am." She gestured helplessly. "By the way, our youngest daughter is Sroh's." She laughed. "It's interesting that the boys especially are so unlike

Gutter and so very like Sroh in demeanor, but Sroh's daughter is so much like me."

Mark couldn't help it. He liked Gzem better than he ought to, liked and trusted her. He had to be careful. She was Gutter's friend, not his. "I find that your entire family is quite remarkable." He couldn't think of anything else to say after she'd revealed so much to a stranger.

"You may think that this doesn't involve you, but our somewhat unusual family is more loyal and devoted than it seems, and you are very much a part of it. Gutter ... he's told me everything about you, and Lord Argenwain, and his mistresses and ... everything. I'm so glad that you're here, and I'm so angry that he never told you anything about us and who we are to each other." She strode to Mark and held out her hand. He gave her the letter, which made her chuckle. She pressed it back into his hand and took his other hand in hers. "He should have told you everything, if not from the beginning, then on the way here. Since he hasn't, I will. If you are ever confused, or afraid, or have any questions at all, ask me and I'll try to answer, or I'll pry it out of Gutter myself."

She shocked a laugh from him, though it didn't have much strength to it. "Thank you."

Gzem's fine brows quirked. They smoothed after a moment and she lifted her chin. "He's told you some of it, hasn't he?"

"Most of it, I think. He had to." He couldn't bring himself to speak Gelantyne's name to her. "A mask forced him to."

Gzem's breath caught. "Is Gutter all right? Are you all right?"

"Yes, I'm fine," Mark assured her.

Gzem gazed past him at the door. "He's not angry, is he?"

"Gutter?"

"No. The sacred sacrifice."

She had to mean Gelantyne. "I don't think so."

"I'd better make certain all is well. They argue sometimes, in ways that we can't hear, and Gutter is very good at covering his pain though I've noticed that lately he's been slipping more." She squeezed Mark's hand once before she let go and hurried out.

They can thresh me like wheat, Gutter had said.

Mark needed to have his letters to Rohn and Winsome leave as soon as possible, but he didn't want to leave Gutter and Gzem and Gelantyne alone. Too much depended on their relationships, and he wanted to stay close by to witness any breaks.

He had to admit that he didn't want to face Gerson Lowell again so soon either.

Sroh? He didn't know the man.

No, that was a coward's way of dismissing the possibility. He didn't want to ask a favor of Sroh without any bond of friendship or payment or anything. Not that payment would help. If Sroh was half as noble-minded as Gzem thought him to be, he'd be offended at the suggestion of payment. Regardless, if something went wrong ... he couldn't accept the responsibility of dragging Sroh into this on Gutter and Gzem's behalf, whether they all considered Mark family or no.

Family. Gzem made it easy to believe that they were his family in a way, but he hadn't been so young when his mother was murdered—

By Gelantyne? The notion made his stomach cramp with nausea.

—to forget his true family.

Maybe Gelantyne knows what happened to my father. Maybe Gzem knows.

He didn't dare stay, much as he wanted to. Questions relating to his father's disappearance and his mother's murder would have to wait a little longer. Meridua had to take precedence. Rohn needed this information, and so did Winsome, and he couldn't be sure that he'd always be able to leave the house without interference. Now, in fact, might be his best and only chance.

Winsome. She'd gotten those letters from her father, letters relating to a plot that Gutter had pretty well admitted to being involved in. Mark had had all that time on the ship with her, but not enough information to ask her some very important questions relating to Juggler and his relationship with her father. He wanted to dismiss his next thought but it nagged him. Had she really gotten those letters from her father's house? He'd just assumed, but now it didn't seem so obvious.

It didn't change the fact that he trusted her and wanted her back in Perida, though later he might regret pressing the matter.

"Gale, heel." Mark hardly had to suggest it, she was so eager to leave her corner. She accompanied him, first to his room and then down the stairs, where Bert helped Mark don Lake's heavy blue and silver cloak. Bert went out with them and signaled a carriage for him. "Will you be back for dinner, lord jester?"

Food. His stomach cramped at the thought of it, both wanting it and dreading it. "I believe so." Mark stepped up into the carriage and made room for Gale to bound in. "Bert, where is the best sacred messenger service to be found in Saphir?"

"The Guilbarabb, lord jester. There are several excellent messenger services that make their home there."

Of course, he thought grimly. He shut the door and the driver took him back to the place he'd just left. With any luck he'd simply deliver his message into the hands of someone capable and be back in time for the next crisis.

Mark waited for an hour in the warm, small room beside one of those potentially lethal gas stoves with nothing to do but mull over what he'd learned and wonder why such a famed and well-paid service couldn't afford a better waiting room than this plain, brown-walled place with inelegant leather furniture. After writing a bit more extensively to Rohn about various fears and suspicions regarding Gutter's plans for Meridua, he lavished attention on Gale, who rolled onto her back and allowed him to rub her belly and tickle her ribs until her leg kicked the air with pleasure.

Gale warned him by rolling to her feet, her gaze hard, just before the door opened. A man in heavy leather garb bowed to him. "Lord jester, this is Karlen and Wit." Two messengers, also in heavy leathers, each carrying their sacred satchels, stepped in and bowed. "Karlen has been all over Cathret, but he hasn't yet had to find anyone who might be difficult to locate. Wit is not fluent in Cathretan and he has not spent much time there, but he is expert at tracking in large cities, wilderness and everything between. He can manage to speak in a great many other languages, though his native fluency is restricted to Hasle."

"Wit," Mark said instantly. The man was older, lean, quick of eye. Karlen looked strong and tough and determined, but Mark had a feeling Wit would serve far better to catch Winsome.

Karlen and the other left him alone with Wit. Mark handed him the letter, as well as a letter case holding his letters to Rohn. Wit tucked both into his satchel.

"Thank you," Mark told him.

Wit shrugged. "Who do you need me to find?"

"Lady Winsome Kilderkin. I last saw her in Seven Churches by the Sea. We had a room there, on Walker Main, over Gerty's Jams and Jellies. She might be looking for her father, a baron from Perida, Franc Kilderkin. He might have come here to Saphir, or not. I have no idea where he might want to go. If she didn't follow him she may have followed me here, either to use me to pursue him, or to try to help me in my cause. She's not sure about my intentions toward her father or my exact purpose. I'm not sure about her intentions toward her father, and she may not know what she'll do if she finds him either. I'm not certain how well she'd manage to track him. She's uncomfortable on the mainland. I tried to convince her to return to Perida. I hope she did. If she did, I think she would have left Seven Churches the same day I last saw her."

"What does she look like?" Wit had a complicated accent with a great many guttural tones. It wasn't the Hasle Mark had gradually grown used to. No doubt he'd come from another region than Saphir.

"She's near my height, medium brown hair with golden tones to it, like fine amber. Gray eyes. Slender, but strong rather than delicate in frame. She may be armed—she's uncomfortable traveling without steel and a pistol. I recently acquired a rifle for her, a long barrel suitable for sharp shooting. She is comfortable wearing men's clothing, military uniforms, formal wear, riding wear, and sits a horse extremely well. She fought in a war, and isn't shy about killing. She has no favored color."

"Her father?"

"Heavy, jowled, and a heavy drinker with blooded eyes and yellowed skin. His hair was once a dark brown, and is now mostly gray with some silver. He is clean-shaven but usually only in the roughest sense of the word. He has only the faintest resemblance to his daughter. He recently lost his jester—he may begin a search for a new one. He wears dull colors, no lace, minimal ruffles, and will likely need some sort of assistant to manage his basic affairs." Mark tried to think of anything else that might identify him. "He is of sour disposition, fairly easy to offend, and readily speaks his mind. He left Perida ahead of us."

"Do you know of any specific connections they may have on the mainland?"

"No." Then he remembered that Juggler may have been promised something by the Church. That was only a guess, but still .... "Perhaps the Church."

"They both have sufficient funds to travel freely?"

"Yes. Oh, and she has luggage. She may have taken it with her. Black leather, dark red wood, brass fittings, few embellishments."

"Please write as many dates of various events that you can here." Wit gave him a piece of paper and a pencil. Mark estimated as best he could in regard to the baron's arrival in Perida, along with his and Winsome's departures and arrivals. With reluctance he wrote *Dainty's* name. "We came in on this ship. Winsome may have sailed back with her. As far as I know *Dainty* did not turn around but sailed south to do trade around the bay first. She may also have stopped at some southern-more ports in Cathret and perhaps even Vyenne."

"Excellent. You have given me enough I think. With your permission?"

Mark nodded and handed him a silk pouch with seven gules worth of coin in payment along with some ar, cupru and bits to help the messenger travel without flashing too much wealth. A year ago Mark wouldn't have hoped to hold such a sum. A fisherman like Grant could have lived on it for a pair of years, or many more if he were careful and didn't mind catching dinner most nights. Now, though it had noticeably cut into what he carried in his purse, Mark could afford to spend it on a single letter. "When you reach the coast, please send the letters in the case by post to Perida. It needs no special treatment. The letter to Winsome, on the other hand—if you can't find her within two weeks of reaching Seven Churches, deliver her letter to baron Rohn Evan of Perida instead."

"You have given more than I need. I'll find her." The messenger made a strange gesture along his face. It seemed like something about his stringy hair changed from gray to brown, or maybe his eyes looked wider, then not—and he left with the casual stride of a man out and about with no important business whatsoever, a floppy, shapeless bag slung over his shoulder. Only with great effort could Mark remember what he'd looked like, and a breath later he wasn't sure anymore.

By the time Mark returned, twilight glowed, sparked by stars, and the ice and snow around Saphir took on an eerie phosphorescence not unlike the foam on waves at night back home. The air cut as sharp as winter in Seven Churches.

Bert hastened down the stairs as Mark shut the door and took his cloak. "How are you feeling, lord jester?" he asked amicably. Gale shook off the cold and padded happily around the entryway, a bit of pink tongue showing. Bert stooped to rub her head.

"I'm well, thank you," Mark lied. He felt cold and weak. "I think I'll go to the banre tonight, but first, I'd like to speak to Gutter."

"I'm sorry, lord jester. Lord Jester Gutter and Lord Argenwain left for the evening."

"May I speak with Gzem?"

"I must apologize again. The lady and her husband are also away this evening."

He knew better than to assume that they were avoiding him or just carelessly left him behind, but he still felt terribly alone and forgotten. "Please tell Petren that I'd like a small dinner, if it isn't too much trouble."

"He will be delighted. I understand he considers you a culinary challenge well worth his skills." Bert spoke the words with purest honesty, but Mark wondered how much Bert knew, and what his opinion might be of Mark and Petren's ... whatever it was they had. "What a good dog you are," Bert told Gale affectionately. "May I see to her meal as well?"

"Thank you. Actually, if you don't mind, I would appreciate it if you looked after her while I'm at the banre."

"I would be delighted." Bert grinned.

"Excellent." Mark started up the stairs.

"May I have the evening gazette delivered to your room?" Bert asked.

He hadn't had much chance to read much of anything since he'd come to Saphir. "I'd like to have a look at all of today's gazettes—that is, any you can conveniently lay your hands on."

"We take all the finest," Bert assured him. "And no one in this household is so crass as to fold them, but I will send for fresh copies if you prefer."

"I'm not that finicky," Mark told him warmly. He continued his way up the stairs, taking them slowly and steadily. His heart still raced with the effort, and he began to pant before too long. *I haven't eaten in too long. So much for ten meals a day.*

Bert followed Gale up the stairs after him. She darted past but the butler slowed to match Mark's pace. "I don't mean to be a pest," he said, "but I just remembered ... Luez, my assistant, wondered if you might not want a full-time valet. I could spare him and he's more than willing."

"That's very kind, but no thank you." He'd rather keep his privacy, and he dreaded the thought that he might have yet another person of staghorn lean trying to wile themselves into a place of greater influence or prestige or whatever Luez might be looking for. "But I will be glad of his help dressing for any other formal events that might come along. He did very well."

"He'll be pleased to hear of it," Bert told him.

"Gale," Mark called, and she hurried back down the stairs. He stroked her face. "Bert, why don't you try to take her with you now. I'll manage without her."

"Certainly, lord jester." Bert trotted down the stairs. "Gale, come here."

She pricked her ears.

"Try Cathretan," Mark reminded him.

"Oh yes." Bert cleared his throat. "Gale, come here." He patted his leg.

She trotted down and Bert rewarded her with a heavy dose of ear scratching and head rubbing, complete with a gushing litany of praises.

When Mark reached the top of the stairs she started to go after him, but Mark gestured and told her, "go on," and she returned to Bert.

In his room, Mark reduced himself to a shirt, underbreeches and a plush robe just before a small meal arrived. After a few bites and an hour of recovery, he made his way to the banre. At last he felt warm again. People stared, but they left him alone to the banre's hospitality. Half-asleep and slack with heat, he dragged himself back to his room and slept well into the morning.

Bert had apparently let Gale in sometime during the night, because she was there when he woke. Mark dressed and took her out for a short walk in the courtyard. By the time he returned, his little table by the suite's main door had accumulated a pile of gazettes. He asked the maid who brought him breakfast if Gutter might not meet him for lunch, but it seemed that Gutter and Lord Argenwain had spent the night away and hadn't yet returned. Gzem and Sroh had returned late, but had gone out again first thing in the morning.

He spent the day in strange solitude, nibbling on treats until he was on the verge of retching, reading about people in Saphir that he didn't know and events that he wouldn't have a chance to see. Finally the combination of boredom and nerves overcame him. "Bert," he said after the butler answered his bell, "I'd like to see the Masked Theater performance tonight. Will you watch Gale for me?"

"Certainly. Would you like me to arrange for an escort?"

"No thank you." He regretted saying no only because he was curious about what sort of woman, or man, Bert might have found to accompany him. "I don't mind going alone."

"I will arrange for the seat while you dress."

Mark bathed and washed his hair and made more of a fuss over his appearance than he had since he'd met the duke and duchess. He debated a while before he finally decided to wear his mask, and painted his face accordingly. The dark lines and the green on his eyelids looked unpleasantly strange until he actually put the mask on, and then it all settled into Lark.

He felt the loneliness more keenly, but he didn't take it personally. Before long he'd take the loneliest journey of all. Compared to death, this moment without friendship or even the pretense of it seemed warm and welcoming.

Bert had the ticket and a coach waiting for him. Lark bent beside the butler where Gale sat anxiously. He stroked her shaggy face. Intense love shone in her eyes, and a little fear. "Be a good girl," he told her gently. "Stay." Her front feet danced but she obeyed. It took effort not to look back at her as he walked out with the help of his cane and climbed into the coach. Weakness hampered him but he didn't lose his balance or trip up the stairs. Anymore, that was a great accomplishment.

Twilight had come again to Saphir. The sky glowed a dark, luminous blue. Guardsman, both sacred and private, lit the street lamps. Most of the well-to-do were at dinner but a few young couples walked slowly on granite sidewalks, impediments to business people rushing about their last chores. In just a few minutes the stars failed to outshine the bright array of lights that glittered everywhere. Some of the finer homes had lights cased in crystal or colored glass, or hung candle and oil lanterns to reflect in private streams or along moats. Lark couldn't travel a quarter mile without crossing yet another bridge or passing a small pond. Down one of the more modest lanes, water sparkled and shattered under blue lamps as it turned a large wheel. Glass inlay adorned the thick spokes. The mill had a grand entry with fluted columns, where workmen in clean uniforms sat and smoked who-knew-what on the stairs. Mark had always thought of mills as modest, unimportant things, but here in Saphir, it was a work of art like everything else.

At last he reached a broad lane crowded with people. The buildings were old and stained dark from smoke, smoke that rolled up from dozens of fires that grilled and baked fresh poultry, beef, pork and fish at elaborate stands set on the sidewalks. Laughter cut through arguments that boiled under a cacophony of conversation. The place hummed with a marketplace melody, but this symphony was not written for common trade. He'd arrived at the old entertainment quarter, where countless romances and adventures both historic and fictional had begun. Balconies jutted out like shells crusting old piers, often occupied by revelers or painters trying to make the most of the festival mood. Under the potent scents of rich cuisine and richer perfume, he detected over-sour sweat, old blood, rot and sewage. The wealthy men and women giggled and played among and with those who begged from, depended on and sometimes preyed upon them. He stepped out cautiously, his town sword and pistol a thin defense against all the unknowns that might be lurking in the crowd.

And he loved it. His frailty didn't make a bit of difference here. He'd become just another reveler on a fine, cold night. No one knew him well enough to pity or praise him. In an instant he'd transformed from a lonely, pathetic creature to an explorer eager to find delight or mischief, and he

Confidante

173

didn't care which came first. "Wait for me by that bridge tower over there at eleven," Lark told the driver.

"Yes, lord jester." The driver tipped his hat and carefully maneuvered his coach around, no doubt hoping to find a fare or two in the meantime.

Lark bought some sort of pastry from someone he couldn't understand at all—he wasn't sure if it was an accent or a completely different language. It didn't matter here. He nibbled it and found it had something tender, savory and spicy inside. A tall child-man with large eyes held out his hand. Lark gave him a coin and the rest of the pastry thing. Both vanished, one into the man's mouth, the other into a pocket. Shortly after, the man slipped away as well. A young woman with a brilliant collar of jewels—the famous Hemirzi collars of Saphir—smiled and moved to slide her arm around Lark's elbow but he maneuvered away toward the theater. A group of young men met another group. Two of the members at each fringe bumped and the two ended up shoving and making obscene gestures. Their friends pulled them apart and moved onward, a cruder form of theater and politics with as little importance and consequence as dogs barking at each other, but no doubt it heralded a larger conflict Lark would never know or understand.

He passed under a sign with a tall dog standing on its hind legs licking a woman's face—no doubt a brothel of a sort that would have been burned down in Cathret if it had been discovered—when several elaborate carts drawn by young men drew up in front of the theater. The diaphanous clothing and elaborate straw hats the occupants wore reminded him of the islands, but these were not islanders. The androgynous, beautiful creatures that stepped out to awed gasps, applause and appreciation could only belong to Saphir. Some wore masks, but most did not, and he noted at least one man in a gown, his hair coiffed like a woman's. He and his slightly more feminine—Mark assumed it was a woman—companion led the entourage of about twenty souls toward the theater's dark, narrow entrance. Like the rest of the crowd Lark flowed with them to catch a longer look. A jester among the beautiful entourage made a big show of taking a mask out from his vest. "I'd suggest we all play cards instead but my mask refuses to miss a single night."

One of them, a tall, elegant man with sharp azure eyes and very long, smooth black hair, paused by the door and looked right at Lark. Lark's knees softened and threatened to unhinge while his breath stopped and his belly and groin hardened. The man wore something like a priest's full-sleeved robe made of a deep blue silk, but a ruffled shirt enhanced his broad chest and covered his hands to his knuckles. He winked and Lark could breathe again. The man turned away and went inside.

I can't go in there.

A moment later Lark couldn't wait to go inside. He hurried to the entrance, trying to look as if he wasn't hurrying, and produced his ticket. The scruffy but well-dressed man taking tickets provided Lark with an escort to his seat.

The elegant, azure-eyed man was waiting for them at the stairs to the great balcony. "And you are ...?" the man prompted in a rough voice much abused by smoke and drink in a tone that suggested that Lark already knew who he had to be.

A hundred inadequate answers rushed to Lark's head, but thankfully the only rational one reached his tongue. "No one of importance." He couldn't say anything beyond that. His tongue seemed to swell to three times its natural size.

"You are a visitor to the jeweled city, I assume?" the man said.

"He is a guest at Avwan Trofal, Your Grace," Lark's escort told him.

Though Lark was grateful for the cue that he was in the presence of a duke, he was less grateful for the potential loss of his anonymity. He couldn't think of anything to say, even if he could have said anything, so he bowed.

"Perhaps you would be my guest in our private box, ambassador" the duke offered. "You are Lord Jester Lark, Ambassador of Meridua, are you not?"

"Yes, and thank you, Your Grace." Lark bowed again. The fact that the duke had some idea of what Lark was supposed to be spoke more of the duke's interest in Gutter than anything, but an irrational, giddy and lust-stupefied part of him leapt with joy at the invitation and recognition. "You're too kind."

The duke led the way to a set of thick stone stairs so ancient they were worn down in the center and rounded across the entire front edge, less so near the walls. Lark employed one of the two rails on the narrow walls and his cane to make his way up. The rail had the cold satin feel of true silver. The designs had long been worn off the tops and sides but underneath a few tarnished embellishments revealed hints of what may have been geometry following graceful, interlocking curves. Portraits, darkened and stained by time, dust and smoke from the days when candles still lit the stair, showed only the ghosts of once-famed men and women.

At the top Lark stepped onto thick, plush carpet into a chamber open toward the stage. His host stood aside and gestured to him. "Lark, may I present Her Grace Katholie, His Grace Bvon, Lwevrai Jasoso—"

"Soso!" giggled one of the women, and Soso inclined his curly-haired head.

"Lord Jester Rurin ...." The duke continued his merciless litany of names. Lark employed several memory tricks to keep them all properly organized in his mind. The exercise helped ease the unbearable attraction he felt toward the duke. "Everyone, this is, I believe, Lord Jester Lark, Ambassador of Meridua." Lark bowed in acknowledgement.

"I'll wager ten sol His Grace hasn't introduced himself," Soso said.

"That's not a wager, that's theft," Lord Jester Rurin chuckled. At least, that's what Lark gathered he'd said. He had a heavy accent and though Lark's grasp of Hasle had improved, it still confounded him more than he wanted it to. It didn't help that the others in the group chatted away, some of them loudly affecting boredom or excitement in a boisterous, almost crass dance of social play where they tried to amuse and win each other over. It was hard to make out anything through the loud chitter.

"Have you ever been to the Masked Theater?" Katholie asked.

"No, Your Grace," Lark answered with a bow.

"You must sit beside Foll—His Grace Folluai Tro—so he can catch you up," she said. He wasn't familiar with the phrase catch you up, and wondered if she hadn't spoken in innuendo. His cheeks and ears burned as if she had. Thankfully his mask covered them.

"Wine?" Foll offered as the servants waiting by began to set up two chairs and a small table slightly apart from the others.

"No, thank you."

"And nothing to eat," the duke said gently.

"No." Lark's blush cooled in the wake of the duke's pity. Once again he was the frail, pathetic thing he'd briefly escaped when he'd left the coach.

"So it's true what they whisper at the Erothis Banre." The duke let out a discontented sigh. "I apologize for listening to gossip, but I prefer to exercise my hearing rather than stoppering it up, and people do love to gossip regardless of who might be listening. Especially Saphiran nobles," he added wryly. "If you like, I will start a little counterword of your design. I wouldn't want you to feel misrepresented, or worse, mistreated."

"There's no need to trouble yourself," Lark assured him.

"It would be my pleasure. I consider Her Ladyship Gzem a good friend, and she is both fond and protective of her adopted family. Which is a shame, really. I would have loved to have taken you out for a turn or two. Instead, I will happily serve as your rumormonger."

Blood rushed to Lark's face and ears. His Grace winked and turned his attention to the stage and a glass of wine expertly and unobtrusively poured by a servant. "Let me test the limits of your memory, lord jester, if I may, with a summary of the theater's recent events. On Amendsday's performance, Tuilder—that's Wellen's and Kollen's father—decided to take Amalise as his wife. But he publicly engages himself to Helaini instead, and she doesn't realize it's a ruse. Amalise hates the intrigue, but she understands that her life is already in sufficient danger from the boys, who fear she may convince Tuilder to have children with her and therefore threaten their rights of succession. On Freeday Amalise realized she's with child and she didn't dare tell anyone except Camber, her servant ...." The duke quickly outlined the royal and servile dramas, finishing just as the curtain began to open.

The theater began with no preamble beyond the opening of curtains. Each set was small and aligned across the stage, with only the active set lit. Some had stairs leading to a second level of sets, all currently dark.

A light focused on a small set near stage left. The mask ... Lark couldn't even call it a mask. The costume dominated whatever actor might exist beneath it, wringing her hands, completely and believably presenting feminine terror to the point that Lark wanted to rush onto the stage and protect her. The room's confines lent a claustrophobic air to her moment alone while suggesting a wider world with shadowed activity beyond her private drama. She didn't speak. Suddenly another set was lit, where two servants began gossiping about her. Then an old man-mask came in the room with the woman. It had to be Tuilder and Amalise. Tuilder tried to pry out of her what might be wrong and she kept insisting that it was his false engagement, but he knew better. The masks timed their dialogue perfectly so that Lark was just able to track both conversations at once.

These masks had known each other for centuries. And the drama they played out was an ancient dance where they knew each other too well, but not well enough to avert the next conflict, a conflict that arose naturally through their own desires and needs. If anything, knowing each other so well amplified their hurt and raised their suspicions. Lark had heard of two incidents within the last forty years where a mask had murdered another, and of course the actor wearing the mask also died. As the drama unfolded, Lark dreaded that it would come to murder again right before his eyes. Now that he understood how the Masked Theater worked, he was surprised that more actors didn't come to mortal harm in them.

When the duke touched Lark's knee, Lark nearly jumped out of his chair. He drew his gaze away from the drama and looked into the duke's azure eyes.

"Are you following the story?" the duke whispered.

Lark nodded.

"I hope you're enjoying it."

Lark nodded again, though the stage and everyone in the box with them seemed far less important than the miracle of the duke's voice and touch and gaze.

The duke leaned forward across the table and Lark bent to meet him in a shy kiss that sent shudders of need up and down his spine.

"Good," the duke whispered, and Lark wasn't sure if the duke meant the kiss or his enjoyment of the theater. "It isn't too tawdry for you?"

"Have you reconsidered your decision?" Lark asked him breathlessly.

"About?"

Lust made him bolder than he should have dared to be. "Taking me out for a turn or two."

The duke's gaze slid to the others, and Lark thought he understood. Maybe the duke considered Gzem's feelings, or perhaps he wondered what a short affair with Mark might do to his standing among the others. They could approve, or not, and their approval meant everything because they were Saphir's darlings. They enjoyed not only the considerable advantages of rank, but public favoritism. They likely had a colorful name, like the Ermine Club, whose famous rise and implosion nearly ruined Vyenne two centuries ago with a political war that nearly erupted into a very real and actual civil war. Perhaps this club did not play with such high stakes, but Lark couldn't afford even what they would consider low wagers in their political games.

"It's just as well," Lark told him, easing away. His lust protested but the comparison to the Ermine Club boxed it in enough that he could control it. "I'm far too fragile for Your Grace."

They turned their attention back to the Masked Theater. Lark basked in the weight and warmth between them, and wished he had the courage, freedom, time, and the stupidity to play in Saphir with men like the duke.

The duke accompanied Lark home under the pretense of employing Lark's coach, due to the chill in the air, rather than his favored cart. They groped and fondled and licked and kissed each other to the verge of madness.

Lark opened the duke's robes but the duke artfully pinned Lark's hands over his head.

"Let me go," Mark gasped between kisses.

The duke complied, but captured him again when Lark dragged his hands down his chest and belly. Lark all but stood up to pin him instead. The whole carriage rocked violently when the duke neatly reversed and rolled them with Lark landing on the seat by the door, the duke looming over him.

"Don't you want me?" Lark breathed.

The duke kissed him sweetly on the forehead. "More than I want my heart to beat."

"Then why?" The words whispered out and he wished he didn't sound so very like a beggar.

"I mustn't spill my seed with you. If I weren't noble ... but I am, and I mustn't. It's not just for my own soul's sake, but my jester's. I thought you understood."

"So this is as far as you've ever gone with a man."

The duke let him go and sat back. "I wish I weren't noble born. And the worst of it is, I'm not entirely sure that the beliefs of my church—" He nearly cut off the word church, as if doubting it might be a sin as well. "I can't take the chance. I can't risk it."

"I'm sorry. I didn't know." He wouldn't have tortured the duke if he'd known, and it had been torture, especially now, being so close and unable to have that simple freedom with each other that Lark had come to take for granted in a very short time.

"Don't be sorry. I'll enjoy the memory of us a hundred times over."

"I thought things were different in Saphir."

"There are many beliefs. Some kill for them, some die for them, some live for them, and some suffer. Most do a little of each over the course of their lives. I say I wish I weren't noble, but I have been honored with that birthright and I must respect that."

The coach stopped. It took Lark a moment to realize they'd arrived. "Good night, Your Grace."

"Good night, Lark."

Lark stepped out. "Please take His Grace home as discreetly as possible." Lark paid the driver a large tip, hoping it would quell gossip.

"Thank you, lord jester."

Gale was waiting for him at the front door, huffing with excitement. Lark told her what a good girl she'd been and rubbed her all over.

Bert drooped with weariness, though he stood up straight and tried to hide it with a smile. "Welcome home, lord jester. I hope you had a pleasant evening."

Light-headedness threatened to pull him off his feet, even with the cane's support. "I did, thank you." He thought he'd explode with lust. He hoped Petren wouldn't mind a visitor in his kitchen. "May I borrow your elbow, Bert?"

"Certainly, lord jester."

"Has Gutter come home?" A petty, vindictive part of him had hoped that Gutter had been waiting up for him.

"No, lord jester, Lord Jester Gutter and Lord Argenwain are still out visiting friends."

It seems I'm still the one who gets to wait at home, worrying. Nothing has changed between us. Nothing at all.

He made it safely to his room, and fortunately decided to eat a bit of bread before he removed the mask. As it was, the moment the lamp's light touched his cheeks his vision spotted red and black and the back of his head and neck buzzed. He barely made it to the bed before he collapsed. His head cleared once he'd stretched out on his back, but his heart pounded wildly, and not from fear. It labored as if it barely managed to limp from one heartbeat to the next.

For a long, unpleasant hour Mark thought he'd reached the end of his life, but eventually his heart calmed. As sleep took him, he wondered if he'd wake again.

Chapter Thirteen

The servant that had brought Mark breakfast knocked on the door again just as Mark started to wobble his way toward his dressing room. "Yes?"

"Doctor Ulaleh is here to see you."

"Thank you. Will you come in and help me dress?"

With help he managed to make himself slightly less unkempt than a sailor who'd been out in the wind all day.

Doctor Ulaleh stood up from a bench by the front door when Mark started down the last flight of stairs, supported in part by the servant. "Lord jester, we have an answer," the doctor said.

Mark's breath caught in his throat. "You have a return letter already?"

"The express is reliably quick, though quite expensive. It would have been here sooner—I've had it make a round trip in four days—but it seems my colleague delayed a bit before he answered. For good reason." The doctor drew the letter from his waistcoat pocket. "It's simple, but I don't imagine it will be pleasant."

"What?" The hope that lifted his chest and his gaze made a lie of his resistance to say the word cure.

The doctor joined him where he'd stopped on the stairs. "It's a concoction usually administered to pigs if they're found alive after they've eaten something contaminated by the poison. You've been suffering with the damage for some time, and it has never been tried on a person."

"What is it?"

"Various substances crushed to powder, wetted to make it easier to swallow, drunk down with water. Although the milk eases your pain, he suggests that you stop drinking it. No more soft bread, only rough grains that may be boiled or baked. Nuts rubbed into a paste to use for fat in place of butter. Chicken, finely ground, white fish of fine texture, no other meat. There's more. I'll give the instructions to the cook. You swallow the paste, wait for it to numb the throat and stomach, then eat. If you respond the same way as the pigs, the powders will make you drowsy. Sleep after every meal should help improve your weight more quickly and aid in the healing. Assuming it works."

He wondered if he'd be in a drugged stupor as he'd been when he'd been forced to use gracian. He couldn't afford to be sleepy or addled, not now.

But a cure .... While part of him wanted to dance and laugh to the slim verge of sanity, he feared that if he let go of his doubts and gripped hope with both hands, he'd be left holding on to nothing at all.

It took him a moment to balance his hopes and fears well enough to ask a rational question. "How long will I have to take it?"

"It's hard to say. A few days at least, but it could take much, much longer. Perhaps months, even years."

"It doesn't have any enslaving drugs in it, does it?"

"Not at all, though it's hard to say what such a diversity of ingredients will do when mixed together. It's quite an amalgamation, and I'm sure half of the ingredients have nothing to do with the cure. Of course no one knows which half are the useless ones." He shifted uneasily. "There is a possibility that you'll have an adverse reaction. Individually, all the ingredients are fairly benign to humans, but in combination—they may make you quite ill. The doctor tested a dose on himself prior to sending the letter. He reported the numbing effect and said otherwise he felt fine. I find that encouraging, but I've seen people die of eating strawberries, so ...."

"I understand." Mark appreciated the doctor's caution, though he doubted that the man, or anyone, appreciated what it was like to live daily with the poison's effects. It might make him 'quite ill'? Mark was already quite ill.

"If you're willing, I'll mix up a batch immediately. It will take me until tomorrow to find some of the more unusual ingredients in a state sufficiently fit for human consumption."

"Please."

The doctor nodded and left in a hurry.

Mark had just turned to go back upstairs when a knock sounded on the door. He resisted the impulse to answer it and left it to Bert, who appeared shortly. "Lord Argenwain, Lord Jester Gutter," Bert said expansively. "Welcome home, my lords."

"Lark." It sounded stranger than usual to hear his jester's name coming from Gutter. "The doctor said there was news but he didn't stop to elaborate. Good news, I hope?"

He still felt more shaky than excited. "I'm not sure."

Gutter took the stairs two at a time to catch up. Despite his age, weight and heavy bones, he was as quick as Mark had been, and stronger than he could ever hope to be. "Is there a cure?"

Mark paused to catch his breath. He didn't want to say, though he couldn't explain to himself much less to anyone else why. "Perhaps."

Gutter hugged him hard. "I knew it," he said fiercely.

Mark pressed him away. "I'm tired. I need to rest."

"Is something the matter?"

What wasn't the matter? "Where have you been?"

"Out and about. It's expected. Didn't you get my letters?" When Mark paused in reaction, Gutter paled. "My letters were intercepted," he murmured. "That's ... not possible."

It seemed like such an irrelevant reaction compared to wondering who got them and why they didn't simply send them on so that no one would know.

"They wanted to isolate me," Mark realized aloud. "So that I'd go looking for you."

"Did you?" Gutter asked. A little color had returned to his face but his eyes had a flat, haunted look to them.

"No. I—I went to the Masked Theater."

"Were you followed? Watched? Did you meet anyone?"

"I met Her Grace Katholie and her coterie." He didn't want to confess it, but it might prove to be important later. "Duke Foll paid particular attention to me."

Gutter let out a short laugh and muttered something like *ellisen*. Irises? "Well. That may have saved you."

"Saved me from what?"

"Use your imagination, boy!"

"No, I won't." The hard declaration startled Gutter, giving Mark a chance to continue. "There's only one conspiracy that concerns me. All these little intrigues and running about, making nice with the usual people so that nothing looks out of place, worrying about assassins and public opinion and who thinks what of me—it's meaningless." Gzem descended slowly from the next flight of stairs above him and stopped on the bottom step to listen. "It's useless distraction."

"Those details can undo us," Gutter growled under his breath.

"In one sense, yes." Lord Argenwain said as he started his own way up the stairs, carefully measuring his pace to his increasingly labored breath. "But for practical purposes, perhaps the boy is correct. Will it really be necessary to waste thought and effort on determining who intercepted your letters, especially with the news we've received today?"

"What news?" Mark asked.

"His Royal Majesty is within an eagle's sight of Saphir. He'll be here very soon." Gutter seemed to settle inside his own skin. "We've managed to gather what I think will be enough strength. All we have to do is to survive until the performance. Which means no more Masked Theater and whatever else you did with Foll until—" It was the barest of pauses but to Mark it seemed to stretch the length of a rapier's thrust through his heart. "—after the performance."

"After," Lord Argenwain murmured. "I wonder what Their Royal Majesties Saphir will do." The last word trembled. "I wonder what will be left for them to deal with, if anything."

"I'm more worried about what you'll do to me. What you'd better do." Gutter stabbed a finger toward his lord. "I mean it, Merrin."

"You are not the master." Lord Argenwain gave him a hard look.

Gzem's breath caught. When Mark glanced at her she looked away from all of them and ran up the stairs. Would Lord Argenwain have Gutter beheaded? He'd almost have to, Mark realized. At least he'd have to order it. Gutter might escape, become a fugitive ... and where would Gelantyne end up?

Not in my hands. They can't mean to give Gelantyne to me. It wasn't just his fear speaking to him. Gelantyne would need a stronger, more clever partner in his schemes, and Gutter had more strength and wit than anyone.

That assumed Gelantyne allowed Gutter to be caught after the performance. The mask would have its own plans.

Gutter and Gelantyne might leave to do as much damage to the royal line as possible, leaving the wake of their destruction to wash over Lord Argenwain, Gzem, Sroh, Mark ... everyone.

The king, the royal line ... Cathret would fall into chaos.

What will all this mean to Meridua? Aren't I supposed to be looking after her interests?

It was too much to consider and his head was still light and buzzing. "I'm tired," Mark told them.

"Let me help you." Gutter took his arm.

Mark shrugged him off. "Help your lord. I'll be fine."

Gutter's eyes seemed to darken even more behind his mask. "Don't leave the house again. It's not safe."

"Where would I go?" Mark turned the landing and started up the next flight of stairs.

"Where wouldn't you go, if you had leave to explore Saphir? I wish I could let you go, but I can't. Not when there might be someone waiting for another chance."

Like the woman with the Hemirzi collar. She could have been angling him for a dagger between the ribs.

Gutter went to help Lord Argenwain, and they began chatting about their visits as if nothing untoward had happened.

I chose this life, he reminded himself. He thought about Magpie, and wished he'd been that brave and had become a sailor. He would have had to run forever but he wouldn't have been poisoned, or caught up in all this—

But I'm not Magpie. It wouldn't have just been the Church, or Gutter, or Lord Argenwain after him, though all three were formidable enough. It would have been Gelantyne.

He hadn't realized it, but he wouldn't have gotten far even if he had decided to run. If anything, bonding himself to Rohn had given him choices about his future when he'd had none, and that bond might yet save his soul.

Rohn might yet save Meridua from all these mainland schemes as well.

"Bless my master," he whispered under his breath. He'd never spoken the words before. Though strange and old-fashioned, they felt true and gave him courage.

Bless Rohn Evan, and blessings upon you, a foreign voice whispered in his mind.

"Who are you?" Mark whispered, hoping no one would overhear him.

The voice didn't answer.

Mark slept until dinnertime, and woke weaker than he had been when he went to bed. He forced himself to clean up and wash his hair, and dressed nicely for dinner. He had to use his cane to get there. Everyone was formal and pleasant, but Gutter kept looking at him with too much concern, Lord Argenwain drank too much, and Gzem looked like she wanted to talk, but couldn't. Sroh didn't speak a word all night. Afterward Mark huddled in misery under a blanket in a soft chair in the library with hot water instead of brandy. His heart had started to labor again and he didn't want to go to bed, though he could hardly keep his eyes open. At least Gale seemed content. She sighed on occasion, keeping his feet warmed but pinned as always so that he couldn't get up without disturbing her.

"You look tired, lord jester," Bert noted, emerging from his little corner where he stood when he wanted to be inconspicuous. It seemed he'd decided that no one but he himself could see to Mark's needs. "Would you like to go to the banre for a massage, or perhaps have a nice soak in a medicinal bath before bed?"

"I should take Gale for a walk instead, but thank—"

"Please, lord jester, let me see to her, if you think she'll allow it."

Bert looked so eager Mark had to smile. "All right."

"And may I brush her for you, lord jester?"

"Please. It's been too long. I'm afraid I've been neglecting her grooming lately."

"Perhaps trim her bangs a bit?"

She was getting so big. He would have sworn she'd gained more weight and height just since they'd arrived in Saphir. "If it brings you pleasure, Bert, you may pamper her until your arms fall off."

"Very good, lord jester." Looking pleased with himself, Bert called to her. "Come here, Gale. Good girl. Come here to Bertie."

Gale looked a little uncertain, so Mark gestured for her to go. "Go on. It's all right."

She followed Bert toward the stairs with only one more glance back. Mark made sure to gesture for her to go before he went out himself and started up the stairs toward the third floor and his quiet little rooms.

Several steps up he began to smell something like incense and milk in the air. The scent grew hot, then sparked in his senses like a fresh fire catching on dry paper. His heart skipped and everything began to go dark about the time he reached desperately for the rail.

He could barely choke in one breath after another. Something like fish, but more simple and ribbon-like with no eyes or fins, lit the darkness with luminous color. Hundreds of them brightened and flowed among each other in patterns, behaving more like a single living thing than separate creatures. They suddenly rushed around him. The larger ones darted out of the flow and bit into him. With a sharp twist they tore bits of him off and rejoined the swarm. Mark tried to scream but he couldn't breathe—

I'm being torn apart. My soul—

The beings who'd followed him since they'd left Seven Churches and several others rushed out of the darkness toward him. Their strange bodies, or perhaps they were clothes, fanned open and grew edges. The beings attacked the fish things but there were so many and the swarm kept grazing Mark's immobile body.

This is not my body. It's my soul. I have to escape—

No, I have to not be this shape, as they change shape—

The next time a fish latched on he imagined drawing that part of him out of his mouth and the pain vanished. The success opened his mind with revelation. He might have been able to flow like a stream of water away, but instead he mimicked his guardians and imagined himself feathered with edges and armor. He spun and the fish retreated. A few writhed with bloodless wounds. The swarm returned, devouring its own wounded—

He focused on the memory of an aria with hard-edged flurries of harpsichord and guitar. When nothing happened he opened a throat he summoned into being and pushed.

Light exploded in vivid gold and silver and pale green, laced with other colors that savaged the darkness. The fish creatures fled and balled up into orbs that whirled and spun away to escape into the darkness. His guardians warded the light with fan-shaped, bladed hands.

Mark stopped pushing the light-noise and they lowered their hands again. The colors from his voice expanded out in ribbons and waves off into the distance, gradually fading like the wake from a ship vanishing into the waves.

The two guardians advanced.

If they even are guardians. Did I anger them? He had nowhere to go to escape from them, and he didn't want to attack them again, in case they were allies. Besides, the light had only made them flinch. It didn't seem to damage them.

Mark imagined his eyes opening on the stairway in Gutter's house—

For a disorienting and terrifying moment he saw Bert and Petren carrying his twitching body up the stairs. Darkness flashed into his mind with a hard snap like being struck with the flat of a rapier.

His eyes opened again, this time safely back in his body. He groped for purchase on Petren's apron.

"He's breathing!" Petren cried.

"Here, set him here," Bert gasped. They lowered him onto the landing. Somewhere below Mark heard Gale snarling and clawing behind a door. He smelled blood. It dripped on his face from Bert's wrist.

"You're hurt." At least, Mark tried to say it but it came out muddled.

"Send for a doctor. I'll stay with him," Petren said.

Mark still felt the echoes of the fish-things tearing away pieces of him and the shock his mind took when he saw his own body. Petren cradled him. Mark wanted to retreat to his room and write, and consider, and shout what he'd just experienced. He'd seized control of ... what? His soul? His mind? The power that made him a Confidante? He couldn't even say if they were separate and different.

"Stop fighting," Petren urged. "Just rest. The doctor will be here soon."

"Gutter," he wanted to say, but his breath and mouth didn't cooperate. Petren was right. He had to rest first. He couldn't even tell anyone that fetching the doctor was a waste of time. There was nothing he, or anyone, could do.

He needed that cure to work. Only, now he wondered what he might be able to do and discover if he could only have more time during his seizures to learn to control his consciousness. It would do him nothing but good to explore and learn to defend himself in that strange landscape before death irretrievably forced him there.

And if he could pass that knowledge on, he could help countless others as they prepared themselves for their inevitable deaths ....

Like sacred poets accept the madness, would I accept dying that much faster in exchange for knowledge that could help others for generations to come?

Though he still couldn't think of another world war without recoiling in horror and terror, he could understand a little better why some would be willing to sacrifice so much to have their minds and world opened to their darkness-starved sight. If he and others like him could share what they'd learned of the hells or whatever places he went during his seizures ....

If we could learn how and why we go there, and what makes a soul worthy while another is destroyed—why did those fish things attack me? Why did those other beings try to defend me?

Gzem hurried down from the upper story. "Did he fall?"

"Not far, my lady," Petren told her.

"These damned stairs are so treacherous." She crouched beside Mark. "Let's get him somewhere more private."

Petren hesitated. "I don't know that it's wise to move him, my lady."

"Lark." She took his hand. "If it's all right to move you to your room, squeeze my hand."

Mark managed to do that much.

"There. See?" Gzem helped lift him. "Is that Gale growling?"

"She wouldn't let us near him. Bert had to drag her into a closet. She bit him." They took Mark off the stairs, through the common room and down the necessary halls to his room.

"The doctor had better have a look at Bert too." Gzem rang for more help after they settled Mark on his side on a rug.

None of the embarrassment and helplessness mattered this time. He wanted to plan what to do the next time a seizure came.

If it came. When it came.

He had a terrible feeling that the next time would be his last.

Mark woke in the dark in his guest room well before morning, hungry but in too much pain to want to eat. A single lamp, the wick set low, lit Sroh's slumped form where he'd fallen asleep in a chair. Despite his terrible weakness the day before and his seizure and the fall, Mark felt better, if a bit bruised. Mark slipped on some clothing, wrote a note, and left it by the lamp, all without waking the man, though Sroh stirred once when the desk drawer whispered open. Gale emerged from beneath the bed and followed him out in perfect silence.

The ovens, even burned down to nothing, still warmed the kitchen to a comfortable temperature. Mark relished a few bits of bread and washed it down with warm water. The familiar cramps made him grit his teeth. A few moments later his mood lifted as the nourishment buoyed his strength. The pleasure of it won through the agony in his belly and made him feel a little drunk.

He wondered if anyone had gotten around to feeding Gale. He took a piece of bread with him and went to the back stairs, this time taking the oil lamp outside the door and lighting his way down the stairs into unexplored territory. They had to have a cellar somewhere down this way.

The dry pantry proved to be behind the first door. The large room was packed tight with enough flour, sugar, soda, pounded grains and other supplies to feed the entire neighborhood all winter. He probably ought to have gone down the hall, but the next set of stairs down beckoned him.

Shivering in the dry cold, he found a root cellar and the room where they hung smoked meats, and a cheese room. He carved some ham for Gale, and gave her a bit of cheese as well. The rich scents drove him mad with hunger. He nibbled a bit of each himself, not enough to hurt him but enough to work the flavors around inside his mouth.

The hall traveled farther than he would have expected. He looked in each door, holding the lamp just inside each one to have a peek. One had stacks of old floorboards, furniture, and apple crates with decent apples and pears in them. Another had what amounted to an apothecary shop's worth of medicinal salves, salts, powders, hanging herbs and clean rags. Considering how many rags and cloths Petren went through in a day, they probably needed yet another room of rags just to keep him in supply for huge occasions like Yule.

The next and last two doors, paired across from each other, were locked. The iron facing, ice cold to the touch, made him shudder from more than cold. One had a sliding window at its center and a locked pass door at its base. He unlatched the window and looked inside.

It could be nothing other than a cell. That stark realization distracted him from his painful belly and made his mouth and throat too dry to swallow. He couldn't see anyone in there, though it smelled as if long ago—who knew how long ago—it had held someone wrapped in misery, fear and pain. The sweat and filth scents of a terrified human being had permeated the dust and old, dry wood.

Gale, who had been more quiet than usual, sat in perfect, solemn silence, watching Mark as if she wanted him to give her some command that would make him feel safe again. He slid the window shut—his fingers had left dark, clean places on the iron. He took out a handkerchief and cleaned the top surface off fairly poorly, then returned to the dry goods storage, uncertain if the extra trouble was necessary. His pounding heart pressed him to continue. He managed to find some dirty flour in a waste bin by the door in the otherwise spotless room. He took it with him and blew it onto the window, shielding the door itself with his handkerchief, matching the thickness of the dust as best he could with what sat on the pass door below. It didn't match the color perfectly, but it was close enough he hoped that anyone passing by would likely not notice. Not that anyone ought to.

Except ...

He explored the end of the hallway. Saphir had been a center of intrigue and war for over two thousand years. He couldn't discount the possibility that the house had at least one secret room or hidden passage down here. He started to press in various places where the mortar seemed absent, but nothing moved.

This hall is too dry.

He was far underground in a city woven through with rivers. The only way to keep it dry ...

There's another level below this one.

The passage down would probably be in a locked room. He went to the door without the window in it and considered using his somewhat primitive skills at lock-picking.

I might ruin the lock, or worse, spring a trap, or ring a bell somewhere.

If he trusted Gutter even by half he'd ask him about it. Gzem, though he hardly knew her, seemed like a better bet.

They're lovers, or were.

He couldn't chance asking about it, not without knowing if it would lead to anything useful. He had to let his curiosity burn unsated, at least for now.

Mark explored the next hall up just in case, as an entrance from the lowest hall would be the most obvious one if someone like him went looking for a secret passage. The architects might have created a double-level stair somewhere higher up to foil spies.

His search led him to a fencing practice room.

It's been too long.

"Gale, sit. Stay." Mark uncovered the dummies and selected a light foil with its tip bent double. He added a leather practice tip over it to limit the damage he'd inflict on the targets.

It only took a few minutes of practice before he felt winded and light-headed. His frustration flashed his temper to life and he pressed on. Gale watched, panting, her half-hidden eyes wide with anxiety. He didn't have the breath or strength to reassure her. He staggered with exhaustion, pushing, fighting, willing his endurance to be anything but what it had become—skeletal and frail.

When he could hardly keep his feet any longer he braced himself into an upright stance and practiced precision work. When he felt rested he worked in the round again. It felt good, if nearly losing what little he'd eaten and staggering around like a wounded drunk could be called good by anyone but himself.

I can still fight if I have to.

When he could barely move more than a step he sat on an old, leather-seated chair and rested his weary arms on his trembling legs. It felt as if he'd been trapped in his own mind, and that the physical exertion had finally freed him. "Gale."

She trotted over and he rubbed her head, massaging the loose skin over hard bone and muscle. She'd bitten Bert. He didn't like it, but he couldn't punish her, not that she'd understand even if he did. He couldn't deter her from protecting him when that was her primary duty and purpose. Still, Bert hadn't meant him any harm.

She'd had this problem before. What if he needed help and she impeded it? He needed someone that she trusted to help train her ....

She trusted Winsome.

Winsome is confused enough about me, and I'm doubly confused about her. Besides, she isn't here.

He might never see her again, and if he did see her here, it wouldn't exactly be a joyful reunion. His doubts about her would rub against her unhappy knowledge of his bend ....

He wished he'd taken her with him.

Mark braced up and put away all the equipment. He'd just left when a servant came hurrying down the hall. "Lord jester, the whole household has been up and about looking for you."

The note he'd left had said he'd be in the kitchen. "I'm so sorry—"

"Not at all!" The servant looked horrified at the apology. "If it pleases you, lord jester, Lord Jester Gutter is anxious to see you."

"Thank you. I should wash up first."

"I believe they expected you to be bedbound, lord jester," the servant told him, leading the way up the many flights of stairs. "To be honest, we all did. If it isn't too much trouble I hope you will consider seeing Lord Jester Gutter first and foremost."

They expected him to be bedbound—where Mark could be easily watched and managed. He wondered if they preferred him to be bedbound.

Mark had to rest at the top of each flight. He didn't let himself linger long. He'd be even more bruised and sore tomorrow, but he didn't care. "Why don't you go on ahead and order some hot water for my room," Mark told him. "I can find my own way, thank you."

"Yes, lord jester." The servant took the stairs two at a time in his haste.

I used to be able to do that.

He didn't envy it so much as marvel. He could barely remember being strong any more. People with their health intact might as well have been another species capable of flight, while he, like a turtle out of water, remained awkwardly earth-bound.

Somehow he managed to make it all the way to his room. Gzem, Sroh and a cluster of servants strode down the hall toward him, Gutter at their lead.

"Where have you been?" Gutter demanded.

"Fencing practice." Gale moved just ahead of him, her head held high as if preparing to savage them all if they dared try to harm him. "If you

don't mind I'll clean up and then you can all come in and sit if you like."
Mark didn't want to offer that, but he felt compelled to, seeing how they'd
all been woken at a reluctant hour. "Gale, heel," he added softly, and she
returned to his side.

Gutter calmed. "You're feeling better?"

I hate this. "I'm seldom noticeably worse. If I got noticeably worse each
time I'd be dead by now." Judging by their uncomfortable expressions he
realized he shouldn't have been so blunt. "Please. As far as I can tell I'm
not in any danger. If you'd rather all go back to bed, seeing as it's still dark
outside, we can meet at a more sociable time."

Gutter narrowed the distance between them. "Don't you ever do that
again. We thought you'd been taken."

He set a hand on Gale's head to keep her steady, just in case. "By
whom?" Gale trembled under his hand.

Gzem took Sroh's arm. Her large, quiet husband looked ashamed,
probably because he felt responsible for allowing Mark to slip away.

I'll have to fix that later.

Gutter only shook his head in answer. "I just received word that His
Royal Majesty has arrived in Saphir. We cannot have him in the house,
so we must leave to meet him immediately. We must all be delighted and
honored and beside ourselves with joy, if you think you can manage it. It
would be best if you wore your mask for this."

Their anxiety wormed into him. "I'll bathe and get dressed."

Gzem tugged Sroh back toward their rooms. The servants dispersed.

A maid let herself in the back way into his room with her cart of hot
water. Mark shut the door on Gutter and the rest of the world. "How is
Bert?" he asked the maid.

"He is well, lord jester. Thank you very much for asking."

I have to fix that later too.

He had to admit he didn't know how, or if he even ought to try. His dog
had injured Bert. Bert had loved Gale. Now he'd likely be afraid of her.
The maid seemed cautious too, though Gale ignored her and sat by the
door where she could watch Mark's every movement.

Gutter would likely chastise him for allowing himself to be distracted
by unimportant details like injured and fearful servants, but those details
happened to be human beings, and they'd all been very kind to Mark so
far, more kind than he would have expected. He'd been a servant before,
and he remembered too well how easy it was to resent a demanding and
potentially dangerous stranger in the house.

A man screamed and Mark heard something like a shout, but cut off in a way that sent a shock through him. Memories of the massacre at Hevether Hall knocked him hard into that cold place where he could hunt men without hesitation. He grabbed up his pistol and rapier and opened the door as if he had the leisure to stalk his quarry, though his heart pounded in his throat and roaring rushed in his ears. He didn't move slowly, just smoothly and quietly and with a calm, cold desire to destroy anything that might harm anyone in the household. A glance out into the hall revealed no one. A servant babbled somewhere near the base of the main stairway, crying for help between gulping sobs. Mark made it to the top of the stairs and what he saw crushed his chest so hard he couldn't breathe.

He set down his weapons in a fluid motion and flew down the stairs. "I'll stay with him," he told the servant, taking Lord Argenwain's weight against his knees so the old lord wouldn't slide any farther down the stairs. "Send for the doctor, then fetch Gutter. Go!" Mark cradled Lord Argenwain's head. It hung heavy from his thick neck like Norbert's had when he and Rohn had moved his body out from the kitchen where he'd been killed. Lord Argenwain's hips lay at an unpleasant angle askew to his torso, and the sharp bend to his thigh marked where his leg had broken. The scent of piss wafted through the old lord's favorite musky perfume.

Gale frantically licked the old man's face. "Gale, go lay down!" He gestured sharply to the top of the stairs, where hopefully she'd stay out of the way. She retreated only a few stairs and settled, her mouth opening wide into a stressed pant.

Mark felt for a pulse, remembering too well how he'd left Trudy for dead. She'd survived somehow, though he'd left her to bleed in her room.

I was such an idiot.

Lord Argenwain still had a heartbeat.

It had been so easy to loathe him, and to pretend kindness at the old man's appearance but deep down secretly sneer at his fishy jowls and his elderly scent and his dry, brittle skin and dry brittle hair ... but all Mark could think about now was reading to him aloud, night after night, while Lord Argenwain listened with closed eyes, his face smoothed by peace. Mark remembered the old lord and Gutter sharing brandy with him while they recounted the hilarity of their youthful adventures all over the wide world, and riding lessons while Lord Argenwain sat his horse as if he'd been born astride, and most striking of all how Lord Argenwain pulled Gutter back not so long ago.

I warned you. And this is what it has come to. We have no choice now, and I can accept that. But you will not be so damned foolish as to speak so irreverently and carelessly of his most noble and sacred majesty, even to illustrate a valid point, he'd said.

Without this flawed, fragile, ancient creature, Gutter would be less than half sane, and there would be no one who could rein him in anymore.

The house unraveled around him. One servant after another arrived, some in hurried silence, some with a cry of dismay. Gale kept her place through it all, though her pink tongue hung out obscenely and she let out little gasps that didn't quite reach the volume of a whine.

The servants parted as Gutter arrived at the top of the stairs. Even at that distance Mark could see Gutter's dark eyes widen and his pupils blow open until Mark would have sworn he saw red within them. Gutter's exposed skin, already pale, turned an ugly ash color as he thundered down the stairs. "Merrin." Gutter took Lord Argenwain's hand in his. "Merrin."

"He's still alive." Mark had a pair of fingers set over Lord Argenwain's neck. The fast but steady pulse reassured him. "He's going to wake in a bad way. Maybe we should move him and straighten that leg before he regains consciousness."

"You." Gutter didn't even look at the servant but one straightened as if he'd been addressed. "Fetch his gracian."

Gracian? Mark had no idea. Perhaps Lord Argenwain began to use it after he left, but then again he took medicine every night to help him sleep. Could it be that he was an addict?

"He only takes a drop in his brandy each night," Gutter said sharply, as if he'd heard Mark's thoughts. "For the pain in his joints. You should know he's not addled. Not one wit addled, though many his age prattle on about nothing of importance or say little at all." Gutter caressed Lord Argenwain's freshly shaved face and then pressed the limp hand against his own forehead, as if trying to will it to stir to consciousness. "Merrin, please. Please don't leave me."

Mark's eyes burned, remembering too well how much it hurt to watch Rohn ride away into danger without him, remembering the agony in Rohn's voice when Mark had been poisoned. Always the same words.

Don't leave me.

"Shouldn't we straighten—" Mark began again.

"Don't move anyone in this serious of condition without a doctor to guide." Gutter pressed Lord Argenwain's hand to his mouth and then rested his cheek against the pale fingers. His head jerked. "You did send for a doctor—"

"Yes."

"Where in the hells is he?"

"He'll be here soon." It was an inane thing to say. Mark couldn't know when the doctor would arrive. He just wanted Gutter to stay calm. So far he seemed to be managing well, but Thomas ....

Thomas had burned a ship full of men when Mark threatened to abandon the life Thomas had planned for them both. What monstrosity would he perpetrate if his beloved master died?

The servant arrived with the gracian. Gutter snatched it from him. A dropper fit into the beautiful cobalt glass and gold bottle. Gutter filled it and pushed the head past Lord Argenwain's lips, then slowly squeezed the bulb.

Under Mark's pinky Lord Argenwain's heart began to slow. "Stop. Gutter, you have to stop."

"This much won't kill him." Gutter gave the bottle and dropper back to the servant without looking away from Lord Argenwain's face. His head jerked again. "You have to go."

Mark's chest contracted with fresh shock. "What?"

"You have to get out of here, and you have to take him with you."

It had to be the madness finally breaking through. "You just said he shouldn't be moved."

"Not Merrin. *Him.* The King will rush here as soon as he discovers Merrin's fallen and he can't be here when the King arrives."

Sroh?

No. *Gelantyne.*

Gutter finally looked away from Lord Argenwain and focused on Mark, his eyes wild behind the mask. "One level below the hall with the fencing room." He quickly worked his belt off with one hand and opened a catch at the buckle's back. Several keys dropped onto the stairs. He selected one and gave it to Mark. "The last room on the right. Bert has the key to it. Find the hidden door by pushing on the largest stone block. It will reveal a key hole. Twice left, and then you must force it to the right. Once the lock slips you'll have to have Bert's help to press the rest of the door open. It's hard going for a reason. Tell Bert to help you close the passage and to lock the room again. At the end of the tunnel is a wire pull. It will ring Gerson Lowell. Don't come back this way whatever you do, and don't leave him alone. If I don't hear from you by tomorrow, I'll send someone to fetch you when I can." He drew out the key to the armoire. "Twice right, once left, then straight in. Be careful, and don't you dare, no matter how stridently he insists ... don't succumb to him. Lie and tell him you have orders from me to leave him behind if you must. Just ... be careful, and don't leave him in harm's way."

Mark hurried up the stairs, Gale close on his heels. He picked up the pistol and rapier on the way. He stopped by his room long enough to grab a hat, a cloak, a dagger, a second pistol, and to put on his mask. His shoulder twitched and a shudder passed through him.

Lark took a long, steadying breath before he walked to Gutter's rooms. Even with Mark's recent experience with Gelantyne in his mind, Lark felt as if had begun a long, groping walk into a sharp and shadowy place of unknown dangers. Gutter had occupied the mask before, which made Mark, perhaps wrongly so, feel at least a little protected. This time Lark faced Gelantyne alone.

Gale heeled as pretty as a well-trained lap dog, but with the wariness of an experienced guard that had taken scent of a yet undefined danger. She stopped abruptly at the door to the suite. Lark left her there.

The armoire seemed to advance toward him faster than his pace could account for. Lark inserted the key into a lock with a face plate shaped like a rose. Twice right, once left ... Lark pressed the key in without centering it again, hoping Gutter hadn't left out an important step in his instructions. Something clicked and he flinched.

The doors felt free. He pulled on the handles and the doors swung open, revealing the golden and lacquer mask on an elaborate stand of silver and a red wood with almost no grain in it. The gold-shot silk flowed along the stand and pooled at its base like frozen blood. The amber eyes seemed to glow with a golden inner fire. It might have been a reflection of the metal shining on hidden surfaces inside the amber, but he knew better.

This is an allolai, most sacred of all things.

The striking design in cream and black lacquer invited his gaze to wander and try to find meaning but he always found himself staring back into those eyes.

He didn't want to touch it. A powerful impulse inspired him to shut the doors partway, but he stopped himself. Gutter was right. Gutter couldn't leave Lord Argenwain, and once the king heard about the accident, he would immediately rush to the house.

They were all, after all, supposedly friends.

Gelantyne could not be here when the king arrived.

Lark touched the silk first. It felt warm, warmer than skin, more supple than a languorous kiss. He tried to ignore the shiver of longing and terror but it intoxicated him. His hands slid up the silk and touched the gold. It too was warm, like a man with fever, or the heat of skin scalded by summer sun. He lifted the mask. It felt strangely light in his hands, though his arms flexed and the cords stood out in his wrists with the weight of that gold and silk.

One hand held the golden mask to his breast while the other gathered the silk over his arm. His heart pulsed with a strange rhythm, as if a hand were massaging it gently into a smooth, steady silkiness rather than letting it run free and wild. It unwillingly calmed him and choked him at the same time, forcing his emotions to walk because he couldn't get enough air to run in a panic. He left the dressing room, the suite, the hall, traveling down back stairs until he reached the lowest floor. Gale fled before him with her tail tucked. When he stopped by the door, she came toward him a few steps, her ears held low and her short tail hidden under her. Finally she sat and trembled.

He had to wait for Bert. After seemingly taking forever to reach the doorway he wondered how Bert couldn't have reached the door far ahead of him. Every heartbeat lasted a long minute, and every trace of sound that echoed in the quiet, stone-ensconced places well below ground scraped the insides of his ears. At last, Gale's ears perked briefly before sinking back down. A short moment later footsteps thundered down the stairs.

Bert came down the hall at a healthy trot, though it seemed to take him an eternity. He fished through a small ring of keys on a silver and silk chatelaine. Mark had ample time to remember how, at Hevether Hall, they'd determined that the assassins had made copies of several keys at the party, allowing them quiet access to the entire house. That silent entry had given them the opportunity to kill the staff and trap the colonel in his room before Juggler finally let himself into Lark's room with the intention of killing him.

Those keys proved to be the undoing of their assassins. The Morbai's Kiss intended to trap everyone in the house, and so locked the doors behind them. With Lark close behind they had no time to let themselves out the back door. That forced them into the colonel's path.

Rohn's swift and gruesome revenge upon them still haunted Lark's mind. He forced the thoughts away as best he could—keys, Grant's death, all that death—but the jangling keys kept luring him back to that cold and lonely place.

Bert finally reached the door with the proper key in hand. Lark placed himself between Bert and Gale while Bert opened the door, favoring a bandaged hand as he worked the handle and lock together—handle up, turn right, handle down, turn left, neutral, left again and open.

Lark immediately spotted the largest of the wall's stones. They both pressed until it slid in with a grinding sound. Lark opened the lock, and they pushed.

An opening widened on the floor at the stone's base. When the door stuck the opening wouldn't have permitted someone Gutter's size through, but it was just enough for Lark.

Except Gale would never make it down the ladder. He knew how to get her down. He wasn't sure Bert—

Just go.

He didn't want to. He didn't like the long, narrow opening that had been carved a long distance through solid rock, much less the terrible, tight darkness that swallowed all but the very top of a rusted iron ladder.

Lark climbed down with one hand, the warm silk slipping off his arm to flow along his body as he went. When he reached the bottom of the damp, dark, narrow place he looked up. "Can you lower Gale down to me?" He precariously wedged the mask into his waistcoat, then crammed the silk into his belt enough to relieve the balance of the weight.

"Yes, lord jester." For a long stretch nothing happened, and then what little light came from the room blotted out and dog feet started waving around over his head. Lark cradled her hind legs in one arm and took the weight of her chest gradually from Bert. "Easy, Gale." She started struggling more wildly. Bert let her go. Lark managed to keep his feet but he nearly dropped her writhing, heavy mass of bone, muscle and fur. She yelped when she bumped on her side to the ground. She got right back up but Lark feared she was hurt and ran his hands over and over her, trying to tell if anything had broken.

She tucked her tail and shivered. He hoped it was just the mask's presence and not an injury.

Maybe I shouldn't have tried to take her with me.

Nothing for it now. "Thank you," he called to Bert.

"Is she all right?" he called back.

"I think so." She'd already taken a few steps down the narrow hall. "Bert, I wanted to say ... I'm so sorry. She shouldn't have bitten you."

"I knew better than to test her like that. It was my fault."

"Still—"

"No, lord jester. Truly. Think nothing more of it. I hope we'll see both of you again soon."

Neither of them would feel right about it. He might try again, next time with something more than just words, but even a gesture from him or Gale herself would never make the scar Bert would have on his hand disappear. "Is there a light you can hand down to me?"

"I'll fetch a lantern."

"And a striker, in case the flame goes out."

Bert was gone only a moment. Lark mulled over the fact that he'd actually timed his apology poorly. Bert might think Lark was simply afraid of being locked in should something happen to Gutter. If Bert decided to leave him there to rot, no one would know where to find him.

But of course it was a false fear. Bert wouldn't take such an extreme action for a dog bite, and besides, Gutter wouldn't let that happen.

Assuming Gutter thought to tell anyone else about where he'd sent his little jester friend.

Nothing is going to happen to Gutter.

He's already half-mad ...

Stop it.

He touched his mask, wondering if it might be slipping. A rush of hysteria began to overtake him, as if one of Winsome's fearful fancies had wormed into him, turning the darkness into a living, watchful thing that waited to tear him into ragged, wet pieces of dead flesh.

Bert returned with an old-style oil lantern that messengers used to carry while on horseback. One side of the handle had a small, ornate weight, while the other held the lamp so that the bearer could brace against his leg or hip or his horse and keep his arm relaxed while keeping the lamp safely away from anything that could catch fire.

Lark climbed partway back up the ladder and Bert got down on his belly and stretched his arm to hand it to him. "Thank you," Lark said.

"Good luck. There should be a crank there somewhere. Lock the handle into the gear."

Lark spotted it, locked the handle in and began turning the crank. The entry began to narrow. Not far from the handle hung an old pull cord, rotted wood dangling from a thin wire.

"Do you need help?" Bert asked. "I can run upstairs and work the crank on the other side."

"No, it's not hard."

"Don't forget to unlock the handle, lord jester," Bert reminded him. "Otherwise, if you're overdue, no one will be able to follow you from this side. Maybe Gutter might want it that way, but there's no telling what condition the door on the other end of the tunnel is in. It's been some years since anyone's used it."

"Thank you. I'll remember."

"Good luck, lord jester."

"Thank you, Bert."

Lark kept turning the crank until it the stone shut out what little light came from the room, kept turning until the stone stopped hard and the crank wouldn't turn anymore. The lock clicked from a far away, muffled place. He unlocked the crank.

At least Gelantyne was safe now.

Lark took in a deep breath and began his journey through darkness.

Chapter Fourteen

Short as he was he still had to duck. He felt his way along with one hand on the ceiling, grateful for his gloves, splashing occasionally through ice-edged puddles or skating over uneven, treacherous frozen water and stone. Gale stuck close to him through it all, at first ahead of him until he'd bumped her one too many times whenever she stopped suddenly, then trailing behind him, shivering, her head held low in misery. At least she didn't seem to be limping, but he worried about her constantly.

The scent of mud and stone and green water reeked in the frosty, still air. Every sound he made returned too close to his ears. The light seemed to hamper his vision more than it helped, blinding him to everything beyond a pair of paces. He held Gelantyne steady with his left hand, hoping the silk wasn't getting dirty. It seemed a foolish thing to worry about, but to soil such a beautiful thing seemed as much a sin as defiling art. The thought of muddied silk started to bother him enough that he gathered up his cloak and did his best to make a sack of it to protect the mask.

Lark quickly lost track of time, though that didn't bother him as much as his body's increasing weariness. He hadn't eaten in too long. His focus protected him somewhat from the light-headedness, and he could distance himself from the pain of an empty belly—a pain slightly less severe than the nauseating agony of an overfull one—but he knew he couldn't press himself too much or he'd collapse. Alone, in the soggy, cold darkness with only Gale and the mask's insistent but too slight heat to help keep him warm, he might die. The fact didn't alarm him. It existed only as an obstacle that he had to avoid.

Lark found a reasonably dry area and braced on the wall for a rest. His treacherous eyes kept giving him false images of wall, ceiling and floor beyond the light's edge. His back and neck ached from stooping. This would have been a tortuous path for a tall man. He was grateful for his hat. It had saved him several times from a nasty knock on the head from unexpected dips in the ceiling.

Gale sat on his feet and leaned on his legs, shivering violently. Could she be cold? It seemed unlikely, but then again she was still young and didn't have the strength or toughness of an adult.

More likely she was afraid. Lark crouched to huddle with her but she shied away.

Not from him, from Gelantyne. She'd gotten used to it enough to comfort him, but not enough to risk its touch.

Lark straightened again. "I didn't mean to test your loyalty, Gale." She ventured to sit against his legs again, and he stroked her broad head. "Good girl. You're my good, brave girl."

Perhaps the way out wouldn't be too much farther ahead. He started moving again, trying not to acknowledge his rising heart rate, and it wasn't just from exhaustion. He had to admit that this place unnerved him. He hadn't been in it for very long and already he felt like he'd been walking for half the day, and it all looked the same. Maybe it didn't end. Maybe there'd be no way back. He could be trapped here forever—

Stop it.

So much weight overhead. What if the tunnel collapses? How long has it been here, untroubled by careless hands. The slightest pressure on the wrong stone might bring it all down—

Stop it!

He didn't dare touch the ceiling anymore, just in case his fears were justified. The sections with solid rock seemed just as treacherous as those that had been built from huge blocks. Cracks ran through almost every stone, and water seeped and dripped, rotting it, crumbling it ....

Lark had to stop again, his breath coming in short gasps. Had the lantern's glow diminished? Was he suffocating, or was it just fear making him feel like he was?

He closed his eyes and tried drawing the mask off his face. It slipped, and he took his first full, deep breath in what had seemed like forever. His eyes seemed to clear, and the oppressive darkness didn't seem so terrible. Mark still panted with exhaustion and the verge of panic, but he didn't feel so alone and pressed and uncertain.

He'd been more afraid with the mask on than off, not of death oddly enough, but of the dark and suffocation and burial. It seemed strange to think that his mask would have fears that he didn't own, but he didn't want to fumble about for an explanation. He had more important things to do.

He started to move as soon as his heart steadied. His gut burned with hunger. He longed for the doctor's faint hope of a cure, and wished he could have tried it before he went this way. His seizure and now Lord Argenwain's terrible accident certainly delayed the cure's construction. The doctor may not have even begun to gather the necessary ingredients for it.

I've waited this long. It doesn't matter.

Despite the rational thought, he still felt as if he'd missed his last chance at life.

Finally he reached what seemed to be the tunnel's end. He faced a ladder, and a crank handle, and a pull cord. He pulled—

The wood handle came free in his hand.

Did it ring before the wire broke?

His insides shrank and his knees threatened to buckle, but he forced himself to examine the wire with the hope that he might find another way to ring the bell.

The piece of wire he held was less than a foot and a half long. Maybe he could reach the broken end.

Mark set down the lantern, and took off his cloak so that he could hang it and Gelantyne over the ancient ladder rung without dirtying the silk. He groped among the webbed cracks and openings around the crank, grateful again for his gloves as he crushed spiders and saw some escape down other cracks, down his arm or drop to the ground. In any other situation he might have recoiled, but more urgent fears forced him to set his revulsion aside. His breath created a lingering cloud of mist, but at the moment his vision didn't matter so much as his sense of touch.

There.

Mark felt around a roughly round opening that seemed to have nothing to do with the crank. The stone had been smoothed, but something didn't feel right along its bottom lip. He reluctantly removed his glove.

A crack had opened along the opening's bottom. From what he could tell, the crack extended a long distance into the tube. No doubt the wire had been pinched in there. Maybe someone had been stuck down here before, and in a panic kept yanking on the trapped wire, weakening it. Or maybe time had made it fragile and the crack only did it in when Mark pulled on it.

Mark cupped his hands around the opening, took a full breath, and bellowed from his diaphragm. "Hello! Can anyone hear me?" After a moment he tried again. "Someone please fetch Gerson Lowell. I'm trapped!"

He listened for a long while. If anyone had heard him and had tried shouting back, their voices weren't coming through.

He could always try reaching the wire.

He'd wait first. If the bell had rung, which he now doubted, or someone heard him, he might perhaps avoid a lot of trouble trying to reach it. Besides, eventually Gutter or someone might send a message to the gerson to make sure Mark made it through. He settled on the stone, cringing at the cold but he couldn't stand up much longer. The walk had bled most of his strength from him.

To measure the time he sang arias, sometimes aloud and sometimes under his breath to save his strength. They were his favorites from his youth, and he knew exactly how long it took to perform each one.

My youth. Isn't this supposed to be my youth?

The bitter thought made him smile.

I am young, even if my body doesn't feel that way anymore. If I'm so lucky as to grow old, there won't be any Petrens and Rohns lusting after me anymore.

The bitterness faded into a gentle humor.

I have had a glorious life, and have had the good fortune of excellent friends and lovers. I've seen fine art, heard and performed music beyond the sweetest dreams, sailed, marveled at a jeweled city from a mountainside, and I've eaten fresh oranges plucked moments before from the trees that bore them. Best of all, I'm a free man with the power to defend what I love most in this world. What is youth, beauty, even strength compared to freedom and the ability to fight for the freedom of others?

His thoughts buoyed his voice for a time, but after about two hours he was too tired to sing even at a whisper. He set Gelantyne back on the ladder after cleaning off the rungs with the cloak, wrapped himself in the cloak and settled to rest. Gale crept close and snuggled against him.

He slept for a few minutes at a time, always waking to shivering. He didn't want to move. He tried adjusting the cloak or the hunch of his shoulders to get warmer but the best he could manage was to avoid getting any colder.

But I am getting colder.

He had felt warmer when he'd slept in the snow that terrible night between Seven Churches and Reffiel.

I have to move or I'll die.

But it's cold ....

Just a few more minutes to gather my strength ....

No. I have no strength to gather. I have to move now or never again.

It took a great deal of effort just to stand.

I don't have the strength to make it back and I can't wait here any longer.

He tried forcing his hand up the narrow opening that the wire once threaded through, cringing at the spiderwebs and creeping things inside there.

It was far too tight and rubbed his skin raw only a few inches past his wrist.

Then he had an idea.

This is really stupid. If I get stuck I'll lose my arm ....

"I should laugh and boldly declare, what is an arm when compared with freedom." His voice wheezed and his throat felt hot and raw. Thinking about how bravely the island veterans got along with various limbs missing didn't make the thought of losing his hand or his arm any easier. The only thing that gave him the courage to risk it was the irrational belief that it probably wouldn't come to that. He didn't let himself consider just how irrational that belief might be.

Mark set his dagger, the sharpest of his weapons, within easy reach. He pulled the laces from one boot, doubled it, slung it over above his bicep and pulled the ends through the loop.

If I'm forced to amputate my own arm I am not going to bleed to death from it.

He doused the lamp and poured out a little oil at a time into his hands, working it well into his skin. He took off his coat, pulled up his left sleeve, and rubbed the oil liberally over his arm. His arms, thinned to sticks by starvation, would served him well, but he still had the same joints widened from a lifetime of fencing practice and gymnastics and every other kind of physical training he once took for granted.

He kept working in more and more oil until his skin felt so slick it felt wet. He then took what little oil remained and coated the opening. The air stank not just with the sharp, heavy scent of oil but sweat, and his breath had gone foul.

His hand slid into the opening, but only just. Even oiled his skin scraped and pinched on the rough rock as he inched farther in. He constantly twisted his hand and groped with his fingers for the wire. As his worries bloomed into horror, a tight, fierce suction began to form that made him suddenly think of thrusting into Petren.

Mark laughed low and fearfully in his throat. "You were not this tight, my love," he murmured.

I'm losing my sanity.

He'd gone in nearly up to his elbow, and still no sign of the wire.

Wait ...

Something sharp glanced over his finger again. It was the wire. It should have been flexible, but it didn't move. It had to be stuck against or in something. He pushed on it. It punctured the end of his pointer finger. He winced and caught it under his nail. After several agonizing attempts that made his lower belly tight with frustration and his middle weak and soft with fear, he managed to flick the wire out of the crack.

He leaned to adjust the angle of his arm and slid in a half inch more. "I don't think you'd like it if I had my arm in this far." He managed to get the wire end resting on his pointer finger, and pinched it with his middle.

His fingers, of course, were slippery. He tugged, and the wire easily followed his pull.

Did it ring? He thought he'd heard something in the far, far distance, but that had to be a mad fancy. No sound would reach past his arm to his ears.

He tried to draw his arm out while holding on to the wire, but as he'd feared, his arm was stuck. His mind blurred as he pulled in growing panic.

He'd studied science. He knew how to break suction.

Mark rested for a moment, then pushed his arm in another inch and worked the wire until it made as good a loop as he could manage. He was now up to his elbow, and his elbow was too large to go into the opening. It took a long time, but he twisted the wire until he felt like he might be able to hold the wire tight. He bent his finger over it, and pressed his middle finger against it to keep it from slipping.

No telling how much slack there will be. I hope there's enough that I can pull the wire out far enough to reattach it to the handle.

Assuming I get my arm free ....

He took a deep breath and blew along his arm. At first he couldn't do anything. He couldn't get his face close enough to the hole to make any difference. His shoulder didn't allow it. Then he thought to get his pistol. He banged it repeatedly and worked the ramrod on the wrong side to unload it, formed a seal over the chamber with his hand, stuck the end against his arm, and blew. It had no effect either. The end of the pistol didn't fit snugly enough to force air past his skin into the opening.

He pulled and twisted back and forth as hard as he could until his skin stretched and his joints cracked and he gasped from the pain. His panic didn't help. It just wore him out.

The feathers in my hat.

It took a long time to calm down enough to make use of his idea. With a trembling hand, he pulled the largest one free. It took some awkward maneuvering to trim the shaft into a straw one-handed, but he managed it. The shaft felt sharp along his scraped and raw skin, but he didn't care. He blew into it—

He felt a little warmth along his arm, but it didn't seem to help. He tried again, changing places until he'd pretty well ringed his arm—

His arm slipped a little. He kept hold of the wire and kept working more air around his skin. His arm slipped far enough that the wire had tension on it. He worked his arm the slight distance he could manage back and forth, hopefully ringing the bell while scraping skin off his hand and arm.

Mark almost let go, then thought better of it. He should wait to see if someone heard.

His arm ached from cold. He might be able to slide it in again after he'd had a chance to rest and warm up—

Except I'm out of oil.

He realized that over time his skin would absorb the oil anyway. He couldn't leave his arm in, or he'd be trapped and might be forced to amputate. He didn't think he could survive an amputation, despite his brave preparations to do just that.

He tugged the wire a few more times, then reluctantly let it go. Twisting, turning, bleeding—his blood proved to be a fair lubricant—he finally freed his arm and sank, shivering, to the wet ground. Gale sat beside him and licked his wounds. Her tongue sent rasping fire up his arm. "No," he told her gently, and held her head with his right arm. She hadn't meant to hurt him, and he didn't hurt her, but she squirmed and he held her long enough to make certain she knew his displeasure. "Behave," he admonished her.

I'll just rest a while and see if someone comes for me.

But of course that was a trap. He needed more warmth. For a moment he considered holding the lamp close, but he doubted he'd find a way to noticeably warm himself with that slender flame without burning himself on the glass.

The mask.

He forced himself up again and, shivering, gathered the Gelantyne mask into his arms. He clutched the mask to his chest, and drew the cloak over them both before settling down. He didn't want to sit in the wet, but his trembling legs wouldn't hold him much longer and he couldn't risk a fall in this place of rough, sharp edges. "Gale."

She refused to approach.

Maybe I should wear the mask.

Gutter had warned him against it, and Professor Vinkin had reminded him that he couldn't cheat using masks. If he grew too weak while wearing it, he'd die the moment someone removed it.

Worse, the *allolai* might do something on its own. Mark didn't dare consider what it might do to survive.

When the time comes, I will claim you. The *allolai's* whisper, especially after its long and seemingly inert silence, frightened and repulsed him. He didn't want to know if it had heard and answered his fears, or what it meant. Better to save his own life somehow then have the *allolai* do whatever it threatened to do, most likely at the loss of his life, his free will, and perhaps his mind and soul.

Twenty minutes and then I'll try something different.

His thoughts reluctantly slid to Lord Argenwain—whether the old lord still lived, or had died on those stairs. He didn't want to think about him at all. It made him uncomfortable. It was so much easier to hate him from a distance, and to pretend that the day he died would be a grand day for the world, having one less man like him in it. The rapists, murderers, slavers and torturers in the world seemed more understandable and human than the creatures who sexualized little boys and girls. Better that such things— he couldn't call them people—didn't exist. A man like Merrin Argenwain, who kept himself free of sin only by way of a few back staircase rules sung by mad poets, still had that same loathsome quality that damned the rest. Why should it matter that Mark had been of age, barely, and only looked like and dressed as a younger boy? Why should something his jester provided for him free him of the sin in the first place?

No one ought to forgive Merrin Argenwain his sins, or give his terrible injury on the stairs a second thought. But Mark had lived unmolested in his house for years, and couldn't escape the memory of Merrin's generosity, not just toward Mark but the entire town, especially its poor.

He couldn't hate Lord Argenwain as much as he wanted to. He wanted to be glad that the old man likely lay dying at this moment, if he weren't dead already. Instead his throat tightened with the threat of tears he didn't want to shed, and frustration at all the things he wanted to say to the old man, as if telling him off or convincing him that the world would be a better place without him would change anything. Mark didn't just fight a losing battle against a shred of sympathy for the old man. He hurt for Jeffrey and for all the other boys he didn't know about that had been bought and bribed and whatever else Argenwain and Gutter had done for and to them, who would never receive any measure of justice or any satisfaction should the old man die.

As much as I hate him, I hate us. I hate myself, for being willing, and for letting myself think of him as anything other than a twisted, ruined caricature that could never be called a human being.

At least there is something that can despise him purely and without entangling thoughts of pity or mercy. Let the morbai *cleanse both worlds of his existence. I'm too entwined to hate him as much as I want to, as much as I need to—*

A realization shocked through him, so potent he stood up and knocked his head against the ceiling. He gasped in pain, not just from the stone but from an awe of the beautiful, dark workings of beings he'd always feared, even when he didn't really believe in them.

Morbai.

They destroy that which is irredeemable with a purity that can only come from objectivity. I can't be objective because I'm ... I'm a part of the pain of the world. I even contribute to it, though I do my best not to. All humans do.

The legal system needed to be the same as *morbai*, or at least as near as a court of human beings could imitate them. That roughshod, primitive thing he'd seen when he'd participated in a Meriduan trial could only be improved with some mechanism that would help it become more impartial. Without objectivity, victims and criminals could only battle and lash at each other, and justice would have no meaning. Without objectivity, a trial was a miniature war, where the strongest, most clever, and most charismatic won the day and the common good was served only by chance, if ever.

Gelantyne began to glow. The subtle, amber light didn't touch the walls, but it warmed the red, gold-shot silk and lit his cloak, making it an unpleasant burgundy color.

Yes, it whispered in his mind.

The glow faded. Maybe he'd imagined it. Could Gelantyne hear his thoughts? The idea disturbed him.

Mark rubbed the sore, bleeding lump where he'd smacked his head and settled on his heels.

He felt more at peace than he could remember. Or perhaps he'd never felt this at peace, even before his parents died. Somehow, the possibility of justice, not just against Lord Argenwain but perhaps for his parents, for everyone, seemed within reach. Let someone else, someone who hadn't been hurt by him, judge Lord Argenwain. All Mark had to do was treat that old man only as someone who'd known him for almost half of his life could treat him.

There was something else, something deeper and even more difficult to accept, but it gave him hope. Gutter had pointed it out, but Mark hadn't related to it until this moment.

Mark had allowed himself to be an instrument of Lord Argenwain's lust. He'd never hated the old lord enough to leave, or kill him, or end it. He'd had the power to run away just as Magpie had fled the Church not once but many times. Mark had been too young, too afraid, and he had to admit, too comfortable, and he lacked imagination or belief in himself. He didn't think he had any other choice, and he'd always believed that it not only could, but would be worse if he left. He'd seen no evidence to the contrary, and he'd lacked the courage to risk it. He also believed, and a small part of him still believed, that he couldn't escape for long. Lord Argenwain and Gutter were too strong.

But it doesn't matter that they're strong. All that matters is that I have the ability to fight them. I have fought them. I've even won a little.

The world seemed to flip end over end. His heart quickened with his own power.

I might have my own reasons for being here, but the reason I'm with them is because part of me still believes I can't escape, and I can't live without them.

But I can.

He shook with fear. He wanted to deny the reason why he remained with them, but it seemed terribly clear.

Because I feel safe with them.

I'm dying. What does safety matter anymore?

He gasped, or laughed, he couldn't tell which.

He could exist without them. And he could leave them, or use them as he saw fit. He'd managed to escape them when Obsidian had handed him his excuse to leave in the form of a book and a signet ring. Now he not only had practice at leaving them, but he had the wealth, the status and the will to return home if he could just live long enough to do it.

The signet ring. He hadn't thought about it in a long time. He'd taken for granted that the duke or the duchess would be RT, but he was Duke Farevren, Lord of Kenwallick and Duthring and she was Anne, Her Grace the Duchess of Jessrill, Lady Dyanne of Prussmile, Angcheswere and Nort. There wasn't an R or a T among the first letters of either of their names. His mind shuffled through all the names of the people he'd met since he'd come here, and none of them had initials that fit. "Huh."

Mark settled in, mulling for the remaining minutes he'd decided to wait for an answer to the bell. There was someone he hadn't met yet, someone very important. If that person didn't come to him soon, he'd have to ask Gutter about it, and if Gutter didn't answer him he'd ask Gzem, or find some other way. He wouldn't depend on Gutter anymore. In fact, he intended to never depend on any one person other than himself if he could possibly help it.

I must never enslave myself again.

Chapter Fifteen

Somehow, despite the terrible cold, he dozed off without meaning to. When he woke, throat sore, nose running, he knew he couldn't wait anymore. He was getting too weak, too cold, too hungry, and he might not wake again. He worried about Gale, too. She had to be getting hungry and he wasn't sure the moisture she licked from the walls and puddles on the stone was good for her. Of course he didn't want to die down here, but Gale, an innocent in all this, didn't deserve to stand guard over his corpse until she died of starvation in the darkness. Help might come for her, or it might not. Besides, even if she survived until someone rescued her, what would they do with her? Bert, who adored her, was now afraid of her and if no one else wanted her, they might just toss her out on the street, or kill her, or give her away to someone who mistreated her.

Mark realized he'd allowed his imagination to scare him just as Winsome sometimes did. He needed to do something about his circumstances and not worry so much about what might happen to him and Gale.

He considered going back to Gutter's manor, but if the King was still there ....

He knew that the King would have not only a human entourage, but a spiritual one as well, and he doubted that they were confined by the physical spaces of this world. He couldn't risk taking Gelantyne close to the house, and he couldn't leave the mask unguarded now that he'd, at least in theory, had rung the bell.

Sorry, he thought as he set the mask gracelessly on one of the lower ladder rungs and wound the silk around it to hold it in place.

An image, not from his memory, flashed—the mask and its silk dripping with mud and blood and gore, all ruined by filth save the gold which remained pristine as it fought in a hellish battle among thousands of screaming men ....

Mark shuddered. He walked a few paces away to relieve himself, Gale close on his heels. After he was finished he moved away, crouched down and ran his fingers through her fur. Maybe it was his imagination, but she felt cold. His fears sprang back to life. She might be large and look as robust as an adult dog of any other breed, but she was still a puppy and needed sustenance. "Good girl," he murmured. "You're a very good girl. Let's get you out of here and get you some breakfast."

He had no choice. He needed to work the locking mechanism from this side somehow.

He groped about with trembling hands, finding all the necessary pieces to give himself some light. After he put the lamp back together, he squeezed the striker over the wick. There would be at least a little oil left in the wick itself, and the wick would also burn nicely, though too quickly for his needs. He hoped there might be a trace of oil that might last a bit longer.

The few times he managed to work the striker with his weakened hands the sparks didn't want to take, but finally the wick lit. A small, rounded flame burned, giving just enough light for him to work.

He looked about the crank, examining the gears and how they were set in order to move the stone. There was a metal track set in the stone in which the gear moved, and the handle shifted over to set into the gear which also caused the rod to which it the handle was attached into the ceiling to swing into something hidden in a wide seam up above.

Bert had said that when the handle was engaged, it would be locked above. No doubt that would prevent someone in pursuit from working the gear above against the gear below, or opening the doorway again should the person who went in in-advance want to stop them.

There was also a lock. Was it separate from all this? It would have to be somewhere in the same seam, wouldn't it? Mark tried shining the light into the seam, but he didn't have much luck.

The rapier.

He memorized as much as he could of the workings, disengaged the handle, set his hand on the seam to keep his mind oriented, and blew out the light to save on oil. The smoke from the doused flame sharpened in his nose even through his clogged sinuses.

He drew his rapier and carefully slid it up the seam. The sensitive steel transmitted something close enough to a picture in his mind to allow him to imagine its progress between the stone faces on either side of the seam. He traced the rod, traced the closer edge on the seam, farther—

Both times he met a bolt, about a half inch thick, that ran from one side of the seam to the other.

If he tampered with it, it might render the entire mechanism useless. If that freed the door, that would be good. If it broke a section of the works that the crank relied upon to open the door, or more likely, if there was a second bolt higher up that needed to slide over to free the door, and the lock jammed thanks to his tampering, then he'd really be stuck.

Perhaps he could find whatever moved the bolt into place and affect that.

He explored deeper into the seam but found nothing.

Shit.

He concentrated past his fears and his hunger and remembered the sound of the lock mechanism when he and Bert opened the door at the other end. The sound that the lock made when the key turned was of a single bolt sliding aside. He hoped this door was the same. That, at least, would help him.

If he were making such a lock, he'd set the mechanism that slid the bolt entirely interior to the stone. It wouldn't matter if someone below were trying to break in or not. They wouldn't be able to slide the bolt against the locking mechanism, even if it were unlocked. Nothing below could gain any purchase on the smooth metal to encourage it to move to one side or the other. And if it were locked, it wouldn't move at all.

Shit!

But maybe he could cut the bolt.

The rapier, as it was, couldn't do the job, and it was the only tool he had that could reach besides a bullet, and a bullet would do no good.

But the rapier ....

What he contemplated would ruin the blade, but he saw no way around it. He drew his dagger, and began sawing edge on edge. He felt with his fingers in the dark, making small notches in the rapier blade. Each took a long time, and they were very small, but he hoped that they would do. When he had about a foot of them he slid the rapier up and began sawing on the bolt.

The bolt hardly dulled the rapier notches at all, which surprised him. He expected the bolt to be steel, but maybe it was brass. Metal shavings sprinkled down, so fine that their only evidence was a strange metallic taste in the back of his throat. It made him cough and stung his eyes.

Mark had to rest often. He had been underground a long time, he hadn't eaten, and it took hours to saw and saw until—

The bolt broke, and the stone settled, startling him. He engaged the handle and began to turn. With the unreality of a mythic tale the stone began to move. When the opening first cracked he took scent of fresh air and realized how stuffy it had become around him. He couldn't turn the handle as fast as he wanted to. He nearly fainted from light-headedness, and his heart tapped too lightly and too fast within him, when he finally opened the way enough for his passage. He wanted to worm through the small gap, but he had to be patient. He opened it completely, lit the lamp and set it to one side of the opening. Mark hoisted Gale into his arms.

Her weight strained his back and threatened to buckle his legs. "Up you go," he gasped, trying to encourage her to place her front feet on the ladder. "Come on, Gale. Up. Go on, girl. Up!"

She tried to place her feet on a rung but they slipped for no reason he could discern. It seemed such a simple thing to set one's weight on a ladder rung and walk up. Maybe she was too weak to grip, or didn't know how to hold on or balance on the narrow rung. "Come on girl. Please, Gale."

Gale scrabbled frantically. She managed, more from clawing than anything, to work up to the next rung, and then suddenly she thrust her hind legs into Mark's chest and vaulted through.

He sagged against the ladder, on the verge of collapse. He tasted blood in his throat. Gale's clawed feet tip tip tipped and scratched on a hard floor somewhere up there. "Good girl," he whispered. "Good dog." He let his eyes close—it hardly made any difference in the dark—to rest.

He startled awake when his head drooped and touched the ladder's cold metal. His arm, oil rubbed into raw wounds, throbbed. Thirst raked his mouth and throat so much he hardly noticed any pain in his belly. That thirst drove him to retrieve all his abused weapons, unwind Gelantyne from its perch and climb the ladder. His cold-stiffened joints and overworked muscles could barely carry his feathery weight. At the top he sank to the floor for a moment, so exhausted he could barely move. He couldn't even shiver anymore.

The small, round room was dry and that more than anything made it feel far warmer than the tunnel. It had stacks of cannonballs and shot of various sizes, and crates no doubt holding more of the same. It also had tools hanging on the wall, most of which he couldn't immediately discern what they might have been used for. He felt a little proud of himself for recognizing a set of files as being files. Especially by the lamp's dim and uncertain light, everything else looked more like torture devices than anything that could be used for proper craftsmanship.

A set of narrow stairs little more than outcroppings of stone from the wall with no rail to hold onto led to a trap door. He forced himself onto his knees, then his feet, and staggered up the stairs. The trap door was unlocked, and swung open easily enough. Gale trailed unhappily after him. At least she did much better on the stairs than she had the ladder.

The next room up was a little larger and full of metal-clad grain bins. An equally insubstantial stair as the one before led to a slightly larger room with a better variety of stores, mostly roots.

He recognized what he'd come into.

A tower.

He could run into someone at anytime. Hastily, Mark wrapped Gelantyne in his cloak before he took another step.

He passed through another grain store, a weapons store, armor store, each with a better staircase, until finally he reached a large room with actual exits on the sides. One was locked, the other was not. He opened the door and was momentarily dazzled by the light from a bright gas lamp.

A sacred guard startled at his post. A window looked out over the river. It was a foggy night, though in his disoriented state Mark couldn't say what time. Judging by the high walls hemming in the rushing river, he seemed to be near the gatehouse that led into the Guilbarabb. Gas lamps set at the tops of the walls lit small swaths of fog into clouds of pale gold.

"I know where I am." Mark let out a little laugh.

"Who—where did you come from?" The guard drew his sword. Gale growled, her still youthful voice managing to summon more menace than the last time Mark had heard her warn a stranger.

"Gale, stay." He touched her to make certain she heard him. Her focus on the guard was so fierce she didn't respond to his hand at all. "I'm here to see Gerson Lowell." Mark tried to stay calm but by the way the guard held his blade Mark knew the man was an expert and Mark, weak, cold and still half-blinded, was at great disadvantage. "I rang the bell but no one came."

"The bell ...?"

"Down there. Down in the tower. You didn't hear it?" The guard might not know about the passage. Maybe he wasn't supposed to know about it. He wondered where the bell line ran to, and who was supposed to be listening for it, if anyone. Maybe Gutter had sent Mark into that tunnel with false assumptions regarding who would be listening for the bell and during what hours. He'd said it would bring Gerson Lowell, hadn't he? "Please. I'm on urgent business. I need to see Gerson Lowell right away. Tell him Lark is here to see him."

"You stay right there." The guard backed a half step and pulled on a cord.

Mark had no intention of moving.

A half dozen guards arrived very quickly. They all drew their weapons. Mark stood very still. "Gale, stay," he reminded her.

"Wait here," the guard told him.

Mark didn't dare move, not even to nod.

By the time Gerson Lowell arrived Mark wobbled with exhaustion even with the support of the wall he leaned against. The guards, of course, were fit enough to stand with weapons drawn indefinitely. "This man is of no danger to me and I accept him into my charge," the gerson assured the guard. The others made way for the gerson and sheathed their weapons. "What's happened?" His long, dark hair hung loose and hadn't been brushed, and he smelled like sleep.

Even though he was starved and exhausted more than halfway to death, life stirred below Mark's belly at the sight of the handsome gerson. "I can't say. Not here." Gale finally relaxed and wagged her tail hesitantly.

"Follow me." The gerson led him down halls and stairs and out into the strange and beautiful splendor of the Guilbarabb, where the smooth, empty darkness of the square was surrounded by thousands of oil and gas lamps that revealed the jeweled entrances and façades of every building. It had to be a late hour. Sacred guards were the only people about any sort of business, and a sleepy silence softened the frigid, misty air. They walked along the wall toward one of the least impressive buildings in the Guilbarabb. The gerson unlocked a small door in an alley between it and a beautiful tower and led Mark through even more rooms and halls and stairs until, on the verge of being befuddled to the point that he might not be able to retrace their steps, Mark found himself in a small cell of a room with only a recently vacated bed, a chair, a short desk, and one bookshelf.

A door on the left wall promised the possibility of more space, though Mark had little doubt it was as cramped as this if not more. The room had smooth plaster walls and a warm wood floor. The gerson's shelves, table and desk were adorned with an excellent assortment of the finest necessities: hand-painted books, good candles, beautiful inkwells that held a wide variety of colored inks, wood-working tools, ornate scissors of a dozen types and sizes, and other useful items each of good craftsmanship.

Gale explored with her nose. She had almost no room to wander, so she concentrated on fine details—sometimes well-handled objects, but more often particular places on the floor. She took special interest in a pair of well-worn, embroidered silk slippers by the door. The gerson slipped off his shoes and put them on.

The room's cozy warmth embraced Mark with Gerson Lowell's subtle, amber scent, and honey tones of good, sweet wax, laced with velvety incense.

Gerson Lowell shut the door. "You have Gelantyne."

Mark opened his cloak.

The gerson took a step back, his eyes flitting over it as if he'd never seen it before. Perhaps he hadn't, or maybe he saw things that Mark couldn't. "What happened?" he asked.

"Lord Argenwain took a bad fall on the stairs—"

"I'd heard you'd taken a bad fall on them—"

"No, I think I caught myself—it doesn't matter. His Royal Majesty Michael has arrived in Saphir and once he hears of the accident, he'll visit the house—" He remembered suddenly that his voice might be overheard, if not by priests then by *allolai* and *morbai*. "My master wanted this safely away."

Gerson Lowell's dark eyes narrowed in confusion. They were neither brown nor gray nor hazel, but an odd, deep color among them, a sort of charcoal but full of fire. Mark had never seen their like in his life. "How did you get in the wall tower?" the gerson breathed.

"Is that really important?"

"I'd rather like to know. There is a way, but the bell boy didn't come for me. A guard did."

"I, uh ..." He realized he'd destroyed what had likely been an ancient and valuable door. "I cut the bolt. I tried to ring the bell but the wire broke, and ... I'm sorry."

"You're smeared in blood. Are you hurt?" By his tone of voice he sounded as if he thought it more likely that Mark had killed someone on the way.

"Just a scrape. Is there somewhere safe I can hide with this?"

"Let me see." The gerson gestured and Mark started to hand him Gelantyne, but the priest flinched back. "No, I mean your injury." He made an impatient noise, and Mark felt like an idiot. "Set the mask on my bed."

Mark obeyed. He hadn't had a good look at his arm yet. He didn't want to, either. He showed the gerson his ragged fingers.

"Let's get these washed. I'll heat some water. Stay here." He said the last as if he expected Mark to wander off. He paused at the door. "How long has it been since you've eaten?"

"Gale's likely more hungry than I am."

"She probably needs a walk, too. Will she come with me?"

Mark hesitated, remembering the last time he'd sent her with someone. "We can try, but be careful. The last time she left me I had a seizure, and—well, she bit someone. All she knows is that people were doing things to me while I was ill and they locked her in a closet when she tried to protect me."

Gerson Lowell crouched. "Gale?"

She left off her explorations and came over to him. He stroked her, not meeting her eyes, until she got that slight look of an almost-smile on her face and a bit of pink tongue showed. "Good girl," he murmured. "Come." He stood and she followed him to the door. Like last time she hesitated and looked back at Mark for approval.

"Go on," Mark told her gently. "Go."

"Come, Gale." The gerson walked and she followed. He left the door open behind them.

Mark waited until they were out of sight before he softly shut the door.

The gerson seemed so perfect in every way, but Mark didn't trust his own judgment, especially since the gerson drew him in so unwillingly. It would be different if ....

What? If it felt more natural and mutual as it had with Petren? That worked out well, he thought sarcastically.

By certain definitions of well, he supposed it had, actually.

Hadn't the gerson said something about someone else?

It came to him, and the memory of the gerson's voice warmed him even though it made him sad.

My lover left me when his wife became pregnant. I don't want another lover. I don't even want to be your friend. You confound me too much.

They had nothing in common, and everything opposite, and soon either Mark would be dead or he'd be going home.

Home. Longing rushed through him with such power it made him shudder from more than just a lingering chill. An ache remained behind, not very different from the ache he felt after he lost his parents.

He wondered how far the messenger had gotten. He probably hadn't yet left the city, making certain that Winsome hadn't followed Mark here.

She might have even beaten me here. I didn't think to look for her among the heavily-clothed riders that passed us.

Please let her be on her way home.

Mark sat on the bed beside the mask.

The next thing he knew Gale was licking his face. The gerson set a large steaming pot of water on the floor beside the bed. Another priest set a stand with an empty bowl while a third carried in a large pitcher and linens. Mark sat up with horror, thinking of the mask, but someone had covered it and him with a heavy blanket. He still felt half-asleep, his sight muddled and his mouth dry as wool.

"Thank you," the gerson told the other priests. They nodded and left. One cast Mark a sidelong glance that wasn't entirely kind on his way out.

"You slept a long time," the gerson told him. "It's past suppertime."

"Does Gutter—"

"I sent word." The gerson's expression tightened for a moment before easing. "Let's see your hands again." He examined them. "You're usually so kempt, it's a little strange to see your fingernails half torn off and a bit of beard on your face."

"And that was with gloves on most of the time. You should see my sword." Mark's face flamed as the gerson looked up, startled. Sword was a euphemism in Hasle, he remembered. "My rapier," he amended in Cathretan.

The gerson went into his other room and returned with an ornate wooden box full of fragrant powder that reminded Mark a bit of chamomile, jasmine and sage. The gerson put a handful into a rag that was hardly a rag—the soft cloth had beautiful embroidered edges to keep it from fraying—wetted it with the hot water, and began to gently work over Mark's hands. The nearly unbearable hot water softened the powder into soap that stung but soothed his dry skin at the same time. The gerson added more water, making it almost too hot to bear again, and it began to foam an ugly pinkish brown. "They do this for injured men at the banre," he told Mark. The massage felt far better than Mark wanted it to. "It sometimes staves off infection. This is my own recipe, with rosemary, soapwort, sage, thyme, cressite, healing salts from the Truvalthan Mine ... I can't remember what all else. I don't know how well it will work. I've only used it on minor things." He worked his way up Mark's wrists. His brow furrowed. "How far up this arm—"

"Just to the elbow."

"Take off your shirt."

Mark took off his coat and waistcoat. They were filthy anyway. He started to pull up his sleeve. The cloth stuck to his arm and yanking it free hurt.

"Don't tell my you're shy."

Mark tried to sound annoyed. "I'm cold."

"Cover up with the blanket, then."

To hesitate would be to admit that it wasn't just the cold, or even shame. Mark stripped the shirt off, feeling more than naked. He felt terribly fragile as the gerson soaped his arm very slowly, very gently, working his way up halves of inches at a time. "That stings," Mark told him.

"I'd be surprised if it didn't. You should have told me about this sooner. You could get a fever from this."

"And die?" He couldn't keep the harsh ironic tone from his voice.

The gerson paused briefly in his ministrations. He kept his gaze on Mark's arm.

"I'm sorry," Mark told him.

"Why are you apologizing?"

"Because I rubbed your nose in something that isn't your fault. And because I'm arguing when you're trying to help me. And because I know how shocking it must be to see what's little more than a skeleton over skin."

"You're not so thin as that. I saw worse, once. A slave. I confiscated her. She was so thin that her skin sagged between the bones on her arms, and you could see rings on her throat and every vertebrae on her neck. She survived. I still can't believe she survived. I thought for certain she would die. If she could survive in that condition, then I think you have little to fear, at least for a while."

Mark shivered with horror. "How could she have the strength to work in that condition?"

"He didn't want her for work. All she had to do was lay there for him. He had a lust for—"

Mark cried out in disgust.

"The Grand Court executed him." The flat words lacked passion or satisfaction. It was a simple fact to him.

Mark shuddered with a dark and uneasy passion. "Good."

"Let that sit for a moment." The gerson drew the table with the empty bowl closer. He poured water in from the pitcher, then began adding scoops of hot water with a ladle that hung from the pot's edge. He tested the water frequently until his skin turned pink from it. "Rinse your hands and soak them in here."

The heat bit him hard. Mark gritted his teeth. The potent glow sank into his bones and his body relaxed so swiftly into languor he let out an involuntary sigh. The gerson sluiced the water over his soaped arm. The water quickly became soapy and muddy with blood and filth.

The gerson left to pour out the water. He returned and filled a fresh bowl of hot water. Again he sluiced water over Mark's arm.

"May I borrow a razor?" Mark asked.

"I should have known your vanity would exceed your wisdom. We need to wrap this arm and your hands and then you need to eat." He stared into Mark's eyes a while before he relented and fetched a shaving kit.

Mark started to reach for the soap but the gerson pulled it away. "We'll do this properly," he admonished. He soaked a cloth in the water after adding a bit more hot, then wrapped it over Mark's face. When it was time to unwrap it the gerson already had hot soap ready, and soaped Mark's face for him. He stopped short of applying the razor, letting Mark do the work while he held a gold-framed mirror. Mark washed his hair for good measure, and under his arms.

"Shall I fetch you a bath?" the gerson asked dryly.

Mark chuckled and blushed and the gerson kissed him. Mark ducked his head, pulling away from the kiss, but kept his cheek close to the gerson's slightly rough skin. His hand wove into the gerson's thick, silken hair and the gerson mirrored the gesture. They held each other, breath blowing across fragrant skin.

The gerson let go first and Mark released him, letting his hand slide down the gerson's neck and shoulder before sitting back. He couldn't look at him. The kiss lingered in his mind. It still felt as if their lips touched. Mark licked his lower lip and tucked it under his teeth, not-quite biting because that was a bad habit he'd fought a long time to break.

"I'll sleep somewhere else tonight," the gerson told him.

"Sleep with me." It sounded more like a plea than Mark had meant it to be.

"Sleep with you in the Hasle sense or the Cathretan?"

"Both." Mark still didn't dare look at him.

"If you're lonely, there's someone I know from the *trerashefral.*"

"I don't even know what that is, and I don't care to know," Mark told him.

The gerson went into the other room and came back with rolls of very fine linen and a pair of small, very sharp scissors. "I was going to make an architectural model with this, but it will serve better as bandages for your hands." He knelt in front of Mark and began unwinding one. "Spread your fingers."

Mark felt more hurt than deprived. He did as the gerson asked.

"I can't," the gerson told him softly. "Not with you. I've had short affairs—"

"With anyone as short as me?" Mark quipped, offering a smile. His heart ached right up through his throat.

The gerson let out a nervous laugh. "You're not that short. You're at least a half foot over five."

"Something like that." The words barely came out.

The gerson wrapped each finger and then wrapped all around them, making Mark's hand into a mitten. He left the thumb exposed. "If I really believed in my heart that you would die here in Saphir, I would be on you before you could blink." Mark's heart squeezed painfully inside him. "But I can't be with you and then watch you leave Saphir forever without another thought spared for me. It's just who I am. The irony is that because I'm so foolishly loyal I've become something of an object of pursuit at *shrefmetyne*."

"I don't even know what that is," Mark admitted.

"It's where men like us go to be free of judging eyes. It's ruled by the *trerashefral*, a group of men and women whose every move is catalogued with breathless rapture in every gazette. In Saphir, the most famous are *Ellisen*."

"Irises? Like the blossom?"

"Yes. They define fashion, which I consider separate from culture, but most in Saphir do not, much to the dismay of anyone sensible. I have to admit, their taste is exceptional. I'm sure they'll find your voice remarkable, and therefore everyone in Saphir will find your voice remarkable, even if they've never hear it. I've seen them lift people of your talent to great heights. I've also seen them cruelly dismember those who foolishly cross them. And if you ever fall out of favor by way of an embarrassment— many who plummet from that height gladly plummet from the nearest cliff for an encore."

"Is Duke Foll—"

A rueful chuckle sounded in Gerson Lowell's throat. "I shouldn't be surprised that you've already heard of him." His eyes widened a little at Mark's expression. "You've met him." Mark blushed. "You've more than met him." The gerson's tone gave too little away. Mark wasn't sure if he was annoyed, jealous, awed, or disapproving.

"You know him well?" Mark asked.

"No." The gerson's matter-of-fact tone perfectly matched the hard judgment darkening his beautiful eyes.

"Well, I'd rather avoid them in general, and him in particular, from now on," Mark assured him.

"You will perform before too long before all of them. You can't avoid them. Gutter might even invite them for dinner in hopes of gaining some advantage in his quest of destruction." The gerson's mouth tightened into a thin line.

"This isn't the first time you've put him down. I find it strange that you're helping him when you seem to think so little of him."

"Our labor is my duty. It's his obsession." Gerson Lowell wound the bandage carefully up Mark's arm, smoothing it as he went with his other hand but not applying any tension to it.

He must think even less of me, with neither duty nor obsession to recommend me. I'm here because I'm caught up in an intrigue and for political advantage, not because I believe in or even trust Gelantyne.

"Is the bandage too tight?" the gerson asked softly.

"Will you stay?" Mark asked him.

The gerson looked into his eyes and Mark's mind slid out of focus. Everything he wanted in the world seemed to be crouched before him, dressed in a painfully exquisite body, mind and soul. "I'm not the sort of person who gives a different answer when asked the same question twice."

"I promise that you won't fall in love with me. How could you, when you know I'm little more than Gutter's puppet half the time." All sense of shame shrank to nothing beside his need to hold the gerson close. "Besides, I'm not someone that people fall in love with. I'm a toy. You'll see. I'm nothing but a toy."

"You're so much more to me than that already."

"I don't understand." The pain in his chest had faded but it grew worse again. "Why is this happening to us?"

The gerson's gaze gentled, and a wistful smile warmed his expression. "Why does anyone fall in love? They just do."

"Is that what this is?" But they barely knew each other.

The gerson snipped off the linen and tucked the edge in at Mark's elbow. "I can't speak for your heart. I can only speak for mine, and I know this road too well. Better to turn back than to go forward. My beloved lies in a woman's bed every night while I sleep alone and wonder if he still thinks of me. I don't want to wonder about two men. If I love again, it will be with a man who stays by me." His gaze deepened and grew hotter. "If I asked, would you stay in Saphir with me?"

Mark didn't want to, but he forced himself to shake his head. "I can't."

"If you need anything, I'll be next door to the left." The gerson started to leave. He stopped by the door. "I'm sorry. You haven't eaten." A short laugh escaped him. "You've distracted me from my purpose again."

Again? "Go. I'll be fine."

Gale, who'd sat quietly near the bed, moved closer after the gerson shut the door. Mark shifted the cleaning table away so she could take her place on his feet and lean on his legs. She slumped as if her heart had stopped and her head leaned bonelessly to one side. Her weight comforted him. He stroked her broad side and thought of Perida. The pain in his chest faded to a more familiar, safer one of homesickness. He stripped off the rest of his clothes. The room, nothing near as cold as his room at Gutter's house, had begun to warm from the steam. The water in the pot had cooled enough to bathe in, but he didn't dare wet his bandages. He slid under the covers, wishing he could at least rub the worst of the sweat off. It felt like a sin to soil the gerson's clean sheets.

Gelantyne warmed his feet. It seemed irreverent to use the mask for such a low purpose, so he forced himself up and wrapped the mask neatly in the blanket before he set it on the chair. He'd just returned to bed when the gerson came in with two plates of food. Gale sat up in swift attention.

"Now you're just torturing yourself," Mark told him, accepting the plate. It was enough dinner for a dozen meals if not more. Gravy pooled richly around a generous portion of pheasant, bright carrots, and dark beets. A thick slice of buttery bread almost as large as the plate sat atop it all.

"I'll leave you to your dinner." The gerson lingered, his gaze held low.

His presence only increased their pain. Why did he stay? "I'll see you soon, I'm sure," Mark told him.

The gerson took a step away. "In a few hours."

For one so wise in love, you're making us both into fools. "Go, then."

He took another step. "Take a bite first."

"Leave first." An unwilling smile started to lift and warm his face.

The gerson's eyes smiled. "Eat first."

Mark peeled off a piece of bread. Gale watched his every movement, rapt. "Go."

"Eat."

"Go." He wouldn't manage hardly any of the food without milk anyway, and he didn't want to try with someone watching, especially the gerson.

The gerson set his plate on the desk and crossed his arms.

Mark had to admit it. "There's no milk."

The gerson's eyes widened. "You are the most spoiled creature I have ever met."

"So get it, or go."

He actually started to look angry, but then the gerson laughed, not entirely pleasantly, and stormed out. "Do not let Gale have my dinner."

"You can have mine when I'm finished," Mark assured Gale. The rich, meaty scent whipped his hunger to near-madness. "I'm sure you'll like it." *Please let me be cured soon.*

The gerson came back with a whole pitcher of milk and sat it down on the desk. He fetched a cup from the other room, poured, and handed it to Mark.

This would be the end of their game. Mark braced himself, dipped a tiny bit of the bread in the gravy and savored it before he swallowed and washed it down with milk. The doctor had told him no more, but he couldn't imagine a meal without it.

It had been too long since he'd last eaten and his belly avenged itself with fire. From long experience he knew he could tolerate another bite of bread so he took it with a half a slice of carrot and a little more milk.

Any more than that and he'd be sick.

The gerson ate, largely ignoring him. After a moment he glanced over. "A bite of pheasant."

"I can't," Mark told him.

The gerson gestured with his fork. "You will."

Mark almost did it just to spite him, but he needed every bit of food he'd just eaten or tomorrow he'd be too weak to get out of bed. "No. I won't."

"You're proud and stubborn and insufferable."

"So leave." His temper lifted but he managed to smother it by focusing on his pain.

The gerson chewed slowly, watching him. Something in his eyes changed. "You really can't, can you."

"I have plenty of time before I starve to death," Mark reminded him bitterly, his temper roused by the gerson's fucking pity, pity as unwelcome as priests at his door. "You told me so, remember? Get out. Get out!"

Gale's hackles rose.

The gerson picked up his plate and walked out, carefully not looking at either Mark or Gale. He shut the door behind him.

"I thought he was different but that man is the worst thing the Church has ever bred," Mark told Gale. "I hate him." But it wasn't true. He curled up around his pain and forced himself to think of Perida. After a few more tiny bites of food, he set the plate on the floor for Gale and finally fell asleep with everything he longed for impossibly out of reach.

After he woke Mark dressed and ventured out into the hall. Once again he was awake at a dark and unseemly hour. He reminded himself that the gerson's door had a beautiful stone arch carved and painted over with red flowering vines so he could find it again. The painted vines continued onto the thick oak door. He walked to the right toward the end of a hall he hadn't yet passed through, the direction the gerson had taken when he told Mark he'd take Gale for a walk.

After a few false turns down various halls parallel to the gerson's, he found an exit into a small, unlit courtyard. The air shocked him with its chill, and the stars looked close and far too bright to be real, and yet they defied their own impossibility by sparkling in a great expanse of black. They glimmered faintly with swaths of smaller lights and something that looked like a master artist's brushwork far too distant and unmoving to be clouds. Gale snuffled near the rosemary beds and squatted. He waited while she walked around some more until she hunched to relieve herself. He let himself into a tool closet and raked her leavings into a small bucket, dumped it into an outhouse and cleaned the bucket and rake under a water pump before he took her back inside.

When he returned he nearly ran into the gerson as he came around the corner.

The gerson caught his breath. "I thought you might have taken Gale out. The doctor has come to see you. He's brought medicine for you."

Mark muffled a flash of irritation. Fear came in its wake. If the cure didn't work then hope would end. "You didn't have to send for the doctor. He has more important things to do. How is Lord Argenwain?"

"The doctor just came from there at Gutter's request, as he's no longer needed. I'm sorry, Lark. Lord Argenwain is dead."

Mark gasped and backed without finding a wall. He nearly fell over and staggered sideways into a pillar in time to steady himself.

"Lark." The gerson caught him by his injured arm but Mark hardly felt it.

Lord Argenwain is dead.

"Lark." The gerson pulled him back to his room. Mark stumbled along like a dumb animal being led to slaughter, still reeling. He shouldn't have cared, or better, he should have been pleased.

He suddenly hated Saphir. Nothing good had come from his journey here. He was too far from home among people he didn't want to be with doing things that had nothing to do with Meridua anymore.

The gerson sat him down. The doctor said things, the gerson said things, and they handed him a cup with a spoon that sat in something gloopy and more or less white. Mark stirred it and sampled it. It tasted like sweet chalk, as much as it tasted like anything, and then it turned so bitter it made him shudder.

His throat went numb. His stomach cramped violently and he swallowed hard before a lurch of bile could erupt from inside him.

Then, suddenly, a blissful nothing. He felt so little pain compared to what he'd felt continuously for so long that it almost felt like pleasure. It had been so long since his belly hadn't tortured him he'd forgotten—

It didn't feel normal. The numbness in his throat had spread into the depths of him and he felt a little swollen inside.

"Eat this." The doctor offered him some sort of mash. Mark couldn't taste it but he didn't care. His hunger reared into an impossibly ravenous thing and he fed it as fast as he could.

"Slow down. Slow down!" The doctor caught his hand. "Slow down. This is the most you've eaten in a long time and I'm afraid you'll be sick."

"I'm not sick." Mark could have danced with joy if he didn't feel so unsteady. "I'm all right."

"You're not healed. Cures don't work this fast. You feel numb in your throat?"

Mark nodded. He pried his wrist loose from the doctor. The gerson took the cup from his hand. Mark wanted to stab him with the spoon.

"Your stomach is numb as well," the doctor told him.

"I know—"

"I don't know if it will work," the doctor reminded him. "You might not be able to digest anything. You might vomit. Anything could happen. Just try to be patient. At least wait an hour before you eat anything more."

I've been waiting for months, Mark thought bitterly, but he knew the doctor was right. He set the spoon back in the cup and sank his head in his hands. He couldn't tell if he was overjoyed or sick with fear or angry or sad or even if what he felt had anything to with the cure or if it had everything to do with Lord Argenwain. He just wanted to weep or bleed or something to release the unbearable pressure of hope and grief within him.

"Do you need me to write the instructions down?" the doctor asked the gerson.

"No. It's fairly straightforward. Thank you, doctor."

"Don't thank me yet." The door closed.

The gerson sat beside Mark. "Are you all right?"

The question was absurd, but Mark forced himself to nod.

A strong hand smoothed down his back. "I'm sorry about Lord Argenwain."

The gerson would never understand. Mark hardly understood himself. He fought it but his eyes ached and burned and his throat squeezed so hard it hurt and he couldn't hold back the tears anymore. He pressed his palms into his eyes until he saw red sparks and still they flowed, this time down his nose and throat and dripped everywhere. A spasm rocked through him but he held back the sob.

"I'm so sorry." The gerson's hand kept smoothing up and down his back. Mark curled, half on the gerson's lap, half on his own, trying to win back a modicum of control.

"Just let it go," the gerson whispered.

Another spasm rocked his body with horrific violence, and Mark let go. His body sagged as if all the life had fled from his body and he lay there, strangely unable to cry. His arms tucked against his chest and stared, seeing nothing, feeling nothing, but he drowned in agony.

"That's it," the gerson soothed. "Let it go." He gathered Mark into his arms and held his head against his chest. The gerson's heart pounded, strong and steady, and his strength held Mark close. Mark closed his eyes. Nothing hurt in this strange, dark, peaceful place that smelled like incense and clean skin. All he had to do was breathe. He wished it wasn't so hard to breathe ....

The gerson held him, and after a moment Mark slipped his hands around the gerson's waist and gently, as shy as an orphaned child reaching for his only hope of security, Mark held Gerson Lowell close.

The music moved in the lower edges of Mark's range and then bounded up two octaves where it traveled a short time before it dove into his strongest voice. He sang savagely—

"No! No no no." Gerson Lowell stopped him.

"Aw!" protested one of the workers at the back of the auditorium. "That was magnificent! What do you know about music anyway?"

"Look at the lyrics." The gerson stabbed the page with his finger. "This isn't lightning and thunder crashing overhead shattering the rocks. This is thunder in the distance, traveling through the clouds until it breaks here." He showed the next octave leap. "Rolling. Understated. Anger, but a quiet, menacing anger that slips the assassin's dagger into the ribs and then twists with a sigh and a smile. Again."

Mark followed his instructions. At the last note a stunned silence muffled the auditorium.

The gerson broke the quiet. "I confess I despise most music, especially vocals, but that curled my toes." He turned in his seat toward the workmen. "Well?"

The workman who'd complained bowed.

The gerson turned back. "Do you understand it now?"

Mark nodded. "It's beautiful. I've never heard this before. *Morbai, allolai*, it's like a song about love but a twisted, dark love ... only pure ... both beautiful and ugly, but beautiful because it's ugly and ... absolute." He wasn't explaining himself very well.

"You've never been in a church during the holy day, have you."

"No," Mark admitted. He didn't want to add that he'd never actually spent any time in a church before his bonding, and he hadn't had a chance since. He'd only been in court.

"It is the one time of year that truths can be spoken and shared, but only as music and poetry, only as sacred lyrics. They must be obscured, but the feeling can remain. This feeling you're describing relates to the sacred. It teaches us things. Here, in Saphir, we have more freedom than most but we are still restricted to music. Most of it can only be performed in Church, where the people who need to hear it most, can't. This is just barely secular enough that doesn't provoke an attack. At least, it hasn't in the past." His hands traced across the paper. "I wish I could interpret this for you, but I must not. I can hint that this song is a warning about lost love. It is grief and anger and despair that gives the lover a terrible strength even as it consumes and destroys her."

"Her." He couldn't tell by the lyrics that it was a woman.

"It warns us about the terrible things that good is capable of. I think it's appropriate. What do you think?" the gerson asked.

Mark nodded. The gerson's casual, almost flip tone didn't ring true, until he realized that the gerson hadn't meant it in regard to himself or Mark at all. He was talking about Gutter and the king.

"The last piece ...." the gerson prompted.

Mark turned the page.

"Is very quiet. This is the lost child."

A shiver went through Mark.

"A lost child's best chance to survive is to overcome his fear and use his curiosity and his ability to notice details that others overlook. This lost child saves himself by relentlessly discovering all he needs to know to live. At the end—"

Mark flipped through the pages, scanning the lyrics. He wished he knew Hasle better. The nuances were lost on him.

"—the music suddenly explodes."

This is the moment.

"Small, delicate, lost voice. You will travel down a narrow, glass walkway over the audience to where the king is seated," the gerson said. "Feather will begin to sing on stage, joining you in the harmony. Another will join, and then you and she and the chorus and a great many vocalists and instrumentalists throughout the audience will execute the final pages from all sides."

Feather? Feather was here?

He remembered her voice. He remembered her way of watching things unseen, too.

It would be an overwhelming amount of music.

It would not be a literal scream as he'd thought Gelantyne wanted him to do. It would be a musical scream, a scream of victory, of life, of the child seizing his fate and survival and wringing his own power from the world.

Mark listened to the music play through his mind as he paged back and read through it. Shivers traveled through him.

"It's as if it was written for you," the gerson said. "But it was written over a hundred years ago."

Mark looked at the composer.

G.

Gelantyne.

When he learned of me, he knew I was the one who could do this.

Later, in the gerson's room where Mark mainly slept and ate and read and wrote and exercised and washed himself alone, he sat on the bed and the gerson sat in the chair and they didn't look at each other.

"Won't this warn the king when it begins?" Mark asked.

"I don't see how it would."

"But it's the mask's music."

"No one knows that. I'm surprised you guessed it."

Mark looked up at him. "It's obvious."

"It's only obvious to you because you are so much a part of what will happen."

"But whatever is protecting him on the other side—"

"—has heard this music before. It just won't have been performed with such ... power. And they will not expect you."

"They'll know the moment I open my mouth, if they don't know already."

The gerson sighed. "It's possible, but we're staging things as best we can. Not just us. The mask as well. He can't protect you, but he is capable of a great deal that we don't understand, and he would not attempt this if he felt there was no chance of success."

Mark wasn't sure he wanted to risk his mind and perhaps his life for this. He still had only their word that the king was a murderer.

"There is one more thing," the gerson said. "You mustn't speak at all the day and night of the performance. It will give away too much of who and what you are and will be. I believe that you're being guarded almost constantly, so we should be safe in this room, but that night, the forces that protect the king will be everywhere, searching for threats. We don't want them to hear you say something that might suggest that he's in danger. In fact, it might be a good idea for you to restrict what you say from this time forward, just to be sure."

Because they can hear me.

Someone knocked on the door. The gerson got up and answered it. He accepted a note, cracked the seal, shut the door and began to sit.

He froze.

Mark rushed over and read the note. An evil cold traveled down his spine and he felt sick to his soul.

Duke Farevren was missing.

"How. How!" Mark hardly knew the man but he knew enough to care that he might be dead or hurt or whatever the king did when people disappeared around him.

"I don't know. They were supposed to protect him. Gutter. Gutter." The gerson stood, shaking violently. "If Gutter used the duke to distract the king I'll kill him."

Mark took the letter from him. "This is Gutter's writing." It was in the RT code. "He wouldn't tell us of it if he'd done something to the duke."

"He would have to when Anne noticed he was missing, and she'd notice in a heartbeat something was wrong." The gerson took the note to a candle and lit it, then cast it in a special burning case for the purpose. He sprinkled in incense before lighting a charcoal held in a pair of tongs. His eyes reflected the candlelight with a dangerous fire. "I feared he would do something like this. Lord Argenwain's death assured it."

Mark wasn't sure the gerson had leapt to the truest conclusion, assuming he was talking about Gutter and not the King, who might also be greatly affected by Lord Argenwain's death. "We don't know what Gutter is up to.

Look. I've foiled his plans before. I might not be much of a threat to him, but I have more power than he likes. If Gutter engineered this kidnapping or whatever it is, I don't think he would have sent that letter for fear I'd muck things up for him again. Besides, Gutter loves the duke. He wouldn't do anything that would put him in harm's way," Mark reminded him.

"Look at what he did to you, the son he'd always wanted but never sired himself," the gerson shot back.

"He wants the duke and duchess on the throne. He wouldn't—"

"He wants the duchess on the throne. The duke isn't strictly necessary, not with their eldest son in position to stand beside her."

"Their eldest—"

"Sir Richard, Duke of Truvalth, known as Rick Talisman."

Mark had never heard of such a person. "Their eldest—"

"Was hidden at birth and given title here in Saphir."

RT. The sense of revelation didn't last. "It doesn't matter who arranged this." For all he knew, even if Gutter had done this, Gutter might also be counting on Mark to get the duke back. "We have to find the duke." He had little doubt that he was still missing several important connections but they didn't matter at the moment. They could sort it out later.

"You aren't doing anything but preparing for your performance. We can't risk you."

Mark walked out, grabbing his hat, cloak and weapons on the way. Gale trotted beside him, heeling without being asked.

"Lark!"

"You can come with me or you can stay here. I don't care which."

Cursing in a language Mark didn't know, the gerson grabbed a hat and cloak and followed him.

"Get me to the duchess."

The gerson grabbed him, pulling him to a halt. "You can't do this. Not like this."

"Why not?"

The gerson stared at him for a moment. Another moment passed. The gerson started walking and Mark and Gale took up pace beside him. "We'll hire a coach. Her Grace is staying at her son's house. It's not far from here, but it's on an island and we're sure to be seen on at least one of the bridges between here and there."

"My running to her in her time of distress won't be particularly noteworthy," Mark said.

"Except that she hardly knows you, as far as Saphir's courtiers understand. It might attract their curiosity."

"Let it. Very few people, since I've hardly been anywhere in Saphir except the banre, know me on sight. By the time they figure out who I am, they'll come up with something more plausible on their own than we can craft for them as to why I arrived at her door." He wasn't sure this was entirely a good idea, but he didn't trust Gutter enough to go to him and he couldn't see Gzem without risking a run-in with the lord jester. "What about Legend? Will he hunt for the duke or stay with duchess?"

"Gutter wouldn't consider Legend of much importance as far as his plans are concerned. He has a distinct disregard for other jesters. They are all beneath his notice." Gerson Lowell picked up his pace and Mark had a hard time keeping up with him. His newfound ability to eat had bolstered his strength beyond his best hopes, but he still had little endurance.

"I think you hate him so much that you underestimate his need for connections and his fear of failure," Mark said.

"I don't hate him. I just don't trust him, and I know how ruthless he can be. I'm surprised that you would defend him."

So am I. "Legend is an asset, regardless of what you think Gutter may or may not think of him. And Gutter doesn't waste assets. Whether he set this trap or is desperately looking for the duke himself, Gutter will employ Legend somehow."

"If Gutter did something to the duke, chances are he would have been forced to do something to get Legend out of the way. Even if Gutter spared his life, Legend would spend all his energy searching for the duke. He'd be a lost asset either way."

"And if Gutter didn't engineer this disappearance?"

"He'll give Legend his head to look for the duke. It will free Gutter to employ means of his own to find the duke. If he cares to find the duke, which I fear he does not."

Mark had a strong suspicion that Gerson Lowell was far more intelligent than Mark's tutors had ever praised him up to be. He feared the gerson's assessment of Gutter's feelings toward the duke might be closer to the truth. "Together you and I can find the duke. You have the intelligence, the knowledge of the necessary politics, and the keys. Gutter will go out of his way to protect me, and I have leverage should he try to stand in our way. We'll find the duke, and we'll save him. Will Gelantyne be safe in your rooms?"

The gerson turned ashen. "Oh. I don't know. I ... I wouldn't hesitate except that if I was wrong ...." His look brightened. "We can use the passageway. There's a hidden cache large enough to hold him."

"Is it close?"

"Not very—you should know. You came that way." The gerson started back toward his room.

"We can't use it. I broke the door, remember?"

"What are you talking about? You—wait. I do remember you telling me something about that. You said you cut—what did you do to the door?"

"Never mind. We can't use the passageway as a hiding place. It can't be locked on our side."

You are not made for this task. You will fail. Gelantyne's thoughts entered his mind from faraway, but though faint they still blotted out the gerson's words. *If you wish to save the duke you must kill Michael before Michael kills him.*

Gerson Lowell put his hand on Mark's arm. "—down?"

Mark kept his focus on his conversation with Gelantyne, though he wondered what the gerson had tried to ask. "The performance isn't for a week." Mark went to the back room. It served as a combined washroom, storage, and draft room. Baskets of dry herbs and yarn and measuring instruments sat on shelves that covered one wall. The mask lay hidden in a large basket among the others. "How long do you expect him to suffer?"

He may already be dead. It doesn't matter. Now that his bloodline is secure, his soul is all that matters, and it is safe regardless of whether he lives or dies.

"He matters to me." Mark's temper started to rise, his old friend and companion when fear and frustration twined like familiar lovers. "If you want me to perform, you—"

Think this threat through. You would sacrifice this cause, a cause rallied for the sake of all humanity, for one man?

"My voice comes from my heart. Do you really want me to sing knowing I did nothing, and that the—" *I might be overheard. Be careful!* "—that he's dead or dying alone, without hope of aid?" Mark wanted to shake the basket. "I can't stand by and do nothing."

"Are you speaking with Gelantyne?" the gerson asked breathlessly.

Mark gestured for the gerson to be quiet.

You can't fetch him out without risking everything. Even if you succeed, what will Michael do when he discovers the duke is gone?

All Mark could think about was how it would be to be tortured, screaming, hoping for help knowing deep down not one of his friends or family could come to save him because of this horrible plan ....

The strange, ethereal expression on the duke's face when they all met in private suddenly made sense. "Why was he taken?"

That is a question for your mortal friends. The questions you ought to ask me should refer to the final night and how we may best succeed so that this monster prince and his line never inflict themselves upon humanity again.

"Or maybe I should ask why this is important to your cause," Mark realized aloud. "I thought you wanted humanity educated."

The war in the All and the war in the Shell barely touch. This is a service I perform for You, the Church Nations. I pray it will help you seize control of your spiritual lives. I cannot help my brethren in the All, now that I'm here. I can only help You, and this is the mightiest of causes.

Gelantyne's thoughts in his mind helped him understand beyond the words, otherwise he wouldn't have understood that the Shell was the living world. "But it still connects, doesn't it." When he heard Gelantyne mention his brethren in the All, which he assumed were the hells and whatever other weird countries there might be for souls to live and die in, something slipped in Gelantyne's otherwise clear and controlled thoughts.

Revenge.

"You're not just destroying the—that family—for our sakes," Mark began.

You are of course free to belittle and question a thousand years of sacrifice, Gelantyne told him with a strange and uncomfortable gentleness.

"Let me at least try to help him. Believe me, I don't want to get myself killed any more than you want my voice damaged. Please."

Gelantyne didn't respond right away. For an uneasy moment Mark felt as if he'd been blundering around in a dream and had woken up to realize he'd been momentarily insane. The gerson's frightened expression didn't quiet his fears in the least.

Yield to me and I will show you.

Mark didn't sense a trap but now that he'd caught the *allolai* in one subterfuge, Gelantyne would likely be more careful with his thoughts. "What do you want to show me?"

I see that you will persist regardless of argument. Let me see.

"I don't understand." But then he did. Without someone to inhabit, Gelantyne had little power. He barely had any voice, trapped inside that inanimate object he'd somehow become. "You'll look for our missing friend?"

I will look and see what may be possible.

Gelantyne could just as easily hold Mark prisoner until the performance.

No, he can't. I'll starve to death in a very short time, well before the performance. The giggle that bubbled out didn't sound entirely sane. It frightened and amused him at the same time. *My poisoning has worked to my advantage for once.*

"No." Gerson Lowell, who'd been standing close by, grabbed Mark as he reached to draw the mask from the basket.

"Do you want to save the duke or not?" Mark demanded.

Gerson Lowell let him go. "I do. But what if we do? What will His Royal Majesty do if we take the duke from him? He'll be exposed and he'll know it."

"I'd like to at least look at the problem and the mask promised to show me." Mark reached for the basket again. Gerson Lowell grabbed his arm and got in his way. "Do you want to leave Geoff to suffer and die without any of us lifting a hand?"

"The duchess—"

"Yes, her." Mark wrenched his arm free. "Think she'll sit idly by? I thought you've been in love before. Would you stop at anything if you knew the man you loved was in danger? We *have* to save him before she does something desperate to save him herself, or we'll lose them both. And if out of desperation or revenge she manages to reveal what's happened with proof enough to demand a trial, what then?" It was an honest question, not a threat. A trial seemed a far better outcome than whatever Gutter had planned. Either way it would lead to war between Cathret and Hasla. But the gerson, rather than answer, let Mark move him aside. Mark's hands started to sweat and shake as he opened the basket and lifted the mask out. This time it felt heavy and cold. He turned it around. The hairs on his neck prickled up and gooseflesh tightened on his arms. His heart pulsed in his ears. He drew the silk that cascaded from the mask's crest over his head—

Terror clawed through him but his arms moved on their own even as he fought to pull the mask away. Something seized his neck with sharp teeth and sank them into his spine, so deep, so real that the masks he'd worn before seemed to just tickle by comparison. He couldn't scream. The floor vanished and he started to fall. The teeth caught him and shook him until a darkness shot with silent lightning swept in.

The lightning vanished and his awareness yawned. The thing within him that felt joy and fear and love and hate emptied as if every artery were cut and bled his soul away. He'd never felt this alone, even in the wilderness. He had no voice, no body, nothing to touch, nothing to see, nothing to hear. Thoughts of the people he knew drained away. He couldn't remember anyone's names, and even the blurred faces faded from memory—

Rohn. He clung to that one name, and the memory of Rohn's strong hand holding his after the bonding, their flesh knitted into one. It had terrified him at the time but now he held on tight. He imagined Rohn thinking of him, an abstract in the dark but the fragments of Rohn he clung to were all that remained beyond the total darkness.

Red light, silk, a flash of gold and Mark took in a heaving breath. He toppled into the shelf, dragging down baskets on himself. His limbs shook, but he had limbs again. Gerson Lowell existed again. The gerson crouched near him, rubbing his wrists and lightly slapping his face. Gale licked his hand and put a foot on his leg, then his shoulder, as if stepping on him would help bring him back to awareness. She was all puffed up like a frightened cat and trembled so violently she couldn't stand still.

She hadn't warned off Gerson Lowell.

"Good girl." Mark had a voice again. The room seemed strange and confining. His clothes felt hard and heavy against his skin, and his belt weighed on him like stone. His neckerchief choked him. He pulled off the confining gloves that stifled his hands and clawed at the heavy collar around his throat. He couldn't unwind it fast enough. His coat, his vest, everything tangled him, bound him, dug into him with hard, sharp edges—

"What are you doing? Lark. Lark, calm down."

"It's hurting me it's hurting—" It wasn't pain. In some ways it was worse, this all-over-body discomfort like he was buried in cold porcelain plates and butter knives and broken furniture, worse than an itch he couldn't scratch, more terrifying than battling fire on a ship's deck.

Gerson Lowell took Mark's face in his hands and looked into his eyes. Mark gripped his wrists, feeling more bone than skin and flesh at first, but the horrible sensations began to fade. Mark stared back into those beautiful dark eyes a moment, then let go. Too slowly, the sense of edges became so faint that he almost felt normal, though the memory of it threatened to give the madness renewed strength.

Gerson Lowell's hands slipped from his face and the gerson eased back.

The room still seemed cramped but the walls kindly kept their distance. "What happened?" Mark asked. He hugged himself to try to control his trembling. "What did Gelantyne say?"

I was insane a moment ago. I didn't fear or guess or think I was insane. I was insane, truly insane.

So that's what it feels like.

He wanted to hide within his mask and be Lark a while, but then he thought of Gutter and his layers of masks holding Thomas together, barely. He closed his eyes and listened to the gerson's voice.

"The duke is locked in a room beneath *Zellenai*, the Cathretan Ambassadorial Summer Palace on one of the islands," the gerson told him. "I have a key to a tunnel that will lead us very near to the room, but door leading to the catacombs beneath the palace is guarded. We can try to make it look as if the duke escaped and killed the guards, and then was swept away by the river and drowned."

Kill the guards. Mark couldn't believe that the gerson could say such a thing so lightly. "Are the guards partners in the king's sin?"

Gerson Lowell hesitated.

"Do they know who they're guarding? Do they know what their master is?" *And what is the king? What does he do?* Mark desperately wanted to know, to see for himself if it was true.

"I don't know. But we either fight our way in, or we have to leave the duke to his fate."

Mark remembered the gentle, resigned expression on the duke's face and opened his eyes. "Show me the way."

Take me with you. I will dispatch them. Your soul will remain clean, and your body will not be harmed, Gelantyne whispered.

The mask is more important than I am. We'll be too close to the King to risk it. Besides, the king's family trapped Gelantyne once before. They might do it again, and this time, they won't let him get away.

True. It startled Mark a bit that Gelantyne had heard his thoughts. A heartbeat later he felt a strange sense of reassurance mingled with fear that this ancient being agreed with him. **But it is also true that both the gerson and the duke are less important than you. You must accept that and you must not hesitate should it come to a choice.**

If you do not keep yourself safe, the king will do this again, and again, as often as it pleases him.

The gerson fetched weapons from the back room, as well as a second set of keys. "What about Gelantyne?" the gerson asked.

Reluctantly, Mark picked it up with trembling hands and wrapped it in its own silk. He placed it in the basket and back on the shelf. "Gelantyne isn't helpless. A locked door should be enough."

I will call you if I need you, Gelantyne whispered in his mind.

Chapter Sixteen

Mark made sure he walked with special care so he wouldn't make any noise in the tunnel when Gerson Lowell slowed down and began to measure his steps. Mark kept one hand on his rapier and the other on his pistol. He carried a bag over his shoulder with clean clothes, a bit of bread, a small flask of wine and a bottle of water.

We're going to murder good men.

And you will send their souls to a place where they will be free of all this evil, Gelantyne whispered from far away. **There is no need to hesitate.**

That doesn't make it right.

You are a jester, are you not? On the surface the inflection sounded snide, even contemptuous, but beneath that Mark caught a hint of something deeper, as if it were a sincere question, as if he wanted Mark to come up with a better answer.

This tunnel wasn't as crude as the one he'd passed through from Gutter's house. Every several paces the ceiling arched high up into a deep opening. Light glowed from the streets and reflected down the opening's white glass facets. It wasn't a bright light, but it was enough to see by. The gerson carried an unlit lantern with them, presumably for whatever lay ahead.

They weren't alone in the tunnels. Several times they'd passed sacred guards walking through, always in the opposite or a cross direction. The guards placed their hands over their hearts and bowed in greeting to the gerson as they passed.

This wasn't going to work. Even if they survived whatever fight they'd have ahead, they wouldn't be able to fetch the duke to a safe hiding place without everyone noticing. Perhaps the gerson had enough influence among the sacred guard to keep their general silence, but it would take only one man to betray them.

If the secret of the duke's rescue escaped, it would lead the king back to the gerson, maybe even Gutter, certainly to Mark who'd been staying with the gerson all this time, and their plan to bring the king down would fail. He wasn't sure what the king would do, but he certainly wouldn't pass an idle evening sitting with his Saphiran friends at a musical performance.

Now you finally understand my fear, Gelantyne whispered from far away. ***Turn back.***

Not until I know for certain that there is no way to save Duke Farevren.

More privately in his mind, he hoped that what they would find would vindicate the king and put a stop to the conspiracy to take his life.

The gerson turned into a narrow side passage and they walked down a set of stairs into darkness. The gerson lit the lamp. Water dripped from overhead and they splashed through puddles.

The ground gave way to a racing stream. They crossed a wet, slick bridge barely wide enough to allow their passage. When they reached the other side the gerson doused the lamp. They felt along the smooth, wet walls. The cold penetrated Mark's gloves. Mark listened for the gerson's breathing and the slight scuff of his feet to keep a proper distance. The gerson fell silent, and Mark halted. For a moment nothing happened.

He heard the gerson draw his dagger.

No.

Mark touched his elbow. "Talk to him," Mark whispered.

Gerson Lowell pulled him back down the passage. "What?"

Mark found his shoulder so that he could lean close and whisper in his ear. "You're a constabulary priest. He may trust you. Talk to him. Maybe, if he's ignorant of what's going on, he'll help us."

"He will never believe us. I didn't believe it until Gutter proved it to me," the gerson whispered back.

"So lie to him. Tell him you're taking the prisoner into custody. If he knows what's going on, he'll give himself away very quickly and we can kill him without regret. If he doesn't know anything about a prisoner, we can tell him that it's a highly delicate and confidential matter because of the prisoner's rank and that he must be moved to Saphiran custody. Give him some legal reason. You're part of the constabulary order, and a priest. He'll trust you." Mark tried not to raise his voice in his growing excitement.

"He'll want some proof that we have a right to him," the gerson objected. "As a courtesy their majesties Saphir allow that this palace is under Cathretan law. We can't just claim jurisdiction and be done."

"Then let's provide something."

"A forgery?"

Mark couldn't force him to accept the idea. Either he would, or he wouldn't. "I barely know the man and yet I want him back by his wife's side. You're willing to kill good men to free him, but you won't let me create a work of fiction on paper."

"It's treason. Doubly so for you."

"I'm not Cathretan anymore. I'm a Meriduan. Besides, I thought we were doing all these things for the sake of humanity. What does nation matter?" Mark kept his voice as low as possible and tried his best to obfuscate his words, but he feared that this close to where the king might be, he'd readily be overheard and they'd soon be under a terrible assault. It didn't matter whether it would be physical or spiritual. They would lose, and the duke would die.

"Jesters," the gerson hissed under his breath. Mark's face flushed with shame. "It isn't possible. A guard will only respond to royal seals, either the Hasle royal seal or Cathretan, better both."

Mark was glad he'd raised the objection because it made him realize something important. "You're wrong. Your seal and a blank will do."

"I don't understand."

"No one of importance would sign their name to that important of an imprisonment, and your nobles would be equally reluctant. Trust me. No one of noble blood ever wants their name associated with the downfall of another noble. They'll avoid it any way they can. And unless the guards understand everything that is going on, you can trust that their shock and horror at his imprisonment will keep them from asking the right questions. Is there somewhere nearby we can gather the needed materials?"

The gerson considered. "Yes."

"Is there someone you trust who can fetch them for us? The fewer who see us developing this forgery, the better."

You are a clever creature, Gelantyne breathed into his mind.

Mark didn't consider it a compliment.

Click. The slight sound made Mark jump. Click. Tap. A scrape, another click, and then silence. Mark's heart pulsed in his ears. The gerson slowly opened the door.

A Cathretan sacred guard, a large man with a red and white tabard over armor and a golden royal crest on his helm, took a step back from them.

The gerson held the scroll case but didn't offer it. "We're here on a delicate matter," he told the guard. "We're here to claim what is under guard in the southeast lower hall at the last door."

The guard's eyes narrowed in suspicion. "You're Saphiran. There is nothing in that room that concerns you."

Mark tensed and then his body became unnaturally relaxed, preparing to kill him as Mark had killed men before—quickly and holding nothing back.

It's an evil thing that I've had enough practice at killing that my body remembers how to do it.

"I have documents of transfer, but it would be best if I didn't show them to you. Who has your charge?" the gerson asked.

The guard looked uneasy. His gaze shifted between them and to the door.

"I have the key because I have the right to it," the gerson told him. "Do you recognize this?" He touched the chain that hung from his neck.

The guard ventured a glance at it. His shoulders settled a bit. "Leave your weapon with him." He gestured to Mark. "Lock the door, and come with me."

Mark held his expression though he wanted to protest. He accepted the gerson's dagger and stepped back through the door.

They locked him out.

Standing alone in the dark, he feared he'd just lost the gerson forever. Had the guard just captured the gerson? If the guard believed but wished to see the documents, would his forgery hold up? It had been easy to be confident of it when he thought he'd be there to help fight their way out. Now that the gerson was alone and unarmed—

No, the guard couldn't know about the duke. If he did, then the guard would have insisted that Mark accompany them to help keep the king's secret. Wouldn't he? That way no one would know what had happened to the gerson, and they'd have an extra person to torture so they could find out how many more knew about the duke's imprisonment.

Of course there might be a back passage into this hall where additional guards could slip in behind Mark and kill or capture him. In that case, separating him from the gerson would make it that much easier to capture them both with far less risk.

He had to remain alert.

Every passing minute dragged to the point where he couldn't measure time in any rational way anymore. He drew his rapier.

Gelantyne.

What do you see? Mark wasn't sure Gelantyne would hear his thoughts, though he made them as loud and clear and distinct as possible. *Is the gerson all right?*

Without a bearer I am blind.

Shit.

Click. Mark startled in the darkness. Click. Tap. A scrape, another click, and then silence. Mark took another pace back from the door and drew his pistol.

The door cracked, dazzling his eyes with wavering lamp light. The crack widened.

Two Cathretan sacred guards dragged someone upright between them. Duke Farevren.

He couldn't see much in the lamp light, and yet he saw too much and for a long moment he couldn't breathe, much less move. Not even his eyes could shift to look away. The duke's shirt hung open, the ruffles dark with blood, framing his gray-pale, ravaged chest like the edges of a wound. His head hung down, shaved, cut along the top in an arc from ear to ear and stitched closed. A long, clean slice traveled down his chest, also stitched closed with neat little sutures. Ragged ends of sutures that had been cut made a line not unlike a ripped seam between them. The line went all the way down to his groin and stopped. His manhood looked wrong, looked ...

He had no testicles. The realization rocked through Mark's body like a physical blow, freeing him at last. He hid his face against the wall and breathed in the wet stone's cold, clean-earth scent, tinged with green moss. Still somehow he smelled the blood. Still somehow he saw, though he'd looked away, the cuts over the duke's left knee, and the top of his right foot. Mark could almost feel the wounds on his own body, and he could imagine too well someone not just inflicting them in the quick agony of a sword's sweep, but with the deliberate care of a surgeon and then peeling back the bruised skin to have a look at what pulsed and twitched underneath.

It took enormous effort for Mark to sheathe his pistol and rapier. The gerson was close behind them. He kept his gaze averted from the duke while he shut and locked the door.

"Is he alive?" Mark asked. The smell of blood and shit made him want to gag.

"I live," the duke rasped. His voice didn't just startle Mark. Everyone flinched from it.

"You will see justice soon enough." The gerson's mouth worked in an exaggerated fashion, mouthing silent words, but he couldn't say what he wanted to. He didn't realize Mark had caught his tone and understood. He'd told the guards something that implied the duke somehow deserved this treatment by whoever had imprisoned him.

It couldn't have been the king. How could any noble do such a thing, much less a royal?

"I hope you can spare some more of your time," Mark told the guards. His voice wavered, but no one seemed to care. "It will only take a moment to cross onto Saphiran soil, where we can properly take custody of him."

"I cannot account for this." The guard sounded bewildered.

"It's a delicate matter," Mark told him.

"What did he do?" the guard asked. "Who did this to him?"

The duke began to say something and Mark slapped him. "Silence."

It shocked all of them. Mark had shocked himself. He hoped the darkness hid his expression until he could smooth it. *I'll travel through a few hells for that, I'm sure.*

"Gerson, if you would lead the way," Mark prompted.

Gerson Lowell gave him a stark look as he passed. Mark took up the rear for a time, then passed them after the bridge so that he could lead the way up the stairs. As he suspected they would, the guards had trouble negotiating their way up while burdened with the duke.

Mark pulled the gerson up into the hall. "Find some guards and have them arrested," he whispered.

"What?"

"We can't let them go back. Even if we explain everything and trust them, if they go back, how will they account for the duke's disappearance? If they're good men I don't want them to be executed for their part in this."

Gerson Lowell nodded and hurried ahead. Mark waited for the guards at the top of the stairs. When they finally reached it, Mark gestured. "This way. I'm sorry for your pains. The gerson and I weren't certain what condition he would be in—"

"This doesn't seem right," one of the men, the smaller one, said. He had keen gray eyes and a short beard. "His Majesty ... His Majesty cannot lie."

Mark's skin prickled up. "And yet, here is the evidence." What lie did his most Royal and Majestic Michael tell these men?

The guard gazed at Mark. "Who are you?"

He had a hundred answers balanced on his tongue, but Mark heard the gerson and the guards coming. Only one seemed fitting that would still make them hesitate. He took a bow. "I'm just a boy of no consequence."

The gerson's presence seemed to relax the Cathretan sacred guardsmen, but then the Saphiran guards surrounded them and they dropped the duke. His savaged body struck the stone ground with a painful crack.

The guards reached for their weapons. The Saphiran guards pounced on them, weighed them down and had them in irons in moments.

Mark helped the duke up as gently as he could, but there was no helping him without hurting him. The noble flesh felt as cold and clammy as fresh fish from Old Gosh's shop. Some of the stitches had torn out, and he bled anew, though the blood smelled off.

The man couldn't bear more than a trace of his own weight. "I'm so sorry I struck you, Your Grace." The inadequacy of his apology shamed him. Mark draped the duke's arm over his shoulder. The smell of blood and excrement and mysterious fluids too vital to be exposed to the air overwhelmed Mark's senses and made him want to vomit, not just from revulsion but pity and horror. The duke's breath came soft and shallow. This close, Mark could hear hisses of pain in it, constant pain more intense than Mark had ever known. It made his bout with poison seem of no consequence.

The duke nodded and braced his wounded head against Mark's head. The trust and weariness imbued in the gesture made hot tears well around Mark's eyes and choked off his throat. Mark didn't deserve that trust. He'd already betrayed it by doubting for a moment that the Cathretan monster capable of this needed to die.

The anger that should have been the duke's woke inside Mark like a like a wounded lion. The king had done this, and had lied, and had done this very thing to countless people, had killed them slowly in the dark. No one had saved them. No one even knew to try but a handful of conspirators, and they'd waited how long to act on what they knew? How many people had died in that time?

Mark doubted they'd saved the duke. They'd only revealed his suffering, and perhaps had spared him the worst of it, but this .... Mark held the duke gently. "You'll see your wife soon, Your Grace," Mark promised him. "And then you can sleep." Mark hoped he would last at least long enough to speak to Anne. How he'd survived this long, Mark couldn't understand.

A pair of Saphiran guards took Duke Farevren from Mark, and their group made their way slowly to the surface.

"Gerson." Mark, shaking with rage and horror, fell in step beside him. "You have to go on ahead and clear the way, or we'll never make it before someone asks the wrong question."

The gerson nodded. He fell back to walk alongside one of the Saphiran guards and spoke a few words in Hasle so quickly Mark couldn't follow their meaning. The gerson caught up with Mark again. "There's someone who should know what's happened. Not your former master. This man's wife."

The duchess, Anne. Mark nodded.

The gerson worked a key off of one of his rings. "One left, one right. Take the next set of stairs up. The door will let out into the wall, and the door on your left will open by the same key and pattern onto the street. Tell the guard you are a red messenger. Lock the door behind you. You will be about a mile from the banre. If she is not with your former master, then the former messenger can deliver the message discreetly to her."

Gzem. Mark nodded. "I understand." He trotted on ahead, tired and hungry and afraid. The king could be at the house with Gutter. Mark couldn't let himself be seen at Avwan Trofal.

The king was likely there comforting Gutter in his grief. How dare he? How could Gutter stomach it? He wondered if the staff knew—no. Gutter wouldn't risk it. They'd all be serving that creature as if it were an honor, and remark on how the king doted on his grief-stricken friend with such grace.

Stop dwelling and think.

He could use the kitchen entrance. If the gate into the garden wasn't locked, Petren could let him in.

He had blood on his gloves from the duke, and blood on his coat. This wouldn't be easy. Fortunately he'd worn a cloak. He still hadn't gotten used to the cold and now his need for extra warmth helped him just as the poison assured that Gelantyne couldn't trap him. Mark reversed the cloak to hide the blood.

The duke was free, but now the king would be nervous and Gutter's plans would begin to crumble. The king might even leave Saphir before the performance, and Gutter ... Gutter wouldn't let him escape. If Gutter made an attempt on the king's life now, he would likely fail, die, and the king would get away. That sickening creature would return to Cathret, to his throne, where no one could touch him, and he would be wary.

And he would kill again, at his leisure, comfortable on his home hunting ground, protected not only in the living world but inexplicably by the morbai and allolai who treasure his bloodline.

I will not let him escape, Gelantyne whispered harshly in his mind.

I won't let him escape either. We'll get him, Mark swore to Gelantyne. *Even if we have to send an army over the mountains after him.*

Mark followed the gerson's instructions. He emerged into an early evening. The blue skies delicately brushed with clouds gave enough light to see by, though Saphir itself rested in the shadows of the mountains that cradled her. He'd never seen such blue, cold and relentlessly bright all the way to the jagged and tower-peaked horizon.

His body began to fail. The light-headedness overtook him without warning. He held his cloak close and forced himself to slow his pace. His ears closed up and his vision wavered. He watched his feet with only an occasional glance up to keep from running into anyone.

The mile should have taken him only a few minutes but he was certain it took him nearly a half hour before he reached the banre.

A long line of fine carriages stood in front of the house. People talked on the steps in large groups, dressed in rich clothing fine enough to wear to a royal ball. Messengers and visitors came and left with such regularity that the door stood open with one of the minor servants merely standing by while others ferried the invaders back and forth.

Mark crossed the street at the far end of the house, unnoticed in the chaos, and slipped into the narrow alley between Gutter's house and the neighbor. He tried the side gate.

It was open.

He slipped into the garden and tried the kitchen door. It was also open. Of course it would be, but after meeting so many locked doors and passages he'd forgotten what it was like to roam in the usual world.

The usual world had changed for him forever.

Mark took the back stairs up, nodding in greeting to a harried servant on the way. He had to cross to the house's center to take the next flight of back stairs up to the third floor. Refined guests stared at him but he refused to stop, even when a dignified woman wearing enough diamonds to buy a warship waved her fan at him. No doubt they were all here to see Gutter in his time of mourning. Mark would never get to him, much less have a chance to speak with him privately. He needed to talk to Gzem. She was the best person to bear the news, and he could find out from her better than anyone else what was happening, and what he might be able to do to help.

The door to her suite was locked. He lightly rapped his knuckles on the carved wood.

Sroh answered and stepped back in shock. Mark slipped inside past him and shut the door.

Gzem had been writing a letter. She sat propped up behind a small desk in a large chair. She stood and set her book aside. "Lark? You can't be here."

"Can we talk?"

Sroh's mouth tightened into a line and he began to leave.

"It's all right if you stay." Mark told him.

"He can't." Gzem's eyes narrowed in pain as Sroh let himself out and shut the door tight behind him. "All of this—he can't. He has to remain free of sin for both of us."

As if their marriage needed any more strain in it. Mark kept his questions to himself about the sins they may or may not commit according to what standards anyone alive could measure. "We have the duke. He's alive."

Gzem gasped. "How is he?"

Who would tell his wife what had been done to him? "Never mind that. Anne needs to know."

"Gutter has her locked in the basement." Gzem's eyes sharpened and her jaw slid sideways with anger before she composed herself. "I'll let her know. You have to get out of here."

"Is—is *he* here?"

"He comes every day and stays for hours. He could arrive again at any moment. Where have you been? Are you hurt?"

Mark shook his head. "I'm well enough, thank you." Actually he felt extremely unwell, and thought he might be sick, no so much from the poison but from rage and impatience and the horrific memories of the castrated duke. The wounds he'd seen obliterated the world around him in flashes like a nightmare trying to battle its way into his waking world.

"You're pale." She cast her hands up in a gesture of helplessness. "Go. Go on. I'll take care of matters here."

"And Gutter?" Mark asked, knowing he ought to leave, but he had to know.

Gzem's expression hollowed. "Better than I expected, but ... you mustn't stay. You're right, he needs you, but he can't have you by him so we'll have to do. He's resting now, and I'm trying to help with his correspondence ...."

Gzem closed her eyes for a long, telling moment. "Sroh and I can hold him together in your absence. Now go."

Anne had to be warned, so she could grieve and scream before she saw her beloved. He just didn't know what words to send to her. It seemed to take an eternity to find them while Gzem waited for him to leave, her impatience fading as she realized he had something important to impart before he left. "We didn't reach him in time, Gzem. He may not survive. I don't know how much was taken from him."

"Taken?"

"He was ... castrated. And more. He's very badly hurt." He couldn't do any more than whisper the words.

Gzem stilled, and the color bled from her face. A breath later her skin blotched with grief and rage. He could almost see the memories of her longtime friend shatter and cut her apart as she absorbed and understood what Mark had told her.

"Gzem."

She startled as if he'd just appeared before her.

"Don't think about vengeance. Stay calm." He had no right to ask that of her, but he had to. "We have to do this right or we'll never have another chance. You have to remind Anne of it too. Any moment we might be discovered, and then it will be over for us, and he'll do this again to someone else's beloved."

Twin tears leaked over her lashes and raced down her face. "You have to go."

Mark went out the way he came.

He wanted justice with a passion more intense than he'd ever known, and he was helpless to do anything about it. He had to wait and hope the king—it was hard to think of that vile thing as a king—didn't flee. The thing he wanted to do he could not. He couldn't confront His Majesty. There would be no accusations, no denials, and there would be no attack. The sacred protections upon the king prevented any hope of that succeeding.

Morbai protected the king, inspite of what he'd done. Mark began to realize why the king couldn't go to trial, why it had to be done this way, if it could be done at all. It overwhelmed him, the enormity of it, the length of time that it had taken to arrange this, and how fragile and unlikely the plan was. Would his voice be enough? What about Feather? What could she do?

He stumbled in the street, alarming a group of passersby. He bowed and turned his back to refuse their concern. A man-drawn carriage walked by. Mark waved for him and hired him to take him to the Guilbarabb.

By the time he reached the gerson's room his gut threatened to crush him and his head pounded. Gale circled around him, panting with concern. He took the doctor's stomach medicine and drank water until he felt ready to burst. An old plate of dried figs and even drier bread eased his belly cramps. He tasted none of it but it didn't matter. The light-headedness and headache faded, but the nausea remained.

Mark washed up, changed his clothes, took Gale for a walk, and then settled back in the room to wait.

He waited for hours, trapped by what he knew. If the plan didn't work, what could they do? Did they have enough men to assault the palace? Perhaps Gutter could try to lure the king to them, or perhaps if the king came here then they could destroy him.

Except that they would go insane. The question was, could they assassinate him before their minds and souls crumbled out from under them? Whose *morbai* and *allolai* had the advantage, the king's, or Gutter's allies?

Gutter and Gelantyne had crafted a way to ensure the king's death by way of Mark's voice. The concert had to go forward somehow.

Would a private performance, with Mark performing alone, suffice?

Gelantyne would not have gone to such great lengths if it would.

As much as his memories of the duke's condition tormented him, the idea that others had died alone in that darkness began to grow even larger in his mind. At the first meeting he'd had with the duke and duchess, he'd learned that she was not at risk from the king's attentions, but the duke and the children were. *I fear for my children, and I fear for him,* she'd said. The screams of victims he didn't know and might never hear of rose in Mark's mind, and some of those screams had the heart-rending, terrified wails of infants.

No doubt, once he'd finished with the duke, the king would have found a way to have her children as well, perhaps even the unborn one.

He's not going to get away. The duke is evidence. We'll put it before Their Royal Majesties Saphir, if they don't already know, and close the borders.

Mark had a terrible feeling that it wouldn't be enough, not with the *morbai* and *allolai* protecting the king. But an army had succeeded in bringing down a king before. An army could do it again.

Did they have an army waiting, just in case?

Hours passed. He had to take Gale for another walk. He took his stomach medicine to ease his hunger pains and changed into clean clothes before he ventured to explore the halls. It didn't take long to find sacred guards sitting down to a late supper in a long dining hall. No one gave him more than two glances as he took up a plate and waited for his turn at the kitchen window. The cooks filled his plate with roasted lamb, black carrots, sausages filled with chicken and cheese, a thick slice of golden squash, and a mound of chopped greens dripping with butter. He took it back to his room and ate. He tasted nothing, but the lack of pain kept enticing him to eat a little more, and more. Over the course of a pair of hours, with a little help from Gale, he'd finished the entire plate.

Warmth radiated all the way to his hands and feet. He barely remembered this feeling of satiety, comfort and ease, but he couldn't enjoy it. It had become inconsequential compared to his desire to protect the duchess' children and see justice for her husband. Unfortunately, as time wore on his fears of failure began to outpace his lust for revenge. He had to prepare himself.

After visiting the necessity room and taking Gale for one last walk, he curled up on the bed and closed his eyes and tried to rest. For long moments he could do nothing but think about Duke Farevren—whether he still lived, what might have been done to ease his pain. Eventually exhaustion broke his thoughts into disjointed pieces. Not long after, his worries vanished in waves of freshly sated weariness that rocked him like *Dainty* on calm, tropical waters.

"Lark." A hand touched his arm. The candle he'd lit had long burned out, but a lamp now glowed from its hook by the door, and Gerson Lowell crouched by the bed, framed in its light.

Mark sat up. "How is the—how is he?"

"He's still alive." The gerson lowered his gaze. "He'll live a while longer," he said more softly. "Anne is with him now."

"And ... the concert. Will I perform?" *Please.* He didn't even know who or what he pleaded with.

The gerson raised his gaze and looked into Mark's eyes. "We don't know. He's only returned to his palace a pair of hours ago. But Gutter believes he will stay. Gutter believes the king may even ask him for his help."

Mark covered his mouth, trying to contain his surprise and shock. "His help?" Had the king confided in Gutter? Had Gutter pretended sympathy, even approval, all these years? "How is my master?"

"Angry." The gerson stretched his legs and sat on the floor. His head bowed wearily. "I'm so tired."

Mark stroked the few hairs that had fallen from the gerson's bun back from his face. He shouldn't have, but the gerson didn't protest.

I don't deserve such intimate privilege as touching this beautiful man.

"I've overslept." Mark shifted his legs off the bed. The whole of the world felt unsteady save for the gerson, and he didn't want to defile that purity with his confusion and hatred and lust. "I should take Gale for a walk. Why don't you lie down in your own bed for once." He got up and fetched his cloak.

"You saved three lives today. Perhaps more."

"No. You saved them." Mark opened the door. "Gale—"

"Stay."

He could have sooner resisted the pull of a thousand men. Mark shut the door. Gale, confused by what probably seemed to her one command given by two men, sat and stayed.

The gerson pulled himself onto the bed and began to strip, beginning with the heavy chain of office around his neck. Mark didn't dare move. The gerson pulled his robes off, revealing a knee-length white shirt belted over red trousers. He pulled the belt off, his head still bowed, and drew the shirt off over his head. He had a strong, beautiful body with perfect skin. His hands worked in his hair a moment. The binding released long locks that fell in perfect undulating curls to the base of his ribs.

Mark couldn't bear to stay. He reached for the door again.

"Stay."

His chest ached, high up almost to his throat.

"Unless ...." the gerson began.

"I ate today," Mark told him. "A whole plate of food. I—" A small, fragile laugh bubbled up from the pain in his chest. "I think I might live a while longer." He knew then that it wasn't just lamb and squash that filled him with contentment. It was hope.

That hope had brought him pain, too. He might see home again, but it would mean that if he survived the performance, he would leave Saphir.

He would leave the gerson behind.

The gerson stood up behind him and caressed Mark's arms. His breath blew sweet and warm in Mark's hair. "You saved my soul," he whispered.

"Is this my reward?" Mark meant it to sting just a little. He couldn't muster any stronger defense than that.

"If it is, would you rather have someone else?" The gerson drew Mark's hair off his shoulder. His mouth pressed tracks of warmth from Mark's shoulder up his neck, leaving a trail of tingles that traveled fast down to Mark's toes.

A rush of lust burned away any thought but having him in his arms. Mark turned against him, pressing him back toward the bed, kissing, grasping—

"Hnnn." The gerson caught his hands and forced them to slowly rake over his chest. "Hnnn," he soothed, and nuzzled Mark's face before he trailed kisses along Mark's jaw. He whispered soft, indistinct words in Hasle to him as he slowly drew off Mark's coat and waistcoat. A kiss followed every movement that then followed a kiss on his throat, his chest, his belly ... slow, an agony of sweetness and care. Mark's trousers slid down, carrying his loosened belt with it and then wet warmth drew tightly over his need and he arched and gripped and poured his hands through silken hair.

Pressure uncoiled and they moved with desperate, urgent grace. Faster, harder, he slipped and slid until Mark's spine shuddered low and deep and he spilled and overflowed with glory beyond dreaming.

The gerson pressed him into the bed. For a fleeing moment Mark tensed with fear but the gerson turned onto his back and let Mark drag his hands down the gerson's chest and then Mark devoured him. He'd never been so hungry and eager and full of power with anyone. The gerson writhed and clawed and Mark played him until he groaned for mercy. With terrible joy Mark licked and nibbled his way up to his starving mouth and kissed him, gripped him and worked his hands low between them until the gerson shuddered, his cries muffled by Mark's mouth.

Too quick. It wasn't enough. It would never be enough. The glory bled away and left him slack and exhausted. Slick with sweat, they melted against each other.

Mark closed his eyes. Nothing troubled his mind anymore. Warmth, skin, another human being's breath and heartbeat close to his—he awkwardly dragged part of the gerson's blanket over their legs to fend off any threat of chill. They dozed, close and warm and content and best of all, together.

He had no idea how long he'd slept when Gale woke him by scratching on the door. She padded to him and stuck her nose inches from his face, her gaze insistent.

Mark felt hungry again. That slight edge of pain didn't bother him in the least. If anything, real hunger without that awful burning and cramping felt like a luxury. He mixed a little powder with water until it was the consistency of pudding and swallowed it. Even the hint of pain vanished. Mark sorted through clothes, trying to find something that didn't have blood or mud on it.

"Someone hurt you," Gerson Lowell said softly from the bed.

"Several someones tried to kill me, actually." Mark had no idea what that had to do with anything.

"Did someone rape you?"

What is he talking about? "No."

"Then ... you flinched—" The gerson sat up and combed through his tangled curls with his fingers. "I'm sorry. I just assumed—I've never been with anyone who—I've had only a handful of lovers. It's only my limited experience revealing my ignorance."

Suddenly Mark understood. "But all your lovers bent over for you."

The gerson blushed. "They never acted like they were afraid of it."

He would yield for this man, but he doubted he could do it without fear.

"I don't mean to imply you're cowardly or deficient in some way—" the gerson said hastily.

"I didn't take it that way." Mark chuckled. "I should say, I didn't misconstrue your words, though the other meaning is also true." He pulled on a pair of breeches and belted them together. "At least now you know you won't miss me. You've had better, and you'll have better again someday. Someone who can stay." It hurt to say it, but it was true.

"You're quite cruel when you want to be." The gerson stood, magnificent and proud and perfect, to light a few more candles.

"I didn't mean to be. I thought—" His temper flared, mostly toward himself. "You're the one who's staying in Saphir with your *shrefmetyne* or *trerashefral* or whomever, whatever, and admirers and the city—this city." *I might have called this home if I hadn't bonded with Rohn.* "I'm the one, should we survive, who will to go home to Perida." He flushed with shame to talk like this about the city he loved, but he couldn't pretend that he belonged there anymore. "There's no one there for me. No one." *I may as well die here.* The thought gave him the strength to face the king. He wanted to do it now more than ever. Mark threw on a shirt and waistcoat and went out barefoot to take Gale for her walk. She followed nervously. "I'm sorry," he told her. "You're a good girl."

She rushed ahead and he let her out. He leaned in the doorway, switching his weight from foot to foot to ease the bite from the icy stone. By way of apology he stayed after he cleaned up after her so she could explore a little longer. It gave him too much time to think about the duke, and the king, and Gutter, and Lord Argenwain. He thought about Anne, too, what it would be like to sit by while her lover suffered and died little by little, mutilated. If it had been the gerson who'd been tortured like that, after all he and Mark had shared, Mark would have lost his mind to grief. He couldn't imagine what it would be like for her, to lose so much of what her husband had been, and to know she would soon lose him altogether after all their years as lovers, friends and parents.

Gerson Lowell walked up behind him. An arm circled his waist. A pair of slippers dangled from the gerson's hands. Mark put them on. The gerson's warm body pressed against him, held him, and soothed the ache in his heart. "Come back to bed," the gerson whispered in his ear.

It was wrong. They both knew it was wrong, but not because it was a sin. They were doomed to tumble and fall and shatter.

"Maybe I'll die at the performance. Or go mad," Mark said, by way of an excuse.

"We both may."

That startled him, though he should have expected the gerson would be there. Somehow he'd thought that the gerson would only open doors for the conspirators and nothing more.

Mark curved his arm to work his hand into the gerson's hair and they kissed, twined together like vines. It felt strange and wonderful to kiss where they might be seen.

Like free men.

The gerson led him back to his room, pulling him along by his hand. "Slowly this time," the gerson told him, shutting and locking his door. "Let me teach you. Wait here."

Mark sat on the bed and trembled. The gerson seemed to take an eternity to return, but return he finally did with a tray of food and pitchers of water and flasks of oil.

He undressed Mark with excruciating care. He fed him tiny honeyed pastries and kissed his mouth with sweetness and smoothed oil over his skin. The luxury overwhelmed his senses. The gerson bathed him with hot, soft cloths and caressed and kneaded muscles and joints until Mark's body squirmed with languid but ever-more-desperate yearning. Only then did the gerson let him draw the robes off his shoulders. Mark ached for him so much he wasn't sure he'd ever find release. He knew the gerson ached too. His flat belly had become as rigid as stone, and his back curved with a telling, animal line. Their bodies formed into an architecture that could not be anything but natural and perfect and human and true. And Mark trusted him.

But the gerson played him with hands instead. Mark dragged him down to the bed. "Impatient—" Mark smothered the gerson's words with a kiss.

They rolled, wrestling, fighting the painful urgency, making war against it with the desire to linger forever. The gerson pinned him—Mark let him pin him—and they breathlessly stared into each other's eyes.

I refuse to be afraid.

His heart pounded in defiance.

The gerson released one wrist to slide his hand down and stroke, then slid down farther, stroking, touching ... and Mark yielded to the touch as the gerson proved to him through pleasure given by talented fingers the truth that had glowed in Petren's eyes when Mark had taken him.

He'd never known such pleasure as what the gerson gave him.

Mark sat up and rolled him onto his back for one last play with mouth and tongue, teaching his teacher what he knew. It was too much. The gerson fought him off but it was too late and the gerson spilled over and over. The gerson forced his shoulders between Mark's thighs and the wet and insistent work he did there ended it all in waves of heat and ripples of blinding pleasure.

After a moment, his chest resting on Mark's belly, his hands protecting Mark's chest from his strong chin, the gerson heaved a great sigh. "You are a spoiled brat. Do you always get your way?"

Mark couldn't think of a counter insult. He couldn't think at all. His fingers played through the gerson's coiled hair, tangling in the heavy locks.

"Why do you shave your legs?" the gerson asked suddenly.

It seemed like an odd question. "Actually, I had them waxed at the banre."

"Waxed, shaved, what difference does it make? I asked why."

"Habit, I suppose," Mark decided. "And I think my legs look strange when they start to get hairy. It's the same with a beard. On any other person a beard and hair would make them look dignified, but on me, it just looks like I'm trying to play the part of a man."

"Looking young is one thing, even acting your age is fine, but putting yourself through this elaborate dress-up to look like a child—"

"You only say that because you're old," Mark joked.

The gerson tensed.

"I was only teasing," Mark assured him. "You're still young."

"I'm forty seven, Lark."

"That's younger than Gutter by a long stretch," Mark reminded him, offering an encouraging smile.

The gerson's grim expression didn't soften. "Gutter is older than a lot of men who've died past their prime."

Mark nudged him. "Why are you always picking fights with me?"

The gerson lay there, staring at nothing. He was so beautiful by lamp light, it made Mark's chest hurt.

"I irritate you, don't I." Mark didn't need the gerson's acknowledgement to know it was true. He wished he understood why. Not that it would matter in the end.

"Yes." But then he smiled, and chuckled low in his throat. "I shouldn't let you. I shouldn't think about you at all."

He shouldn't, but he did, and that made Mark painfully happy. He stroked the gerson's face, and then kissed him. Ardor began to glow within him again, but the gerson gently fended him. They caressed each other tenderly, hands sliding over warm, bare skin. Mark wished the gerson felt the same urgency he did, but the languid, luxurious kisses they shared were enough for the moment. They would have to be enough.

The gerson caught Mark's fingers in his and exposed Mark's wrist, kissing him there. Mark never thought the touch of a mouth there could be so erotic. "You're driving me mad," Mark breathed.

"Good." The gerson kissed the scar on his palm, inspiring a fresh glow of passion. "It's your turn to yearn for me like I longed for you the moment I saw you."

Mark drew his hand away and touched the place the gerson had kissed, suddenly shy, but not because of the power of the love between them.

"Does it hurt?" the gerson asked.

"What?"

"Your scar. Does it bother you sometimes?"

Mark shook his head. "Do you know what it is?"

The gerson settled a little behind Mark and held him close, his chin resting on Mark's shoulder. He traced a hand down Mark's arm, sparking tingles that chased and gathered along Mark's spine, and wove his fingers with Mark's, exposing the scarred palm. Most of it had faded to a soft gray, but the center was darker, like the dusty skin of a blue plum. The scar had settled into the shape and size of an eye with little tendrils that followed some of the lines on his palm. "They're rare." The gerson's voice soothed Mark's uneasiness. "I've seen two others, but only when they were fresh."

"You've bonded jesters with lords?"

"Yes." The gerson kissed the sensitive skin below Mark's ear. "I wish I could speak of it, but I can't. You should be proud of it. It's a sign of your devotion. I worry for you, though."

That made Mark shiver deep in his belly. "Why?"

"I can't say. I'm so sorry. I mustn't say. I just hope he's worthy of you."

"Rohn?"

"Is that his name?" The gerson hugged him possessively and Mark reveled in their nearness, in being wanted, in being loved. "Do you love him?"

"Not like this."

"Is he a good man?" the gerson whispered.

Mark wished he hadn't hesitated, but he did.

"I shouldn't have asked. I'm sorry—"

"No." Mark drew in a deep breath and let it out, releasing his doubts, his cares, everything that weighed him down when he thought of Rohn. "Don't apologize. He's a good man. Noble. Too noble." Mark blushed. He shouldn't think of Rohn and their desperate passion for each other while wrapped in another man's arms.

"I don't know why I asked. I didn't want to know." The gerson ducked his head and kissed the mound where Mark's shoulder met his neck, rounded and firmed from fencing practice but now shrunken from long starvation.

"It's just as well. I'm hungry."

The gerson laughed softly. "Then let's wash and get some food."

Chapter Seventeen

A letter with Gutter's seal waited for Mark when he returned from the tailors. The gerson waited by, swinging a large set of keys hanging from an ornate jeweled chatelaine's ring from hand to hand. He watched while Mark cracked the seal and read.

The performance will go forward as planned.

"Are you ready?" the gerson asked.

Mark nodded and they walked out, Gale on his right, the gerson on his left, and crossed the Guilbarabb. Another evening had come, a rare evening. There would be no performance at The Summer Sky Hall tonight, as there had not been for the past three nights, for she was being dressed for the most important performance in her long history.

Mark spotted no less than three dozen guards at her face. They allowed the gerson and Mark passage only after searching them both for weapons. Mark had to give up his pistol, rapier and dagger.

The gerson led them down through the same passage as before and up onto the stage past guards who watched the people gathered there.

Feather stood out in a ruby gown among eleven other men and women of widely disparate ages and races. All together they made a group of lucky thirteen, loosely grouped beneath an incredible construction of crystal glass. He'd envisioned a literal staircase, but the Vicalli Stair was more like a delicate chandelier inspired by a waterfall. It didn't look like it would hold a child's weight, but then, he had little weight on him.

Feather approached him while the others stared at Mark with varying degrees of suspicion. She looked pale and afraid, but a fragile smile warmed her face a little. She touched her mouth to his. "You've grown taller," she told him, stepping back to have a better look at him, and oddly, the air around him..

Mark bowed with an almost-forgotten flourish. "We parted on uncertain terms. I wish ...." *I wish I'd known then what I know now.* "You said something to me, and I've been puzzling over it ever since. You said you ought to hate me, and that you would miss me. Do you remember?"

Her gaze shifted to one side and lost all focus. "That was a strange night."

"Did you know there would be an attempt on my life?"

Shock drew her attention back to him. "No. I had to leave by the end of the month. The assassination attempt was coincidence."

"You wanted to hate me," he reminded her. "Why?"

"Because of this. Because I will never see Perida again. It was easier to blame you and the existence of your voice and the powers your soul possesses than to resent ...." She bit her lip.

Gutter.

"But we must perform, and soon. I don't know how much longer they can hold," Feather told him. "If only the performance were tonight."

"The young always want things to be over," growled an older man. He had the richest voice Mark had ever heard, full of depth without falling too low, entirely free of burrs and nasal tones. "I wish it would never come. And it will come, even if we fail! They'll be here. They'll kill us all. Everyone will die, or lose their minds."

"Or both," added another performer.

"You should not speak so freely," a large, dimpled alto told them. She flicked a theatrical glance toward Mark.

"They don't know we're here," Feather told the older man calmly, ignoring the alto.

"They always know." The young, dark-skinned woman of about Mark's age lifted her chin. "They may be attacking our defenses already. It doesn't matter. I will do my duty."

"Gutter will keep us safe," a middle-aged woman told them. She crossed her arms, her shoulders bent. She had the clear voice of a supreme soprano.

"I fear that we will begin something that will sunder the world rather than heal it," the older man said ominously. "But turning back now will only give the enemy a sure victory."

Enemy. They all spoke in an almost abstracted way. They hadn't seen the king's handiwork. They likely didn't know the duke, or his wife, or care. Duty, loyalty to the cause, devotion to Gelantyne—somehow Gutter had collected them and convinced them to risk everything, but all of them had the air of poets passionately at work rather than soldiers.

All but one. Pinched, quiet, the little mezzo-soprano clutched her music so hard that the paper rumpled and her hands shook. She had seen something, perhaps lived it, and she was terrified, but she would not leave. She had come in spite of her terror, and when she looked at Mark he knew she would perform for the sake of someone or something she'd lost, not because of some ideal, or for a greater good.

I'm with you. Together we will bring him down.

"We're here to practice," Mark reminded them. "Let's practice."

Feather touched his arm. "You don't seem as confused as you ought to be. Has Gutter ...?" Her brows knotted closer together and worry shone in her eyes.

"Maybe I've learned to stop asking questions when I know the answers will do me no good." *If only,* he though bitterly as she drew away. She seemed satisfied, but he wasn't sure he could have detected doubt through the armor her feathered mask provided so effectively. *How much do you know, Feather? Did you just trust Gutter, or did you demand proof? Did Gutter tell you lies, or the truth?*

This time they didn't even have workmen to hear the performance, just guards, a few members of their accompanying orchestra, and to Mark's surprise, Legend who sat where the king would sit. And it was Legend who coached them.

Mark lost all sense of his own voice. The others—they were true masters of music, and it seemed to him that his clumsy pronunciation of the Hasle lyrics ruined everything.

He couldn't stand it. "I can't be the lead," he told Legend. "Put Capadro as the lead. I can't do it. I can reach the notes but—"

"You will perform the lead. No excuses." Legend's sharp tone startled Mark. It shouldn't have. Legend's lord and master was dying, and Mark hadn't thought to even ask after him. He'd just assumed they would tell him—what? That the duke was doing better? Worse? Worse than what had already been inflicted on him? That he was dead?

Duke Farevren could be writhing in fever, even dying at this moment, yet Legend was here with them.

Mark tried again, this time more gently. "I can read Hasle but my accent is getting in the way."

262

"Your accent is your greatest asset," Feather told him. "Don't be afraid of it. You're only having trouble because you're fighting it." She moistened her lips. "You curl toes with your accent when you speak Hasle."

"She's right," the gerson told him. "You have nothing to be ashamed of. Sing ... sing like we practiced. Don't try to sound like the rest of them. Sing with the heart of a Meriduan, and the knowledge of the musician you are and have always been."

"Gutter bet our lives on this nervous little diva," muttered Capadro, his rich voice carrying in the hall with ease.

"It wasn't Gutter that laid that bet," Feather told him sharply.

Gelantyne. The name whispered through them without anyone saying a word.

"Everyone is tired." Legend stood up from his seat. "Dress rehearsal tomorrow, and the following day, you perform."

"What?" Mark's startled exclamation beat everyone else's.

"His Majesty King Michael's suggestion," Legend said dryly. "To align with Lord Argenwain's funeral rites." A great deal more lurked behind those words. "Good night. Rest your voices as best you can, and be sure to hold back tomorrow, especially those of you who aren't accustomed to long performances. We can't afford any broken notes." He walked to the main aisle and started up toward the grand entry.

Mark hurried down the stairs and up the aisle after him. "What's happening?"

"That's no concern of yours. You play your part, and we'll play ours." The great jester looked down at him like the neophyte Mark knew himself to be.

Mark didn't know how freely they could speak here. He'd unforgivably indulged himself in Gerson Lowell's arms and now he had no knowledge of anything of importance. "Your lord and master—"

"Is no concern of yours."

His temper flashed to life. "I helped save—"

"All right!" Legend halted, his breath coming hard now. "This way." He led Mark back the way they'd come, up onto the stage, and under everyone's shallow attempts not to watch, back behind all the curtains. The gerson began to follow but Legend warned him off with a glare. "Make certain no one follows us," he told the gerson, and moved on.

Legend tried several doors until he found one unlocked. It opened into a small dressing room. Legend shut the door and locked it. "I will answer your questions as best I can as a courtesy for what you've done, with the understanding that you'll do nothing more but sing."

"I can't make that promise."

Legend started to leave.

Mark barely managed to duck the broad, deadly swing of Legend's fist at his head. Mark backed up, catching himself on a chair that caught his heel on his retreat. "Wait!"

Legend hesitated.

"I won't put myself in danger. Honestly I feel more in danger from you at this moment than I did fetching your master."

"Yet you allowed me to bring you here, defenseless, when you cannot know whether I might have a dagger hidden somewhere. You're an idiot." Legend's anger burned red around his orange and gray mask, whitened around his scar, and his hands shook.

Mark blushed. "I am sometimes, but I don't think I'm being foolish now. No, I think you're afraid. And rightly so. Did your master tell you how a certain someone got his hands on him?"

Legend's gaze dropped and he retreated a step. "Perhaps I'm the one who's an idiot. How much do you know?"

They were both dancing around the unavoidable. "Too much."

Legend retreated another step. "Put your assumptions aside. We're not certain of who attacked my lord."

"I know who did it," Mark told him. "You can't shelter me. I don't know why you would even want to try to protect me, especially now that it doesn't matter anymore."

"You have no idea of your importance."

"My importance? Even if I really do have any, it won't save me tomorrow. Only victory in the All can do that." Mark wanted to shake him. "Just tell me what happened. How did your master end up there in the first place?"

Legend blanched. "You know everything. Your voice ... you're vulnerable. They could find you and destroy you before you ever reach the stage."

Mark wished that he knew everything. Unfortunately, he knew only just enough to make himself vulnerable to the *Trokellestrai*. "Just tell me. How did they catch him? Who caught him?"

Legend averted his gaze. "It was a mask. A strange mask, one I hadn't heard of." Legend's words came out dry and sticky, as if he were dying of thirst. "It ... it went to the house, his son's own house, and convinced a servant to fetch him without waking the duchess. And ... my lord left with the mask. Willingly. At no time did my lord have even a moment of doubt that what he was doing ...." Legend reached for a rapier that wasn't at his side. His hand settled on a vanity instead and he leaned against the gaudy, gilded surface. "It was the mask that came for him during his imprisonment. It may have even been the mask that tortured him. He's ... confused."

The king could have worn the mask, of course, but it sounded as if Legend weren't sure. "The person behind the mask had a certain stature, a certain coloring ...?"

"My lord can't speak of it. I have a terrible, terrible feeling ...."

He has to know. A fresh rush of doubt slashed through his chest. "We must be sure of the target."

"It will make no difference to you either way. The sin is ours, not yours." Legend started to leave.

"I don't give a fuck whose sin it is. I know which direction my mind will start to twist once it begins. I've felt it."

Legend stopped short. "They attacked you?"

Mark couldn't be sure if it was Gelantyne or something else. He didn't want to answer either way. "I'm already in it. I just want to know the truth. Do you doubt our target's guilt?"

Legend's gaze slid sideways. "No. If it were only this I would doubt, but there's ... there's more. But the mask—Gutter doesn't care that there's a mask involved. I don't know how much he understands anymore. His mind is failing at this, our most critical moment."

Horror raked down Mark's spine and clawed his gut. "Can you take me to him?"

"Not without exposing you. Our target hasn't connected the two of you beyond the fact that Gutter is your host during your stay in Saphir. No one outside our confidence knows that you were trained in Gutter's house. You must not betray your intimate relationship with that household or the target will suspect that Gutter's madness did not arise from Lord Argenwain's recent death."

"Madness. Was he attacked?"

"We're not sure. His grief is so great, it could be that alone."

"You're telling me that his mind isn't just failing—that it's gone." Mark couldn't comprehend the idea that Gutter might be completely mad.

"Not entirely. He's holding on, and the king is helping him. As always, His Royal Majesty is an excellent friend to Gutter. His Majesty has always been an excellent friend." Legend put his back to the door and braced on it. "If I didn't know what I know, I would doubt everything."

The duke had followed someone or something willingly to his doom, though he knew everything. Because of a mask.

Something about the mask's ability to convince people to do things they knew better than to do reminded him of something he'd heard in a lesson long ago. "The mask that took your lord ... it reminds me of Honesty."

Legend looked up sharply at that. "That mask was destroyed."

"But it still sounds like Honesty. Someone may have tried to recreate it, and managed it. Either that, or it's an *allolai*, or a *morbai*—"

Legend flinched, but he didn't look surprised. "I fear that more. Our only advantage is Gelantyne. If there's another mask like Gelantyne, we'll lose that advantage, and it's likely that any of us that survive will either be insane or executed for crimes against nobility. Not even Their Majesties Saphir could protect us ... and they will be there, at the performance. They have to be. We all have to be, and will be, except my master, of course, otherwise our target will become suspicious that his secret is out, and run." His hand clenched on the vanity. "The duchess is a fine actress, publicly holding a proud and uncaring countenance as if she fears the gazettes write the truth of the matter."

"What have the gazettes written?" It seemed painfully inconsequential but he had to be aware of whatever fiction their conspiracy supported, just in case the matter came up in conversation somewhere. Not that they'd let Mark put a toe out into a public place.

"The duke is presumed to be ensconced somewhere with a mistress. It suits our purposes to appear to believe this while we deny it and promote the fear that he has come to some harm. Our friends, of course, support our fear and are in a panic. Anne indulges that too, and has gone to Their Majesties Saphir for aid, and that aid has been, of course, supplied. Naturally they will find no trace of him."

"Does the king know your master has escaped and that two of his men are missing?"

Legend's eyes lit a bit. "That was a clever piece of work. I do believe the king will suspect that his guards discovered the duke and helped him escape. He will also believe that the three of them are in hiding, and may attempt to escape Saphir. If he has been as private in regard to his hobby as he's been in the past, he will have only a handful of men at his disposal to help him search for the duke. I believe this is the only reason he has chosen to linger in Saphir. He hopes to find the duke before the duke can surface and accuse him."

"If he has a mask like Honesty ... all that mask has to do is ask someone who knows your master's whereabouts, and they will tell him. If he has trusted men, he might even loan it to them so that they can enter the confidence of one of our inner circle." He felt like he was trying to open a puzzle scroll without the proper key. "Why does he torture people? And why your master? Why would *allolai* protect the king but not the duke?"

"Be careful of what you say. We don't know what might be listening." Legend closed his eyes for a long moment. "I thought you understood more than you do." When he opened his eyes again, he looked thin and frail. "You haven't spent any time studying sacred poetry, have you."

"I began only recently, and most of it doesn't make sense to me," Mark admitted.

"No matter." He traced his fingers over the door's lock. "The relevant part is that the king once courted Anne. She refused him in favor of my master. That alone wouldn't have troubled the king for more than a day, but the duchess' family was against her choice. The Church sided with her family. My master defied Church and King to run away with Anne, and married her in Saphir."

"What reason did the Church state for its objection?" Historically the Church intervened in marriages in only a handful of cases, all usually due to some infirmity in a family line that passed from parent to child.

"The duke is a commoner's bastard," Legend told him baldly. "Her family didn't know, but the Church did, and they let that slip to the king, which gave him the freedom to continue his studies and plot to undo my master's familial line."

He'll kill the children. "Studies?" Mark asked weakly. *Is that what that monster thinks he's doing? Furthering science?*

"He studies anatomy." Legend's fragile façade broke. His eyes glittered, and somewhere from behind the mask a tear emerged, forming a jewel that glittered along his jaw. "After he castrated my master, he opened his belly and began to chart his organs." Legend's voice blurred and broke with grief. "Fortunately, he very tidily stitched his butchery back up. The doctor has little hope that Geoff will survive the week, but he relieved my master's pain and there's always a chance ...."

Rage kept him from throwing up, but only just. "I'm so sorry."

"I wish I understood why some *allolai* are so fixated on bloodline while others only care what we do in life. I once believed that if I did all the right things and chose the right master, everything would come out all right after my death." His words, already marred by pain, began to sob. "I thought my master would be safe, and he would protect me, no matter what happened. I don't understand anything anymore. All I can do is try to save my family, and perhaps spare others what mine has suffered. If the *morbai* hunt me down for that, so be it. My soul ... I wouldn't want to exist in a beyond where souls are destroyed for protecting children while others are cherished because the body they once housed had an elegant brow."

"Is that what's happening? Is that why—" He had to think to remember what Gzem had called him. "Is that why the sacred sacrifice is here?"

A flicker of doubt flashed in Legend's eyes, then vanished. "You'd have to ask him."

Even if you doubt me, you cannot deny that this course is right, Gelantyne whispered.

You're right. I can't, and we can't do this without your help.

His clothes started to feel uncomfortably hard and unyielding. Mark pulled off his gloves and rubbed his fingers together, then smoothed his hands over his face. The feeling passed. *Did I speak too freely? Has a morbai loyal to the enemy won through to cripple my mind?*

No. That is my fault, Gelantyne told him.

Legend wiped tears away from under his mask. "You have a tic."

"It's new. Hopefully it won't bother me again." Mark shuddered and moved toward the door. "I know everything I want to know. I'll stay hidden away until the dress rehearsal."

"Don't come to the dress rehearsal." Legend opened the door. His words fell hard, overly bright from his pain and determination. "Don't budge from the gerson's side, and keep yourself armed and safe at all times. Don't venture out, don't talk to anyone you don't already know. In fact, try not to speak at all. If you're right about this mask and it learns of you, there's nothing we can do to keep you safe."

Chapter Eighteen

Mark smoothed his hands over the fine paper, warming it, afraid to begin, afraid he wouldn't finish before he had to leave.

My beloved Rohn,

I never hoped to be a captain of a sailing ship. I just wanted to be a sailor. I spent my happiest days running around on a cold, wet deck while my father paid little or no attention to me. Dressed up in oilskins far too large, flopping about in boots that fell off my feet when I lifted them too high, I rode a ship on waves as large as hills for the love of travel. I never cared for ports or presents or toys. I loved tying knots and splicing ropes and sleeping in a tiny hammock slung from my father's bedpost to one of the lamp hooks on his wall. I can't even remember what kept me so busy in those violent northern waters. I should have been afraid. But the only thing that I dreaded was being left at home with my mother, forever helping her tend the wine shop.

I don't regret the life I've led in place of my dreams. There's only the memory of that longing for the sea in me now. The boy that left Seven Churches lacked the imagination to foresee the things I regret now. I'm sorry that I waited so long for things to sort themselves out, instead of seizing hold of my life and claiming it for myself. I wish I'd listened less to your own regrets and demanded a full accounting of your dreams so that I might have helped you more while we were together. Most of all I regret that I brought sorrow, pain and death to everyone I loved, and brought so little joy to so few.

I will not end this note like some funeral march, nor indulge myself in more self-pity. I want instead to leave you with all my well wishes. There's no need to worry for me. I am better than I have been since a certain night. I've eaten a full meal, slept well and long, and my body is full of contentment. My soul

The gerson came into the room. "It's time to leave."

burns, Mark wrote, thinking of *Mairi* in the bay, *with life and death and all that is between. Every breath and heartbeat and step has become part of a great and terrible symphony that I hope no one will remember, especially you. I want you to remember me only as the one who hopped from rock to rock on a stormy seashore and listened to words no one else wanted to hear, the one who loved you most, especially for who you really are instead of what you wished you were, the one who would have died for you but managed to live for you instead.*

"Lark—"

"Mark. Mark Seaton." Mark signed his given name with handwriting his hand had almost forgotten in favor of Lark's practiced flourishes. He folded up the paper and wrote Rohn's name and address on the outside. "I need this sent before we go."

"I know someone who can see it's delivered. Is it private?"

Mark caressed the paper. "It's not important."

The gerson opened his desk drawer at Mark's waist and impatiently melted wax to it, pressing it closed with his own seal. "Gutter wants you to sign this for him." He drew papers from his vest and unfolded them. It took only a glance at each to realize what they were. "Gutter is leaving me his paintings? What is this? His last will?"

"Only an addendum to it. Sign here, and here."

"This page—oh." The hull fund. He'd forgotten about it, and Gutter's plans to build a ship, a ship that was already being framed in a shipyard somewhere.

His paintings. The gift made Gutter's likely impending death too real. *I don't know if I can watch whatever is left of him die.*

"We have to leave now," the gerson told him curtly. He went to his back room while Mark stood and brushed off his pale slate coat. If it weren't for the ruffles, the ensemble would have been something Rohn would have worn comfortably in public. He strapped on his dress sword. It would be his only defense, and he'd have to give it up before the performance.

"Gale." She came to heel by Mark's side, recently bathed and beautiful and soft-eyed. Of all of them, Gale risked the least, but had the most to lose. He crouched beside her and stroked her gentle face. The duchess, who would not attend the performance, would take care of Gale until she could be sent to Rohn should anything happen to him.

The gerson emerged carrying the basket with Gelantyne. He paused, moved the covering aside, and placed his hand on the gold face.

A jolt rocked Mark up to his feet. "What are you doing?"

"I thought you understood." The gerson stared back at him with gentle, dark eyes. "I'm the only one who can. You'll be on stage, and Gutter will be beside the king, and Geoff ...."

He'd understood nothing. "I thought you would only unlock the necessary doors and direct the guards."

"That was before Geoff—" The gerson sucked in a shuddering breath. "before. The sacred sacrifice chose me to take the duke's place."

"No." Once again he'd become so buried in his own troubles, he'd neglected the people closest to him.

When will I learn this lesson?

"You can't be late." The gerson walked out and Mark had no choice but to follow him.

Mark caught up with him. "My letter. You have to send my letter before we go." It was the only thing he could think of that could delay this.

The gerson stopped. "Oh. Yes. And the contract must be given over to the Church."

He wanted to offer to wear the mask instead, but he had to perform, and he could offer on no one else's behalf. "I don't even know your name." The question came from the depths of his mind for no reason he could fathom.

"We don't have time for this." The gerson marched back to his room and snatched up the papers. He nearly ran into Gale, who trotted between them in confusion.

"It's one word."

"You gave me your name, so I must give you mine, is that it? It won't matter after tonight. Even if our minds and bodies survive, you're leaving."

Mark knew they couldn't talk about this so openly in the hall. "One word. Please."

"Verai." Gerson Verai Lowell tossed the name over his shoulder as he passed Mark in the hallway once more. "The guards are waiting."

Verai was right. It didn't change anything, and it didn't matter. But he held that name safe in his heart and somehow it comforted him.

Mark followed him out, Gale trotting neatly beside him. They met the guards outside, a group of six sacred guards with the wary ease of lions who had nothing to fear but remained watchful anyway. At least it seemed so, initially. Their crimson and white coats, blackened weapons and black hats with long, white plumes made them seem all of a kind, a sea of martial prowess, but as they formed up, their individuality revealed their human fragility. The youngest watched their leader's every move with too-wide eyes. A swarthy, heavy guard tapped his fingers one at a time at the base of his palm on his right hand as if he was counting one two three four, four three two one, over and over. Two handsome and fit men that may have been brothers grinned nervously at each other, like boys going to their first formal ball. They were the only ones smiling. The largest man stood still with his arms tucked against his chest, his gaze unfocused, until the leader tapped his rapier. The large man straightened, overly formal compared to the others, and brought his heels together while the leader performed the last check on each of the man's two pistols and returned them to him.

The leader, a man about Verai's age, slapped each man's rapier and checked each pistol with the grace of long practice and constant repetition. It had become a ritual, and that ritual brought the men into focus.

The physical danger they might face before the performance came from a quarter that Mark didn't fear, only because it seemed so distant and unlikely. Of the many strange sects that thrived in Saphir, the *Mrallai Uss*, sometimes known as The Silent, supposedly crafted ways to discover the identities of Stricken in order to kill them. Before he'd learned what little he knew now of the sacred, he'd supposed that they mainly killed unfortunates tormented by various mental and emotional maladies. Now he wondered how accurate they might be. If they had arcane ways of discovering Stricken, the chorus that performed tonight would be too tempting a target for them to resist.

No one else would know enough or care enough to threaten Mark before he could sing. So why were these men, hand-picked and trained as well as any guards in the world, nervous?

They must have a role to play beyond getting me to the Summer Sky Hall safely.

He wondered if they had any doubts. He would be in a great deal of danger if even one of them had the same doubts Mark had once had before he'd rescued the duke. A sure and unexpected attack would kill Mark before anyone could stop it, and Mark's death would end all hope of the plot succeeding. Mark kept a wary eye on all of them, his hand balanced carefully on his sword.

We are all about to kill a king.

They crossed the Falleon Orb too quickly and before Mark could really prepare himself, one of his guards uncoiled a leather leash. "I will take your dog now," he said.

He couldn't part with her. "Please let me keep her. She can stay in the dressing room."

The guard looked to Verai, who nodded. They progressed through heavily guarded doors and halls to the dressing room. The door shut, and locked. He and Gale sat in silence, waiting for the summons, he on an ancient, highly varnished stool of the sort that ladies in hooped dresses sat upon while being coiffed, Gale on his feet, braced against his legs so that he couldn't move. He buried his hand in the fur behind her ear and massaged her, but she didn't relax into it and it didn't comfort him either. He didn't stop because her feared the loss of connection with her would sunder his courage. He glanced at one of the many beautiful old mirrors that made the room seem brighter than the lamps could account for. He looked even more pale than usual. If it weren't for the bit of color he'd applied to his mouth and the soft brown he'd used to darken his brows, lashes and around his eyes, he would have looked as featureless as a sandy beach.

He wondered if Rohn could feel his heart pounding.

Rohn. What will he think when he hears of this? He will die of shame.

Panic seized him. If it weren't for Gale he would have vaulted out the chair and rushed out the door, calling for help. He wanted his mask. He didn't want to do this bare-faced.

I need to calm down. All I have to do is sing.

I should warm my voice.

His breath labored too much to do anything but gasp. He started to open his throat to work a scale, then stopped himself.

What if the king's protection is already here? They mustn't hear me before it's time.

Stop panicking. All you have to do is sing. It's not like you'll be the one to—

Cathret will riot with grief and rage when they hear of this. Riders will bring the news within a pair of days. The world is now experiencing its last moments of peace. No one knows it except we few who know that everything will change forever.

A king has not died a violent death in over three hundred years, and on that terrible day, even the chanting armies howled and soldiers tore their hair and men cut their own throats to escape the horror of it.

A knock startled him. Mark stood up, trembling, and opened the door. The sacred guard, one of the handsome brothers, gestured. Mark half-expected the man to stab him, but the guard made no unseemly movement except to glance at Gale with curiosity. Mark slipped his sword belt and set it aside. If anything, the guard seemed far more concerned that someone might come upon them than with Mark himself.

Just beyond the hall with the main dressing rooms, the backstage area lost its aged if fancy decorum. The bones and guts showed—battered wooden beams, dusty curtains, props in large boxes, as much rope as would be found on a sailing vessel, but in less tidy coils, thick stone columns that spanned between the foundation and roof soiled by the brushing-by of countless sweating people, some in staining makeup that still remained on wood and stone a century later. Gale might have even smelled traces of them past the thick atmosphere, but she didn't explore as she usually did. She stayed close, nose twitching and flexing, mouth closed, head held low and her eyes wary.

The air burned his throat. Smoke from hundreds of lanterns both oil and gas mingled with the distinct narcotic smoke he'd once tasted when he first arrived in Perida, and not since. The lanterns burned the dust and scent of varnish in the air, making the place smell like it might catch fire any moment.

The guard led him through a maze of impossibly tall curtains. Here, in the farthest place back from the stage, they could barely hear the music already at work on the audience.

Finally they reached a rough staircase that would take him to the top of the Vicalli stair. The guard gestured for him to go first. Boards and beams lay at odd angles and the narrow steps only accommodated half his foot, but it had sturdy rails and only creaked a little when he set his weight on it.

"Stay," Mark whispered to Gale before they went up.

The guard kept his distance as they climbed up the stairs into the rigging. Music, still muffled by the many curtains, grew steadily louder as they approached along gangplanks precariously dangling from the rafters high above them. They moved around various stage hands who kept watch over the intensely bright lanterns that lit the backdrop. Mark was forced to lean out against the thick rope rails to get by. At last, with the guard blocking the only access point, Mark crossed behind the highest curtains along a narrow, wood-railed plank to the top of the stairs. From that great and deadly height he stood poised beside the top of the Vicalli stair. The first narrow crystal pane, beveled and edged in ornate silver, sparkled in the reflected light from the stage. It had taken a dozen people days to polish the entirety of the staircase, and they had done an exquisite job. The metal and glass, curving back and forth during its descent over the stage, paired perfectly with the white stage floor and blue, violet and aquamarine curtains. Long crystal spears, beveled to catch the light better, formed curtains of their own that framed the center stage for the primary performer below it. Arched supports, crusted with jewels and silverwork, didn't just hold up the many tons of glass and metal but formed their own artful framework within which other performers could stand. Huge paintings of what looked like columned ruins served as a backdrop, staggered to allow performers to enter and exit the stage with grace.

The stage was lit softly except where Feather stood. The blazing white light reflecting from the stage floor seemed to float into the air like a mist around her flowing ruby dress. The audience sat in rapt silence, their presence like a great expanse of heavy velvet lit with stars. Though they sat in twilight with only a few lights glowing against the carpet in the aisles, the ceiling above them glowed a mysterious blue, like a summer sky for which the auditorium was named. The balconies, gilding sparkling in the dim light, were adorned with hundreds of brilliantly dressed nobles, all unified by the blood red seats upon which they sat on-edge, fanning themselves. The beauty of it etched itself into his mind, all the more vivid because he knew it would devolve into a scene as hellish as the sacred murals hidden away in the caverns beneath the world's churches.

The royal box dominated the center of the hall. Closest to the stage, elevated and separated from the orchestra pit by a broad aisle upon which servants and royal guards stood ready to address every whim, framed in ornate iron rails of purest black set in for the purpose of housing royalty, sat the most elegant, most beautiful, and most powerful people on the continent. He couldn't tell from his great height which of the crowned heads was Michael's, and he couldn't recognize Gutter from above, but they were all there save for a few empty seats.

Some of those empty seats would belong to the duke, the duchess, and their son.

The music ravished him in not entirely pleasant ways. Feather was in the midst of her solo. The orchestra accompanied her with heartbreaking fragility, thin notes dancing at the edges of her voice. She sang about young life, and young love, and how thoughtless passion raped the promise of a young woman's future. Feather's pain rang out too true, blossoming from direct and present experience. *You drew me in,* she sang in the delicate poetry given to Hasle that translated so poorly into Cathretan, *and I'm inside you, caged in your ribs, drowning in blood.*

His body tensed as his cue approached. He thought of Verai, perhaps already lost somewhere in Gelantyne's darkness. Who did Verai cling to while he fought for his memory, identity, and sanity?

Is it me? Is it his lost love? Or has he forgotten everything, even himself?

He thought of Gutter and whether he would do what he had to—kill his friend, so soon after losing his lord, all while he was losing his mind. He thought of the other performers, and the guards—he startled when he heard a creak behind him. His guard was leaving him. Was that part of the plan?

He thought of Rohn as he stood there, alone. He could never explain or justify what he was about to do to his lord. This would be the first and worst secret between them, one that might break them apart at the very point that they could finally hope for a future together.

The time to sing rushed up to him. He remembered and held the memory of the duke in his arms, that suffering, the betrayal of it, and the use of a mask that could have done so much good in the world but instead was employed to torture and kill. He embraced his anger, and focused it like the point of a rapier upon the box of nobility below.

It ends tonight.

Mark descended as she concluded. With no lights upon him, he began his piece. In the quiet of the auditorium, unable to see the audience except as a mass of colors and sparkles, he felt utterly alone. He remembered Verai's coaching, not as a criticism but as a guide through the dark places between stars. He sang to Verai, sang to the memory of their bodies together and their minds working as one to build Gutter's monstrous war machine. It seemed impossible that so much effort had to be applied to kill one fragile man, but history had taught him that anything less would fail utterly.

I would rather be alone, he sang at the end of it, *than be a slave to valiant folly. I will lie on the ice and breathe the sea. Bind me in the chains that bind the world, and my writhing soul will break them.*

The enthusiastic applause at the song's conclusion surprised him. He made his way down a few more steps, singing along with the chorus the moment the applause began to fade. Their voices smothered the audience's appreciation. The light shone on him now, if indirectly. The hot reflection glancing off the glass blinded him. The vast expanse of Summer Sky Hall seemed like a deep crevasse filled with hungry shadows. If he hadn't been singing he might have fallen, but the music kept him grounded and held his balance for him. He seemed to have no control of his own voice. The music drew it out of him, stealing the air from his body and transforming it into something inhuman and perfect.

I left you, they sang. *I can't breathe, I can't move, I'm too small to be seen. The wind blows and I tumble and fly and fall. No weapons of war, no chant, no grace, there will be no final tears of joy. The fire burns and I'm ashes and smoke and light that fades and wisps away.*

The next soloist sang, and the next, and the next while Mark provided choral support with the others, and then it was time. Mark measured his way down and the lights focused on him, dazzling him with rainbow sparkles. He still couldn't see much of the audience. Fear of what might happen and what might not happen raked his ribs and threatened to strangle him. He opened his mouth, knowing he'd be alone in the beginning. No instrument would play but his own voice.

Softly, Verai had coached. Trust the hall. Trust yourself.

Your skin, my skin, silk on silk ...

His throat opened and the air seduced him.

My mouth, your lips, velvet and sweet
I remember but will never feel again
Only war will touch my flesh
Only steel will slice my heart
Only screams will grace my ears
I will never love again

He'd nearly reached the base of the stairs when he saw her.

Mark had thought that his first sight of the king would overwhelm him, or that he'd be drawn to stare at Gutter, who sat beside His Sacred Majesty Michael. But it was the little girl sitting behind The Second Queen that captured him. She wasn't much older than three years. Her eyebrows were darker at the center and frosted pale at their ends, the classic sign of Cathret's most royal lineage. Her hair, coiffed for the performance, flowed smooth as glass but seemed to ripple due to its ashen, oak and hazel brindle. She sat unnaturally still for a child, her gaze focused on Mark's eyes, her milk-and-tea complexion too perfect to be human, hands folded amid the ample silk, velvet and fur of her midnight-blue gown.

The king had brought his youngest daughter Laura with him.

The stairs halted over the orchestra pit on a short platform before the royals and their guests, who were all seated on one long row of fine chairs draped in gold cloth. Gutter and Their Sacred Majesties Saphir sat to Mark's right, King Michael due ahead, and the two others of the royal family along with the Cathretan royal guests sat to Mark's left. At the king's feet, two magnificent and bizarre wolfhounds with coats like a strawberry roan horse rested their massive heads on long, ungainly legs. Behind them, surrounded by an empty chair on his left and two empty chairs on his right, sat Legend.

The music began to build into the storm. Mark feared that he'd begin to go mad, as the *morbai* that protected the royal family certainly would detect a threat at any moment now, but the girl kept him captive in her cold, gray gaze.

The king's gaze shifted and Mark looked into periwinkle eyes. A smile gathered in the faint smile lines around them, and something hungry. The king's gaze raked over Mark's body, seeming to see not just past the clothes, but beyond the skin. Those unusual eyes caressed Mark's hollowed cheeks with that pale, verging on lavender gaze. They grew luxurious with a delicate lust that yearned to expose what Mark's fragile, starved skin failed to obscure. Of course the king would be intrigued with him. Mark's voice hardened with anger. Naturally the king would find Mark's immodest covering, his skin made thin by starvation, akin to an attractive woman stretched on a bed with only a translucent sheet of silk to cover her.

The last trace of doubt, fragile as a needle of glass, broke, and Mark's heart broke with it. The atrocities the king had committed had not been due to the influence of an evil mask, or implied by the careful crafting of a mad conspiracy. The monster reveled in his desire, yearned for it, may have even considered how he might take Mark away with him back to Cathret for a little dalliance in the palace with his scalpels and sutures and vials and calipers.

Mark's voice rose with the gathering crescendo backed by the passionate orchestra. The singers placed throughout the audience joined in on cue. His throat opened so wide he could have swallowed the world. His voice unleashed a roar of rage and pain. He didn't sing with the others, though that didn't make them falter. He sang the words in Cathretan, his own words, his own pain.

"Traitor to love, thief of trust! You are death, you are unworth, soul of scars that hide the truth!"

The king stood to his full six and a half foot height, his perfect teeth bared with startled joy as if Mark had released him from a prison. His Horrible Majesty exuded an air of unabashed passion. He seemed certain that no one but they two knew or cared, as if they could fuck each other on stage and the audience would think it an artful performance, as if no one would dare believe that the words Mark sung were an accusation. And of course, he was right.

"In the dark you peel them, rape them, feel them." The words poured out with frightening surety, as if his heart had written them and all he had to do was remember.

The startled, enraptured audience stood with the king—

"Tears of wine, you drink and drink them."

The lights began to darken, Mark thought by design but then phosphorescent phantoms emerged from the darkness, adrift near the ceiling. Shards and blades grew from their bodies—

Mark fought to control the scream of anguish and terror exploding inside him. "Beg your innocence, beg me, beg them!" The next line came to his mind in a flash, brilliant in its symmetry. He tried to temper his voice ... and the music that came from him when he did sent shocks of power and heat into his heart and up through his throat. "*Morbai ulleth ellanai iwei.*" *Morbai will sunder all you are.* Light seemed to come from within him and the creatures in the darkness hesitated—

Gutter reached under his seat and drew out a strange and terrible single-handed axe with a long, narrow, graceful blade counterbalanced by a thin spike.

The audience drew a collective gasp as Mark repeated the line. Though he didn't have time, didn't dare to look away, somehow he noticed Duke Foll in the crowd among his coterie. The duke's mouth had drawn open into a terrified rictus.

The axe flashed.

The king's head tipped sideways and fell and the darkness shattered and erupted into dark flames. The wolfhounds went mad and attacked Gutter.

The audience screamed like a seething organism being torn apart. Their horror momentarily drowned the music and the phantoms in the darkness collapsed into the bloodshed and panic. Mark kept singing Gelantyne's beautiful music, and its glory was an abomination soaring over the chaos. *The pridemen howl* ....

The king drew his jeweled sword with the grace of infinite practice. The blood that jetted from his severed neck halted and a gossamer black blossom opened in its place, spreading roots down into the royal neck and over his skin. Gutter desperately fended the dogs, wounding them but they didn't seem to care.

Gelantyne emerged from the secret door under the orchestra, all razors and amber and crimson light boiling out of darkness. The sacred guards poured out behind Gelantyne and the king's guards in the aisle below Mark rushed to defend their dying king who should have been dead.

People in all their finery crawled over each other like animals to escape, while some howled with madness, attacking anything and everyone near. The madness came like waves rolling up to the rocks. An undercurrent of confusion among hapless, terrified people in their finery foamed to life among a pack that surged against their neighbors and each other like starving lions. The darkness and phantom shapes within the chaos had faded, but he could still almost see the *morbai* doing their work, groups of them attacking the minds of anyone who might be a threat to the king.

A king that should have been dead, but fought with terrible efficiency.

Mark stood frozen, trying to direct his voice to fend the *morbai*. It seemed to help, but not enough. *I need to do something. Run!*

But he couldn't. He didn't dare stop singing. He was one of only a few that still sang while the orchestra played as if it were a terrible storm keeping a wildfire at bay. Somewhere, he heard Feather screaming. If he stopped ... he didn't dare stop, though he didn't know what would happen if he did. For the moment at least, his voice and the musicians in the pit seemed to keep those within several yards of him safe from the madness.

Those cruel waves of madness forced people to try to claw out their own eyes or savage anyone near with teeth and bare hands or with weapons if they had enough facility to take them into hand. Whatever violence they did they inflicted with the pure ferocity of beasts. Crude overhand stabs. Fists wielded like clubs. One man tried to dig into another's mouth, breaking teeth and cutting his own fingers.

Saphiran guards stabbed and slashed the king's body, often heedless of the Cathretan royal guard, to their peril. The king's body fought on, defiant, attempting to reach its head. His corpse killed and maimed the sacred guards but couldn't quite get past Gutter's axe and blade even with the dogs distracting the master jester.

Gelantyne leapt with inhuman grace, hacked off one of the king's arms and then skewered the cowering queen in a display of artful and continuous motion as fluid as water.

Little Laura ran.

Mark broke free of his terror and leapt off the stage just as one of the gerson's trusted guards tried to seize him. Mark's hand found a jeweled, bloody rapier as he scooped up the little girl. He had no more air to sing. All he could do was gasp for breath, for life.

Gelantyne came for him.

The dogs rushed after Mark as he desperately fended Gelantyne's flawless and lightning-quick attacks. He crawled and leapt over chairs, kicking whatever he could find loose at Gelantyne as he retreated with the little girl screaming under his arm.

An eerie howl pierced the auditorium just before one of the wolfhounds finally caught him and leapt. Teeth sank into his off-arm. He punched the wolfhound in the side with the base of his rapier but the dog only sank its teeth deeper. The dog frustrated Gelantyne's attempts to finish Mark off.

Give her to me!

Gelantyne's voice shattered his mind. Mark's clothes slashed him with fire and cold and wires digging past the skin into flesh. The air felt like chunks of cold marble, smothering him. Mark finally beat the dog off of his arm, curled his body around the little girl and tried to run. He tripped over broken bodies, hindered by the dogs snapping at his clothes, their teeth tearing through cloth and flesh. He crammed Laura under a chair. "Run," he told her hoarsely, expecting a blade to slice through his spine or the teeth to savage his throat at any moment.

Gale flew in, crushing him under her weight and the dogs tore at each other. Blood splattered over him and her claws dug into his flesh. He huddled under her. Her heavy feet raked and trampled him as she desperately held her ground against the bigger dogs.

Verai screamed. Mark rolled from under Gale onto his back in time to see Gutter ripping the mask from Verai's head. Only it wasn't Gutter anymore. His porcelain gone, the Gutter Rose split by a wound across his nose and cheeks and smeared with blood, only Thomas' wild eyes stared out from his ravaged face. Thomas attacked Verai. The youngest sacred guard intervened just in time, only to lose his hand and then his life.

"Thomas!" Mark struggled past the warring dogs. He wanted to tear away his own clothes and flesh, tear the very air that crushed him but he engaged Thomas' blade instead and kept it from hacking Verai.

A numbing crack and pain shot through his head as Thomas hit him with the butt of his axe. Sword in one hand, axe in the other, the bloody Gelantyne mask looped by its silk around Thomas' arm, Thomas took another slash at the king's failing body. The attack gave the guards trying to kill the king a brief advantage. Thomas deflected a sword attack, then tried to charge past Mark to get to the girl.

Mark kicked a chair in his way but couldn't bring himself to skewer his beloved master.

It was a mistake. Thomas attacked him with far more skill than Mark expected. He retreated as best he could, unable to think about attack or defense. He barely had time to defend himself, and too many of Gutter's attacks sliced and wounded him by bits.

Merely responding to attack is a losing game, Gutter told him from the past.

Gutter had taught him to survive, not to duel and this was too near to a duel. Worse, all around him people were fighting, pistols and long rifles were going off, and acrid white smoke had begun to fill the great hall. He had to focus on Gutter with everything he had but the constant threats from the battle all around kept jerking his attention away, and Gale needed him—

Gutter is better than me. I have to try to kill him.

Abstracts. Thoughts. He had no time to plan or think.

Do it!

Mark managed to catch Gutter in the elbow, crippling his axe arm. Mark tripped—

—his hand found a dagger—

—Gutter lunged as Mark continued to fall sideways—

Gutter's rapier tore through the back of Mark's clothes. Mark sank the dagger into Gutter's knee and rolled. The rapier ripped free of Gutter's hand when Mark rolled onto it and the mighty jester collapsed.

Give her to me!

Gutter screamed the words at the same time that Gelantyne shook Mark's mind again.

"She's just a child!"

And that child cried for her mother, "mannaneh mannaneh mannaneh" *mommy mommy mommy* while she ran wildly toward the heavy-set Saphiran sacred guard.

A guard who'd no doubt sworn to kill her.

Mark's heart leapt into his mouth. Somehow he launched himself to her, his feet kicking off the seat and then the back of a chair while he drew Gutter's rapier from his clothes, and he had her in his arms. She screamed in rage and terror.

"She has to die," the Saphiran guard told him.

"No!" Mark held her close. She didn't want him to. She squirmed in his arms, her body rigid, her hands pushing against his chest and his throat and his face. He had to drop the rapier to hold on to her.

"If I must kill you I will," the guard told him.

"Don't touch him." Verai, as bloody as any of them, struggled up an aisle and put himself between Mark and the guard.

The girl suddenly went quiet and still in Mark's arms. He thought she might have fainted, but when he glanced at her beautiful little face she kept her head close to his chest. She stared over her shoulder at the guard whose sword was streaked with her father's blood. Behind them, Gutter struggled to his feet, favoring his devastated knee.

"Not by the sword." The Hasle king, His Majesty Saphir, dark and silvered and fearsomely handsome, stood unstained and apart from the carnage. "She is in Our power now. We will deal with her in ways more merciful than cruel steel."

The guard bowed, lowered his weapon, and stepped back. Verai stood closer to Mark, shielding his side. Much as Mark appreciated it, even longed for that show of friendship and trust, he braced in case Verai produced a dagger to end the girl's life.

Gale—

Somehow Gale had survived, though she was a wreck. One of the wolfhounds was dead, and the other ... he had no idea where it might be. Gale limped toward him, hurt but proud, and sat by his feet.

Thomas, Gutter, whatever he'd become, stood up straight amid a tangle of dead and dying men. Behind him the Saphiran royal family, all unblooded and watching from afar, began to move toward him. Gutter reached into the still-writhing mess of flesh and black blossoms that had been the Cathretan king and drew out a satin-backed mask. He placed it on his face.

Mark gazed into the eyes of an innocent young woman, frightened, wounded and alone. His skin prickled up in warning and his mind jarred in all directions, trying to reconcile the blood dripping from gray hair, the broad torso and that innocent visage.

The young woman picked up the Gelantyne mask and limped from Summer Sky Hall unmolested. Mark held the little girl in his arms and hoped the young woman would reach safety. If anyone could be trusted with Gelantyne, it would be someone like her.

"Your compassion is admirable." His Majesty Saphir approached Mark, holding a hand up to keep his guards with his family. Gale, a horror of open wounds and matted, bloodied fur, growled at him. "And We will be compassionate, but We must also be practical. It is Our purpose, as it is yours, to eradicate this line. She is part of it."

"No one need know." Mark's voice emerged as thin as thread. He'd sung and screamed himself beyond hoarse.

"It is written all over her, within her, and in her *meillai*." Mind-soul.

He couldn't comprehend how he could be having this conversation with a royal family member, and not just because of his defiance. It was as much a betrayal to hear His Majesty Saphir demand the death of a child as it had been to learn that His Royal Majesty Michael was a murderer. "I can disguise her. Anyone could with a little hair dye." She huddled in Mark's arms as if she finally understood the danger and realized that he was the only one protecting her. He wished he could trust Verai in this. He turned slightly so that she'd be better protected if Verai moved. "She's innocent, and she is not entirely her father's daughter. She's her own person." He could barely force the words out.

"And when she's grown, w—"

"With the understanding of what her family had become, with the whole world's understanding when we publish what had become of the Cathretan lineage ...." *I just interrupted His Majesty Saphir. I'm arguing with His Majesty Saphir.* Mark held her close, trembling all over. He feared his blown voice and poor Hasle would convince no one, let alone royalty. "She's no threat to whoever you put on the throne. She's three years old. And no one will know about her but those of us in this room, none of which—none of us want anyone to know about her. Please." He had only card to play. "If you want Meridua's support, you'll let me take her home with me, and I will devote myself to raising her to be a good person."

Apparently all the words they'd traded before had been cat and mouse. Now it had become negotiation, and he'd just promised something on behalf of his chosen nation.

Is this how it feels when one makes a historical decision—half-blind, ad hoc, speaking in an unfamiliar language, forced by desperation?

The king's expression changed ever so slightly. He lifted his fingers to someone unseen, no doubt a sharpshooter who had slowly been positioning themselves to kill Mark and his charge.

I'm not getting out of this alive.

Any moment metal would pierce his brain. He fought the urge to duck and cringe. "Did you hear me?" Mark asked desperately. "I make no threat to withhold Meridua's support in war. I mean to offer support if you give me her."

"I have your oath that you will support Saphir in her endeavors in this war?" the king asked.

"No one but a Hasle citizen could make that oath without calling himself traitor to his own nation. I will convince the new Meriduan government to oppose the Cathretan nobility. I have that right and power. You know I do."

"You will oppose the tainted blood of Cathret and Her Corrupt Church?"

"And Her Corrupt Church." A shudder went through him. Even as a child, not knowing that the Church might be different in other places, he'd always sensed something was wrong. Maybe he could help pry that rot from the nation it marred and save the Cathretan people.

284   E. M. Prazeman

He had to. He'd just sworn an oath to a noble. If the sacred poetry had any truth to it, his soul would be scarred forever if he broke that oath.

Depending on who won the war in the All, that might not change the fact that his soul could be slated for destruction, but it mattered to Mark.

I will not be damned and shattered because I broke my word, or did evil. If I'm damned for doing good, so be it.

Her Majesty Saphir stepped up to stand in her husband's shadow. The lovely creature might have appeared subservient and shy, but something about the way she stood and moved suggested instead that she used her husband's body as if he were her weapon and armor rather than her protector. This was no shy and cowed woman, but a power in her own right. Perhaps the main power. "Will you consider giving the child to me?" she asked. "With my oath to never harm her?"

The queen might even mean it, but it wasn't practical. "In Perida, she can be free. Here, she'll never see the light of day. It would be no life for her, to hide from people who might recognize who she is. What chance would she have to be good and loving? And what of Cathret? How would they regard your holding her should they discover it?"

The queen touched her husband's shoulder.

The king nodded. "It is done. We will grant you and the princess protected passage from our shores to your homeland."

Mark bowed. His arms ached, and he was bleeding he couldn't tell from how many places. Gale moaned a low, soft whine. They were both hurt badly and they needed to get out of here.

Where's Gutter?

Shit.

Mark retreated with Verai close at his shoulder, accompanied by a pair of Saphiran guards he hadn't yet met. "Will someone please carry my dog?" The large, battered guard lifted Gale gently into his arms. He grunted a little from having to heft her weight, and she whimpered from her wounds.

Summer Sky Hall looked like something from a sacred painting, full of horror and agony. There were men and women in there still dying, and men and women who would soon be dead among knocked-over chairs and abandoned accessories of inestimable worth, including a jeweled purse and a delicate gold fan, bent and useless. Somewhere on a balcony, a broken pile of pink and cream silk lay very still on the burgundy carpet, a casualty of the mad crowd as it clawed its way out of the building.

A war had begun, perhaps the war that Obsidian had feared as well as the war in the All, as Gelantyne had called it. And Mark had helped begin it. How many would die to end the reign of a vivisectionist and his twisted family?

And what if Laura is also twisted? What if she grows into a monster?

Verai walked alongside him, silent and pale, looking only straight forward as they progressed toward the main entrance. "I need a cloak to cover her," Mark said, and a guard provided it.

"You're very like Gutter in one important way," Verai said just before they emerged into the clean, unbloodied air of the Guilbarabb where onlookers and survivors of the slaughter and panic gathered to stare and gibber and spread the word. Most seemed to be asking if they'd actually seen the impossible things they had seen. A group tried to restrain a man who tried to claw the skin off his own face. Others huddled, weeping, or screaming. They were the bowels spilled from the gut of the hell they'd created inside the theater. "I wouldn't have guessed when I first met you, how paternal you are," Verai told him gently. "It makes sense, though. You're coming into your own as a Confidante." Verai produced a handkerchief and, with trembling hands, tried to clean the blood off of his face. He sounded so calm, but he was pale as flour.

Mark had nothing to say about it. It seemed a strange time to pay compliments.

"You'll have to be very careful," Verai continued. "Once word spreads of your abilities, you will be a target. You will have proved what The Silent have always feared—that people with a connection to the world outside our living world are dangerous. They won't understand why you did what you did, and they wouldn't care even if they did understand. They'll want you dead."

The Silent will be looking for all of us.

What will happen to Feather now?

It seemed so inconsequential compared to all that had happened, but he cared nonetheless.

Mark held Laura close. He couldn't afford to consider anyone's safety but hers now. For the first time since he'd gone to Perida, he thought of his home city as a safe haven. But to reach safety, he would first have to leave Verai.

Come with me, Mark had pleaded, and they'd held each other close. Those words colored the silence between them as they sat on the bed and watched Laura play with a toy horse a guard had brought her. Apparently it was her most precious and favorite toy, made of fine silver suede with velvet reins embroidered with gold thread. The toy also had a velvet and gold saddle studded with jewels and a gold cloth blanket and silk-lined barding of silver. She liked to make the horse gallop about free of its tack. It had a rider, a handsome porcelain doll of a bearded knight whose dress clothes fit under silver, jeweled armor, but she left him in the bag that had room to hold them both along with a few other toys.

"I know it seems," Verai began softly, breaking the silence so suddenly that Gale lifted her swaddled head, "that your heart is utterly broken. I remember when I was young, and every love seemed like the best and last and only love I'd ever want. But you'll soon find another one. Young men always do. Even if I came with you .... And there I'd be in Perida, with no means to return, no hope of regaining my position here, no friends except you in the most dangerous city in the world."

"It's not that dangerous," Mark protested.

"Says the man whose entire household was murdered."

That stung him. "I think the carnage in Summer Sky Hall more than matches that." His temper bared its teeth only briefly before he sank back into a terrible loneliness like he'd never known.

"This is my home," Verai said. "This is my life. You can't expect me to leave it any more than I would ask you to leave your master and stay with me." It sounded almost like a question.

Historically, it had happened, of course, but it always ended badly when a jester traveled so often and so far from his master that their bond existed in ritual only.

He doesn't want me anyway. Rohn never wanted me.

Mark couldn't sustain the lie. Even if it was true, he had to go home. He wanted to go home. And to fulfill his oath, he had no choice but to go home.

A knock startled them. Laura clutched her horse to her chest and fled to Mark's knee. "The carriage is here," the sacred guard told them.

Mark's heart felt as if it would shatter in his chest. He gripped Verai's hand, but it wasn't enough. He clutched and Verai hugged him hard, their heads close. "I love you." Mark's voice croaked. He smoothed it but it would only come out in a whisper. "I love you."

"Go home." Verai drew away and stood up with him. "Go." He gestured to the door. There was something more than heartache in Verai's expression.

Fear. Their Majesties might try to delay it a while but their desire to bring down Cathret's Church as well as the royal family made it inevitable. War would come to Saphir, and he'd be in the middle of it. "Verai. Please."

"No." The strength in his voice gave Mark courage he didn't own himself.

It also gave Mark the strength to lift Laura into his arms and turn away. "Come, Gale." She limped alongside him. He opened the door and walked out, Verai's presence like the empty nothingness he'd fallen into within Gelantyne.

His escort of twenty men walked at a slow, executioner's pace so that Gale wouldn't hurt herself trying to keep up. For all he knew a jester loyal to the cause or The Silent might be in position to take them. He could be going to his and his charge's execution.

He looked over his shoulder, but Verai's door was closed.

I'll never see him again.

He didn't want it to be true. If he survived, he could come back to Saphir and visit.

But by then, Verai might be back with one of his old lovers, or have a new lover, or he might be killed as the war went from this one terrible act and spread into what would likely be a mutual invasion of military forces and assassins and jesters and messengers ....

Despite the danger, Mark wished he could stay, but Laura couldn't remain in Hasla, and they didn't dare linger. Every hour that passed increased their chances of being caught.

Their chances of cutting overland without being intercepted, even in Vyenne, were slim. Even if they managed it, there was no guarantee that they'd be able to hire a ship headed for Meridua that wouldn't be challenged by a Cathretan ship somewhere along the way. They'd have no chance at all to hire a Hasle ship that could win a fight to keep them from being captured, assuming the captain and crew would even care to try. If they wanted to avoid Cathretan war ships eager to take Hasle prey, Mark and Laura had to circle around the continent from Saphir's eastern shore to round the infamously dangerous waters of the Southern Talon.

Once they were on the open water past the Talon they'd be safe.

Maybe.

Cathret's fleet would be mobilized against any Saphiran ship it might chance across, and Cathretan ships and sailors were superior to Hasla's. And it would take a long time to round the Talon. A successful blockade near Meridua wasn't out of the question. Cathret had blockaded Meridua before, in the last war. She might do it to stop Mark from reaching home.

Meridua's ships could challenge Cathret's, but Meridua wouldn't involve itself quickly even if she were blockaded, so long as trade ships were permitted to pass. Besides, Meridua couldn't afford to fight. She didn't even have a president yet. And she might not want to go to war with Cathret without Lark's influence. Meridua might even listen to Cathret's grievance against him and deliver him into Cathret's hands.

After all, Rohn hadn't known Mark for very long, certainly not long enough to trust him about something this horrible.

If Winsome hadn't gone home, she would have been caught in a precarious position. This conflict would blindside her. Nonetheless, he wished he'd had her by his side. If she'd been with him, she could have helped in countless ways. But he'd left her behind, and now he'd be alone and there might not be anyone who'd be willing to listen long enough for him to explain himself.

All those dangers, and others he suspected he had no knowledge of, seemed meaningless while his heart flailed and ached for Verai.

A dozen mounted men stood guard around the carriage, spare horses in hand, waiting for the rest of his escort. Fog deepened the darkness of the moonless hour, making it difficult to see more than a few paces away. A guard helped Gale into the armored carriage after Mark carried Laura in.

"Doopa Mommy?" Laura offered Mark the horse. He hadn't figured out what doopa meant. Verai, who knew a great many more languages than Mark did, couldn't make it out either.

Mark made the horse dance about for her and she took it back, satisfied. She was a very solemn little girl. He hadn't seen her smile once. She hadn't even cried since they'd left Summer Sky Hall. She rarely spoke. The only time he'd seen much emotion from her was when her mother had been assassinated. Sometimes when he looked at her he could still hear her screaming mommy mommy mommy—

His own mother's murder kept returning to him. He hadn't thought about it for what seemed like a long time, certainly the longest time since it had happened, and now it roared back as if the memories were water rushing over a broken dam.

He hoped Laura was too young to remember her parents' murders for long.

They were strangers to each other, but their maternal murders made him feel connected to her in ways she wouldn't understand until, perhaps, she was much older.

If either of us get any older.

When they finally left the city's confines, Gale heaved a sigh of relief. Mark couldn't relax, not even when it seemed his mind had escaped the madness that struck so many at Summer Sky Hall, and continued to ripple throughout the city, emerging in unexpected places.

Once they'd left the mountains they began a journey across the strangest landscape he'd ever seen. Like they'd failed to describe Saphir herself, all the texts and paintings he'd seen of Hasla's Edryan Plains did not do them justice. Painfully flat, maddeningly endless, the twisted scrub and ten foot tall grasses primarily housed the famed two ton Saphiran buffalo and large tribes of lions, wild dogs, herds of the slate and golden-striped yunfa horses with their strange tooth-tusks, and of course red elephant. Their train carried four small cannonades but by their expressions the guards doubted their weapons would succeed against a red elephant tribe should it charge them.

But the thing that dominated the plains most of all was the sky. It yawned with a vastness that felt both heavy and empty at the same time. At night the stars blazed with a brightness only exceeded by the bold jewels that hung over the Saphir herself, but they made up what little luster they'd lost in comparison by their uncounted number. Without mountains or hills to veil them at the horizon, the stars outnumbered and outweighed the glories of the earth.

Mark had never felt so small and helpless as he did at under those stars. He didn't just feel mortal and frail. Laura constantly reminded him that she needed protection and that he had little or nothing that could protect her. Just a promise, one he wasn't sure he'd be able to fulfill.

It had been the worst of arrogance to think that he could be her guardian.

But he couldn't have yielded her, not to the Hasle queen, not even to Verai. She was too dangerous to their cause, and they had too many enemies, and the war .... Even Meridua would be too close to the center of things to afford her the safety she needed. Unfortunately he didn't have the connections or enough money or anything sufficient to take her anywhere better.

Laura didn't sleep well. It took him longer to figure out than he would have admitted to anyone, but he realized that she responded to his voice, and he learned that a simple lullaby could usually send her back to sleep. To help keep his mind off of his worries, he spent some of each day composing new lullabies for her.

Mark didn't sleep well either, not on the plains where he feared one of the guards might end both their lives in service to Gelantyne's war, and not in the villages they hid her away within, her face and hair covered. He managed to procure some hair dye used by the local women to make their gray hairs dark again. The color was too deep and strong on Laura against her soft complexion, and she hated when he applied his makeup to her brows to match the hair. At least searching for a better dye along the way served as another welcome distraction from more fearful concerns, though late at night, shifting from one side to another in bed, his worries crowded back.

Somewhere out there, Gelantyne and Gutter together ... would they hunt her? If they wanted to destroy her, he wouldn't be able to stop them. Perhaps the only reason that she still lived had everything to do with priority and nothing to do with mercy. Or maybe it had a little to do with Thomas and his feelings toward Mark. Gutter could afford to wait and kill the girl some other time, when Mark wouldn't be able to get in his way. Gutter could bide his time, and once he knew Mark had the princess with him, he could easily find her.

Gutter had the power to do anything he wished. He had the king's mask.

No wonder Honesty had been destroyed. The mask Gutter had taken from King Michael, which Mark had nicknamed Innocence for the moment, might even be more potent and deadly, and Gutter was the last person who ought to wield it.

Maybe not the last. It had been worse on the Cathretan king's face. It was a good thing that Gutter had taken his head off before the king could use it.

A good thing to take a man's head off. It might have been, looking at the situation from a political and social perspective, but witnessing it, Mark couldn't accept it on such pure terms. Every death in Summer Sky Hall had been a brutal, horrible, barbaric atrocity. Historians might call it a victory, depending on who came out as the winner in the war, and for humanity's sake it had been a small but important strike against evil and sin, but death itself wasn't clean and the heroes who'd taken part would forever stink of blood no matter how history tried to wash them of it with euphemisms.

"That is as it should be," he whispered under his breath as he watched Laura sleep. If killing wasn't hard and messy and ugly and painful, it would be trite, or worse it would become a pleasant for anyone who wished to have his or her way. Mark decided that war, no matter how rightly waged, ought never be easy and blameless and good, or no one would ever yearn for peace, or love that peace enough when it graced the world.

The heavy-hulled ship with its steel bow and iron-clad sides groaned, squeaked and crackled like a huge old wheelbarrow breaking under a load of big rocks. Mark held Laura close, his cloak wrapped around the both of them, his knees bracing them in place under the desk where they sheltered. Even in the fine cabin they'd been given, the wind blew the seawater in the door whenever they had to go out or food was delivered in, and everything was soaked—clothes, blankets, hair, his dog, the floorboards. Their wool clothing kept them just barely warm enough to survive.

He didn't dare look at the waves, but what he remembered of the southern seas returned to his eyes every time he closed them. Waves big as mountains. Ice. Horrible wind that strained the limits of *Uthwierta's* heavy sails and stout masts. She sailed slowly along the east coasts, but here she surfed like a swift trader, icicles blown in strange angles and spirals in her rigging. The unearthly icicles often shattered, only to reform once more, and ice sometimes formed on the sails too, to break off in dangerous, sharp shards whenever the sails luffed.

The ship suddenly lurched onto its side. Gale scrambled hopelessly to keep her place by his feet and ended up tumbling over the bunk. Laura let out a squeak and began to cry again. For a terrible, long moment it seemed this time they would stay knocked over, or worse, be turned entirely upside down by the next wave, but *Uthwierta* slowly, reluctantly rolled back into a more comfortable lean.

He hoped no one was on deck. This was the first ship he'd ever seen, much less sailed upon, where the sailors seldom worked on deck, and the wheel was entirely enclosed in what they called a bridge. It restricted the navigator's view terribly, but it made his work much safer. Apparently they mostly sailed by compass. He hadn't even heard of such a ship. Apparently she was of Osian design and build, but she was Hasle, purchased only a few years ago for diplomatic and postal purposes. In that time, the captain proudly told him, she'd rounded the Talon in the southern winter four times with no lives lost.

"We're all right again," he told Laura softly, and then he began to sing. She quieted in his arms. It was a strange feeling: being so constantly afraid that fear had ceased to be a novelty; damp and chilled so long he didn't remember what it felt like to be dry; to know absolutely that the ocean could decide to sink *Uthwierta* and they could do nothing about it except drown and vanish. Presumed dead. It would take months before the gazettes would suggest that they might have sank while going around the Talon.

Those facts alone weren't all that strange, except that the very folly of their attempt to round the Talon in winter somehow helped him let go of his sense of weakness. Here, everyone and everything that wasn't seawater was as fragile as frost. Everyone was weak. Comparing one man's strength to another's made no sense. All he could do, all any of them could do, was endure and hope, and strive with what little they had. It gave him a sense of peace like he'd never imagined. It leant a soft but strong quality to his voice, and a warmth he'd never before possessed.

Gale settled by his feet again. He stroked her head and sang.

Someone was listening outside his door. Mark closed his eyes and in his mind the monstrous waves soared high above their sails. He sang to soothe the water, but mostly he sang for the sailor who listened, and Laura, and Gale, and the ship. He could think of no greater honor than to sing in this place, where nothing lasted and everything mattered.

Chapter Nineteen

Mark rode up to Hevether Hall with his weary little princess sleeping on his lap and Gale, scarred but much healed, trotting alongside with her tongue lolling happily. A strange man left his work scrubbing the salt off the stone arch over the hall's entryway and took the borrowed horse's reins. He had old, white burn scars on his face and the skin on his hands looked like molten wax. "Sorry, baron," he said in the island's easy lilt, "we weren't expecting anyone."

Mark shifted Laura's weight to one arm, carefully balanced himself on one stirrup, legged over, slipped the stirrup and dropped before the man could help him.

"Eh you're quite the horseman there, baron," he noted.

"Actually, I've just been eating well lately." He'd gained some weight, and strength, and had limbered himself on the long voyage. It had only been a matter of balance and mental planning to get down.

He remembered how everything used to be easy like this, but more importantly he remembered how hard it had been when he'd been ill. He'd never take his health for granted again.

Mark strode up to the front doors and knocked. Sweat soaked his clothes and hair. After being chilled by the mainland's spring and nearly frozen to death while sailing by the Talon where summer was winter and they'd all lived with dread of icebergs, late autumn in Meridua felt hot and intensely humid. But he loved it. Though he sweltered in the relative warmth and his face had already gone pink from too much sun, he felt alive and well.

Trudy answered, her poor savaged throat still bearing the ugly red scars. "Mark!" She looked ready to launch herself at him but held back, no doubt because of Laura. She danced in place with barely-contained excitement a moment before she spoke again. "Everyone, Lord Jester Lark is home!" She dashed toward Rohn's office. "Colonel!"

Colonel Rohn Evan slammed open his office door. Laura woke halfway and squirmed a little before settling back to sleep in Mark's arms. Her dark-dyed hair stuck to her sweaty face. Gale trotted to Rohn as Mark's lord and master formally closed the distance between them. Gale sniffed Rohn over suspiciously as she did all strangers now. She didn't seem to remember him.

Mark felt as if he barely remembered the man as well. He'd forgotten how handsome and poised he was, and how cold in demeanor.

Rohn glanced at the little girl, his height and pride and perfect posture familiar and new at the same time. "You look taller," he remarked. "Who's the girl?"

"I'll explain later," Mark told him softly. "I'd like to settle her in to the Pearl Suite for now, if you don't mind, but it might be better to put her in—"

"Lark." Rohn spoke Mark's jester's name with a trace of pain in his voice. "Welcome home." He crouched and Gale went to him to sniff him over again. His hands gently and expertly worked through her fur, flinching at her scars. "She's been in a bad fight."

"We all have."

"What news of the conspiracy?" Rohn asked. The words carried an ugly tone.

Mark couldn't look at him when he answered. "There's too much to tell and my arms are getting tired. What news of Winsome?" He turned his gaze back toward Rohn. He was so handsome ....

Rohn hesitated and looked away briefly before he answered. "We're engaged to be married."

The news stabbed Mark's heart, but he forced himself to smile. "Congratulations."

"Lark." Rohn moved close but didn't venture to touch him. His gaze lowered, sheltering his eyes with his long lashes. "I've missed you."

Mark's eyes blurred. He closed his eyes to calm himself. "I've missed you too."

Mark hadn't craved gracian in a long time, but in the darkness, so near the room where he'd recovered from terrible wounds while Rohn read from a passionate if often overwrought romance ....

Where he'd been poisoned.

Where he and Rohn had slid skin against skin.

Where Grant had died.

While he waited for Rohn to come home from a visit to Winsome—he had no idea how she felt about him now.

While he wondered if Verai would love again, or become a casualty of war, or would forget him as quickly as he'd taken Mark into his arms ....

Mark poured himself a brandy. It wouldn't satisfy that strange, not-quite-urgent but constant desire for a just a little .... Gracian tempted him like the desire to taste his favorite dessert when someone kept offering and he had to keep saying no, thank you, no, never again, no.

Just a little.

One dose, or better, a half dose, a quarter dose, just to relax and feel truly good with no worries or fears. He could be surrounded by soft beauty, and sing without being haunted by what his voice had done.

He feared that, given the slightest excuse, he would say yes. He didn't know if it was because his belly had healed enough for him to notice the cravings, or because he felt like an unwelcome stranger in his own home, or both, or something else. All he knew was that tonight it was particularly difficult to ignore.

He remembered how Gutter had offered him muoduo—exotic vanilla cognac from Bel. He wanted to taste it now that he could have it. It would be a welcome distraction. Maybe one of the merchants in town had some. If not, he'd find a way to procure it.

Grismotael abarti would take wallowing in self-pity one step too far, but he wished he could have a glass of Verai's favorite wine nonetheless.

Later. It's too soon.

Laura was safe, truly safe, at least for now. It still seemed like they had passed in front of a whole line of loaded cannons and somehow had emerged unscathed.

The jangling of harnesses and hooves striking soft sand came through Mark's open window. He didn't dash to meet Rohn. That would have been pathetic, and useless. He blew out his lamp and sat in the dark. He took a careful sip of brandy, just enough to warm his mouth, and let it spread over his tongue like hot velvet. Only at the end did its fragrance remind him a bit of the wine it had once been.

296   *E. M. Prazeman*

This had been good wine, once. In a way, its distillation had ruined it, but he didn't want good wine. He wanted to be drunk.

Unfortunately, he couldn't. His stomach hadn't healed enough to drink alcohol, not in the quantities required to get him truly pounded.

He took another sip, and another. By the time he heard the colonel on the stairs his stomach hurt enough that he had to get up and take his medicine. It numbed the pain, but he'd learned the hard way that it wouldn't keep him from getting sick if he overindulged.

An open hand softly drummed the door.

Ignore it.

Against his better judgment, Mark walked through his sitting room to the front door and opened it. They stood there facing each other a long time before Rohn pressed past him. He had gazettes in his hand, and he smelled like cheap rum. He set them on the coffee table.

Mark lit a lamp, then picked them up and leafed through them. Some of them dated back to when he'd first arrived in Seven Churches.

Lord Argenwain and Lord Jester Gutter left for Saphir with a handsome young jester about which there has been much speculation. This writer learned that the young jester had arrived on a ship from Perida and was once a member of Lord Argenwain's household ....

Mark leafed through more gazettes from Cathret and Vyenne and Hasla, wondering if Jeffrey had been paid well for the information he gave.

He skimmed past the articles screaming war between Cathret and Hasla in the Seven Pages gazette.

.... believed to be a young jester from Meridua, possibly Lord Jester Lark of Perida. Little is known about the chorus, but one of the survivors remembered seeing him entering the Erothis banre from Avwan Trofal's private access. A separate source confirmed that someone of his description was a guest there. It is unknown whether the musicians that performed that terrible night had any foreknowledge of, or involvement in the regicidal assassination ....

Mark set the gazettes aside.

"Did you know?" Rohn asked him.

"About?" Mark countered.

"This!" Rohn grabbed up the gazettes and fumbled with them until he held up one that blared "His Royal Majesty King Michael of Cathret Assassinated in Saphir!" The paper rustled in Rohn's trembling hand.

Mark's heart leapt to match Rohn's suddenly crashing heartbeat. "You can't ask me things like that."

"We agreed. We agreed that you will not do things that you—that I mustn't know about. I chose you because I believed you were different! And now you are involved in something so abhorrent I couldn't bring myself to believe it was really you."

Mark wanted to fight back with angry words, but he forced himself to calm. His heart still matched Rohn's, but a strange exhaustion settled in and he slumped into its embrace. "That's not fair."

"Am I not permitted to demand an explanation?"

"I look at these gazettes and I wonder what you've assumed about me. The worst, I'm sure. I understand. It's much harder to trust a man you've known a month than it is to believe what all this paper suggests."

"So you deny it?"

A long silence smothered them. The ocean rumbled and hissed. The sea breeze blew freely in Mark's window. It was too late for gulls but monkeys and strange birds called out to the stars. The mist and sea spray that hung in the air dulled the glitter of those stars. "Do you think I'm the sort of person who would kill a good man?" Mark countered softly.

Rohn didn't answer. The uncertain light from a single lamp in the otherwise dark room disguised what little Mark could make of his expression. It saddened him that Rohn hesitated.

No, it was more than hesitation. Rohn didn't want to admit that there was in fact no trust between them. It was as if they hadn't been through ... everything. The bonding. The massacre. Especially their one moment of passion.

Mark had been away longer than they'd been together. In fact, the sea voyage from Hasla had taken more time than the entire span that he'd spent in Perida. He couldn't expect Rohn to trust him on that very short experience.

"I didn't kill the king." Mark bowed his head, trying to smother the memory of the king's death, and all that blood and suffering.

"I believe ... I hope ... I hope that you were involved unwittingly." Rohn's voice hushed. "Can you assure me of that?"

"You'd rather I were stupid and blind?" But now he was being unfair. "It doesn't matter if you trust me, I suppose."

"It matters a great deal." Rohn tossed the gazette aside. "Your letters ...." He stood uneasily a moment before he stripped off his coat.

Mark's heartbeat leapt faster and higher into his throat, but Rohn moved away from him and tossed the coat aside.

"Say something," Rohn demanded.

Mark leafed through the gazettes. None of them had anything about the duke or the duchess. It had to have been by design, but he had no idea why they or Gutter or Their Majesties Saphir would want to keep secret one of the many reasons why King Michael had to die.

Maybe because it wouldn't be believed. Mark wouldn't have believed it. "He was a vivisectionist." He could barely rasp it out.

"What? Who?"

"His formerly Royal Monstrous Majesty. He lured a Cathretan duke from his rooms and sliced him up and stitched him back together for his amusement. I was involved in the duke's rescue. He's probably dead by now. There wasn't much left to save." He found an article about Lord Argenwain's tragic death. It vomited praise and mourned the beloved lord's passing. Another article elsewhere speculated that Gutter's involvement in the assassination had been due to madness aggravated by his lord's passing.

Lord Jester Gutter Hunted by All Nations

Rohn stared at Mark as if he'd gone insane. Mark didn't blame him.

Royal Cult Suspected of Harboring Mad Jester

Famed Jester Seen Near Cathretan Border

Bodies of Royal Family Burned in Arcane Ceremony

"I saved her," Mark said softly. "Her Royal Highness, Princess Laura. She likes the name Ellen. It was her nursemaid's name."

Rohn walked to him and took the gazettes from his hands. "What did you do?" he whispered.

"I don't know," Mark confessed. "I thought I was going to save the king. I wanted to save him, but it all turned out—" He tried to swallow but his throat was too numb and too dry.

"Start at the beginning," Rohn suggested.

Mark smoothed a wrinkle on Rohn's vest. Rohn slid his arms around Mark and Mark wrapped his arms around Rohn's waist, tucking his head under his master's chin. For the first time since he'd come home, he felt safe. As he relaxed something broke loose inside his mind and the enormity of all he'd experienced poured through him. He couldn't begin to try to describe any of it, not even one small piece.

Rohn stroked his hair. The ribbon got in his way and he pulled it free. His hand traced around Mark's ear, making him tingle, and then he ducked his head toward Mark's face—

Mark pulled away, though his body and heart fought to yield to the promise of that almost-kiss. "Don't. That's not fair. It's not fair to Winsome, or me, and you know you'd hate yourself if you stayed with me, tonight, tonight, when I want you so much."

Rohn heaved in a hard breath and stepped back. His hands drew back to rest on his hips and his shoulders hunched. It was hard to tell if it was shame or barely restrained anger that shadowed his face. "I was such a fool to bring a jester into my house," he said roughly.

Mark let out a pained laugh. "I never wanted to be a jester. But you—you offered me freedom, and you inspired me and you made me feel like I could do some good."

"Is that what you did in Saphir? Good?"

"Yes." The word hissed out with a passion he thought he'd all but lost.

"I believe you." Rohn's voice smoothed like gentle hands over Mark's face and Mark calmed in an instant.

In that calm, loneliness crept in. Mark moved, as if shifting to one side or another could help him escape his own feelings. "May I offer you a drink?"

"That doesn't sound like an innocent offer." Rohn wore a sober expression, but Mark thought he heard a smile in the words, so he went to his liquor cabinet and poured a brandy. Having his back turned to Rohn seemed to intensify their nearness. The distance felt more like a handspan than the breadth of the room.

When Mark brought the drink to him, their fingers touched. A lustful heat roared freshly to life, warming his face and pulsing through the depths of him. Mark lingered too long but finally relinquished the glass. He raised his own. "It's good to be home."

"I missed you," Rohn confessed.

That made Mark smile, and he relaxed a trace. "I missed you too. Very much."

"Your letters ...." Rohn lowered his gaze into his glass.

Ah yes, my letters. And now he was here, where he'd wanted to be, and he couldn't do all the things he'd wished he could do when he wrote them.

That knowledge thickened the air between them and pulled them closer, though neither of them moved. Mark hoped Rohn would step closer, but his master didn't yield. Or maybe Rohn didn't feel anything except those urges he wished he didn't have.

Or maybe he isn't keen on the idea of me rejecting him again, as I should.

He didn't want to reject Rohn. He wanted something of what he'd had with Verai, maybe even something stronger. Something lasting.

Could something like what I feel for Verai last, or was Petren right about love?

"You must be tired—" Rohn began.

"I met someone." Admitting it reignited the pain he'd felt when he'd left Verai. And it was real pain, pain like he'd felt when his mother died, like when Grant died, as real and as potent as the pain he'd suffered from the poison. But while he'd healed somewhat from the poison, the pain he felt when Grant died hadn't faded, and losing Verai had fresh, jagged edges that opened in his heart whenever Mark thought about him. "I tried to convince him to come with me." Rohn didn't seem to react, so Mark limped onward. "I wouldn't have mentioned it except that I think ... I need some advice."

"I will do my best," Rohn said quietly.

He had a difficult time framing his question, but Rohn was patient with him and waited. He'd taken a few sips of brandy before Mark managed to put it together. "You feel it's a sin for us to be together. And I aggravated Verai more than I pleased him, I think. Regardless, he didn't feel strongly enough about me or he didn't trust me or ... I guess it doesn't matter what was going through his mind. He didn't even put up a fight to try to stay with me." His breath shook when he drew a breath though he tried his best to maintain a certain academic disinterest. "Am I wasting my time looking for someone who will stay? Or is it as I was told—that love is an invention of women to keep their men faithful when it's more natural—"

"Lark."

Mark gratefully yielded to Rohn's interruption.

"Love is real, and it can and does exist between men, and some men spend the entirety of their adult lives together. And despite my fears of what is sinful and what is not, that should in no way—please don't ever think that I would condemn you to a life of loneliness. It's clear you're a *velsheer*."

The Hasle word, at least he thought it was Hasle, spoken in Rohn's voice with such eloquence and an almost native Saphiran accent sent a shiver through Mark.

"You wouldn't, couldn't find happiness with a woman. And you're not noble. There's no reason for you to deny yourself in favor of empty acts with a woman in order to produce children. You have the freedom to be with whomever you choose. You should exercise that freedom and experience love." He flinched. "Again." His gaze lifted and found Mark's eyes. "You do love him, don't you." Before Mark could summon an answer he looked away. "I heard it in your voice."

"I loved you first." He hadn't meant to say it. It slipped free of him before he considered the wisdom of it.

A knock nearly made him jump out of his skin. After a slight hesitation, Rohn answered the door.

Winsome stood there. Her gaze moved from Rohn to Mark and back again. The nuances of expression, especially in her eyes, proved to be too complex for Mark to interpret. She held out her hand, and Rohn obediently went to her and drew her hand around his arm.

"Good night," Mark told them, and they spoke 'good night' slightly off unison in answer.

Rohn stopped just a few paces away. "I'll be one more moment," he told her. She waited while he returned to Mark's door. "First thing tomorrow, we need to talk about the war." He gripped the door jamb.

"Of course," Mark said, more than a little puzzled. Why would he leave Winsome's side just to declare the obvious?

Unless he's inclined to torture us both.

Rohn loomed close, almost threatening in his demeanor, but his voice softened. "Don't disappear. Don't run off on the next ship, don't ...." He took a breath and squeezed harder on the jamb. "Promise me you'll stay at least until spring before you run away again. Swear."

"I can't swear that. There's a war," Mark reminded him. "Why—"

"Please. Stay."

Something in his voice, an understated but clear pleading that had nothing to do with fear or politics or masks or the sacred, eased the ache in Mark's chest. He wasn't sure, but he let himself believe it was love. He smiled, and a hint of smile lit Rohn's eyes in return. "I'll see you in the morning," Mark promised him. "Early. We have a lot to talk about."

What can I say about E.M. Prazeman?

Well, for starters, it's a pseudonym. The artist known as E.M. lives and loves and sometimes brawls in the Pacific Northwest, a big change from being an illegal alien refugee from the old Eastern Bloc.

Fully naturalized now, E.M. writes and gardens and raises livestock. Has a fondness for swords and history. Is a better shot with a bow than with a gun, but isn't too bad with a .45.

In the last year the Prazeman household has hosted Kurdish expatriates, SWAT medics, former special operations soldiers, (ostensibly reformed) criminals, Finnish martial artists and the occasional author or school teacher from a remote village.

These people come to E.M. to decompress and think.

I know. I'm one of them.

Rory Miller
Author of "Facing Violence"

VIOLENCE

A Writer's Guide
Second Edition

"... a superb resource ... written by a man who knows his stuff" – Barry Eisler, NYT best seller

"... as a long-time martial artist and a writer ... I can tell you, it's the real deal ..."
— Steve Perry, NYT best seller

RORY MILLER

Best Selling Author of *Facing Violence*

Click through the Wyrd Goat Press website
and buy your copy today

WYRDGOAT.COM

What could be more fun
than chasing goats around the orchard?

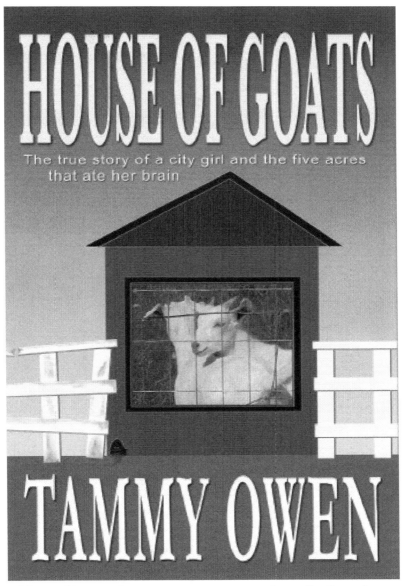

Reading about someone else doing it.
Click through wyrdgoat.com and enjoy the disaster.

Innocence & Silence

Book Three of the Lord Jester's Legacy

Available soon at Amazon, Smashwords, Barnes & Noble, CreateSpace and other fine retailers You can also order other great books through Wyrd Goat Press www.wyrdgoat.com

Here's an excerpt from Innocence and Silence:

They held the meeting at the Court. Rohn, his various secretaries, governors or their representatives from every island, Lark and all the other officials' jesters crammed themselves in a long double line where the judge, herald, primary defendant and the defendant's witnesses usually sat. The podiums, seat boxes and table had been removed to make room, and a few narrow tables allowed each of them space for a little paperwork and a glass of water. Behind them, a long line of various servants, including William, stood by. All the citizenry of note that could fit in the pit and the surrounding stadium seating had packed themselves in, sometimes with men standing, kneeling or sitting in the aisles. A few women sat in their husband's laps with as much decorum as could be managed under the circumstances. A large number of citizens who couldn't make it into the meeting had gathered outside. Listeners at the door passed on what little information reached their ears as it came.

The air warmed past stifling in short order. Those who hadn't brought fans made them from anything they could find at hand. Lark loosened his neckerchief to no avail.

Just as Rohn called the meeting to order a sacred messenger arrived with a puzzle box. Under everyone's unrestrained curiosity, the messenger stopped behind Lark's chair, asked for his signature and accepted the traditional gratuity.

Gutter's seal covered the keyhole.

Lark felt a little faint. He couldn't exactly excuse himself from the meeting to read it.

Rohn's body shielded him from much of the audience, but not from his neighbors. It would be in code, but that would only shelter the contents. Inevitably, codes became recognizable to those who hunted and studied them. Lark couldn't afford to give anyone even a glimpse of any of Gutter's codes in case that same person saw it again and made a connection that they shouldn't.

He'd read it under the table. He gave his closest neighbor, Bell, a sharp look. With a laugh, Bell, turned just enough to make it awkward to glance in Lark's direction. "Thank you." Their duties sometimes put them at odds, but he considered Bell the closest thing he had to a friend among the island jesters.

Lark fished out the key Gutter had given them for their shared puzzle boxes— he always carried it with him—and broke the seal.

What if Gutter is trying to kill me? He knows which key I'd use, and if he gave me the wrong puzzle lock on purpose ....

He'd been poisoned once before. He didn't want to repeat the experience.

Hells. Nothing for an entire year. This couldn't have arrived when I had nothing to do but take Ellen to the beach?

Lark carefully slid the key in. It successfully turned to the left on the first cut. He flinched when it clicked. He slid it in deeper. It easily turned left again. Three, right, click. Four, left, click. Five, right—click-pop. The delicate metal sheaves parted as the puzzle scroll hinged open, exposing the unharmed pages of a letter written over in the convoluted cipher Gutter had taught him as their own private code. The central chamber had nothing in it.

Rohn read a report aloud about how the Church in Cathret had begun to prop up some sort of government independent of the nobility. The priests wanted to organize the Cathretan commoners behind them to oppose Duchess Anne and her followers. The duchess, her entire family and all her supporters were declared regicidal schemers and treacherous Saphiran agents whose only ties to Cathret were land rights to which they had no moral connection or sense of obligation.

Lark, the first page began in a hasty scrawl. Lark held it under the table at a shallow angle and huddled over the table so that anyone trying to read it would make themselves obvious. *pleas come to port deep where ill leaf sign if can i knew its dangerous but no one anywhere no safe haven i trst only you saphiran regents have accord to plan declared me murdrer an only bearer of regicide sin but none of us expect my survival or the long trot the allolai took upon me and now alone*

A shock rushed through him. Had Gelantyne abandoned Gutter? If so, who had the mask? He hoped that Gutter only meant he had no allies to help him, but the cold, tight feeling in his gut suggested otherwise.

in cathret with no way out and i cant death without passing on the kings mask to someone Good no one could resist abusing her but you my boy my son come claim your inheritance and then deal with me as you will i would make an excelling bargain for your beloved meridua in her dealings with saphir cathret and in fact any nation in war or out of it if your love if it still exists for me prevents such use i would consider it a kindness if you brought gracian with you to end my life so that i may dissolve beside my beloved lord who i miss more than i feared i would and also perhaps i might ask sorry of the friend I killed for I love him as i love my lord in spite of their unforgivable flaws be careful take no chances i would not ask but for this masks sake love

Thomas

The grammatical errors and occasional misspellings could have been deliberate but Lark's gut tightened even more. Madness danced too clearly in the pen lines to dismiss the possibility that the words accurately reflected a deteriorating mind.

And Gutter had signed as Thomas. Gutter had written no date nor a location. He could have written it anywhere at any time. He might even ....

Mark couldn't allow himself to believe that Gutter might be dead.

Made in the USA
Charleston, SC
04 August 2015